DRAKE - TUDOR CORSAIR

THE ELIZABETHAN SERIES

TONY RICHES

COPYRIGHT

All rights reserved. No part of this publication may be reproduced, stored in a retrieval system or transmitted in any form or by any means, electronic, mechanical, photocopying, recording or otherwise, without the prior permission of the author.

This book is sold subject to the condition it shall not, by way of trade or otherwise, be resold or otherwise circulated without the consent of the publisher.

Copyright © Tony Riches 2020
Published by Preseli Press

ISBN-13: 9798673053379
BISAC: Fiction / Historical
Cover Art by Gordon Napier

ALSO BY TONY RICHES

OWEN – BOOK ONE OF THE TUDOR TRILOGY

JASPER – BOOK TWO OF THE TUDOR TRILOGY

HENRY – BOOK THREE OF THE TUDOR TRILOGY

MARY ~ TUDOR PRINCESS

BRANDON ~ TUDOR KNIGHT

KATHERINE ~ TUDOR DUCHESS

ESSEX - TUDOR REBEL

THE SECRET DIARY OF ELEANOR COBHAM

WARWICK: THE MAN BEHIND THE WARS OF THE ROSES

QUEEN SACRIFICE

ABOUT THE AUTHOR

Tony Riches is a full-time writer and lives with his wife in Pembrokeshire, West Wales, UK. A specialist in the history of the early Tudors, Tony is best known for his Tudor and Brandon trilogies.

For more information visit Tony's author website: www.tonyriches.com and his blog at www.tonyriches.co.uk. He can also be found at Tony Riches Author on Facebook and Twitter: @tonyriches.

For my wife
Liz

1

OCTOBER 1564

The towering *Jesus of Lubeck* creaked at the quayside, an impressive relic of the late King Henry VIII's navy. The ship's design betrayed her age, yet the tang of freshly tarred rigging assaulted my senses. Shouts filled the crisp morning air as men climbed high in the ratlines, while others loaded sacks of supplies and wooden casks.

I needed to find a passage on a ship before the money I'd saved ran out. I'd grown tired of drinking in noisy taverns, and wouldn't miss my damp, rented room above the candlemaker's shop. My lodgings reeked of rendered tallow, and I'd promised myself the miserable place would be a temporary home.

I suspected there would be a good reason for the rumours of mystery surrounding John Hawkins' flotilla. The air of secrecy put me on my guard the moment I set foot on the scrubbed deck. My old skipper had called this sense of danger a sailor's instinct, to be ignored at your peril.

'Trust your instincts, Drake,' he'd said in his Kentish accent, a twinkle in his rheumy eye. 'More than any maiden's promise, they'll not let you down.'

My skipper's deep laughter turned to a hacking cough. My

instinct had been right enough then, as the old man died within the year. He left me the coasting bark in which we'd scraped a living piloting merchant ships to safe harbour. I'd learned to use the winds and currents, calculate tides and read the stars. I enjoyed the skill of knowing the dangerous rocks and sandbanks, but dreamed of sailing the great oceans.

Captain Hawkins' voyage could be the opportunity I longed for. I'd listened to my old skipper's stories, never sure which were fanciful sailors' tales. He'd talked of far-off islands, ruled by cannibal kings, surrounded by half-naked women and fierce warriors. He'd told me tales of Spanish treasure ships so laden with gold and silver they sat low in the water.

Once, he'd unfolded an old parchment map, won from a Portuguese merchant in a game of cards. I'd stared in wonder at the coastlines of Spain and Africa. Mysterious islands and exotic sea monsters embellished uncharted seas which beckoned brave explorers. This was the reason I'd abandoned my easy life in Kent, and sold the ageing bark to pay for my new life in Plymouth.

I'd spent the last of my money on the wool coat I wore over a high-necked jerkin and Venetian breeches. I'd cut my hair as a precaution against lice, trimmed my beard, and treated myself to a pair of sturdy boots, and a dagger in a leather scabbard.

All I owned was in the bundle I carried. A change of clothes, my 'black jack' tankard of thick leather, sealed with pitch, and my old pewter bowl, knife and spoon. My most precious possession, wrapped in a square of white linen, was my father's volume of the Psalms, from which I read each day.

A muttered curse sounded behind me and I stepped out of the path of a man carrying an oak cask. A squeal of alarm made me turn to watch as they hoisted a struggling pig aboard. Men called out to each other as they loaded the last sacks of grain

Drake - Tudor Corsair

and barrels of beer. The ship would soon be ready to depart, and I needed to see the captain.

I made my way to the captain's cabin in the aftcastle, and knocked on the door before trying the handle. Captain Thomas Hampton, his florid face framed by a greying beard, frowned as he checked papers at a cluttered desk. He looked doubtful when I asked to join the crew.

'We've all the crew we need.' His Devon accent marked him as a local man, and his tone sounded final.

'I've made a study of navigation, and can read the Psalms to the men.'

The captain raised an eyebrow as he spotted the dagger at my belt. 'You are to address me as *captain*. Is that understood?'

His voice carried the authority of many years of command, but he didn't dismiss me. Despite his gruff manner, his eyes betrayed a hint of sympathy. I guessed he'd once been in my position, so the time had come to play the one card which might win him over.

'I should tell you that Master John Hawkins is my cousin, Captain. I give my word I'll work as hard as any man aboard.' At least the second part would be true, although I was less certain of my blood ties with the Hawkins family. I held my breath as he studied me with an appraising stare.

'I believe the *Tiger* is short-handed.' His face lit up with an unexpected smile. 'Tell the captain I sent you.'

I thanked Captain Hampton, although I regretted having to rely on my tenuous family connections. Once at sea there would be opportunities to prove my worth. I would sail to the mysterious West Indies my old skipper spoke of, and might return with my pockets weighed down with Spanish gold.

At twenty-three years old, my quest for adventure had cost me everything, including the auburn-haired girl I'd left behind in Medway. She would have been content with the simple life of a Channel pilot's wife. My mood darkened with the pang of regret at her tears when I left, and I tried not to think about what had become of her.

The last sight of Plymouth slipped into the grey Devon mists and I settled into the *Tiger*'s routine, marked by the clanging of the ship's bell. Each morning at seven o'clock and each evening, when the night watch came, the crew assembled to recite the Lord's Prayer and hear me read the Psalms.

The sense of freedom felt exhilarating as I breathed fresh sea air and scanned white-crested waves. I'd never been so far from land, and knew I could never return to my old life. I slept in a cramped corner of the gun deck, and ate hardtack with greasy pottage. The work proved physical and the hours long. My hands became blistered and black with tar from hauling ropes, but this was the life I'd wished for.

We'd not been long at sea when I clambered down the wooden steps into the hold. A rat scuttled past, and I caught my breath at the foul odour hanging in the air. I'd boarded many ships during my time as a Channel pilot. They could stink like an open sewer, but this would not be sluiced clean with a bucket of seawater. I recalled the same smell on the old hulk used as a prison ship in Chatham Dockyard.

My eyes adjusted to the dusky gloom, and I stopped to work out what troubled me. The hold should be crammed full of trade goods, yet it looked as if space had been left for a special cargo.

A metallic rattle echoed as I picked up an iron bar which passed through holes in two U-shaped loops. Wide enough to fit around a man's wrists or ankles, and locked to the bar with an iron ring, they shone with regular use. More shackles spilled from a canvas sack. I'd found the reason for the secrecy.

I shared the evening watch with the ship's navigator, Master Gilbert, who acted as the *Tiger's* second in command. Well educated, with an easy-going manner, Gilbert passed the time answering my many questions.

'We carried a haul of spices and a good number of slaves on our last voyage. Captain Hawkins made a handsome profit, and so did the crew.' Gilbert grinned. 'We'll all be rich, Drake, soon enough.'

'Why is our true purpose such a great secret?'

'We must be wary of those who could betray us to the Spanish.' Gilbert frowned. 'They control the trade, and declare it illegal for us to sell slaves to their settlers. Captain Hawkins has an agent in Tenerife, a plantation owner, Pedro de Ponte, who brokers his deals.'

'Why take such risks, when there are many other goods to trade?'

'The Spanish settlers have need of workers, and the captain takes pride in making sure the trade is fair.' Gilbert gave me a conspiratorial grin. 'Captain Hawkins discovered trading routes used by Portuguese merchants. We've learned it's easier to sail westward to the Indies after first going south to Guinea to pick up the trade winds. On the way home we follow the currents, and use the westerly winds.'

'Will you show me how you plot our course, Master Gilbert? I served my apprenticeship as a pilot and know the Channel well, but I've never been this far from sight of land.'

'Any fool can sail the open ocean.' Gilbert gave me a knowing look. 'It's the land that sinks ships, so your piloting skills might yet prove useful.'

'The furthest south I've sailed is La Rochelle.' I grimaced at the memory. 'The weather in the Bay of Biscay tested our nerve – and our ship. We took waves on the beam in a heavy swell and I feared for our lives.'

'Many good ships have been wrecked in Biscay storms. We shall need to keep our wits about us. We'll take fresh water and supplies in Gascony before heading down to Tenerife, and on to the Guinea coast.'

I began to understand the enormity of our venture. We would sail halfway around the world, and challenge the might of the King of Spain's navy. The risks were great and we might never return – yet this voyage could be the making of me.

I woke to find a crewman shaking me and shouting, 'Look lively, Drake! There's a storm in our way. It's all hands on deck.'

The ship lurched as I pulled on my boots and coat over my nightshirt. I clambered out into the darkness and struggled to stand in the stiff breeze. Wet spray stung my face and I tasted salt in the air as mountainous waves crashed against the side of the ship.

The bosun shouted orders as the crew struggled to put a reef in the flapping sails. He spotted me and yelled over the noise of the storm, 'Drake! Attend to those hatches, quick as you can!'

I tied the ropes lashing the heavy canvas cover over the nearest hatch. As I made my way to the next hatch the ship bucked like a stallion, rising from a deep trough in the violent sea, and heeling over. I lost my footing on the slippery deck, plunging towards the dark waters of the deep ocean. With a yell, I scrabbled to save myself. A strong hand grabbed my floundering arm.

'Have a care, Master Drake!'

I stared up into the rugged face of the bosun, who must have seen my fall. The *Tiger* heeled hard over, and freezing seawater sluiced over the deck like a swollen river at the flood. If I'd slipped overboard no one could have saved me. I owed him my life.

'Thank you, Bosun.' My clothes were soaked and I struggled to see in the dark, but in that moment, I'd become part of the crew. I scrambled to the forward hatch with a lighter heart and a renewed sense of purpose. Dealing with storms was part of the adventure.

Our fleet found shelter in the natural harbour of Ferrol, on the Galician coast, where white-painted buildings lined the quayside. Unlike Plymouth, which greeted visiting sailors with the stink of rotting fish, Spain offered prosperity. Rows of bronze cannons also showed the Spanish could defend their harbour.

As we departed for the island of Tenerife, Captain Hawkins ordered the *Tiger* and *Swallow* to keep 'in good company' with the *Jesus of Lubeck* and to watch for her signals. A flag flying over the stern, or at night two lights, would mean to come close for new instructions.

I took my turn on watch with Michael Morgan, an experienced crewman ten years older than me. Morgan's scrawny build reminded me of the fighting cocks, battling with such bravery in the pits. He spoke with a lilting Welsh accent and would take on anyone, once he'd had a drink or two, yet I could trust him with my life.

In a rare melancholy moment, he'd told me his wife died of the sweating sickness. His life at sea offered a way to cope with his loss and, like most of us, Morgan dreamed of making his fortune from Spanish gold, and one day reclaiming his two children, who lived with his parents in Cardiff.

We scanned the horizon each day until the chain of islands appeared. Many ships anchored in Garachico, the main harbour of Tenerife, so we sailed along the coast to the Caleta de Adeje, the home of Pedro de Ponte, Captain Hawkins' agent.

The sharp crack of a gunshot rang out as we approached the old stone quay. A group of men, armed with arquebuses, swords and pikes, shouted threats and insults in Spanish across the water. I'd been looking forward to setting foot on the island, and turned to Morgan.

'This isn't the welcome I'd hoped for.'

Morgan seemed unconcerned. 'Let's pray it's only for show.' He spoke with a glint of amusement in his eye. 'They can't be seen to be helping us, can they?'

We lay at anchor, waiting for two long days before Captain Hawkins' agent arrived to discuss business. As usual, Morgan had a theory.

'Those men are local militia. I'll bet they've been told to look out for English corsairs.'

'Will they allow us to take on fresh water?'

'Captain Hawkins promised we'll be off as soon as we have, but he's ordered lookouts posted to warn of Spanish warships.'

I scanned the horizon, half expecting to spot an approaching flotilla. 'Let us hope we don't have to take on the Spanish before we're past this island.'

Morgan shrugged. 'Captain Hawkins will fight if they offer us no choice. He has eighty fighting men on the *Jesus of Lubeck*, so he'll be ready enough if there's trouble.'

'It's said the Spaniards torture their prisoners.'

'True enough. They force men to convert to the Catholic faith or face a martyr's death.'

'I would choose death before I could deny my faith.'

Morgan grinned. 'Let's hope it doesn't come to that, Master Drake.'

'We've done nothing to provoke the Spanish, or the Portuguese.'

'Not yet,' Morgan admitted, 'but it'll be a different matter once we're in Africa.'

The tropical heat of Guinea made the chill air of Plymouth a distant memory. We cursed the north-east wind, which left everything covered in a fine dusting of golden desert sand. Our fleet anchored at the island of Sambula, and we scanned the shore for signs of life.

Strange trees covered the shallow banks with a tangle of thick roots, rising from the clear blue-green water like writhing snakes. Scampering monkeys chattered in the branches and bright-green parrots flew overhead. A well-worn path led from a shingle beach into thick forest, which concealed the native village.

Morgan remained with the crewmen tasked with keeping watch on the *Tiger*, while boats were lowered and rowed to the shore. The men looked wary, and stayed silent, except for the rhythmic splash of their oars entering the water.

The warm scent of woodsmoke carried in the still air, and I sensed we were being watched. 'The question is, have the natives run away, or do they lie in wait to ambush our men?'

Morgan frowned. 'Captain Hawkins won't give up until he has as many slaves as we can carry, and the natives won't surrender without a fight.'

I watched the landing party haul their boats up the beach and make their way into the forest. As they disappeared, a lone native carrying a spear emerged from his hiding place. He showed no fear as he shaded his eyes from the sun, scanning each of the ships in turn.

He stared at me before melting into the trees like a ghost. We'd moored too far out to be certain, but I could sense the man's intelligent curiosity. I'd been told the natives were savages, but I doubted it. The man studied us as if noting our vulnerability.

After a long wait, raised voices drifted in the still air, and the landing party reappeared. They'd taken a dozen natives prisoner, and led them to the boats with their hands bound with rope. They also carried woven baskets of fruit, scavenged from the village.

The only casualty, a crewman from the *Tiger*, grimaced in pain and bit on a piece of wood as the ship's carpenter removed an arrowhead and stitched his wound.

'They hid in the trees.' He scowled. 'We were lucky. They outnumbered us but most ran off.' He cursed. 'We found fifty or more of their dugout canoes, so if they'd attacked the ships you'd have been in for it.'

I agreed. 'We could never have defended the *Tiger* against so many.' I thanked God for my narrow escape, and resolved to learn to use a weapon to defend myself.

We continued down the Guinea coast and sailed into the turquoise waters of a wide river estuary, dotted with islands. Glad of my broad-brimmed hat to shade my eyes from the glare of the sun, I kept watch for dangerous shoals and rocks under the shallow, sparkling water.

Gilbert noticed me studying the circle of high mountains in the distance.

'The Portuguese call them Serra de Leão, the mountains of lions. We call it Sierra Leone, the greatest natural harbour in West Africa.'

Towering palms fringed endless beaches and the distant mountains were the highest I'd seen. I relished the prospect of seeing fierce lions, great elephants and strange creatures I couldn't even imagine existed.

We reached the bustling Portuguese outpost at the mouth of the river, and Captain Hawkins rowed ashore to barter with the merchants.

I stayed aboard the *Tiger*, yet this time Morgan left with the shore party and returned in the late afternoon with news.

'Captain Hawkins purchased two caravels loaded with slaves, and learned of gold in a nearby village. He's paid a Portuguese guide to show us the way.' He clapped me on the back. 'We're going to search for the gold at first light, Drake. Will you join us?'

'Try to stop me!'

I'd grown tired of remaining on the ship and wanted to experience something of Africa. I armed myself with an old sword, and found a leather bag to carry anything of value I discovered. For years I'd dreamed of searching for gold in this wild country, and now I had my chance.

Morgan cursed as the dark mud at the landing place chosen by our guide clung like glue to his boots. We walked in single file down the narrow path and I hacked at the undergrowth with my sword, mindful of stories of poisonous spiders, deadly snakes and dangerous animals.

The village came into view, in a clearing surrounded by thick forest. I was surprised by the silence; it seemed the villagers had learned of our approach and fled. We'd been ordered to keep together, but the men began rushing from hut to hut, their discipline lost in the search for gold.

The first arrow flashed through the air and struck the man ahead of me in the throat. He fell with bright blood gushing from a deep wound. More arrows flew from the forest, finding their targets with deadly accuracy.

I froze in panic. We'd walked into a trap and were a long way from the boats. An arrow thudded deep into a tree close to where I stood, and Master Gilbert yelled in pain as another hit him in the shoulder.

A native ran towards me, his spear raised high in the air. Painted with red earth, he wore a necklace of curved white fangs. His muscular arm drew back, ready to put all his strength into the throw.

I turned and ran back the way we'd come, the yells and cries of pain urging me on as my heart pounded and I ran for my life. The low branch of a thorn tree scratched across my face, drawing blood, and I expected an arrow to strike my back at any moment.

I called out the words of Psalm 7 as I raced for the safety of the boats. '*O Lord, my God, I come to you for protection.*' I gasped for air as my lungs threatened to fail me. '*Rescue me and deliver me from my pursuers, lest like a lion they tear my soul apart.*'

2

JANUARY 1565

Captain Hawkins rowed from the *Jesus of Lubeck* to bring a keg of Portuguese wine for New Year's Day. The rich red wine made a welcome treat, yet few of the *Tiger's* crew were in any mood for celebration. I swilled the wine around my dry mouth, the comforting warmth like the smoothest silk as it trickled down my parched throat.

Lines of concern marked the captain's face, and he stared up at the canvas sails, hanging like shrouds on the yards. The trade winds, supposed to carry us to the West Indies, had failed to appear. Our fleet drifted, becalmed and helpless on the open ocean – a sailor's worst fear.

'Keep your faith, men.' Captain Hawkins glanced in my direction. 'Pray for wind. God willing, we'll be under way soon enough.'

I prayed the captain was right. We would be lucky if our water lasted for another week. I tried to forget my old skipper's tales of ships lost on the open ocean, their crews turned mad with thirst and blind from drinking seawater.

Some of the crew argued we should draw lots to decide who would row back in the longboat. I hoped I might be one of those

13

with a chance of survival, until Master Gilbert told me what we knew in our hearts. We'd drifted too far from the Guinea coast.

It troubled my conscience to recall how I'd run from the dangerous natives without any concern for my crewmates. Seven of them were killed in the raid and many more suffered serious injuries, including my friend Master Gilbert. The navigator wore a bloodstained linen sling over his injury. He made light of it to the men, yet confessed to me the injury refused to heal, and he feared he might lose his arm.

Two crewmen from the *Tiger* died in slow agony from foul-smelling wounds. When the end came we were relieved to commit their bodies to the sea. I lay awake that night, troubled by the memory of how close I'd come to a pointless death.

Morgan survived unscathed, and offered his own theory about what happened. 'It was a trick, don't you see?' He watched for my reaction. 'The Portuguese turned our greed for gold against us.'

'What would they have to gain by betraying us? They seem content to sell slaves to Captain Hawkins.'

Morgan shook his head. 'The Spanish and Portuguese are all the same, if you ask me. The village was well defended.' He scowled. 'They hoped enough of us would be killed so they could seize our ships.'

'What happened to our guide after we reached the village?'

Morgan, as always, had an answer. 'He ran off in the chaos when we were attacked.' He gave me a knowing look. 'The Portuguese merchants hoped the King of Spain would reward them for preventing our venture.'

The attack at the village came close to ending our mission. All the men who went ashore in search of gold could have been killed or captured, yet Captain Hawkins continued undaunted with his plans, and carried over two hundred slaves on the *Jesus of Lubeck*.

The crew cursed our luck when he'd ordered the weakest to be transferred to the *Tiger*. We soon learned that tending to the slaves could be the most unpleasant work on board. Many suffered with sickness, so we risked them bringing some strange illness or disease to our ship.

Captain Hawkins' orders were for the slaves to be kept clean and well. The difficult task could only be done by bringing them up on deck, ten at a time, and washing them down with seawater. This became a regular ritual, with each member of the crew having to take their turn.

'You have to watch them, Master Drake,' one of the deckhands warned me, 'or they'll jump as quick as look at you.' He gestured over the side. 'They'd rather drown than work, see.'

I peered into the hold. Dozens of dark faces stared up at me, some wide-eyed with fear, while the faces of others were contorted with misery. Young and old, men and women, were manacled and chained by their wrists and ankles. My conscience told me we were wrong to treat them so harshly.

Two crewmen, waiting below for my signal, unfastened their manacles and urged the first ten slaves up the ladder. The natives emerged blinking in the bright sunshine. Some limped from being manacled so long in the cramped hold. Several were unsteady on their feet, but all seemed relieved to be out in the fresh sea air. Most looked about my own age, but some were little more than children and a few had greying hair.

The women made no effort to cover themselves, drawing ribald comments from the crew. I noticed one of the younger women shivered, despite the heat, and I worried she might have a fever. I'd never imagined I would become involved in the slave trade, and the reality of it troubled me.

Lowering the leather bucket on a rope, I swung it into the waves to fill with seawater. I'd seen others have sport by throwing the water over the heads of the slaves, but I pulled the full bucket on deck and placed it in front of the first man.

'Wash.' I dipped my hand into the bucket of water and ran it over my own face, tasting the tang of salt on my lips. 'You must wash. Do you understand?'

He eyed me warily as he reached out to pull the leather bucket closer, and poured it over his head. There were more derisive suggestions from the watching crewmen as I retrieved the empty bucket. It would take the whole afternoon to wash them all this way, but we had little else to do.

I enjoyed the challenge of helping Master Gilbert plot our location as we drifted at the whim of the tide. We measured the heading and speed of the ship and the estimated currents to calculate our position. Clear night skies and calm seas made it easier to measure the angle between the horizon and the North Star with the cross-staff.

Pointed at the star, or the sun during daylight hours, the cross-staff had sliding markers which were moved to line up with the horizon. Master Gilbert showed me how to calculate our distance from the equator using reference tables to find our latitude.

Estimating our longitude could be a different matter. We needed to develop a feel for our speed, or lack of it. We tried the old method of throwing a piece of wood overboard and seeing how long it took to float away, but it proved I'd been right to worry.

I passed the time studying Gilbert's map and trying to commit it to memory. More detailed than any I'd seen, the map extended past the familiar coasts of England and France, past Spain and Portugal, all the way to the mysterious cape of Africa.

Chains of small islands, offshore rocks and shoals were marked by symbols and Gilbert's cryptic notes in black ink.

'How did you come by this?'

'Captured from the Spanish, and worth its weight in gold.' Gilbert's forehead creased with concern as he estimated our position and traced a line with his finger. 'I'll not lie to you, Drake. If the winds don't return soon, our only hope is that the prevailing current will carry us to the coast of South America.'

I read aloud from my book of Psalms, a parting gift from my father. The young woman I'd seen shivering in the sunshine a few days ago died in the night, and Morgan stood with me to watch two crewmen lower her sailcloth-wrapped body to the sea. I said a prayer for her soul, despite her lack of faith.

The haunting singing in the strange language began again, the deck vibrating under our feet to rhythmic chanting. Watching the shrouded body slide beneath the green-grey waves, I knew any of us could be next.

I stared at the black leather cover of my book and recalled my father's parting words: 'Keep your faith. Stay true to your roots and believe in the will of God.' We both believed we would never see each other again.

I'd inherited more than my West Country accent from my father, Edmund Drake. He'd farmed in Tavistock before making our home in the hulk of an old ship at Chatham Dockyard. A Protestant curate, his sermons at the parish church were well attended, and he read prayers to the boatmen of the Medway. Together with my eleven rowdy brothers, I grew up surrounded by ships and men of the sea.

I said a silent prayer for my father, who'd taught me to read and write, but suffered with failing eyesight. He would not be able to send letters or make the long journey to Plymouth. I doubted I would ever return to my old life in Kent, yet hoped the girl I left behind would not forget me too easily.

Another week passed without any improvement in the weather. The men grumbled about the water being given to the slaves in the cavernous hold. Five had died from a sweating sickness since we left Guinea, and I feared more would be lost if we didn't reach landfall soon. I began to worry about how long we could afford to give so many our precious remaining water.

My daily prayers included a reminder to the crew that God would not abandon us, although my throat felt drier than old parchment as I spoke. '*Lord God, you send us forth to be lights in a dark world.*' I looked around at the faces of the men and knew my father would be proud of how I helped them keep the faith.

'*Thank you for the power of your spirit and for the sword of your word, without which we would have nothing to say. Give us courage that in our time we may confess our faith in your son Jesus Christ, in whose gracious name we pray. Amen.*'

In the second week of February, I was snatching some sleep when Morgan's shouting woke me. I rushed on deck to see the topmast pennant fluttering as wind began to fill and flap the sails. Our prayers had been answered by a light north-westerly wind. I offered thanks to God as our fleet set a course for the island of Santa Dominica.

After two weeks of sailing, the first promising signs appeared. The trunk of a partly submerged tree floated past, followed by bright-green seaweed, and an exotic, long-tailed yellow bird, which landed in the rigging.

The men gave a ragged cheer of relief as a small, green-forested island appeared on the distant horizon. We moored close to a deserted beach and I went ashore with Morgan and two crewmen in search of fresh water.

It felt good to be on dry land after two long months at sea. The forest grew denser and we struggled to cut a path through the thick undergrowth, yet kept a good pace. The prospect of slaking our thirst drove us on, like eager pilgrims close to reaching a holy shrine.

We found a shallow rainwater pond, shaded by tall palm trees. We knew the dangers of drinking still water, however thirsty we might be. Undeterred, Morgan cupped his hands and bent to taste the murky brown water, but spat it out in disgust.

Our thirst became so great we sailed through the night until the lookout sighted the mountains of the island of Margarita. Wary Spanish settlers there allowed us to take on the desperately needed fresh water, but refused to trade with us.

On evening watch, I spotted the flag hoisted at the stern of the *Jesus of Lubeck*, the sign for new orders. A messenger rowed across to the *Tiger* and climbed aboard. As he stood to address the men, I recognised Captain Hawkins, who'd come to address us again in person.

John Hawkins looked confident, and wore a silver-handled sword in an ornate scabbard at his belt.

'I've persuaded the settlers to sell us some mutton and beef.' He paused while the crew cheered. 'Their governor refuses to meet with me but sent word they are under orders from the King of Spain. They are to repel foreigners who trade in slaves, so we must make a show of force at our next landing.' He smiled at the assembled crew. 'We'll give our trading partners good reason to part with their gold.'

The men cheered at the mention of Spanish gold. I understood. The voyage would be at risk if our slaves remained unsold, although it might be at the price of our own lives or liberty if our ships were seized by the Spanish.

Captain Hawkins studied our faces. 'Keep your wits about you. There could be Spanish warships lying in wait to ambush us. If we sight any, the *Jesus of Lubeck* will fire a cannon to alert the fleet, and you are to do the same.'

At the next island we spotted a group of native men and women watching our arrival from the shore. Olive-skinned, with long black hair, they were naked except for a narrow belt of woven grasses. The men were armed with light hunting bows, and carried quivers of arrows. I turned to Morgan, who watched at my side.

'They look more curious than afraid, which could make them dangerous.'

'Carib Indians!' Morgan swore. 'These are the cannibals we've been warned about. They use arrows tipped with poison which make you beg for the release of death.'

'I'll not be the first to volunteer to go ashore.' I studied the bowmen. 'At least until we know what sort of welcome we'll have.'

With disregard for his own safety, Captain Hawkins took a boat to discover whether the Indians were prepared to trade. I admired his bravery. One of the Carib men raised his bow and nocked an arrow, but the captain didn't draw his sword. Instead he showed them glass beads and pewter whistles, which he traded for baskets of sweet yellow corn and ripe pineapples. They were the first I'd tasted, and were relished by the hungry crew.

By April our fleet reached a thriving Spanish settlement on the coast, where all the armed men who could be spared went ashore to make a threat of force. I carried a long pike and wore an uncomfortable iron helmet, although Morgan joked it would take more than old armour to make a soldier of me.

The Spanish militia formed a defensive line, beating drums and waving their swords in the air. As well as some one hundred and fifty armed townsmen, I counted thirty mounted cavalrymen armed with long lances. They shouted insults and threats in Spanish and ignored Captain Hawkins' request to parley.

We watched as two brass falconet cannons, carried on the boat from the *Jesus of Lubeck*, were prepared. I'd never seen one fired but guessed they would cause carnage at such close range. Holding my hands over my ears, I said a prayer as the small cannons thundered with such a boom the ground shook.

The Spanish militia broke ranks and ran, some falling to the ground. Several of the cavalry horses threw their riders and galloped off in panic. I turned at the sound of laughter. Morgan pointed at the falconets.

'They were only loaded with cotton wadding, but have done their work well enough.'

Captain Hawkins had ordered the men forward to press our advantage, when a rider approached carrying a white flag of truce. The Spanish militia wished to surrender, without a single man being killed or injured.

It took several days to find buyers for the slaves, as the wealthiest settlers had fled to the hills and refused to return. The Spanish governor demanded payment of the tax of thirty ducats for each slave, until we threatened to use cannons again.

We used the time to replenish the water and supplies and prepare the ships for the voyage home. As we left, the cannons of the *Jesus of Lubeck* roared in a final act of defiance. A thunderous blast of cannons boomed in reply. The Spanish could have defended themselves after all. They had chosen to make a token show of strength, rather than risk a battle.

Our intention had been to sail for Jamaica, but the winds and current took our fleet several leagues wide, and the island passed on the far horizon. We continued along the Florida coast, exploring every inlet with small boats in the search for any sign of fresh water.

Morgan was first with the news when we found a French Huguenot colony. Short of food, the settlers were marooned, having lost their only ship in a storm.

'Captain Hawkins has sold them the *Tiger* and twenty barrels of corn, so we're transferring to the *Salomon*.' He grinned at my surprised face. 'They've paid him in gold and pearls, as well as some diamonds.'

We found the trade winds, which drove our three remaining ships homeward to the Irish Sea and the Bristol Channel. I stood in the bows of the *Salomon* as the Camel estuary and sheltered haven of Padstow came into view, and I said a silent prayer of thanks to God for our safe delivery.

The ship's log showed the twentieth day of October. I'd been at sea for twelve months and returned a changed man. I'd experienced my first fight against the Catholic Spanish and defended the true faith. I turned to Morgan, as ever at my side.

'It's you I must thank for this adventure. I might not have gained a command, but I've learned water is worth more than gold, when you have none.'

Morgan agreed. 'And not to believe stories of gold for the taking.'

'That time in the African village was the closest I've come to losing my life.'

'Seven were killed by natives that day, twelve died of wounds or fever and one man fell overboard.' Morgan counted on his fingers. 'In all, twenty men were lost.'

I took a deep breath of the fresh sea air, glad to be alive, and answered softly, as if to myself, 'But Captain Hawkins and his investors have made their fortune.'

3

NOVEMBER 1566

I shivered in a chill breeze as I kept lookout at the weather-worn rail of the *Pasco*, a forty-ton carrack with a Cornish crew, under Captain Robert Bolton. I found myself reflecting on how my life had changed.

The Spanish ambassador protested to the British government about Captain Hawkins, who'd been made a freeman of Plymouth after the success of his last voyage. To appease the Spanish, he'd paid a bond of five hundred pounds, and promised not to sail to the Indies or in Spanish waters for one year.

Ever resourceful, he'd found backers for this new venture on the same trading route, using ships owned by his elder brother, William Hawkins, not subject to restrictions from the admiralty. I suspected the Hawkins brothers were supported in this venture by the Queen of England herself – or at least her senior ministers.

Our fleet sailed under the command of another of my distant cousins, Master John Lovell, captain of the hundred-and-forty-ton carrack, *Paul*. Tall and arrogant, with a reputation for discipline, Captain Lovell lacked the natural authority of John

Hawkins. A devout Protestant, he sailed with his own minister to read the Psalms.

Morgan remained with the crew of the third ship in our fleet, the *Salomon*, now owned by William Hawkins. Morgan was stoical as we shared a last drink together the evening before we sailed. Rowdy seafarers crowded the Plymouth tavern, shouting and cheering as they drank, gambled with cards and rattled dice.

'I've seen captains come and go.' Morgan took a swig of ale. 'My new captain is a Plymouth man named James Raunce. He has less experience of the Indies than either of us!' He scowled at the luck of others.

I shook my head at the news. 'I'd hoped to secure command of one the ships, but settled for a position as second officer of the *Pasco*.'

Morgan took a deep drink of ale and wiped his mouth on his sleeve. 'Captain Bolton's leaky old ship?' He pulled a face. 'They say he's a strict Lutheran.'

'He wishes to discover any Catholics among the crew and ensure their conversion.'

Morgan grinned. 'He'll be busy enough, then.'

The dark local ale began to numb my senses, improving my mood. I took another sip before replying. 'He's required the crew to attend a reading of the Psalms each day. We can't allow our men to have qualms about taking on Catholics, either Spanish or Portuguese.'

We could not expect a welcome from the merchants of Sierra Leone, so our fleet patrolled the blue waters of the chain of islands off Cape Verde for Portuguese slavers. Portuguese ships were known to be well-armed and would not part with their captives easily.

I scanned the foreshore of one of the larger islands as we sailed past. The sea was so clear I could make out the shadowy rocks and occasional large fish, swimming lazily under the surface. The island appeared uninhabited, but we'd been told the natives lived in the forest which gave Cape Verde its name, and hid when they sighted ships.

My pulse raced with apprehension as I spotted a Portuguese carrack of some four hundred tons, anchored in the lee of one of the islands. I pointed and called out to alert the crew. Captain Lovell's ship, the *Paul*, changed course and headed towards the carrack.

Blue castles decorated the stern of the carrack, under the gilded crown of Portugal. The dark noses of menacing cannons poked from open gun ports, and more guns were mounted on the deck. The Portuguese crewmen furled their sails, unaware of the danger they faced.

Captain Bolton gave the order for the crew of the *Pasco* to prepare for action. Steel breastplates and helmets were strapped on and the decks were cleared as the gun crews readied our bronze cannons.

I held my breath as the *Paul* sailed within range of the Portuguese guns. Her cannons boomed, sending a warning shot thundering across the Portuguese ship's bow.

Someone on the *Paul* called out in Spanish. 'Lower your standard and submit as our prize!'

The Portuguese crew shouted back in reply. I couldn't understand what they said, but the raising of their anchor told us they planned to make a run for it. I braced myself for a broadside. On a shouted command from the captain, our helmsman swung our bows into the path of the Portuguese ship to block her escape.

I feared we would be rammed, as there was no clear water for the Portuguese. The *Pasco* would come off the worse, and I had a vision of their bowsprit crashing into our side like a giant lance. My armour wouldn't help if I ended up in the water. I'd sink like a stone.

I recited a Psalm, learned by heart from my father's prayer book. *'The Lord is my light and my salvation. I will fear no one. The Lord protects me from all danger. I will never be afraid.'*

The sharp crackle of a volley of arquebus fire from the *Paul* cut through the still air, followed by shouts of alarm and cries of pain on the Portuguese ship. Unlike Captain Hawkins, Captain Lovell had no qualms about injuring the Portuguese crew.

A cheer rang out as the Portuguese carrack lowered her standard in surrender. The *Paul* went alongside with grappling hooks, and armed soldiers swarmed on to the deck to seize her. Once they had their prize, all available longboats and pinnaces were used to ferry the disarmed Portuguese crewmen ashore.

We watched from the *Pasco,* and I turned to Captain Bolton. 'What will become of them?'

He shrugged. 'It could be a while before they are missed, by which time we'll be long gone.' Bolton scowled. 'Don't waste your pity on the Portuguese, Master Drake. They plunder this coast in the name of the pope, and should be grateful for our gracious mercy.'

The next Portuguese ship we sighted looked smaller and was under way. I flinched at a muffled boom and turned to see a puff of grey smoke as she fired a warning shot from a small cannon. She wasn't going to be taken without a fight.

Captain Bolton smiled as he stood at my side. 'A good sign. They have something worth defending.'

'Their livelihood, I don't doubt, Captain. They're under full sail, and without the element of surprise, we'll not be able to stop them.'

Captain Bolton pointed. 'Captain Lovell has a plan.'

We watched as the prize ship sailed past, a Portuguese pennant flying at the mizzen-mast. As she gained on the other ship her cannons roared with the flash and sulphurous smoke of black powder, the blast of her salvo reverberating across the water.

The mast of the escaping ship shattered with a crack and hung at a drunken angle, supported only by the rigging. Captain Lovell seemed more concerned with pillaging the cargo than the damage done to captured ships, or the Catholic crewmen who sailed in them.

By the time our flotilla made ready to sail for the West Indies, we'd seized three more Portuguese ships off the largest island, Santiago, meeting little resistance. One of the Portuguese carracks was sent home to Plymouth, laden with elephant's teeth, sugar and spices.

The least damaged of the Portuguese ships, a galleon valued at fifteen thousand ducats, sailed on with us, slaves filling its cavernous hold. I transferred from the *Pasco* to the Portuguese prize ship as her second officer, not a promotion I welcomed.

I went into the hold to inspect the slaves and couldn't believe my eyes. I turned to the crewman guarding them. 'They're so close together it's difficult to tell how many there are. How do you make sure they can be cleaned or exercised?'

'They'll have to remain as they are.' The crewman scowled. 'It would take all day to bring so many topsides.'

'I'll pray we aren't becalmed on the crossing. Our water will surely run out with so many to provide for.'

I took one last look into the dark hold, fixing the sight in my memory, and resolved to make my mark on this venture. I rowed across to Captain Lovell on the *Paul*.

The captain scowled at me. 'I understand you've insisted on seeing me, Master Drake. What is it?'

'I'd like to suggest the slaves are shared among the ships more equally, Captain.'

Lovell sat back in his chair and studied me with an appraising stare, as if I tested his patience. 'You presume to tell me how to do my job?'

'Captain Hawkins would have distributed them between the fleet as a precaution against disease.'

'Captain Hawkins is not in command of this venture.' His tone sounded uncompromising.

'With your permission, Captain, there is room on the *Salomon*.'

Captain Lovell frowned. 'As you are so concerned about the slaves, they can become your responsibility. If you wish to transfer them, Master Drake, you had better get busy. We sail with the tide.'

I recalled that fateful conversation as I studied the terse letter from Captain Hawkins. Our flotilla had arrived back at Plymouth in early September, with some fifty unsold slaves, after ten months at sea. Now I'd been summoned to meet Captain Hawkins in London.

The letter, written in a business-like hand, and signed with a flourish by John Hawkins, offered no clue as to the reason for the meeting. If our venture had been a success, the summons might mean promotion, perhaps to become captain of one of his newer ships.

None of the crew were lost, or any of the slaves who

remained on board, but any goodwill Captain Hawkins struggled to build with the Spanish and Portuguese had been squandered, and his ships failed to cover their costs.

I picked up a second letter, kept safe by the dockmaster's clerk until my return, and ran my finger over the unbroken seal of dark wax. It seemed a miracle the letter had reached me, yet instinct told me the news would not be good.

Breaking the brittle seal, I unfolded the short note. The scrawled words were from my brother John, who'd remained in Medway. I wiped away a tear as I read of our father's death, a week before Christmas. I'd been on a fool's errand to the other side of the world when I should have been at my father's funeral.

I set out on the two-hundred-mile journey from Plymouth with mixed feelings. I'd been disappointed with my share of the meagre profit I'd earned on the voyage with Captain Lovell. The ownership of the prize ship was disputed, so I couldn't hope to profit from her sale, but the terse summons intrigued me.

Captain Hawkins' London house proved to be a grand mansion with high, mullioned windows overlooking the River Thames. A liveried footman led me to an oak-panelled study, where a log fire burned in a cavernous grate.

At John Hawkins' side sat an older, well-dressed man with a similar stern expression. I'd not seen him since childhood, but knew this could only be another of my distant cousins, the wealthy ship owner and merchant trader, Captain William Hawkins.

'Take a seat, Master Drake.' John Hawkins gestured towards one of the velvet upholstered chairs and glanced at his brother. 'We've heard differing accounts of your last voyage, which is why we've brought you to London.'

'I can only tell you as it was, Captain Hawkins.'

William Hawkins raised an eyebrow. 'I'm not accustomed to losing money, and neither are our investors. We want to understand how it has come about.'

'We were in luck with the Portuguese at Cape Verde, as you are no doubt aware. As well as the galleon, now in Plymouth, we seized more goods than we could carry, and a fair quantity of slaves.' I looked from one to the other. 'I had little involvement in the fighting, but was ready if needed.'

'What happened at Margarita?'

'We sailed there after our success at Santiago, and sighted a fleet of ships at anchor close to the island. I recognised some of the pennants as French, from my days in the Channel.'

Captain Hawkins turned to his brother. 'They belonged to the French corsair, Jean Bontemps. The man is little more than a pirate, who makes it more difficult for the rest of us to go about our trade.'

'Do you suspect he might be in league with the Spanish?'

John Hawkins shook his head. 'I doubt it. He cares only for himself. I never trusted him, so anything is possible.'

'I was relieved they were not Spanish ships.' I told them the truth. 'I'd been glad we got off so lightly against the Portuguese, and didn't wish to test our luck again so soon.' I glanced at William Hawkins. 'I also had concerns about the slaves. Captain Lovell made me responsible for them.'

William Hawkins nodded in understanding. 'What happened when you met the Frenchmen?'

'I was placed second in command of the Portuguese prize ship. We anchored alongside the *Paul*, and were told we would join forces with the French when we went in for water and supplies.'

John Hawkins scowled. 'The governor there made threats to us last time, although we were able to win him over.'

'Captain Lovell intended to make a show of force. I suggested we might negotiate with them first, but he said the time for talking had passed. The Frenchman told us the Spanish merchants would only trade with us under duress.'

'But were they persuaded to buy slaves?' William Hawkins sounded impatient.

'Captain Lovell sent a deputation under a flag of truce with an offer of a hundred slaves in exchange for a licence to trade. While we waited for the governor's reply, Jean Bontemps took several of the townsmen hostage and threatened to take them to France. He only released them when they agreed to buy twenty-six of his slaves.'

'Then you sailed on to Rio de Hacha?'

'The local militia stopped us from landing to take on fresh water. We arrived on the eve of Pentecost and waited until Whit Sunday, while Captain Lovell tried to obtain a licence to trade. We tried our best, Captain, even after the French ships sailed off.'

John Hawkins turned to his elder brother. 'The governor, Miguel de Castellanos, previously agreed to trade with us.' He summoned a servant and told him to bring wine. He turned back to me.

'Is it true Captain Lovell ordered the guns to be fired at the town?'

'Out of desperation. Captain Lovell ordered the *Paul's* gunners to fire a salvo of blanks, but this only provoked the Spanish militia.'

'That was when Captain Lovell put the slaves ashore?'

'We were running out of fresh water and many of the slaves were falling ill. I believed they might *all* die if the sick were left aboard, so we waited until darkness fell, then took the sick slaves to a riverbank where the militia couldn't prevent us from landing.'

A servant entered, and poured each of us a goblet of wine. I took a sip. The wine had a subtle aftertaste of spices. The opulent study was a reminder of how different my cousins' lives were from my own. They sat in the comfort of this fine London home, while I'd been dining off worm-riddled hardtack, and rationed water.

William Hawkins wanted answers. 'Is it true the fleet sailed to Hispaniola, without waiting for payment?'

'We had no choice, Captain. Our only hope was to find buyers for the remaining slaves in Hispaniola, but the Spanish governor there refused to meet with us.'

John Hawkins glanced across at his brother, and back at me. 'This venture has taught us some lessons. Captain Lovell is not the easiest of men to impress, yet he spoke highly of you, Master Drake. He told us of your concern for the welfare of his slaves, and how you kept the faith with your reading of prayers.' He glanced at his brother. 'I've kept my word to the admiralty, but my time ashore is over.'

William Hawkins leaned forward in his seat. 'You must be wondering why we brought you all the way to London.'

'In truth, I am.'

He smiled, revealing uneven teeth. 'You've shown you can remain loyal. We have a secret to share with you, which cannot be trusted to a letter. But first, you must swear to secrecy.'

'You have my word, as God is my witness.'

John Hawkins continued. 'One of the queen's ministers has engaged us to test the resolve of the Spanish.'

'They might declare war against believers of the true faith?'

William nodded. 'The command has come from the highest in the land, and we must never give the Spanish reason to suspect our true intentions.'

My pulse quickened. 'What do you plan to do?'

'We've been provided with a map of gold mines close to the African coast.'

'I've not forgotten how I nearly died last time we followed stories of gold in Africa. Can we be certain this map is genuine?'

John Hawkins raised his eyebrows at my question. 'Who can know? The map was obtained from Portuguese merchants by William Wynter, of Her Majesty's navy. I'd like you to sail with me on the *Jesus of Lubeck* for a share of the profits. What do you say to that, Master Drake?'

'It will be an honour, Captain.' This was the opportunity I'd been hoping for – a position of trust.

'Good man.' John Hawkins smiled. 'We shall take a flotilla of six ships, including another of the queen's ships, the *Minion,* captained by Thomas Hampton. Now we shall learn the King of Spain's plan – and whether there's a good profit to be made.'

4

SEPTEMBER 1567

A startled flock of oystercatchers took to the wing, piping my approach as I strolled along the bank of the River Tamar. After the noisy bustle of the harbour shipyards, I liked the quieter pace of life in the sleepy parish to the north-west of Plymouth.

It would have been easier to ride, but I used the four-mile walk from my home to rehearse my words aloud. Harry Newman, a fellow crewman on the *Pasco*, shared my Protestant faith, and had invited me to speak at his parish church in St Budeaux.

We also shared a passion for exploration, as well as a sense of humour. I smiled at the memory of Harry's poor impression of Captain John Hawkins, and how I'd teased him that his deeply tanned complexion, dark hair and well-trimmed beard made him look more like a scheming Spaniard than a Plymouth man.

I found Harry waiting to welcome me as I arrived at the village church. He held up a hand in greeting, and turned to a young woman at his side. 'My sister, Mary, has come to listen to your talk.'

'Welcome to our church.' Her eyes shone as she looked at me. 'I've been told much about you, Master Drake.'

I guessed she would be about fifteen, and she had the same dark hair as her brother. Her grey woollen dress showed off her slim figure, and a silk ribbon, the colour of a soft peach, fastened her bonnet. The twinkle in her brown eyes suggested she teased me, and I suspected Harry made more of my connection to John Hawkins than I deserved.

I smiled as I raised my cap. 'Your brother has an admirable talent for exaggeration, my lady.'

She held my gaze and returned my smile. 'Then I shall have to discover the truth for myself.'

Harry pulled open the door of the church to reveal a full congregation. I sensed curious eyes on me as we took our seats on a hard oak pew at the front. While I did my best to listen to the service, my mind filled with questions about Mary Newman.

I recalled Harry saying his late father was a gentleman mariner. In their father's absence, it would fall to Harry, as her older brother, to find Mary a suitable husband. I kept my eyes fixed on the carved oak pulpit, although I longed to steal a glance at the attractive young woman at my side.

When I stood at the pulpit, I spoke of how faith kept a ship on a true course. I held up my father's leather-bound book of Psalms, and told them how daily prayers helped a crew survive the miserable heat and thirst of the doldrums.

I avoided looking at Mary Newman, yet when I did my heart raced. She stared at me with unconcealed admiration, and gave me the briefest nod. I doubted anyone could tell but, in that shared moment, we both knew our lives had changed.

A chill October dawn shimmered in pastel shades on the waters of Sutton Pool, our Plymouth anchorage. A wave slapped the side of our sturdy rowing boat and I shivered at the thought of falling in. I'd not learned to swim, and my heavy boots would soon drag me down.

When I worked as a Channel pilot I'd witnessed a man's fall from the high yards. I'd turned at the sound of his yell of alarm and the splash as he hit the water. His eyes wide with fear, he'd flailed his arms in panic as he failed to keep afloat, and vanished under the waves.

I had more to live for now. On one of our walks along the banks of the Tamar, Mary asked when I planned to return from this voyage. I couldn't be sure, but took her hand in mine and asked if she would wait for me. Her reply was a soft kiss, and I asked her to marry me. Taking my mother's gold ring from my little finger, I found it fitted her perfectly. A good omen, sealing our betrothal.

The swarthy ferryman grunted with the effort of rowing, despite the calm day. He had a reputation for knowing everyone's business, and in a talkative mood as he took me out to the *Jesus of Lubeck*, my home for the next year or so.

'You'll be serving under a new captain, Master Drake.' He grinned as he heaved on the oars. 'Captain Robert Barrett of Saltash is a hard man to please.'

I acknowledged him with a smile. 'He's become Captain Hawkins' right-hand man.'

The ferryman nodded. 'True enough.' He glanced over his shoulder towards the *Jesus of Lubeck*, where a tall figure waited. 'That'll be him now. Looks like he's planning to greet you in person.'

'Captain Barrett is a kinsman of mine.' I doubted the captain took the trouble to meet every new member of his crew, and I recalled my conversation in London; I was no longer an ordinary member of the crew.

Robert Barrett raised a hand as we reached the ship. Well-dressed and handsome, he looked younger than I'd expected, and wore a silver-handled sword in a black leather scabbard at his belt. His dark eyes studied me, and he made no effort to help as I hauled my heavy chest up the dangling rope ladder.

'Welcome aboard, Master Drake.' His voice carried the rich accent of my West Country cousins. 'That's a grand new sea chest.'

'I have more to carry with each voyage, Captain.'

Despite its cumbersome weight, my new sea chest was empty apart from my plate armour, a change of clothes, my tankard, battered pewter bowl, knife and spoon. Hidden in a fold of cloth was a ribbon of peach-coloured silk, a keepsake with the power to make my pulse race with its promise.

My collection of books had grown, for I'd bought a translation of *The Art of Navigation* by Pedro de Medina, cosmographer to the King of Spain. As well as my father's book of Psalms, I'd brought a Bible, bound in black leather with a gilded cross on the cover. I'd also brought a journal, goose-feather quills and two bottles of ink, to keep notes of our voyage.

Like all the men aboard the *Jesus of Lubeck*, my hopes of making my fortune were invested in the success of this venture. My privileged knowledge of William Wynter's map meant I had reason to be more confident than most that we would discover gold in Africa.

The queen's well-proportioned carrack *Minion*, of three hundred tons, sat at anchor alongside the *Jesus of Lubeck*. Close by was the *William and John,* of a hundred and fifty tons, under the command of another of my former captains, Master Thomas Bolton.

I peered out to the mouth of the River Plym, where several of William Hawkins' smaller ships, including the familiar *Swallow* of my first voyage, sat alongside the fifty-ton *Judith*. With the thirty-ton supply ship *Angel*, they all flew the red cross of St George at their mastheads and sailed in support of the queen's ships.

Although not the grandest fleet to set sail from Plymouth, our venture had been well planned and provisioned. Thanks to his royal and government connections, Captain Hampton had his pick of the most experienced crewmen, over four hundred in total. We also carried bales of fine linens from Ireland and rich cloth from the northern weavers to trade.

I knew John Hampton well enough to believe him to be sincere in his wish not to provoke a war with the Spanish or Portuguese. At the same time, every man aboard knew we hoped to trade in slaves, and any Catholic ships we encountered would be plundered without mercy.

On this voyage I shared a cramped corner of the gun deck with the sardonic navigator of the *Jesus of Lubeck*, William Saunders, a Cornishman with a thick beard. He welcomed me with a broad grin. 'I hear you're to read the Psalms to the men, Master Drake.'

I couldn't miss the scorn in his voice, and suspected my new companion might be one of the Catholic spies I'd been warned about. 'My father was a preacher, Master Saunders.' My voice faltered with an unexpected sense of loss at referring to my father in the past tense 'He taught me well.'

Saunders pointed a nail-bitten finger across the harbour at the gathering clouds. 'You might pray for good sailing weather.' His eyes narrowed in a frown. 'I fear this poor old ship will be tested if we meet a storm.'

I agreed. 'We were unlucky to be caught in a Biscay storm on my first voyage with Captain Hawkins.' I shook my head at the memory. 'The fleet was scattered, and I expected at least one ship to be lost, but we all made it to Tenerife.'

William Saunders' concern about the brooding skies proved right. After only four days of sailing, the winds whipped up to storm force. I fastened my warm cloak and clambered out on deck. One of the mainsails had ripped from top to bottom and the torn canvas flapped like the cracking of a whip.

I watched as the crew wrestled with the damaged sail, trying to control the *Jesus of Lubeck* in the heavy seas. For once, her lumbering weight worked in our favour. Her bows carved a path through the waves like a plough behind a team of oxen, but her age was beginning to show.

Built as a floating fortress rather than for speed, windage from the top-heavy forecastle placed great strain on her rotting timbers in storm conditions. The old oak creaked in protest, and we made poor headway, despite the efforts of the crew. Staring up at the worsening skies, I said a prayer for salvation. We would need God's help to ride this storm.

The ship rolled in the heavy seas, a sign the men on the pumps were fighting a losing battle to keep the water from the bilges. I climbed to the gallery at the top of the sterncastle, where John Hawkins stood with the captain. They both wore heavy capes, and even from a distance I understood their concern as they looked out to our wake.

Captain Barrett called out to me. 'Our fleet has been dispersed, Master Drake.'

I gripped the rail as another wave slapped against the side, sending a shower of salty spray high into the air. 'They might have turned back for Plymouth, Captain.' I spotted a small ship, forging bravely through white-crested waves, and pointed. 'I'll swear that's the *Angel*.'

John Hawkins squinted at the distant ship. 'She does well to keep up with us in these conditions.' He glanced up as lightning flashed in the sky, followed by the rumble of thunder. 'Have the men keep up their good work on the pumps, Captain Barrett. The *Jesus of Lubeck* leaks like a broken bucket. If this storm doesn't improve soon, *we* will have no choice but to turn back to Plymouth.'

We battled on for another three days before the storm blew over, our flotilla scattered like dry autumn leaves. Captain Hawkins ordered us to set a course to the island of Tenerife, and I gathered the crew on deck for prayers of thanksgiving. Followed by our supply ship the *Angel*, we reached Tenerife, where we made repairs and waited for the rest of the fleet.

There was a rousing cheer as the rest of our fleet were spotted two days later. They'd all been blown off course by the storm but, by a miracle, survived in good condition. Now the fleet had been restored we could resume our planned course, and make our way to Cape Verde.

I had misgivings about raiding the native village under cover of night. Although we'd have the element of surprise, I'd seen how fiercely African warriors could fight. I wore my plate armour and my new sword, but worried I might not be able to kill a man – even in self-defence.

The burly pikeman in front of me cursed as he stumbled on a thick root crossing the narrow forest path. I watched for any movement in the trees, and a pair of luminous eyes caught the moonlight. Some strange animal watched us from the cover of darkness. Dry leaves rustled close by, and I recalled the sailors' stories.

We'd been warned of fearsome snakes that killed with one strike of their poisonous fangs, deadly black scorpions, and spiders the size of a man's hand. I flinched as something wailed like a ghost in the darkness. This jungle was no place to be exploring at night.

We'd landed after midnight, but with more than two hundred men blundering about in the dark, it was impossible to keep our approach a secret. My throat felt as dry as parchment, and I wished, too late, I'd voiced my concerns to Captain Hawkins when I'd had the opportunity.

Once again, we risked our lives to capture more slaves, yet we still had the fifty we'd taken on our last visit to the islands of Cape Verde. John Hawkins had been critical of Captain Lovell for returning with unsold slaves, but much had changed since our first venture. At least Hawkins was leading us, so if the raid proved a failure he would take his share of the blame.

The forest path widened into an open clearing, and the dark shapes of native huts were silhouetted in the moonlight. The village was shrouded in eerie silence as we crept closer, the only sounds the occasional metallic clank of armour, muttered curses and whispered reminders to keep quiet.

We planned to surround the encampment and prevent anyone escaping. I followed the men in single file as we encircled the huts, watching for any sign of movement. I began to believe the place deserted when a snarling dog ran towards me, its bark echoing until one of the men gave it a kick in the ribs. The dog skulked away, whining, but had served its purpose, as the villagers began to wake.

A sharp whistle blast sounded, our signal to close in. We carried ropes cut into lengths for binding our captives. Captain

Hawkins' orders were to leave the young and old, and to take care not to harm or injure the rest, who would be taken to the West Indies. He'd made it sound simple enough, but we'd not expected such chaos once the villagers woke.

The shrill screams of women and children mixed with the angry shouts of men. The natives fought for their lives but were outnumbered, and began running for the cover of the trees. Some were caught as they tried to escape, others were dragged from their huts and ushered into the clearing.

I was thanking God our plan had worked when Robert Barrett called out to me for help. Captain Hawkins lay on the ground, the broken shaft of an arrow sticking from a bleeding wound in his shoulder. As I rushed over to him, men began falling to the ground, yelling in pain and alarm, as more arrows flew from the darkness.

John Hawkins clenched his teeth as Robert Barrett wrenched the arrow free. Captain Barrett frowned as he studied the bloodied tip. The arrowhead was still attached. He threw it to one side and tore a strip of linen from his shirt, fastening it over the wound.

He turned to me, his face grim. 'Help him back to the boats, Master Drake, quick as you can.'

I pulled my cousin's good arm over my shoulder and helped him to stand. 'Can you walk, Captain?'

John Hawkins forced a weak smile. 'Hurts like hell – but we'd best get going.'

I turned for one last look as woodsmoke drifted on the still air. Bright orange flames leapt high from the palm-thatched huts, set ablaze by our departing men. The destructive act was not one I would have condoned if I'd been in command.

I said a prayer of thanks for being spared when we returned to the ship. Events in the village unfolded so quickly I'd not even drawn my sword. As well as Captain Hawkins, some twenty men suffered serious wounds, mostly from arrows. A dozen more were lost, and only nine slaves were captured.

Many of the injured men began to shake and shiver with a strange fever, which made them clamp their teeth so tight they couldn't eat or drink. The superstitious crew of the *Jesus of Lubeck* became restless. There was talk of poisoned arrows as eight of them died, one by one.

Captain Hawkins recovered from his injury, risking a poultice of garlic rather than endure the agony of having the wound cauterised with a hot iron. His young nephew Paul, who'd proudly told me he would soon be twelve, added nursing duties to the many other tasks of a boy on board a ship.

A bright, cheerful lad, he'd congratulated me for rescuing his uncle. I'd dismissed his words with a shrug, and said I'd been following Master Barrett's orders. In truth, his gratitude meant a lot to me, a reminder of the son I'd like to have one day.

As we continued south, the lookout shouted 'Sail ahoy!', and the order was given to prepare for action. After our brush with disaster at the native village, I hoped they were more Portuguese slavers. Captain Hawkins studied the ships and turned to me as they came nearer.

'French corsairs. It looks as if they've captured a Portuguese caravel.'

'I believe the French made our work harder by taking hostages on my last voyage, Captain.'

Captain Hawkins agreed. 'Have the men ready a boat, Master Drake. I shall speak with their commander under a flag of truce.'

I was impressed by my cousin's bravery as we watched him cross to the French ships in the longboat. When he returned, he called for me and Captain Barrett to meet him in his cabin. He confessed his shoulder wound still troubled him, yet managed a smile.

'The Frenchmen wish to join our expedition, and sail with us to the West Indies. I've agreed, in return for their stolen Portuguese ship, which is named the *Gracia Dei*, together with its cargo.'

Robert Barrett frowned. 'Does she carry slaves, Captain?'

'She does not, Captain Barrett, but she's a good ship, with eight guns and a hold filled with casks of wine and loaves of sugar.' John Hawkins turned to me. 'I'm putting you in command of the *Gracia Dei*, Master Drake. You can take a crew of a dozen men to keep an eye on the French.'

I couldn't believe my luck. 'Thank you, Captain. I'll not let you down.'

For the first time since I sold the old coastal bark, I had my own command, and men would call me Captain Drake. I hummed an old tune as I packed my few belongings. I would appoint my old crewmate Morgan as bosun, to help me choose my crew.

Robert Barrett was the first to visit my new ship and brought news. 'Captain Hawkins is dissatisfied with our progress. He's gone ashore to meet with a tribal chief to see if we can enlist his support.'

'For another raid on a village?'

Robert Barrett shook his head. 'He plans to attack a town near Sierra Leone. Captain Hawkins suffers with his shoulder wound, so he's asked me to lead it.'

'This time we must be better prepared, and wait until dawn.' Now I'd become a captain, the time had come to show leadership, and I didn't wish to lose my command after so short a time.

Captain Barratt gave me an appraising look. 'I'm going to discover how the land lies. Captain Hawkins says the town is fortified, so I want to make sure we aren't walking into a trap.'

My men stood ready at the guns while we waited on the *Gracia Dei* for news. I'd chosen good sailors, rather than fighting men, for my small crew, and placed Morgan in charge of some of the more experienced men, to be ready to support the raid if needed.

The order finally came for the *Swallow, William and John* and my ship to follow the *Jesus of Lubeck* up the river to provide reinforcements. Captain Barratt reported that a high fence of sharpened stakes protected the town, which would make the attack more difficult.

I watched from *Gracia Dei* as my small group of men joined over two hundred from the *Jesus of Lubeck* and were ferried to the bank. Morgan raised a hand in a wave as they disappeared towards the town. I fought against the premonition this venture would not go well.

Several hours passed before I spotted a thick pall of smoke rising into the air. Our boats left the shore, the oarsmen rowing with an effort against the wind and tide. I counted my crew. One of them had not returned. Morgan sat in the stern of the boat, calling the stroke in his Welsh accent, yet didn't seem his usual cheerful self.

'It was a massacre.' Morgan shook his head as he clambered aboard. 'We stood back and watched while the tribes fought each other. A good number of the natives were killed or wounded.'

I poured him a cup of ale. 'What about the other crews?'

Morgan frowned. 'At least four men from the *Jesus of Lubeck* were killed. The townspeople were putting up quite a fight until the town houses were set alight.'

I later learned we took some two hundred and fifty slaves, with nine of our men injured in the raid. More died later from the strange malady that meant they couldn't open their mouths. Two men were drowned when rowing close to the swamp. A savage sea horse with huge tusks, as large as a fully grown bull, reared from the water with a roar. They tried to defend themselves with their oars, but the creature swamped their boat.

At last, we were to sail for the West Indies. Our fleet doubled in size with my ship, as well as four other smaller vessels, captured en route. As I prayed for the success of our next adventure, I was struck by an inspiring realisation. *Gracia Dei* meant the grace of God, a good omen. By the Lord's grace, I'd been offered this chance to show what I could do.

5

MARCH 1568

'Land ho!'

Our lookout pointed to the familiar shape of the mountains of Margarita, like a giant beached whale on the otherwise empty horizon. We needed to take on fresh water, and trade linens for salted pork and fruit, yet there were always risks this far from home.

As we drew close, the sun glinted on a row of new cannons pointing out to sea. The Spanish claimed their defences were to prevent piracy, but I imagined they wouldn't hesitate to use their guns against our vulnerable ships lying at anchor in the bay, within easy range.

I buckled my breastplate over my doublet as a precaution, and carried my sword at my belt, which at least gave me the appearance of authority. The islanders were not to know my sword had yet to be drawn in anger, or that we feared for our safety. Heavily outnumbered, there would be little we could do if they attacked us.

The Spanish militia remained within the high stone walls of their fort, yet we were conscious of flashes of sunlight glinting on their armour as we carried the heavy water casks back to our waiting boats. We were under orders from Captain Hawkins not to sell any slaves, although I longed to see the large white pearls which made Margarita so wealthy.

Relieved to return safely to the *Gracia Dei*, I set sail to follow the fleet to the port of Borburata. We waited while Captain Hawkins led a shore party in the hope of meeting the new Spanish governor. When he eventually returned to the *Jesus of Lubeck,* he sent his messenger, summoning me to meet with him in his cabin.

I found him alone, and sensed from his mood the meeting ashore had not gone well. He loosened the aiglet of his high collar, rubbing a red mark on his neck absent-mindedly. Gesturing towards an empty chair, he poured a generous measure of wine into a silver cup, which he handed to me.

'Master Drake, I need you to do something for me.'

'Of course, Captain.' I sat down and sipped his stolen Portuguese wine. John Hawkins' cabin looked expensively furnished, with beeswax candles flickering in silver candlesticks. Even the chair I sat in, upholstered in burgundy velvet, served as a reminder of the life I hoped to lead.

Captain Hawkins studied me in silence, seemingly lost in his memories. 'My plan was to acknowledge to the governor that we have no permit to trade. I'd hoped his conscience would not prevent him paying for our slaves.'

'What did he say?'

'Our reputation precedes us, Master Drake. The governor told me the king's men arrested his predecessor for illegally dealing in slaves – with me.'

'He turned you down?'

'I decided to go behind his back, but had to threaten the merchants before they would part with their money.' Captain Hawkins gave a wry smile. 'All for show, but the governor will no doubt alert neighbouring ports to our presence.'

I recalled Morgan's warning, a world away in the Plymouth tavern. We played this game of chance for the highest stakes, with severe consequences if we were captured by the Spanish. Morgan said a swift execution would be merciful, as the Spanish tortured confessions from their prisoners using the cruellest of methods.

I kept my concerns from my voice and looked John Hawkins in the eye. 'What is it you wish me to do, Captain?'

'We need to know if it's safe to sail into Rio de Hacha. I'm putting you in command of the *Judith,* as Captain Dudley has died of his wound from a poisoned arrow.' He grimaced, no doubt recalling his own wound. 'You are to sail ahead with the *Angel* to prepare the way for the rest of the fleet.'

I sat back in my chair, taken by surprise. The *Gracia Dei* was a prize ship, taken by force from the Portuguese. My presence there had been administrative, to keep an eye on the crew and cargo. I'd hoped my command would be a stepping-stone to greater responsibility, but had not expected to progress so swiftly.

'Rio de Hacha.' I studied the long sandy beach, punctuated by leaning palm trees and thatched huts. A few old fishing boats were pulled up on the sand but there were no signs of activity. 'The place looks peaceful enough. Why do they call it the river of the axe?'

Morgan, transferred at my request as bosun of the *Judith*, stroked the grey stubble on his chin. 'The Spanish used the native name. There was an old legend—'

His words were cut short by the thunderous boom of a cannon from the shore, followed by a puff of smoke and the sharp, staccato cracks of arquebus fire. A splinter flew from the thick mast, leaving a scar of bright wood. I'd ducked by instinct but my heart pounded at how close it had been.

The cannonball splashed into the sea twenty paces away, but several arquebus bullets hit the *Judith*. What the Spanish lacked in accuracy, they made up for with volleys of repeated fire. They'd waited until we were within easy range, the mark of trained militiamen.

My steel breastplate might have stopped a bullet at such a range, but I had no wish to test its effectiveness. I told Morgan to sail us out to safety before the Spanish could reload their cannons. The *Judith* was small but nimble, and we were soon weighing anchor with the *Angel*, out of range in the wide, sweeping bay.

As captain, I had to decide our course of action. I'd answered John Hawkins' question about the greeting he could expect, yet could do more before the fleet arrived. We flew the red cross of England, and had done nothing to justify being fired upon. Morgan must have seen my indecision, as he offered a suggestion.

'I'll take the longboat ashore, and ask for fresh water.' He squinted towards the sandy beach, from where the dark figures of a group of men were watching. 'It's a risk, but we're not at war with the Spanish.'

I agreed. 'Carry a flag of truce as a precaution, and request a meeting with the governor.'

With a grin, Morgan shouted instructions to the crew, enjoying his role as bosun. I watched as the longboat made steady progress towards the shore. The sun, rising high in the clear blue sky, reflected on the tranquil, sparkling water of the sheltered bay.

They rowed towards the beach, the makeshift white flag held high, a symbol of our good intentions. Shouts in Spanish echoed across the water, followed by the rattling cracks of another volley of arquebus fire. I cursed the Spaniards, as I'd taken a risk with the lives of my men with no risk to my own.

After more yelling and curses, the longboat turned and headed back. As it came closer, Morgan tore a bandage from his linen shirt and bound it over a wounded man's head. The only physician with the fleet sailed aboard the *Jesus of Lubeck*, which would not arrive until too late.

I watched as they carried the wounded man aboard and lay him on the deck. I recognised him, although I didn't know him by name. A Bristolian, popular with the crew for his ready wit, his wide eyes stared and he called out in pain.

I pulled the soaked cloth from his wound. I'd hoped the bullet had made a glancing blow, but found shards of the man's skull, awash with bright-red blood. He didn't have a chance. Putting the cloth back in place, I watched as Morgan bound the wound with a fresh bandage, torn from his ragged shirt.

All sailors knew they might endure the loss of a hand, even an arm or leg, but wounds such as this were beyond our modest skills. We stayed with him, and I said a prayer for his soul as his strength ebbed, and his breathing stopped, a pointless sacrifice of a good English sailor.

Morgan cursed. 'They never let us come close, and ignored our flag of truce.' He pulled off the remains of his bloodstained shirt and used it to cover the dead man's eyes, still wide and staring, as if he accused us of his murder.

'He shall have a Christian burial.' The guilt that I'd not troubled to ask his name was followed by anger at the Spanish militia who'd taken his life. 'First, though, we shall have our revenge on those who did this. Call the men to action stations, Master Morgan. We'll sail in close and show them what our gunners can do.'

. . .

The governor's residence, a whitewashed building with a roof of decorative terracotta tiles, offered a good target for our gun crew. The militia who killed our crewman were acting on the governor's orders, so it seemed fitting he should suffer the consequences.

Shots from the deck-mounted swivel guns scattered the Spanish militia, gathering on the shore as we approached. Their bravery in taking on an unarmed longboat deserted them, and they ran for cover. It would not be long before we came under fire, but that was a risk we must take.

The heavy cannons on the *Judith* were made ready by the gunners, the iron shot so heavy it took two men to lift each one into place. I recalled grim stories of rarely used cannons such as these exploding and killing the crew, so with trepidation I gave the order for firing to begin.

Our cannon boomed with a deafening roar, and the gun crews cheered as we scored a direct hit with the first shot. The masonry of the governor's house flew into the air, and the gunners fired a second shot, which crashed into the roof, scattering the ornate tiles.

I was about to order a third reminder to the governor when our lookout alerted us to a ship approaching from the seaward side. A caravel, she flew the flag of Spain and made good progress towards us. I was sure they'd witnessed our attack, although they would have no idea of the reason for it. Her huge lateen sails gave her speed, yet she proved no match for the *Judith*.

Morgan shielded his eyes with a grubby hand as he studied the approaching ship. 'They're coming for us.' He frowned. 'Do you think we should fire a warning shot?'

'Have the men make ready, Morgan. I'd like to take her as a prize if we can.' Intrigued to discover what she carried, I knew Captain Hawkins would be glad to capture another caravel.

One of the starboard cannons boomed our warning yet, despite the shot splashing close to his bow, the Spanish captain held his course. We were going to have to fight for our prize, and there would be no going back. Either by luck or good judgement he'd trapped us in the bay, too late for the *Angel* to help.

The experienced captain presented his bows to us, the smallest target for our guns, while attacking with arquebus fire. With a thunderous boom our cannons fired again, this time with chain shot, ripping into the rigging of the Spanish ship. Her mainsail tore and the mast leaned at a rakish angle, to another cheer from our gunners.

Their reply was another volley of arquebus fire, at closer range this time. One of our crew suffered a fatal wound as a bullet struck him in the face. Another was hit in the arm, and a third died when a bullet struck him in the chest.

I cursed the Spanish, and was about to give the order to take evasive action when the approaching caravel changed course and headed for the shore. 'They're going to run her aground!' I turned to Morgan. 'Follow her in, as close as we can. We'll use her for target practice.'

We watched as the damaged caravel crunched into hidden rocks and foundered in the shallows. Her crew made their escape to the beach in a longboat, a few men choosing to wade in the chest-deep water. Now we had the chance to find out what the Spanish ship carried.

'Take a boarding party, Master Morgan, and tell the men they shall have a share of the spoils for their trouble.'

By the time Captain Hawkins arrived with the fleet, we were in position with the *Angel* to control the approaches to Rio de Hacha. John Hawkins raised an eyebrow when I told him we'd found nothing of value on the grounded Spanish caravel, and was displeased to learn we'd lost three crewmen.

He studied the governor's ruined house, no doubt wondering if there was more I could tell him. 'We'll take no more chances, Master Drake. We'll go ashore with two hundred of our most experienced men.' He scowled. 'Let's see if the governor changes his tune when we threaten to burn his town.'

I wore my armour and stayed to the rear, after seeing how effective the arquebusiers could be. This proved wise when the Spanish militia began firing volleys, killing two of Hawkins' men, and wounding half a dozen of those in our front ranks.

Determined to resolve our differences with the governor, Captain Hawkins persisted with his demands for a meeting. When these were refused, he ordered his men to set fire to twenty houses in the town, including the governor's damaged residence. The tang of woodsmoke filled the air as a light breeze fanned the flames, carrying grey smoke across the wide bay.

I was starting to believe we should leave the island when Morgan appeared, grinning with his news. 'One of the Spanish slaves showed Captain Hawkins where the Spanish hid two cartloads of valuables!'

'And we're going to take them?' Any pretence of our good intentions had gone. 'We could find they send the entire Spanish fleet to pursue us.'

Morgan laughed. 'Don't you see? The governor will be made to pay a ransom in return for their possessions, and pay for a good number of our slaves into the bargain!'

As we sailed to our next port, I was surprised to find Morgan in a dour mood, and learned that Captain Hawkins had handed over the slave who'd led us to their secret hoard. The governor promptly ordered the unfortunate man to be strung up from the nearest tree, as Captain Hawkins surely knew he would.

The news troubled me, yet nothing would be achieved by confronting Captain Hawkins about his actions. At best, he'd tell me not to question his authority, but I'd also risk a charge of insubordination and could be marked as a troublemaker.

We reached the settlement of Santa Marta, a peaceful town ringed with tall palms. Once again, we made a token attack. This time our cannons fired only wadding before the Spanish governor agreed to buy a hundred of our remaining slaves.

We had less luck in Cartagena, where cannons were fired to warn us off, but only fifty of our slaves remained unsold, and we'd made a good profit.

The dazzling sun and oppressive heat we'd complained about was replaced by a squall of rain which lashed the deck, a reminder the hurricane season loomed. I would command the *Judith* for the long voyage home, but first our fleet of eight ships would seek refuge in a sheltered bay on the Florida coast.

Captain Hawkins said we had no choice. 'The *Jesus of Lubeck* has succumbed to her great age.' He shook his head. 'Her planking lets in the sea on both sides, and fish have been seen swimming in the bilges.'

The leviathan of a ship was careened on her side with thick hawsers, while her crew did their best to caulk the gaps. We beached the smaller *Judith* on a high tide, and all joined in, scraping barnacles and the slimy growth of green weed from her hull in preparation for the challenging journey ahead.

September winds were thrumming in the rigging before we were ready to depart, and autumn storms drove us west into the Gulf of Mexico, where we rested in the port of San Juan de Ulúa.

I counted eight Spanish ships at anchor, and watched a sailing tender deliver a delegation of Spanish officials to the *Jesus of Lubeck*. We later learned this included the deputy governor, who Hawkins held hostage to ensure our safety while we made final repairs.

Despite this precaution, word had been sent to summon the Mexican fleet, which arrived with two warships and a dozen converted merchantmen.

We were outnumbered, but Captain Hawkins ordered all ships to send as many men as could be spared ashore to seize the fort and cannons intended to defend the harbour.

The fortress looked no more than a stone tower, with a gun platform on the top, and a wall to fortify the quay. By seizing control, we could at least ensure it wasn't used against our ships. Morgan volunteered to take our gunners in the longboat.

'It will give me great satisfaction to blast the Spanish with their own guns.' He grinned, but I guessed he was thinking of the Bristol man we'd failed to save.

I unbuckled the leather fastenings of my breastplate and handed it to him. 'Strap this on, Morgan. You still owe me a drink in the Plymouth tavern, and I don't want some Spaniard leaving me thirsty.'

As they rowed for the shore, a messenger arrived in a tender from the *Jesus of Lubeck*. He didn't come aboard but shouted our orders. 'An exchange of hostages has been agreed. Captain Hawkins wishes to be certain the repairs are sound, then we'll be on our way.'

His words were greeted with a cheer from the remaining crew. We'd been through a lot together, and were ready for the rewards of risking our lives, and a spell ashore before our next adventure. I retired to my bunk to dream of buying a house with sea views, with a young wife for company, perhaps one day a son and heir...

.   .   .

I'd been fast asleep when the night watchman roused me, his thick cape dripping with rain. 'The Spanish have boarded several of our ships, Captain.'

After months of taking Portuguese ships with impunity, and trading in slaves without permission, the might of Spain had caught us napping, and now, so close to leaving for home, we would face the consequences.

'Call the men to action!'

I reached for my breastplate, and remembered I'd given it to Morgan, so grabbed my sword and rushed up to the deck. The clash of steel, murderous yelling and the cloying smell of gun smoke told me all I needed to know. The Spanish had ambushed our fleet under cover of darkness.

A barrage of cannon fire thundered from the Spanish fleet and the shore batteries. A direct hit smashed into my old ship, the *Gracia Dei*, and another shattered the mainmast of our sister ship, the *Angel*, which toppled and fell with a crash on to her deck.

They turned their attention to the tired timbers of the *Jesus of Lubeck*. At such close range the cannon fire shredded the once proud ship, holing her at the waterline. She would not be sailing back to Plymouth, and I feared for her crew.

The shore battery continued to pound us, and the dreadful truth dawned on me. The men we'd sent ashore, including Morgan, must have been overrun by the Spanish. I recalled the heavy chests of gold, silver and pearls in Captain Hawkins' cabin. If we couldn't salvage our fortune, the whole venture would be for nothing.

I called all hands to set the sails. 'We are not going to surrender our share of the treasure to the Spanish!' Taking an axe, I hacked at our thick anchor rope, cutting us free of our mooring. Every second could mean the difference between life and death.

The *Minion*'s luck changed, as their gunners must have hit the magazine of one of the closest Spanish warships. My ears rang and I was deafened as she exploded with a blinding flash which lit up the entire bay, throwing men and shards of timber in all directions.

We came alongside the *Jesus of Lubeck* and threw our grappling hooks. Her crew began jumping aboard with whatever they could carry, and I feared we'd be overburdened. We were joined by the *Minion*, and Captain Hawkins leapt across, shouting commands to the men struggling with his heavy sea chests.

Roaring orange flames reached the tarred rigging of the *Jesus of Lubeck*, flaring even brighter, and lighting up the night sky. We had to pull clear of the burning ship, leaving the men on her deck torn between jumping into the sea or taking their chances with the Spanish.

I recognised one of them as Captain Hawkins' eleven-year-old nephew Paul, who stood clutching a gilded plate. He called out to his uncle in a shrill voice, yet the gap was too wide for him to jump, even if he had the strength, and tears glistened on his young face.

I froze with indecision, torn between the desire to save him and the risk to our ship. Captain Hawkins shouted for us to help save more men, but the crackling flames and smoke of an approaching Spanish fireship spurred me into the only possible course of action. I ordered my crew to take advantage of the offshore breeze to make for the safety of the open sea.

As captain, my first duty was to my ship and crew. Our situation looked hopeless, and Spanish warships threatened to block our escape. The *Angel* was sinking, and I was determined the *Judith* would not suffer the tragic fate of the *Jesus of Lubeck*. I would see her safely moored in Plymouth, or die in the attempt.

6

MARCH 1569

I leaned on the old harbour wall and stared out across the grey sea. A lone herring gull shrieked like a lost soul as it skimmed the waves in search of sustenance. The same familiar fishing boats bobbed at the quayside, and a familiar, misty rain added a salty edge to the onshore breeze. Nothing much had changed in the town of Plymouth – except for me.

We'd returned home in late January, exhausted and in desperate need of water. My brave ship, the *Judith*, had been battered by fierce storms, her sails in tatters and her crew exhausted. The leaking bilges meant working the pumps day and night, yet we were alive, and able to enjoy our freedom.

Although we'd not sighted her once on the crossing, the *Minion* moored at Mount's Bay in Penzance a few days later. Only fifteen men – including Captain Hawkins and Mary's brother, Harry Newman – survived from the crew of over a hundred who'd escaped the attack at San Juan de Ulúa.

Harry looked thin and close to tears as he told me how men had begged to be put ashore. 'Others died from illness or starvation.' He shook his head at the memory, but managed a smile. 'We boiled the ship's cat, tail and all, to make a stew, and drew lots to eat our talking parrot, brought home as a trophy.'

Our spirits were lifted by word that the *William and John* had been blown off course, but reached landfall on the coast of Ireland in February. Then came the shocking news that she'd been lost with all hands in a fierce winter storm on the voyage home to Plymouth.

I'd kept a tally of known survivors in my notebook, and had been chilled to count only seventy returning from over four hundred men who'd sailed with our fleet from Plymouth, full of hope, in October 1567. All our other ships were lost or seized by the Spanish, with most of their crews.

This meant I had more than my fair share of our salvaged fortune. Although now a wealthy man, able to rent a fine house in the town, the true cost weighed heavily on my conscience, and left me in a dour mood. I caught Mary looking at me with concern in her dark eyes. She seemed to understand I needed time before I'd be ready to make plans for our wedding.

I prayed every day for those we'd abandoned to their fate, yet knew the lucky ones were those who died in the battle. Any who were captured and taken prisoner by the Spanish would have faced torture before being executed, or spared for the final irony of our voyage – to be sold into a life of slavery.

Captain Hawkins looked as if he also had the lives of those we'd left behind on his conscience. The frown lines in his thinner face were deeper, his once dark hair and beard tinged with grey. He'd summoned me to his large Plymouth house and offered me a seat by his blazing fire.

Although he'd not mentioned me by name, I knew he'd accused the *Judith* of abandoning the fleet, when he'd followed us soon after in the *Minion*. I'd been furious at first, as we'd saved as many men as we could from the burning *Jesus of Lubeck*, but I sensed he now understood. We had no choice – to have stayed any longer would have meant death or capture.

'I fear my days of adventure at sea are over.' His voice sounded flat, and he gave me a questioning look, perhaps wondering how much I knew.

'The disaster at San Juan de Ulúa has made me determined to return, Captain. I've sworn an oath before God to avenge our lost shipmates.'

As always with John Hawkins, I struggled to read his mind. Despite losing his ships, and a heavy case of silver and pearls, he'd returned with a great fortune, and had the power and influence to help my plans – or, if he wished, to prevent them.

He crossed to his desk, picking up a letter, then returned to his place by the fire and unfolded the square of parchment.

'I've received the worst news from my agent, Pedro de Ponte. I regret to tell you a number of the men we left behind were publicly hanged as pirates.' His voice wavered. 'Some were flogged, with as many as two hundred lashes, enough to finish them in their weakened state, or leave them scarred for life.'

I dreaded to imagine the fate of Michael Morgan, and recalled his cheery goodbye as he rowed ashore. My friend had a way with words, so I hoped the brave Welshman persuaded the Spanish Inquisition of his innocence. I would find his parents, and let them have his share, for the care of his children.

Captain Hawkins glanced down at the letter in his hand, and appeared to be struggling to compose himself. 'The Spanish Inquisition tortured our kinsman, Captain Robert Barrett, and burned him alive in Seville market square.'

I sat in silence for a moment, shaken by the news. 'You should not blame yourself, Captain. We all knew the risks.'

He shook his head. 'Robert volunteered to board the

Spanish flagship under a flag of truce. I could have stopped him, but it seemed a good plan. He never came back.' Captain Hawkins looked up at me, as if reaching a judgement. 'I would like to provide you with the opportunity to redeem yourself, Master Drake. My brother William and I have a task for you.'

He returned to his desk and handed me two parchment letters. 'These must be delivered to William Cecil. One is addressed to the Royal Privy Council, the other must only be seen by him. Do you understand?' His tone sounded conspiratorial.

'Of course, Captain.'

'While we were at sea, a fleet of ships carrying a fortune in Spanish silver coin sought shelter here in Plymouth, as well as at Falmouth and Fowey. They carried the pay for the Spanish army in Flanders, and were impounded by the Crown.'

'Might I know what is being asked of William Cecil?'

Captain Hawkins nodded. 'We intend to ask for a share of the silver, in restitution for our losses. Master Cecil will have questions about our conduct, and I've chosen you as the man best placed to answer them.'

I passed the time on my long ride to London planning my future. I'd learned much from my last voyage, particularly the advantage of a smaller barque like the *Judith* over a leviathan like the ill-fated *Jesus of Lubeck*. Captain Hawkins might lease me such a ship, and crewmen from the *Judith* and *Minion* would sail with me for a share of the spoils, in lieu of pay.

After what I'd witnessed on my last voyage, I would train the crew of my new ship to use deck-mounted swivel guns, as well as heavy cannons, and provide them all with steel helmets and breastplates. I'd learned from being vulnerable under Spanish fire, watching men die for no good reason.

London bustled with activity as I made my way to William Cecil's office in Westminster. The starched ruff at my neck itched and I wished I'd worn my fur-lined winter cloak, as a chill breeze carried the stench of raw sewage from the Thames. Merchant ships and barges jostled for space at the busy wharves, but none flew the flags of Spain or Portugal.

A grim-faced secretary kept me waiting outside in the long draughty corridor for the best part of an hour before ushering me in to William Cecil's grand, high-ceilinged office. I bowed as a mark of respect.

'Captain Francis Drake, at your service...' I realised I had no idea how I should address him, and quickly added, 'My lord.'

William Cecil sat behind a polished wooden desk. Older than I'd expected, his hair and beard were white, and so fine I could tell his pale face had not seen much sun. He wore a velvet tunic the colour of rich wine, with a ruff edged with lace and a gold collar of the Order of the Garter, decorated with Tudor roses.

He gestured for me to take a seat and his intelligent, blue-grey eyes examined me, as if passing judgement. I resented these men of noble birth, looking down their noses at me. I came from humble stock, but my father taught me to take pride in my family connections.

Reaching into the leather wallet, I pulled out the letters I'd guarded with such care on the long journey. I passed them to him across his polished desk.

'I've brought these for you, my lord, from Captain John Hawkins—'

'You work for Captain John Hawkins?' William Cecil took the letters and lay them on his desk, but didn't open them.

'I do, sir. I served as captain of the *Gracia Dei*, then the *Judith*, and have sailed with my kinsman, Captain Hawkins, these past four years.' Pride at my achievement carried in my voice. I hadn't left Plymouth as a captain, but I had returned as one, with more experience than some men gained in a lifetime at sea.

William Cecil's pale fingers stroked his beard. He reached for one of the letters, and cracked open the wax seal, skimming the contents before laying the letter back on his desk. I suspected the report to the Royal Privy Council concealed more about Captain Hawkins' activities in Spanish waters than it revealed.

I watched his face as he opened the second letter, addressed to him in person, which I guessed might have more controversial contents. His eyes narrowed at first, then he looked up at me with a raised eyebrow. John Hawkins warned me there would be questions and, for some reason, believed I could answer them. Now this would be put to the test.

'Do you have any idea, Captain Drake, of the difficulty your *adventuring*,' he made the word sound disparaging, 'causes your country?'

'If you mean from the Spanish, my lord, they fired upon us without cause, and murdered our countrymen without reason.' My voice echoed, louder than I'd intended, and I looked him straight in the eye.

William Cecil appeared taken aback at my forthright outburst. 'Her Majesty gave her word to the King of Spain that we would not indulge in illegal trade.'

'Captain Hawkins respected the laws—'

'The Governor of Rio de Hacha complained that Captain Hawkins burned his town to the ground, and threatened to execute innocent Spanish prisoners.' He spoke softly, yet his voice sounded accusing.

'No more than twenty houses were burned.' The scowl on William Cecil's face made me regret my words. My tone became more contrite. 'The Spanish were not innocent, my lord. They shot my unarmed crewman, sent under a flag of truce to ask for fresh water.'

William Cecil sat back and shook his head. 'Atrocities have been committed, yet Captain Hawkins has no doubt told you there is little appetite in Westminster to demand restitution from Spain for his losses.' William Cecil looked again at the letter, as if checking something. 'The silver coin he refers to is the property of Genoese bankers, and you should remind your captain that the *Jesus of Lubeck* was Crown property.'

'We've lost our entire fleet, my lord, apart from the *Judith* and *Minion*.' Again, his expression showed I'd spoken out of turn, but an idea occurred to me. 'Captain Hawkins will not sail into Spanish waters, yet if the King of Spain believes we are beaten—'

William Cecil's chair creaked as he leaned forward. 'I have a busy day ahead, Captain Drake. What is it you've been sent here to propose?'

'I intend to return to the West Indies, not with a great fleet of ships, but in lighter, swifter vessels, armed with the newest guns. I've sworn to avenge the deaths of our crewmen who were murdered by the Spanish.'

William Cecil gave me a stony-faced nod. Not an official commission from the Crown, but we'd reached a tacit understanding. John Hawkins would be disappointed there would be no share of the impounded Spanish silver, but I'd secured a greater prize. In one short meeting, I'd changed from a captain without a ship to a player in the great game of chess between Queen Elizabeth of England and King Philip of Spain.

I walked with a spring in my step as I made my way back down the corridors of Westminster. I planned to make the most of this unexpected development in my report to John Hawkins. William Cecil might even mention our meeting to Her Majesty the queen.

I waited at the church on the hill in St Budeaux, glad of the bright July sunshine – a good omen. The bells chimed tunefully in the square tower, calling the faithful to witness a marriage and see two lives change for the better. I was ready for the solitude of my life as a single man to be at an end, and to start a family of my own.

My younger brother John looked unrecognisable in the dark velvet doublet and breeches I'd paid for. He fidgeted with his new ruff of linen cambric which, like mine, was thicker and wider than we were used to, in keeping with the new fashion. We also both wore tall felt hats in place of our usual caps, as a mark of our importance on this auspicious day.

John leaned over and whispered, 'Father would have been so proud to see you do so well, Francis.'

His words affected me more than I would have expected. I'd achieved a great deal since my return from London. As well as agreeing the arrangements for my wedding, my ambitious plans for a new venture were falling into place.

'Thank you, John. John Hawkins, and his brother William, have agreed to invest in my return to the Indies.'

'The talk in the Plymouth tavern is that you are to command your own fleet.'

'Two ships are not a fleet, and the *Swan*, although a fine barque, is only twenty-five tons. The *Dragon* is only a little heavier, but they're perfect for swift attacks on Spanish treasure galleons.'

His eyes widened at my mention of treasure. 'Will there be a place for me on your new venture?'

'There will, but I can show you no favour. You'll have to work as hard as any man before I might find a promotion for you.'

He grinned, as he had when we were mischievous young boys. 'You can count on me, brother.'

'I hope I can, for if we make a success of my venture, I intend to buy both ships and be free of the Hawkins brothers. They are hard taskmasters, with high expectations, and willing for me to take all the risks—'

'While they enjoy the lion's share of the profits?'

'You can help me by overseeing the ships' refit, while I choose the rest of the crew.'

John smiled. 'I shall start today, Francis, as I imagine you will be otherwise occupied.'

I raised an eyebrow at his suggestion. Mary would see little enough of me once we were ready to sail. I glanced at the waiting congregation. The minister, a white-haired man, looked busy with his prayer books. I doubted they could overhear our talk, but kept my voice low.

'I wish to alter the *Swan* and the *Dragon* to conceal their increased armament, so they appear like merchant traders.'

The church bells stopped ringing, and I turned to see Mary enter with her brother Harry at her side. I'd never seen her look more beautiful, in a gown of delicate cornflower-blue, embroidered with shining silver thread, and her dark hair worn long, as a sign of her purity.

Harry led her up the nave and nodded as I caught his eye. He'd regained the weight he'd lost on his last voyage and had become invaluable to me. He enjoyed his new responsibility, helping me choose my crews, yet never admitted contriving my betrothal to Mary. It no longer mattered whether my suspicions were right.

The minister addressed the congregation in his rich Plymouth accent. 'Dearly beloved friends, we are gathered together here in the sight of God, and in the face of this congregation, to join together this man and this woman in holy matrimony, which is an honourable state, instituted of God in paradise, in the time of man's innocence, signifying unto us the mystical union that is betwixt Christ and his Church.'

He turned to me. 'Wilt thou have this woman to thy wedded wife, to live together after God's ordinance in the holy estate of matrimony? Wilt thou love her, comfort her, honour, and keep her, in sickness, and in health? And forsaking all others, keep thee only to her, so long as you both shall live?'

I stood tall and proud as I replied, 'I will.'

Mary spoke her vows in a confident, clear voice, her dark-brown eyes never once leaving mine. She smiled as I took her left hand in mine and placed the gold ring on the fourth finger. I took a deep breath, and held it as unexpected emotion threatened to reveal the depth of my love for her in my voice.

'With this ring I thee wed; with my body I thee worship; and with all my worldly goods, I thee endow. In the name of the Father, and of the Son, and of the Holy Ghost. Amen.'

7

FEBRUARY 1570

Mary waved goodbye from the quayside until she no doubt believed I could no longer see her, then fell to her knees. Her despair at our parting left me with a heavy heart. Standing alone in the freezing wind, I watched at the stern for a good half hour as the last sight of Plymouth vanished into grey winter mists.

That icy November day haunted my dreams all the way to our first port of call in Guinea. We'd sailed with another of Captain Hawkins' ships, the fifty-ton *Brave*, posing as merchants and taking care not to alert anyone to our true purpose. The *Swan* and the *Dragon* slipped away unnoticed in the middle of the night, bound for the warmer seas of the West Indies.

My mind often returned to a magical July day in St Budeaux, and Mary's smile as she shook the tangles from her long dark hair. After the grand wedding feast in the church hall, with over-long speeches and well-intended advice, we were finally alone.

She'd laughed as the ropes supporting our mattress creaked in protest when I lay back to test it for comfort. Lightheaded from drinking rich wine, I pulled off my leather boots, unfastened the starched cambric ruff and threw it to one side. Taking Mary in my arms I held her close, speaking softly in her ear.

'There is one more thing we must do—'

She pulled back and stared at me with pretended innocence. 'Before we are truly man and wife?'

Her eyes flashed with mischief as she slid the iron bolt on our door. She turned to face me with a shy smile as she unfastened her cornflower-blue dress, letting it fall to the floor to reveal her cotton shift, trimmed with fine white lace. Her passion no longer hinted at, she began to pull off my clothes, and I surrendered to my longing.

The first months of married life passed too quickly, a shadow hanging over our future as the time for my departure drew closer. She understood I'd had much to do, with refitting to complete, provisions to arrange and men to recruit. She made no attempt to dissuade me from my ambition, yet I woke early, a week before we sailed, to find her crying.

'What is it, Mary?' I struggled to see her face in the dawn light. 'What's the matter?'

A tear glistened on her cheek. 'I worry for you, Francis.' She wiped her eyes with her hand. 'You risk your life to make our fortune.'

'There are risks whenever men put to sea, but now I have something more precious to me than all the gold and silver in the world.' I leaned over and kissed her. 'I shall return for you, Mary.'

'Truly?' Her voice sounded like that of a girl, hardly daring to ask.

'I give you my word. I promise to return, safe and well – and wealthy.'

This brightened her mood a little. 'I'm the daughter of a mariner, and sister to another, so am used to long absences with no news.' Mary managed a smile. 'I knew what to expect when I married you, Francis. Half the women in Plymouth wait for ships to return.'

As I headed out into the dangerous waters of the Indies, I said a silent prayer that I would be able to keep my promise to Mary. If not, I'd left a generous bond with William Hawkins, who'd agreed to make sure my wife would be provided for if I failed to return.

Mary worried about not giving me a child after more than five months of married life. Coming from a large family, I'd assumed it would be easier. I reassured her there would be plenty of time to start our new family once I returned with my fortune. She'd smiled, but I sensed the doubt in her eyes.

As we said our farewells, she'd pressed her purse, made from soft kidskin, into my hand. The purse was her favourite, a token to keep the memory of her as fresh as sweet-scented lavender. I would keep from opening the purse until I set out on the return journey.

The thump of boots sounded on the wooden deck and I turned to see my first officer. Harry Newman had become my right-hand man. He'd earned his new position, although I doubted I should have been persuaded to make my brother John master of the *Dragon*, which threatened to leave us in her wake.

'The men are ready for prayers, Captain.'

His formality made me smile. We'd agreed it necessary in the interests of discipline, although it was unlikely anyone could overhear.

My reading of prayers set our ship's routine: I would report on our progress and choose one of the Psalms from my father's book – yet this time would be different.

I studied their serious, bearded faces, proud of my loyal crew of twenty-five men, chosen with care. Most were trained gunners and two spoke Portuguese and Spanish, a useful skill in the West Indies. All were experienced sailors and known to be faithful Protestants. Most had sailed with me in the past, and understood the risks we would take, as well as the rewards to be brought home.

'Before we ask our Lord to keep us safe, I wish to tell you our true purpose.' The wind had eased and my voice boomed across the deck. 'There will be no slaves in our hold this voyage, and you will know we don't carry goods for trade. We sail to the West Indies in search of something of greater value.'

'Spanish gold!' A deep voice called out from the back. 'A shipload of silver?'

'You all sail for a share of the spoils, so keep vigilant for Spanish treasure ships, but the greatest prize we seek is *information*. We know where Spanish gold and silver comes from, and where it goes to, so our mission is to discover the weakest link in their chain.'

I watched as they took in the news, which I'd had to keep secret until we were certain not to return to Guinea. I glanced across at our sister ship, the *Dragon*, and would cross to share the news with them once we reached calmer waters. But, for now, I had more to tell the crew of the *Swan*.

'We must learn from San Juan de Ulúa. You've all heard what happened to those we left behind.' I paused, recalling John Hawkins' letter. 'We are only two small barques, while they have a fleet of warships, so we must outwit the Spanish. We will strike swiftly, but no one will be killed unless we have no choice, and if we find slaves, we'll set them free. I swear to bring every man home, with a clear conscience and gold in his pocket.'

The men cheered, as I'd known they would. I suspected many would have guessed my plan, as the clues were there to be seen. The concealed gun ports, the new swivel guns, the supply of chain shot for disabling rigging, and the time we'd spent learning to convert the *Swan* from a merchantman to a fighting ship.

They bowed their heads as we repeated the Ten Commandments, the Creed and the Lord's Prayer, their rich, West Country voices carrying out to sea. I opened my father's leather-bound book and read aloud my favourite Psalm, although I'd known the words by heart since I'd been a boy, back in Medway.

'They went down to the sea in ships. They conducted trade on many waters. They saw the deeds of the Lord and his wonders on the deep. For he spoke and stirred up a violent storm, which produced large waves. They were raised up to the sky.'

I paused, staring out across the white-crested waves, allowing the men time to recall such storms. We'd all seen fierce seas more than once, and thanked God we'd lived to sail another day. Looking at the faces of the crew, I knew I held their attention.

'Then they cried out to the Lord in their distress. He brought them out of their troubles. He calmed the storm. Its waves were hushed. They were glad when it grew quiet, and he guided them to the port they desired. Let them give thanks to the Lord!'

Mindful of the lack of fresh water at Santa Dominica, our first port of call was the sheltered bay of the island of Margarita. For once, we'd been favoured by the trade winds, and made the long Atlantic crossing without incident.

We replenished our water, and bargained in the bustling marketplace for baskets of freshly caught fish. One of the merchants watched me mop my brow, and poured me a cup of Spanish beer. Unlike the warm, bitter-tasting ale in Plymouth, it had been chilled, with a sweet aftertaste.

I nodded in appreciation. Unused to the heat, I regretted wearing my doublet and the starched ruff I wore around my neck like a badge of rank. I recalled a Spanish phrase I'd picked up on my last visit. *'Muchas gracias.'*

'You are most welcome, sir.' He seemed amused by my surprise at his reply, and I looked at him more closely. Deeply tanned, he wore the loose cloak favoured by the islanders. His sharp eyes shone with good humour, yet warned he wasn't to be underestimated.

'You speak good English.' I smiled. 'To my regret I speak little Spanish, although I'm keen to learn.'

'I'm sure the Spanish will be most pleased.' This time a note of scorn carried in his voice.

'You're not Spanish?'

The merchant smiled. 'Venezuelan – and I have no love for the Spanish. They treat my country with contempt.'

I raised my cap in salute. 'Captain Francis Drake. I'm pleased to make your acquaintance – and I share your view of the way the Spanish claim the Indies as their own.'

He smiled. 'Ruben Díaz, at your service, sir. What brings you to this island, Captain?'

I trusted my instinct about Ruben Díaz. 'Is there somewhere private, where we might talk?'

He led me to a paved inner courtyard and gestured for me to take a seat, shaded from the fierce midday sun. Ripe yellow lemons hung from a tree, growing in a cracked terracotta pot, and a green lizard eyed me as it sat motionless on the top of the wall. My host had brought his jug of beer and refilled my cup before giving me a questioning look.

'We've come to learn the route taken by the Spanish treasure fleet.'

He nodded. 'You are not the first.'

I took a sip of beer, savouring the taste. 'With a guide, we could save weeks of searching.'

Interest flashed in his dark eyes. 'The Spanish come to Margarita to trade for pearls, and I learned there are not one, but two treasure fleets. The first sails to Veracruz to load porcelain and silk from China, brought overland from Acapulco.' He kept his voice low. 'The *real* prize is aboard the second fleet.'

'Gold?' I'd made promises to my crew, as well as the Hawkins brothers, and Mary, waiting for me in Plymouth.

Ruben Díaz shook his head. 'Silver, loaded in Nombre de Dios. They say it's kept in the governor's house, heavy bars, stacked as high as a man.' He smiled. 'The silver comes from Peru. It is shipped from the port of Callao, then transported fifty miles across Panama by the *recuas*, long mule trains, guarded by soldiers.'

'They sail back to Spain?'

'They stop in Havana, where a fleet of warships wait to escort them.'

I took another drink of the sweet beer. I'd found two weak links in the Spanish chain. The mule train, laden with heavy silver, and the unprotected ships sailing from Panama to Havana.

'Will you take me to see these mule trains?'

He frowned at the suggestion. 'The road from Nombre de Dios is impassable in the rainy season, from the end of May right through to December.' He seemed to reach a decision. 'I'll not come with you, Captain, but I know a man who could act as your guide. You would need small boats, with a shallow draft, to travel upriver.'

I hadn't expected this. 'Could we buy such boats here, and tow them to the coast?'

Ruben Díaz frowned and scratched his head. 'The oyster fishing boats would be too slow if you had to leave in a hurry, and are the owner's livelihood.'

I sat back and savoured the Spanish beer, enjoying the taste. I held up my empty cup. 'I would like to buy five barrels of your beer, for my crew. I shall return, early next year, with shallow-draft boats, and hope to find your guide ready to show us the way upriver.'

I handed him a purse of silver coins. 'This is more than enough, so think of it as a retainer for your services.'

Ruben Díaz grinned. 'It is my pleasure to do business with you, Captain Drake.'

'Strike the flag!'

My order sent the crew into the drill we'd rehearsed several times on the outward voyage. As well as sending a silent signal to the *Dragon*, sailing to our starboard side, lowering the red cross of St George from the masthead could buy us valuable time.

The lone Spanish ship we'd sighted, a merchant galleon of good size, lay at anchor in a tranquil, secluded bay off the southern coast of the island of Tortuga, named by Columbus because the rounded mountains reminded him of a sea turtle's shell.

A small boat on the shore suggested they'd stopped to take on water. I studied the Spanish ship's rig. Her sails were furled and she rode low in the water, so she might be carrying a valuable cargo. Her escort of warships were not far away, but this could be our best chance of winning the prize we'd come for.

The *Dragon* acknowledged our signal by following our example, and sailed into position to cut off the Spanish galleon's escape. I watched as our gunners pulled away the wooden covers and prepared our guns for action. The work of moments, the *Swan* transformed into a formidable fighting ship.

The master gunner raised his hand to show he was ready as we drew closer to the Spanish merchantman, and I gave the order to open fire. The sharp boom of the guns reverberated across the bay, filling the air with the sulphurous tang of gunsmoke, but we fired wadding – a warning shot.

The effect was like poking a stick into a nest of wood ants. We watched the commotion on the deck of the Spanish ship as sharp orders were shouted. There appeared to be no more than a dozen crewmen on board.

One of my Spanish-speaking crewmen called out '*Rendición!*', for them to surrender, but his answer was the crack of arquebus fire. I ducked instinctively as the shot rang out, but we were ready. I'd ordered chain to be loaded in our guns and gave the order to fire.

The lengths of deadly chain flew faster than the eye could follow, and could cut a man in two. Our gunners aimed high into the Spanish rigging. The top section of the merchant ship's mainmast shattered in a spray of splinters, before toppling into the sea in a tangle of shrouds.

My gun crew were ready with a second salvo. The long bowsprit of the Spanish ship exploded into fragments, her decorated prow following the mast with a splash. Crippled, she had no way to escape, and my crew cheered at the sight of a white flag being waved.

We drew close enough for my Spanish-speaking crewman to shout instructions across the water. They would be spared if they threw down their weapons and surrendered. At first they looked defiant, but our threats to blast them at the waterline had the desired effect, and they raised their hands as we drew alongside.

It took several trips to ferry their crew to the shore, after searching them for weapons or valuables. I followed Harry Newman to the captain's cabin at the stern while the *Dragon* approached and tied up to the other side.

Surprisingly compact for such a large ship, the low-ceilinged cabin had a narrow bunk but a good-sized chart table, spread with an annotated chart, as well as other papers, a notebook and an empty silver goblet. It seemed the captain, like me, also acted as the ship's navigator, or at least took a close interest in their course.

Harry Newman grinned as he pocketed the silver goblet, then discovered a locked wooden casket hidden under the captain's bunk. He tried to prise the lid open with his dagger, but the iron lock proved too strong. Cursing, he went in search of something to break the lock.

I studied the captain's papers, although they were in Spanish, and gathered them into a bundle. I also rolled up the chart, and took his notebook. Any conscience I might have felt at robbing a fellow mariner was left behind at San Juan de Ulúa.

The chart covered the Gulf of Mexico, and would be a valuable addition to my growing collection. I would have to trust the literacy of our Spanish-speaking crew members, as I was intrigued to discover what secrets they might contain.

Harry returned with a crowbar and grunted as he forced the lock of the casket open. Inside a velvet bag lay a fortune in large white pearls. I took a handful and rolled them in the palm of my hand. These islands were famous for their pearls, and these were of the best quality, their silky patina glowing in the dim light of the cabin.

I looked up at Harry. 'A good find, which will more than cover our costs.'

Harry began searching the rest of the captain's cabin, scattering clothing on the floor before he discovered a silver plate, engraved with the arms of Spain, hidden in a locker. He held the plate to the light and tried to decipher the inscription. 'I'd hoped to find more silver.'

'From what my contact at Margarita told me, I'd guess this is a ship from the first convoy, which sails from Veracruz. It seems she made a detour to these islands to collect your casket of pearls.'

We carried our finds back on deck, where our men were busy stripping the wrecked ship of everything of value. I turned to Harry as we watched them carry rolls of rich silks and woven baskets of Chinese porcelain.

'I've no idea of the value of our finds, but they'll fetch good prices in England.'

As the *Swan* and *Dragon* turned for home, our holds filled with booty, I opened the little purse Mary handed me when we parted. Inside were a dozen sugared comfits, of little worth in Plymouth, but a rare treat after long weeks on salted rations.

Plymouth lay shrouded in darkness by the time I climbed the harbour steps. No one waited to greet us, as they had no idea when we might return. I'd made the decision to avoid the risk of winter storms. Our holds were full and I'd uncovered enough information to plan my next voyage.

A dog barked as I made my way through the dark streets of Plymouth, to the house I'd feared I might never see again. I tried the handle and pushed the door open.

Mary stared at me in disbelief, then embraced me so hard she took my breath away.

'I prayed each day for your safe return.'

I kissed her, and reached into my pocket. 'I have something for you, brought from the Indies.'

She took her little purse and smiled. 'Were you surprised to discover what I'd given you?'

'Only a mariner's daughter would know how welcome they were on the voyage home.'

She looked inside her purse. The twelve white pearls were

Drake - Tudor Corsair

perfectly matched, the best from Harry's casket. Mary stared at the pearls, gleaming in the flickering candlelight, entranced.

'I've never seen anything so beautiful.' She smiled. 'These will see us through the winter.'

I shook my head. 'No. I shall have them made into a necklace for you. We are wealthy now, Mary. I'm rich enough to buy a ship of my own, and shall be master of my own destiny.'

8

FEBRUARY 1571

Squalls of stinging rain made it unpleasant to be on deck, and thunderous, slate-grey skies threatened storms. We had to avoid the start of the West Indies rainy season, yet it grieved me to be leaving Mary so soon. I confided my concern to Harry Newman as we shared a late watch.

'Mary has few friends. She must find it lonely on her own.'

'She has our sister, Margaret, to keep her company, and knew what she was doing when she married a sailor.' Harry grinned. 'Although I doubt she expected to be a wealthy woman quite so soon.'

I smiled at his taunt. 'We're comfortable, Harry, but no longer wealthy. William Hawkins demanded a high price for the *Swan*.'

Harry patted the polished wooden rail. 'She's proved her worth in the Indies, and will do so again.'

'Owning her raises the stakes. I risk losing everything if this venture fails.'

'Then we must ensure our venture is a success, God willing.'

'For the first time since I first arrived in Plymouth I'm my own man, answerable only to God.'

'We have a good ship and an experienced crew, although your brother has not taken well to losing his command.'

'Am I my brother's keeper?' It sounded harsher than I intended, but my argument with John left a bitter taste. 'I couldn't afford a second ship, Harry, and this voyage has a simple purpose.'

'Nombre de Dios?'

I stared out to the vast emptiness of the choppy sea, talking to myself as much as Harry. 'Ever since my contact, Ruben Díaz, told me about Nombre de Dios, I've been looking forward to seeing it with my own eyes. With luck, Harry, we shall also establish a base for our future operations.'

After stopping in Guinea for fresh water, our next port of call, the sheltered bay of the island of Margarita, seemed like a different world. Since our last visit, new harbour defences had been built, and stone buildings replaced the ramshackle wooden huts.

A Spanish man-of-war sat at anchor, her sinister row of snub-nosed cannons guarding the approach to the harbour. A figure on the deck shielded his eyes as he watched us rowing to the shore. The *Swan* still flew the red cross of St George, and I prayed the Spanish lookout didn't know who we were.

I held my breath as I knocked on the door of the merchant, Ruben Díaz. On my last visit, I hadn't noticed the flaking, olive-green paint on the door, and the missing terracotta roof tiles. It suited me that Ruben Díaz might be short of money. With less than three months before the start of the rainy season, we depended on his promise of help.

The door opened and there stood Ruben Díaz. His eyes

widened in recognition. 'Quick, Captain.' He glanced down the narrow street. 'The Spanish are here in good numbers.'

He led me back into the private courtyard, and gestured for me to take a seat. 'French corsairs have been causing trouble, and made the Spanish more vigilant.'

'Is that why there's a man-of-war in the bay?'

He frowned. 'You must take care, Captain. There is a new Spanish commander, Diego Flores de Valdez. He's no doubt been watching you from the moment you arrived.'

'I've no wish to cause you trouble with the Spanish, but do you have the guide you promised?'

'One of the best, he is a leader of the Cimarrons—'

'A Cimarron?' I'd heard the band of escaped slaves had become dangerous outlaws, and were not to be trusted. 'How well does he know the River Chagres?'

'The Cimarrons live off the land and are skilled at outwitting their former masters.' Ruben Díaz smiled. 'This man speaks English, as well as some French and Spanish. There is no one better as your guide, Captain Drake.'

The muscular African wore a large, wooden-handled knife in a leather sheath at his belt, and a jagged scar disfigured his cheek.

'You are Captain Drake?' His deep accent had a Spanish edge, and his dark eyes looked at me as if making a judgement.

'I am – and you must be our guide?'

'My name is Pedro Mandinga.' He glanced across at the Spanish man-of-war. 'We should leave this island while we can, Captain.'

I agreed. 'I wish to find a safe haven, not too far from the River Chagres, to use as a base where we can assemble our pinnace. Do you know of such a place?'

He pointed to the horizon. 'To the east of Nombre de Dios are the islands of the Cativas, close to Point San Blas.' He grinned. 'A safe hiding place.'

The string of small islands were deserted, and large enough for our needs, with tall palms and long beaches of white coral sand. Wary of hidden rocks and reefs, we steered a course to a sheltered bay and dropped anchor. I went ashore with Harry Newman and Pedro, to assess the island's suitability.

A pile of burned wood in a circle of stones on the beach caught my attention, and I picked up a piece. I couldn't tell how old the charred wood might be, and handed it to Pedro Mandinga. 'Are you sure we won't have unexpected visitors?'

Pedro frowned as he studied the burned stick. 'We must keep a lookout, Captain, but this island is not inhabited.'

I stared at the raised ground behind the beach. 'Post a man up there, Harry, and send others to search for fresh water. We need to set up camp and assemble the pinnace.'

It took the efforts of most of the crew to unload the unwieldy sections of the pinnace and lay them out on the beach. We'd rehearsed the reassembly in Plymouth, yet it proved difficult to make the shallow-draft boat seaworthy. The leather straps, used to lace the sections together, had stiffened on the crossing, and needed soaking in seawater before they could be used.

A wit among the pinnace crew called her the *Cygnet*, and the name stuck. All strong oarsmen, the crewmen were trained to fire the bronze culverin, mounted on a swivel in the bows, as well as to use the new design of arquebuses. Each man carried a knife, although some preferred to use bows, swords, or pikes.

Leaving Harry Newman in charge of setting up our camp, I set out in the pinnace with Pedro Mandinga and my brother John, for our first sea trial. Light enough to be manhandled into the water, the *Cygnet* proved watertight, and responded well to the efforts of our rowers.

I called out to the men. 'We need to use our shallow draft. Keep close to the shoreline.' She'd been designed for use on the river, and I worried about how she would cope in the open sea. It might be better for us all to be within wading distance of the beach.

An idea occurred to me. 'Now we'll try a landing.' I pointed to a nearby island with a sandy foreshore.

The *Cygnet* sped towards the beach and the men swapped oars for weapons as they leapt into the shallow water, taking possession of the island. Exactly as I'd hoped, we had a new capability. With the *Swan* and her *Cygnet*, we could move swiftly, strike, and leave before the Spanish knew what had happened.

Each day we explored further along the coast towards the mouth of the River Chagres. Pedro Mandinga took us to a headland where Spanish ships were known to seek shelter from the prevailing winds.

One of the men pointed as we skirted the cliff. A Spanish frigate lay at anchor in a bay of mangroves, an opportunity for my pinnace and her crew to be put to a real test.

'Ready the culverin!'

We'd rehearsed this several times and they prepared the gun to fire in moments. Rowing in tense silence, we approached as close as we dared. I said a prayer my plan would work. I hoped they wouldn't be expecting such a small craft, so close to the shore.

The sharp crack of arquebus fire broke the silence and spouts of water sprayed our bows. I gave the order to fire the culverin. The boom shook the pinnace, and the heavy cannonball punched a hole through the hull of the ship above the waterline.

The Spanish crew cut their anchor cable, and as they struggled to ready their sails, the frigate drifted inshore in the current. Even while we reloaded our culverin, we watched men abandoning ship and wading into the thick forest of twisted mangrove roots.

John pointed at the escaping crew. 'They have a woman with them!'

A lady was being carried ashore by two Spanish sailors, her silk gown trailing in the water, while another man struggled with the weight of a heavy chest. Some of the Spanish carried arquebuses. We were exposed in the *Cygnet* and would make an easy target at such close range.

'Quick as you can, before they find firing positions.' I'd not forgotten my close shave with an arquebus ball at Rio de Hacha.

Within minutes we drew up to the seaward side of the frigate and threw a grappling hook to board her. My brother John drew his sword and hauled himself up first, a typical act of bravado which highlighted the difference between us.

He disappeared for an anxious moment before returning with a grin. 'All clear!'

Leaving two men to guard the *Cygnet*, the rest of us clambered aboard the frigate and began searching for anything of value. I made my way to the captain's cabin and collected together another hoard of papers. The navigator's bunk proved a gold mine of parchment charts, including one I recognised as the local coastline.

Pedro grinned as he appeared, carrying a large cured ham. 'We've caught them on the inward journey, Captain.'

I showed him the chart I'd found and he studied the markings. 'I guess they were headed for Casa de Las Cruces.'

'A harbour?'

'A way station, where the Spaniards have a warehouse.' He pulled out his sharp knife and carved a slice from the ham, nodding in approval as he took a bite. 'I can take you there, if you wish.'

'I'd like to see these warehouses. If this ship was headed there, they must hide treasure. How well are they guarded?'

Pedro shrugged. 'The Spanish keep a lookout since the raids by the French, so we must be ready for a fight, Captain.'

'I don't want to risk the *Swan*, and we wouldn't be able to carry much away in the *Cygnet*.' I turned to my brother. 'It would be good if we could take this frigate as our prize.'

John leaned over the side. 'By God's faith! I can see the bottom. They've run her aground, to stop us taking her.' He cursed the Spanish. 'We'll not be able to pull her off with the *Cygnet*, and don't have time to wait for the tide. Shall we set her on fire?'

'No. The Spanish would see the smoke for miles. We must take what we can and be on our way.'

John didn't reply but shook his head, and I sensed he would be critical of me behind my back. 'There are barrels of wine in the hold. We can only manage two in the *Cygnet*, so what do you want us to do?'

'Take any food, but leave the crew the water. They have a woman with them.'

I didn't miss his scowl. I realised I'd made a mistake bringing him on this voyage, although I'd had little choice. He still bore a grudge but, at the same time, expected special treatment. I'd also noted he could be harsh with the men, although he seemed to have earned their respect.

We rowed back to our sheltered island mooring where the *Swan* waited at anchor. The *Cygnet* sat low in the water, laden with the two heavy barrels of wine, crates of stores and a small amount of silver plate. My brother looked across at me.

'If they had anything else of value they hid it well, considering how quickly the crew fled.'

I agreed. 'It seems they'd been warned of the dangers of piracy, and weren't taking any chances.'

Leaving Harry and enough men to safeguard the *Swan* and our camp, we set out the following morning in the *Cygnet*. Glad of the light breeze and clear blue sky, we tracked along the coast, with Pedro Mandinga guiding our way.

We carried enough supplies to last a week, although I would have to ration the water. We planned to test the defences of the warehouse at the way station of Casa de Las Cruces, and hopefully return with silver, or even some Spanish gold.

The River Chagres flowed more slowly as we rowed further from the sea. The barren, rocky foreshore turned to lush green forest, with palms and spiky thorn bushes. Pedro pointed out a crocodile, watching us as it sunned itself on the bank, its mouth gaping open.

'They seem slow, but move fast when they wish to. The forest here is full of creatures that can kill you, Captain.' He smiled, showing white teeth. 'Snakes and jaguars.'

'Are the crocodiles the most dangerous?'

'They have no fear of man.'

'We need to keep watch for them, when we camp.'

After a long day of rowing, the light began to fail and the men needed to rest. I was disappointed with our progress but concerned to replenish our water, so we went ashore.

While my brother John led the men in search of a source of fresh water, I studied the Spanish chart with Pedro. He told me he'd seen mule trains using the way station, which was regularly visited by Spanish merchant ships.

'We must approach with care.' He traced his finger down the

path of the river. 'Keep close to the bank, so we can escape ashore if we have to.'

I looked out into the clear night. 'If there are Spanish ships moored, we could use the cover of darkness.'

Struggling to sleep, I stared up at the stars and thought of Mary at home in Plymouth. She'd seemed different when I left, as if resigned to our way of life. She'd shivered in the wintry wind, despite her woollen cloak, as I held her close.

This time her gift had been practical; she'd sewn me a dozen shirts from linen, which I wore every day. As I finally drifted off to sleep I recalled the softness of her parting kiss, and her words, whispered in my ear.

'I love you.'

After three days of rowing in the oppressive heat we were relieved to see a row of wooden buildings, and two flat-bottomed barges, moored at a low stone quay. The call of an exotic bird echoed in the still air. John shaded his eyes with his hand and scanned the shore.

'If that's Casa de Las Cruces, it looks deserted.'

Disappointment carried in his voice, but I was relieved we didn't have to fight. We tied up the *Cygnet* at the shallow end of the quay and went to explore. I led half the men towards the warehouse, while my brother and the others went to search the remaining buildings.

I wiped the sweat from my forehead as we approached the warehouse, not sure if we'd be welcomed by arquebus fire. Pedro gestured for us to wait while he scouted ahead. He soon returned, and led us to see piles of dung, drying in the sun, surrounded by the hoof prints of mules in the dusty soil.

'They bring the *recuas* here, then load the ships.' He looked up at the warehouse and scowled. 'They used to keep goods here, until the French raided.'

I understood. We'd arrived too late. One of my men forced open the door, but the warehouse was empty. We found open crates, stacked high against the wall, and a small office at the far end. A small inkpot and an old quill sat on an ornate desk, although I couldn't see any papers.

I turned at the sound of shouts and cracking wood, followed by a rousing cheer. We rushed back to the quay in time to see one of the barges sinking. As we watched, my brother used a large axe to batter the hull of the second barge, which seemed to be resisting his efforts.

John turned at our approach. 'We'll teach the Spanish—'

'What do you think you're doing?'

John scowled. 'There's nothing here of value. Our only reward for three days of rowing is some clothing and a few odds and ends. What would you have us do now, *Captain*?'

'The French have beaten us to this prize, but there will be others. We've been unlucky this time, but we know the lie of the land, and will capture the next Spanish merchant ship we see.' I managed a smile. 'You will all return home wealthy.'

We'd settled into a routine at our secret island, each day setting out to search for food and water. Pedro led a hunting expedition to the mainland and returned with a large forest pig, which we roasted on the beach and washed down with Spanish wine.

Conscious of the need to show a profit, we set out in the *Swan* to a cove on the Cativas headland. Pedro believed more merchant ships would return before long and, after hours of watching and waiting, a sail appeared on the horizon. A fat-bellied merchantman, she flew a colourful Spanish pennant, and sailed without an escort.

We fired one shot from a culverin and were rewarded by the sight of a white flag, waving in surrender. Wary it might be a trick, my crew were armed and ready as we drew alongside, but the captain handed me his sword and spoke in rapid Spanish.

I turned to Pedro, who stood at my side. 'What is he saying?'

'This is an advice ship from Cartagena, taking messages and letters to Nombre de Dios. There is nothing of much value aboard, but he pleads for their lives to be spared.'

'Tell him we're English, and honour their surrender. We will take his ship – and his letters. Everyone aboard will be put ashore unharmed, but first I have a few questions.'

The Spanish captain nodded in grateful agreement. 'Where is the gold and silver kept in Nombre de Dios?'

The captain mopped his brow, and spoke again in Spanish. He looked at Pedro then back at me.

'He says the silver is kept in the governor's house, and the gold and other valuables in the king's treasure house, on the waterfront.'

'Ask him when the flota come to collect it.'

The captain glanced out to sea as if hoping to see the flota on their way to rescue him. He spoke again in Spanish. 'They visit only once a year, and are escorted by Commander Diego Flores de Valdez.'

Pedro scowled. 'He is the man who sent the French away.'

We began searching the ship while the crew were ferried to a white sandy cove near the headland. My brother emerged from a cabin with a trophy, a large Spanish flag, and I called him over.

'Will you take command of this ship, John?'

He held up the flag for me to see. 'Of course, and I have a suggestion. You could hoist this on the *Swan* and pretend to be our escort.'

Once the Spaniards were ashore, we continued towards the wide, sheltered bay of Nombre de Dios. Before long, our lookout called, 'Sails ahoy!'

I glanced up at the topmast of the *Swan*, where the Spanish flag flew in place of the red cross of St George, and prayed our plan would work. There were more ships than I could count; too many for us to risk taking on.

We held back, and our luck changed as the wind veered, causing the Spanish merchant fleet to spread out. Closing on the last in the line of barques, we pulled alongside and Pedro called for their captain to surrender. Again, they proved to be unarmed merchants, and stared at us with terrified faces.

If we could hold our nerve, this would make us all rich. I counted fourteen barques ahead, and wondered how many we could capture before I should give the order to stop. I climbed up on the rail, springing on to the deck of the merchantman, and drew my sword. It had never yet been used in anger, but our prisoners fell to their knees at the sight of it, begging for mercy.

9

MAY 1572

Word of our success spread through Plymouth and beyond as swiftly as a moorland grassfire, so I wasn't surprised to receive the invitation to visit William and John Hawkins. No longer their employee, I'd become a guest, instead of their servant.

John Hawkins looked back to his old self, his silver beard neatly trimmed, his starched white ruff trimmed with fine lace in the latest court fashion. He smiled, yet raised an eyebrow.

'I hear stories about you freeing slaves, Master Drake.'

'I have, and with good reason.' I enjoyed our reversed roles, and the luxury of having more than one ace up my sleeve.

William Hawkins studied me with a glint in his eye. 'Why is that?'

'I had a Cimarron guide.' I savoured their good wine, taking my time. 'The Cimarrons are my allies now, and a few slaves are a small price to pay for the advantage. We took four merchant ships, two with slaves aboard, so I allowed our guide to take one ship as his prize, with the former slaves as crew.'

John Hawkins frowned. 'Once your guide had shown you the lie of the land, he served no further purpose.'

'Quite the contrary. I could not have brought back *this*

without his help.' I reached into my pocket and handed him a blue velvet bag.

He pulled opened the silk drawstring and poured a fortune in gold nuggets into the palm of his hand. The pick of our haul, they shone in the sunlight from his window. For once lost for words, he exchanged a meaningful look with his brother.

I smiled. 'The real prize is silver, so much it takes a whole train of mules to carry it to the town of Nombre de Dios, where I'm told it is stacked to the height of a man.'

William Hawkins refilled his Venetian crystal glass and raised it in the air as he proposed a toast. 'To our prosperous future partnership, Francis.'

I had no need of their financial support. Instead, I hoped their connections at the highest levels of the royal court would be the key to unlocking something of much greater value.

'I must have an official letter of marque, a royal commission from Her Majesty, Queen Elizabeth.'

William Hawkins smiled. 'That will allow you to plunder Spanish ships and ports in her name?'

'Without such authority, we are nothing more than pirates.'

I recalled that conversation as I sailed their refitted carrack, the *Pasco*, back to the West Indies. Thanks to William and John Hawkins, and their connections in Westminster, my letter of marque and commission were granted. Her Majesty, Queen Elizabeth, had become a shareholder in our expedition.

Although wealthy enough to buy the *Pasco*, I'd instead proposed they bear part of the risk of this venture, and encouraged my brother John to use his profits from our last voyage to take a share in her. I also made John the captain of my own ship, the *Swan*, with our younger brother, Joseph, as his first officer.

I'd chosen to captain the forty-ton *Pasco*, with a good Plymouth man, John Oxenham, as my second in command. The men looked up to him, and he had a reputation as an expert with the eleven heavy cannons on the *Pasco*. I planned to make him a captain if we had a suitable prize ship.

We carried two new pinnaces, the *Lion* and the *Bear*, while the twenty-five-ton *Swan* carried a new pinnace, named the *Minion,* in place of the cumbersome *Cygnet*. After many hours of rowing, we'd built our pinnaces lighter and faster, with more capacity to carry our loot. We also had a second culverin at the stern, in case of attack from the rear.

Not all of those who'd sailed with me previously were able to wait for my voyage, but Harry Newman helped me select seventy-three good men, all under the age of thirty, and train them in our new way of fighting. I'd watched them race the pinnaces on the Tamar, using their bows in silent attacks.

Now we approached the sheltered bay we'd named Port Pheasant, after the easily caught birds, resembling English pheasants, which lived there in profusion. Before leaving, we'd buried as many supplies as could be spared, including weapons and tools.

We also carried fresh provisions to last at least a year, twenty-six new arquebuses, and six fire-pikes. The long, sharp-pointed weapons carried a burning torch to add drama in a midnight attack, making us seem like an army of much greater numbers.

As our safe haven drew closer, our lookout called to me.

'Smoke, Captain!'

He needn't have pointed. The wisp of grey smoke rose high into the clear blue sky, and could be seen for miles. My first thought was of the Cimarrons, who knew we'd chosen this bay as our base of operations.

Not wishing to take unnecessary risks, I ordered the long-boat lowered and took Harry Newman with a dozen armed men to investigate. The only sound was the dipping of oars in the clear water as we rowed up the channel, which widened out into the secluded anchorage.

Landing on the beach, we made our weapons ready and crept towards the source of the fire. Boot prints showed in the soft sand and a tall pile of wood, like a beacon, smouldered with a silent, ominous warning.

One of my men called for me to see a message, carved into a piece of lead, and nailed to a tree.

CAPTAIN DRAKE

If you fortune to come to this port, make haste away, for the Spaniards which you had with you here, the last year, have betrayed this place, and taken away all you left here. I depart from hence this seventh day of July, 1572.

Your very loving friend,

JOHN GARRET

I read the scrawled message with a sinking heart. John Garret, previously the second mate of John Hawkins' ship the *Minion*, claimed he had been here only days earlier and found our store of supplies were gone. I regretted sharing the news of our success so freely in Plymouth.

Harry Newman cursed. 'Garret took on several of our crew from last year. Do you think he's also taken our supplies?'

I shook my head. 'It matters little if the culprit was John Garret or the Spanish. Our base is no longer a secret, so we must find another. The nearest Spanish settlement is over thirty-five leagues from here, so we might as well stay overnight and assemble the pinnaces, as we'd planned.'

It would be difficult to find anywhere as ideal as Port Pheasant. Sheltered from the wind, with good fresh water from a clear stream, I'd believed it close to paradise, my safe haven. I recalled the look John Hawkins gave his brother when he held my Spanish gold. I'd trusted him with the details of what I'd discovered, yet it seemed he'd planned another venture behind my back.

The *Pasco* and the *Swan* anchored close off shore and we felled trees to build a defensive stockade. Lookouts were posted on the highest ground, and the guns on our ships made ready to fire. If the Spanish returned we would be ready to welcome them.

The next morning one of our lookouts sounded the alarm as two ships appeared at the entrance to the cove. I recognised James Raunce standing on the bows of the first, an armed barque. The other ship looked like a Spanish merchant vessel, taken as a prize.

I frowned as I noticed the barque towed a lug-sailed Spanish shallop, ideal for sailing these shallow waters. It seemed they'd not only followed in our footsteps but were already profiting from our success the previous year.

James Raunce beamed as he raised a hand in greeting. 'Ahoy there, Captain Drake!'

I knew Raunce from his days in command of the *Salomon*. Ten years older, and more experienced than me, he'd been in dispute with the Hawkins brothers after abandoning the *William and John* in Ireland. She'd subsequently been lost with all hands off Land's End, so I was surprised he'd been given a second chance.

I watched as he was rowed ashore. 'How do you come to be here, Captain Raunce?' I tried my best to hide my annoyance.

'I've come to join you – if you'll have me. Our patron is Vice Admiral Sir Edward Horsey, and we have thirty good men, some dozen of whom you will know.' He pointed back at the Spanish caravel. 'The *Santa Catalina*, a fine ship.'

I had to admit an extra thirty men would be useful once we reached Nombre de Dios, although I wasn't keen to share any silver and gold with James Raunce. I studied the lines of the Spanish caravel. Newly built, she looked like a good prize.

'What cargo does she carry?'

'She's well provisioned with supplies, including sugar and salted pork, intended for Spanish settlers, so we have more than enough to share.' He glanced back at the *Santa Catalina*. 'We put her crew ashore on one of the islands.'

Captain Raunce agreed to guard the ships in a cove close to Nombre de Dios while I led our three pinnaces ashore, with my brother John sailing the Spanish shallop. As well as being armed with cutlasses, pistols, arquebuses and fire-pikes, we had trumpeters and carried two drums.

Our plan was to slip into the town under cover of darkness and catch the Spanish militia in their beds. We hoped to alarm the people of the town with our fire-pikes, drums and trumpeters, and fool them into thinking they were invaded by a much greater force.

We landed in the shallows and made our way towards the harbour battery to silence the guns. We crept up the steep bank and found only one man left on guard. The heavy cannons looked far from ready for use against us. The Spanish were clearly not expecting an attack.

The young Spanish guard dropped his arquebus and raised

both hands. I couldn't understand his gibbering, but guessed he begged us to show him mercy. I wished to set him free, but my brother disagreed.

'He'll rouse the town, and knows our strength – or lack of it.' John spoke loud enough for everyone to hear.

It irked me that, again, my brother challenged me in front of the men. 'We'll have him show us the way to the governor's house, and the treasure house on the waterfront.'

The sky turned from a dusty pink to vermillion streaked with orange as we waited for the sun to sink below the horizon. We'd timed our arrival to be in Nombre de Dios before the Spanish fleet, and a bright moon now cast an ethereal light on the sleeping town.

My brother looked up at the moon, and frowned. 'Rain clouds are gathering, but we have no choice other than to wait.'

I agreed. 'Tell the men to lie low, and keep as silent as possible. We'll march before dawn.'

The long wait did little to ease my nerves. My brothers managed some much-needed sleep, but I kept watch on the town. This was the moment I'd dreamed of, yet my heart raced as I considered the consequences of our attack failing. Every man had agreed to the risks, but their lives were still my responsibility.

The urgent clanging of church bells echoed in the darkness like a death knell, telling us the alarm had been raised in the town. Our raid would be more dangerous now, but we'd come too far and waited too long; there would be no going back.

John drew his sword and gave me a nod, then took his sixteen men to the marketplace. I led the rest of our men up the broad street and gave the order to light our fire-pikes. We marched like an invading army to the beat of our drums, blazing torches on the pikes lighting our way.

As before, our attack relied on bluster and bravado, as we

were certain to be outnumbered by the Spanish militia. I had no wish to injure any of the townspeople, but if they needed an excuse to abandon the town, we were ready to offer them one.

The sharp crack of my brother's arquebus was the signal for our trumpeters, who began their fanfare. The Spanish militia would be forgiven for fleeing such an attack, and we helped them on their way with a fusillade of arquebus fire, aimed high into the air.

Marching into the centre of the town, we found the governor's stone house. The great wooden door stood ajar, with lit candles showing someone was awake. A black horse waited, saddled and ready to ride, and I guessed the governor had yet to make his escape.

Barging into the house, we found bars of solid silver, stacked in a pile against one wall, three feet high. Ruben Díaz had told me the pile was said to be as high as a man, yet there were still more silver bars than we could carry away in our pinnaces.

I turned to Harry. 'Guard the silver with six men – and make sure no one touches a bar of it. We need a wagon to move them, but first we have to find the king's treasure house, which is close to the waterside. That's where we'll find the gold.'

As we made our way to the waterfront and met my brother John and his men, an unfamiliar voice called out.

'Captain! The boats are in danger!'

I turned to see a young Cimarron running towards us, waving his arms. He gasped, out of breath, as if he'd run some distance.

My brother John recognised him. 'He's the one who begged to join us. He said the Spanish threatened to hang him.'

'What's the matter with our boats?' I didn't want to turn back now.

The young Cimarron pointed back the way we'd come. 'The Spanish discover your men. They need help, Captain.'

I had no choice, and turned to John. 'Take some men and go back with him to secure our boats.' I understood the scowl of resentment on John's face, but he called out to his men and disappeared into the night.

The first drops of rain spattered on the ground as we watched him go. We'd chosen to come in the wet season, before the treasure fleet arrived, and now we would pay the price. The sky turned black as thunderclouds obscured the moon, and the storm began with a bright flash of lightning, followed seconds later by a rumbling boom of thunder.

'Keep your powder dry!' I led the remaining men to the shelter in the lee of a large building in the town. One of them cursed the rain. 'Have faith. We're close to the treasure store, where they keep gold and jewels.'

The heavy rainstorm eased as quickly as it had come and, led by our drummers and trumpeters, we marched on further into the town. The buildings were closer together here and the streets narrowed. I scanned the shuttered windows and rooftops, watching for movement. My plan had worked. We'd taken control of the town and the treasure would soon be within reach.

The bangs of arquebus fire startled me, and the young trumpeter in front of me dropped to his knees. His trumpet clattered to the cobbled street, and he slumped on to his face. More shots rang out, and I fell to the ground in agony, as if a burning-hot iron had been stabbed into my thigh.

I cursed my luck and shouted, 'Take cover!' I groaned at the sight of bright-red blood, flowing down my leg from a deep wound. Gritting my teeth, I pulled myself up and leaned against a wall. I could not be captured by the Spanish. I would rather die fighting.

I watched as my men hammered at the locked door to the treasure house. It proved too well made, and we were running out of time. The militiamen would be reloading their arquebuses and regrouping for a new attack. We made an easy target for them, exposed at the open waterfront.

The wooden door cracked and splintered in two. I stayed to guard the entrance, holding the wound on my leg, while the men crawled through the wrecked door and disappeared inside. Blood flowed through my fingers and my head was spinning. Slumping to the ground, I closed my eyes and surrendered to the darkness.

The delicate scent of woodsmoke floated in the warm air, and the soft patter of rain on a roof muted unfamiliar voices. I lay on a straw mattress, thin enough for the stony, uneven ground to press into my back. Opening my eyes, I stared up at the bearded face of the man shaking me.

'You must drink, Captain.' His voice was edged with concern, and I recognised him as one of the Cornishmen from the *Pasco*.

'Where am I?' I stared down at the bloodstained linen covering my thigh. It took me a moment to recognise my white shirt, sewn with such care by Mary last winter, now torn into bandages.

'With the Cimarrons.' He tried again to make me drink from his leather bottle.

'Cimarrons?' My head filled with questions, but I struggled to make sense of my situation, or how I'd come to be there.

'They helped us, Captain. When we couldn't get back to the boats.'

'How is my leg?' I fought off the horrifying prospect of losing it. I'd seen strong men faint in agony when the ship's surgeon did his gruesome work, and didn't relish a future as a cripple.

'We couldn't believe anyone could lose so much blood, and

live.' He grinned, revealing stained and uneven teeth. 'God must have further work for you, Captain – you only have a flesh wound.'

'The treasure?'

He shook his head. 'The treasure house was empty.'

I lay back on the straw mattress. It had all been for nothing. The Spanish would not allow us back into Nombre de Dios. I recalled the stack of silver bars, and cursed my decision to leave it. My ruin wasn't only financial. My reputation would be tarnished by this disaster, and I would understand if the men resented me.

'How many of our men survived?' I held my breath as I waited for his answer.

'Many are wounded, Captain, but the only death was your trumpeter.'

'I saw him fall. He was the youngest of our crew, and had no armour to save him.' I winced as the pain returned to my leg. 'What of our ships?'

'All safe, thanks to your man Diego.'

'Diego?'

The bearded man smiled. 'Young Diego brought us to this place. We've named it the Isle of Victuals. The Cimarrons showed us fresh streams, and tasty roots and fruit, as well as fat hens, which make good eating.'

I held the leather bottle of water to my lips, and tasted the metallic coolness as I parched my thirst. The Cornishman handed me a fruit which tasted like a sweet ripe peach, and the juice ran down my cheek as I took a bite. I thanked God for the men who'd saved my life, and swore they would be well rewarded before we returned to Plymouth.

10

JANUARY 1573

I led the men in the Lord's Prayer, and fought back tears. My brother, who'd followed me to seek his fortune, had paid the ultimate price. Two men carried his body, sewn in sailcloth, and waited for my signal. I nodded, and watched as they lowered it over the side.

Joseph Drake sank into the deep blue water, at peace with God. Seventeen years old, he'd succumbed after New Year's Day to what they called 'Yellow Jack', a strange and painful fever which stole the lives of a third of my men.

Another dozen lay groaning in the hold, likely to die, as we knew no cause or cure. I promised myself that I would ensure my brothers hadn't died for nothing. We'd failed to capture a treasure ship, and our raids only made the Spanish more vigilant – yet we would not give up, or return empty-handed.

Harry Newman remained at my side after the funeral party left, his head bowed. 'I blame myself, for persuading Joseph to sail with us.'

'No.' I put my hand on his shoulder. 'Both my brothers—' My voice faltered. My other brother John, shot in the back while plundering a Spanish ship, had died from his wound. 'Joseph needed no persuasion. He'd have stowed away if we'd not signed him up.' I stared out to sea. 'My regret is that I had no chance to explain to John about the *Swan*.'

'The *Swan* had to be abandoned, Captain. We were short of men, and needed her crew – and you gave John command of the *Pasco*.'

'It was the manner of my doing it, behind his back.' I frowned at the memory of John's anger when he learned I'd ordered the *Swan* to be scuttled by our ship's carpenter. 'You know he never spoke to me again?'

Harry shook his head. 'You had no choice.'

'I will make sure his wife, Alice, has John's proper share, once we've discovered anything of value.' I stared out to the empty sea and said a silent prayer.

Diego sang a melodic African song as we made our way to the Cimarron village to meet my former guide, Pedro Mandinga. After five months of waiting, the rainy season ended, and we'd had word the Spanish treasure fleet sailed to Nombre de Dios.

Young Diego had become my shadow, keen to learn, his sharp brown eyes studying my charts, and asking questions. He climbed to the topmast faster than any man aboard, and speared fish by shooting them with his bow. Most importantly, he knew much about the country we planned to cross.

'You need strong boots, Captain.' He showed me the scars on his bare feet. 'There are thorn bushes, and stones as sharp as knives.'

I relied on Diego, as only eighteen of my men were well enough to make the fifty-mile journey overland. My leg ached when I walked, but I didn't complain, as others were less fortunate. Twenty-eight good men had died, and a few were left to guard the ship, and do their best to care for the sick.

Pedro Mandinga waited on the shore to greet us. He'd become a Cimarron chief, and wore an old Spanish sword on a thick leather belt, with a string of seashells around his neck. He raised a hand and called out in his deep voice as we approached.

'El Drako!' He grinned and waved.

I laughed at his joke about the Spanish calling me 'The Dragon'.

'Pedro! It's good to see you.'

He led us to his village, a collection of palm-roofed huts with views out to sea, hidden from sight of passing ships. Pedro had chosen his best men to make the long trek with us, a dozen Cimarrons armed with bows and large knives.

'They care more about revenge on the Spanish than silver.' Pedro glanced at the sun. 'Your men must be ready at dawn, Captain. We have a long walk ahead.'

I spent an uneasy night in the Cimarron camp, worried about my men. They'd followed me in good faith, yet a third of them were dead, and at least ten more unlikely to see Plymouth again. I prayed for Mary, alone and so far away, and wondered if she'd received my letter.

I'd spent long hours choosing my words, and paid James Raunce to ensure the letter found its way to her. He'd abandoned us once he knew we had no gold. I'd also written a sealed letter to William Hawkins. I didn't trust Raunce not to paint a bleak picture of our prospects when he returned to Plymouth.

An ethereal mist hung over the forest as we set out at first light. We marched in silence, except for the occasional muttered curse, and the clank of a weapon on armour. Pedro's men carried the equipment for our camp and our supplies, as my crewmen looked tired before we began.

Cimarron scouts led the way, hacking at the overgrown path with long-bladed knives. I followed with Pedro and Diego. As well as my sword, I carried a loaded pistol, taken from one of the Spanish captains. If I needed to use it I would only have one chance, so I'd been improving my aim by shooting coconuts from the palm trees.

I also wore another useful prize, a silver whistle on a chain around my neck. The bright sound carried well, so a single sharp blast would be the signal for the men to attack. Two short blasts on my whistle would be the call to regroup.

The forest grew thicker, with trailing green vines over-hanging the stony path, and blue-and-yellow parrots screeching through the tree tops. We'd have found the walk easier on the wide road used by the mule trains, but our guides led us up into the hills. As well as being more direct, there was less risk of being spotted by the Spanish.

After four hours we stopped to rest in the welcome shade. The relentless sun made us sweat, attracting buzzing flies and biting mosquitos. Diego produced a green lime from the bag he carried, and sliced it in two with his knife, handing half to me.

'Rub it on the bites, Captain.' He grinned as he demon-strated on his bare arms. 'Soon we will be in the hills, which are cooler.' He seemed in his element, at home in the woods. I did as he said, and found the refreshing coolness of the lime soothed my skin.

We continued on the stony track to our next stopping place, a Cimarron village surrounded by a deep ditch and high earth embankment. More permanent than the last, it had a wide road and was full of laughing children. They delighted at the shrill sound of my silver whistle, and called me 'Captain Drako'.

The women made us a meal of roasted pork and plantains, with sweet beer made from fermented roots. Later, we sat around the fire and the village elders told us how the Spanish raided the village, murdering many women and children. The men were beaten and tortured before being hanged from trees, the punishment for escaped slaves.

I thanked God for our alliance with the Cimarrons, our secret weapon against the Spanish, our mutual enemy. Diego and Pedro were as loyal as any of my men. Without them we would soon perish in this remote and desolate country.

Starting at dawn, we climbed a steep path to a high ridge. The air grew fresher as we left the low-lying forest, although we had to travel more slowly. At the highest point stood an enormous tree, which Pedro beckoned me to climb, using footholds cut into the thick trunk.

From the tree, I stared at the mysterious South Sea. The shimmering blue ocean belonged to a different world. I could also see all the way we'd come, and the familiar shore where our boats waited.

The welcome breeze restored my spirits, and I prayed the Lord would allow me to live long enough to sail an English ship in the Southern Sea. John Oxenham climbed to join me, and stared into the far distance, a glint in his eye.

'What wonders does that sea hold, Captain, for those brave enough to explore?'

The last part of our march took us through sharp-edged pampas grass, as high as a man. We followed meandering paths made by long-horned cattle, until our scout held a finger to his mouth, the sign to keep silent. The spire of a church, and distant tiled rooftops glinted in the sun. We'd reached the city of Panama.

We hid in a grove near the high road, while one of our scouts continued alone, to find out when the treasure would be taken to Nombre de Dios. We prayed it would be the next day, although we might face a long wait, which increased the risk of being seen by the Spanish.

Night fell before our scout returned. Unable to light a fire for fear of being spotted, we huddled in the darkness to hear whether our long journey had been wasted. He spoke to Pedro in the Cimarron language, but I could tell from his tone he brought good news.

Pedro grinned. 'An important Spanish official, the Treasurer of Lima, travels to Nombre de Dios with his family tomorrow night. He has fourteen mules, half of which carry gold, and there is talk of jewels. A *recuas* of fifty mules, carrying supplies, will leave Panama at the same time.'

My pulse raced at the prospect of so much gold. 'Did your man learn how many guards ride with the treasurer's mule train?'

Pedro spoke again with his scout, but shook his head. 'We don't know how many, but must be ready for a fight.'

Marching until we found a suitable place for our ambush, I lay down with half our men in the long grass on one side. Pedro, with John Oxenham and the other half of the men, concealed themselves on the other side of the road, and we waited for nightfall.

Several hours passed before the distant tinkling of the mule bells carried in the still night air. One of the men stifled a cough, but otherwise we lay in silence, waiting for my signal and holding our breath. My men were to capture the leading mules, while John Oxenham and the rest of the men would take those at the rear.

Iron-shod hooves clattered on the stony track, and a Spanish soldier rode into view. He stared into the tall grasses on each side, and I guessed he'd been sent ahead of the mule train. One of the bowmen at my side nocked an arrow and gave me a questioning glance, but I shook my head.

A Cornish crewman from the *Pasco* ignored the order to stay out of sight and sprang up to pull the Spaniard from his horse. The rider spun his horse around, and galloped back in the direction he'd come from, shouting a warning in Spanish to the others.

I cursed the crewman's stupidity. The bells of the mules became fainter as they turned back to Panama. With no need for silence, we scrambled in pursuit, but they'd gone. We'd marched close to the South Sea, but would have nothing to show for it.

I gathered the men together. 'There are too many soldiers in Panama, but *recuas* rest at Venta Cruces, not far from our way back to the coast. We shall salvage something from this after all.' I forced a smile. 'Who knows what we'll find there?'

The soldiers guarding the village waited in ambush, and fired a volley of arquebuses. A bullet glanced off my breastplate with a numbing thump, leaving a dent and a bright scar on the metal. A young crewman at my side screamed out, his face peppered with shot, blinding him in both eyes.

The Cimarrons charged, yelling and firing arrows, hacking with long knives as the Spanish struggled to reload their arquebuses. The brutal battle ended in moments, as the rest of the soldiers dropped their weapons and fled.

Making our way into the town, we searched every building, taking any plunder we could carry, including two horse loads of silver. The men began drinking, and set fire to several houses, so I gave the order to return to our ships. Although our plan had failed, we'd seen the stories were true, and would return.

Our stores low, we set out in our pinnaces along the coast to find fresh supplies. My crew in the *Minion* captured a Spanish caravel, and found a chest of gold coins. The *Bear* took a frigate laden with livestock, including goats, pigs and chickens. A well-built ship, she would be refitted for the homeward voyage.

Our prisoners would usually be set ashore, yet we worried about them betraying our presence. We kept them below decks, with promises they would be well treated.

The next day we went in pursuit of a carrack but, as we drew closer, the eighty-ton ship turned and approached us under a flag of truce. Her white-bearded commander rowed across to meet me, and clambered aboard with some difficulty, as he carried something wrapped in blue velvet.

'Captain Guillaume le Testu.' He smiled and spoke in English, with a strong French accent. 'We need your help. We have no fresh water.'

'Captain Drake, at your service.' I looked back at his well-armed ship. 'We have water we can share – but how is it you've remained here?'

'France is not safe for us, Captain. I'm Huguenot, and too old to end my days on French gallows. I prefer to take my chances in raids on Spanish settlements. Perhaps we could join forces?'

'I need good men, Captain. I confess our first attempt at an ambush failed, but we've had news of another mule train carrying silver from the Spanish mines to Nombre de Dios.'

'I have seventy men I can put at your disposal.' He smiled. 'I confess we've been looking for you, as we cannot take on the Spanish treasure fleet alone.'

I could only muster twenty men, including myself, and had no wish to be outnumbered by Huguenots. 'I'll take your best twenty, and you're most welcome to come with us to command them.'

Captain le Testu uncovered the velvet-wrapped object and revealed a gilded scimitar. 'This belonged to King Henry II of France, and I would like you to have it, a gift to seal our alliance.'

I examined the polished blade of the well-balanced weapon. The handle of engraved gold was set with rubies, worth a fortune. 'In return for your help, Captain le Testu, you shall have a half share of whatever we find.'

We sailed with the captured frigate and two pinnaces towards the Rio Francisco, a wide river estuary to the west of Nombre de Dios. The sheltered beach proved ideal for our pinnaces, but didn't have enough depth for the frigate, which Harry Newman anchored off shore to await our return.

Marching in silence through the woods, we found the bank of the river and the stony road to Nombre de Dios. I chose a clearing for our camp for the night, a mile from the road, and gathered the men together.

'We hope the Spanish will be tired after their trek from the silver mines.' I waited while one of the English-speaking Huguenot soldiers translated for the others. 'Last time we lost the element of surprise. That will *not* happen again.' I held up my silver whistle for them all to see. 'No one moves until I sound the order to attack.'

Diego woke me at dawn. 'Captain! The *recuas* is coming!'

The tinkle of mule bells brought me to my senses, and I

followed Diego to the viewpoint. The straggling line of mules was visible in the distance as far as we could see. As before, we formed into two groups, and waited for the Spanish to walk into our trap.

Holding my breath, I watched the lead mule come within range, and gave one sharp blast on my whistle. The Spanish guards panicked. Several fired their arquebuses, without taking aim. Others turned their mules back, but our rearguard were waiting for them.

One of the Cimarrons lay face down in a pool of blood, but the Spanish were routed before I'd drawn my sword. Diego took a firm grip on the bridle of the lead mule while I opened the leather straps fastening the heavy woven basket it carried.

Under a scrap of sacking lay a quoit of solid gold on top of ingots of solid silver. I looked down the line of mules, stretching into the distance. If each mule carried a full load of silver, the total would weigh several tons. We'd found our fortune, but now faced the problem of how to carry so many silver bars.

'Take the mules, Captain.' Diego pointed back the way we'd come. 'There's no need to unload the silver.'

'The mules will slow us down, and the Spanish could regroup and find us before we reach our camp.'

John Oxenham arrived in time to overhear my reply. 'The banks of the river are full of land crab burrows, Captain. We'll use the holes to hide what we can't carry.'

I agreed. 'Have the men bury what they can, and place a light-coloured stone close by to make them easier to find.'

One of the Huguenot soldiers who spoke English called out. 'Captain le Testu has been shot!'

I followed him to where the captain lay in the shade of a tree. 'How bad is it?'

The Huguenot captain winced as he held his hand over the red stain on his shirt. 'A flesh wound, but deep.'

I called for Diego. 'We'll fashion a stretcher, and carry you back to the boats.'

We made slow progress on the return journey, following the riverbank through the woods to the sea. Four men carried the captain, while the rest struggled with the weight of a fortune in silver bars. Captain le Testu's condition worsened, and we had to leave him with two of his men to tend to his wound.

When we reached the sea, Spanish ships patrolled the coast, so the Cimarrons helped us make a temporary camp to lie low. A tropical storm kept us awake, threatening to tear the roof from my shelter. By dawn there was no sign of any Spanish ships – or of our own.

John Oxenham offered to follow the coast on foot. 'The going will be hard, Captain, but I don't see how else we'll discover our boats.' He stared out to sea. 'They must be sheltering in a cove, and won't be far away.'

Diego held up his sharp axe. 'I can build a raft, and make a sail from sacking. It will be quicker.'

I agreed. Dark storm clouds loomed overhead and we had to leave as soon as we could. I prayed Harry Newman and his men hadn't been taken by the Spanish. If we couldn't find them soon, we'd be marooned with our fortune.

The makeshift raft looked seaworthy, as Diego fashioned a strong mast for a canvas sail, a rudder and paddles. I chose to sail the raft with Diego and two of the Huguenot soldiers, who claimed to be good swimmers. My heart thumped in my chest as we launched into the surf.

The first wave soaked us to the skin, and I choked as I swallowed a mouthful of seawater, but Diego's raft held together and the small sail filled with wind. We sailed and paddled some three leagues along the coast in worsening seas, but veering winds made our canvas sail flap, so we paddled until our hands blistered.

Seawater sluiced across the raft with every surge of the waves, making me gasp. I watched a tree on the headland, and cursed our lack of progress, paddling harder, despite a growing sense of futility. We were being dragged further out to sea.

'Keep close to the shore. If all fails, we must find somewhere to land.' Glancing at the rocky cliffs, I prayed to the Lord to save us.

After battling rough seas for half a day in the parching sun, we cheered at the sight of our two pinnaces coming towards us. We shouted and waved, but they didn't see us, and sailed into a cove behind the headland. Guessing they would anchor for the night, we paddled desperately for the shore, and abandoned the raft in waist-deep water.

Exhausted by the effort of paddling, we lay on the rocks to regain our strength before finding our way around the headland by a narrow coast path. Harry Newman looked surprised and relieved to see us.

'Captain! What happened?'

I handed him the solid gold quoit as my answer. 'We must thank God for our good fortune, Harry. There's more gold and silver than these pinnaces can carry.'

I kept my promise to Captain le Testu, dividing the treasure we'd carried back with the Huguenot soldiers. John Oxenham returned grim-faced from his mission to rescue their captain and the rest of the silver we'd buried.

'It seems Captain le Testu and his two men have been

captured.' He cursed. 'They might have been tortured to confess our hiding places. Most of the buried silver is gone. We only found a dozen bars and three more quoits of gold.'

I sent Diego with Pedro to see if they could learn more. I owed it to the old Huguenot captain to do what we could. I'd only known him a short time, but we'd discovered a shared interest in navigation, and had both been charting the many islands along the coast.

Diego returned at dusk with Pedro. 'Captain le Testu has been executed. His head put on a pike in the town square at Nombre de Dios.' Pedro cursed the Spanish. 'He was a good man.'

I stared at him. But for the grace of God, it could have been my head on the pike. I went to my cabin and found the gilded scimitar, given to me by Captain le Testu. Even if it hadn't belonged to the King of France, the weapon had great value. I presented it to Pedro.

'We owe you a debt. Without your help we could not have survived this expedition.'

We gave our Spanish prisoners the *Pasco*, and said farewell to the Huguenot ship, which sailed for Cartagena. I ordered the flag of St George to be flown from the main top of the refitted frigate, renamed the *Falcon*, and we prepared for the long voyage home. In less than a month of favourable winds we passed the Isles of Scilly, arriving at Plymouth in bright sunshine on a Sunday in August.

Mary came running from St Andrew's Church, close to the harbour. She'd not received the letter I'd spent long hours writing, and confessed she'd feared she would never see me again.

I held her close, her slender body trembling as she sobbed

with tears of relief. 'I'll make you a promise, Mary.' I pulled back and stared into her shining brown eyes. 'I shall spend a year ashore with you.'

'A year?' Mary put her hand to her mouth.

'You have my word. We will start a family.' I smiled at the thought. 'What use is our great fortune, with no one to inherit it?'

I had one more task before meeting with William Hawkins. Alice, my brother's young wife, stared at me in silent despair as I promised she would have John's share, enough to live in comfort for the rest of her life. Alice blamed me for John's death, and no amount of Spanish silver would make amends.

11

MARCH 1574

We strolled together down the long avenue in bright spring sunshine, past the homes of wealthy merchants and traders, men who made the real decisions in Plymouth. Mary wore a long coat, trimmed with fox fur, over her new gown, her necklace of gleaming pearls a reminder of our success.

I wore a new black doublet with silver buttons, a box-pleated ruff, and a cloak of black velvet, edged with gold. People would know the sumptuary laws forbade the wearing of velvet cloaks unless their income was more than two hundred pounds a year.

I'd been made a freeman of the city of Plymouth, and needed a house in keeping with my new status. My old life as a penniless sailor, living in one room over a candlemaker's shop, seemed a world away. Determined to become a good family man, I'd promised myself I'd be a better husband to Mary.

A light breeze carried the familiar clanging of a ship's bell from the nearby harbour, and I imagined the crew assembling on deck for prayers. I missed the routine of life on board a ship and the excitement of the West Indies, but I'd returned to unexpected news. Queen Elizabeth wished to agree a peace treaty with King Philip of Spain.

William Hawkins warned me I would be well advised to keep my promise to remain ashore. I yearned to explore the mysterious Southern Sea, yet accepted I would have to wait. I told myself I didn't need the money, and it would be too dangerous to sail without a letter of marque.

We reached the address I'd brought Mary to see. The house was one of the best in Notte Street. A short walk from the waterfront, and facing the sea, the well-built property seemed a fitting reward for the great risks I'd taken. I stopped and turned to her.

'This is the one.' I watched her face, trying to read her thoughts.

Mary stared up at the substantial timber-framed house. The walls gleamed with fresh whitewash, and sunlight glinted from leaded casement windows. Wisps of grey smoke drifted from the towering red-brick chimney, one of the highest in the street.

'Can we truly afford such a grand place?'

I smiled at her question as I unlocked the front door and led her inside. I'd dreamed of a home like this, although I never imagined I would be able to buy such a fine home outright. The previous owner, an elderly merchant, had already accepted my offer, yet I must choose my moment to tell Mary that.

Only I knew the full extent of my wealth, as I'd learned to keep such matters secret. After sharing with my crew, and reaching a settlement with William Hawkins, I'd been quietly selling my portion of silver ingots and a hundred thousand pounds in silver coins, but kept my share of the gold in a hidden strongbox.

I led Mary from room to room. Some were empty, others left partly furnished by the previous owner. The most impressive feature was the long gallery, designed for entertaining. It had an ornate plaster ceiling, and leaded windows flooded it with light. There were views across open parkland to the sea beyond.

I'd been watching for Mary's reaction, but she followed me

in silence, as if the house was nothing to do with her. 'You haven't told me what you think, Mary.'

She looked surprised at the challenge in my tone. 'This house is too grand for our needs. My conscience would trouble me if we lived in such a place.'

The argument was one we'd discussed often since my return from the West Indies. Mary only wore her pearls at my insistence. My conscience was clear, yet I found it difficult to help her understand. I had to remind myself she had never left Devon, so it would be hard for her to imagine life on the other side of the ocean.

'I've earned my fortune as truly as if I'd dug the gold and silver from the ground with my bare hands. I had a royal commission, and took care not to harm anyone, if it could be avoided.' My voice echoed in the empty room. I'd spoken more sharply than I intended.

'People died...'

I reached out and took her hand. 'The Spanish murder good Christian men for believing in the true faith.' I stopped myself from adding details of the cruel torture inflicted by the Inquisition. 'They hang the Cimarrons as escaped slaves.'

'You swore to have your revenge.' Her voice carried a note of accusation, which I couldn't miss.

I guessed Harry might have told her, in an unguarded moment, but I'd made no secret of my true intention. Word would have spread easily enough in a town like Plymouth, where my adventures and rapid rise had become quite a talking point.

'As God is my witness, I treated our Spanish prisoners as well as I could, and set all the slaves I found free.'

She stared at me as if she wasn't sure how to reply, but turned and continued our tour of the house. A huge table dominated the dining room, and Mary seemed lost in thought as she ran her fingers over a scratch in the polished walnut top.

'This would seat ten people – or more.'

I smiled. 'Perfect for a growing family.'

'Our present house is enough for our needs.' She sounded terse, but subdued, as if she knew she couldn't win.

'Our present house is only rented, and has no land.' I led her to a window which overlooked the grounds, and opened it to let in the fresh spring air. 'There are rose beds, and a well-stocked herb garden.' I pointed to the stunted trees at the far end. 'We have an orchard, and I'm told to expect a good crop of apples in the autumn.'

She stared up at dusty cobwebs in the corner of the ceiling, and frowned. 'A house this size would be a lot of work to look after.'

'We'll take on more servants. You will have two maids, a cook, a scullery girl, a cleaner and a laundress. There is also Diego, and I believe we will need to employ a gardener.' I gave her a meaningful smile. 'Perhaps soon, a nursemaid.'

'Is Diego to live here as your servant?' She sounded surprised.

'Diego saved my life.' I sounded defensive, even though she knew the story. 'I plan to make him my assistant, and will teach him to read and write.'

I tried to hide my disappointment that she'd ignored my mention of a growing family or a nursemaid. Seven months had passed since my return, yet there was still no sign of a child, and Mary avoided my efforts to discuss the reason. It seemed the Lord had other plans for us, but I'd had an idea.

'There's enough room here for your sister Margaret to come and live with us, if you wish, and I thought of sending for my young nephew John, as company for Jonas.' I watched for her reaction.

Mary brightened at my suggestion. 'It's time Margaret came out of mourning, and she will be able to help me with the running of this grand place.'

I breathed a sigh of relief. Margaret and her son Jonas would be destitute if not for our charity. Her husband had sailed on a merchant ship two years before, and never returned. With no news, the ship was declared lost, and he'd been presumed dead.

If it was God's will for me not to have a son to inherit my fortune, I planned to make sure my nephew John would be set up for life. I would also do what I could to provide for young Jonas, and see they both had the best education.

I wished in some way to make amends for the loss of my brothers John and Joseph, although their deaths were no fault of mine. John's wife still refused to speak to me, yet had already been courting a man from Saltash. I suspected he wished to get his hands on Alice's newly acquired fortune.

I wasn't suited to a life of leisure, and intended to put my fortune to good use. It had taken time to sort out my late brother's affairs, and I'd kept busy overseeing the refitting of the *Falcon* with new armaments and better accommodation.

Inspired by William Hawkins' well-appointed offices, I bought a commercial property within walking distance of our new house. With views across the harbour and out to sea, the location provided a perfect base of operations for my new merchant shipping venture.

William Hawkins was one of the first visitors to my new offices, and seemed impressed. He sat in one of my new leather chairs and admired the parchment chart of the West Indies, a gift from the ill-fated Huguenot Captain le Testu, which I'd had framed on the wall.

'Did you know your adventuring is being talked about in Westminster?'

'What are they saying?' I tried to sound as if it was of no consequence, but my heart raced at the news.

His face turned serious. 'Our queen has agreed to stop her sailors seizing Spanish ships, or raiding Spanish settlements. In return, King Philip has promised to end his persecution of Protestants.' William Hawkins frowned. 'You've been named as an enemy of the King of Spain. That could prove a serious charge.'

I sat back in my chair. 'I carried the letter of marque, a royal commission, which you helped me to secure.'

William Hawkins raised an eyebrow. 'Be that as it may, the Spanish ambassador said you seized Nombre de Dios by force, looted the King of Spain's treasure house, and burned a nearby town, as well as seizing many Spanish merchant ships.'

'We held Nombre de Dios only briefly, and I nearly lost my life into the bargain.' I tapped my leg. 'The wound still troubles me.' I crossed to the map on the wall and pointed. 'As for the nearby town, they must mean Venta Cruces.'

'Is it true that you burned it to the ground?'

'We were fired upon by the militia. They killed one of my men, as well as several of our Cimarron guides. My men were angry and burned a few old buildings, but we took nothing of any consequence.'

William Hawkins frowned. 'These incidents don't help negotiations with King Philip. They have a way of being exaggerated in the retelling, and there are some in London who suspect you returned with more gold than you've reported to the Crown.'

'By God's faith, I hope you've put them right, William?'

He hesitated for a telling moment, before returning my smile. 'I trust we'll remain partners?'

'I need your help; despite my experience at sea, I know little enough of how to run a shipping business. I plan to commission the building of a new ship, of my own design. She'll have the speed to cross the ocean in less than a month, and a hold large enough for the rest of King Philip's gold.'

He didn't respond to my joke, but stroked his beard as he considered my idea. 'Building a new ship is a costly business, which is why we used old carracks like the *Jesus of Lubeck*. You know she once fought off the French invasion of the Isle of Wight?' He shook his head. 'I was sorry to hear of her loss.'

'I will never forget that day in San Juan de Ulúa. You know the Spanish attack was unprovoked, and your brother did all he could to save your ships?'

He nodded. 'I do.' He seemed to come to a decision. 'I will lease you more ships, if you find the crews, but the success of your venture will depend on finding the right routes.'

I poured us both a glass of wine, and handed him one, before sitting at my new desk. 'What routes do you suggest?'

He sipped his wine and nodded appreciatively before answering. 'I've been thinking of developing trade with Ireland. There's demand in London for Irish linen, and we always need suitable timbers for ship-building.'

'What would we carry on the outward voyage?'

William Hawkins held up his glass as an answer. 'Whatever sells, Francis. One month it might be wine, another grain or wool.' He grinned. 'The trick is to watch the market. We'll make an honest merchant of you yet.'

Mary had a question for me after we'd retired to bed. 'Harry tells me John Oxenham is recruiting men for a voyage back to the West Indies.' She looked into my eyes. 'Did you know Harry's thinking of sailing with them?'

'I've advised him against it. John Oxenham has bought the Spanish merchant ship we returned with, and is refitting her with new guns.' I frowned. 'Now the queen has agreed terms with the Spanish, he can't expect to have a letter of marque.'

Mary's eyes filled with concern. 'Does that mean Harry could be in danger?'

'If they approach Spanish ships they'll be treated as pirates. The Spanish had little enough care for a flag of truce in the past.' I took her in my arms. 'Your brother has good experience of the West Indies, but I have better plans for him.'

'Will you make him a partner in your new business?'

'I need men I can trust to manage my trade with Ireland. I'll appoint him captain of the *Falcon*, the flagship of my new fleet. He'll be safer sailing the Irish Sea.'

'It would mean a lot to me.' Mary kissed me. 'I'm sorry I didn't wish to move to this house.'

I pulled her close and kissed her on the forehead. 'This house proved to be one of my better decisions, and you've settled well into the role of lady of the household.'

She smiled. 'I confess I'm happier with my sister Margaret for company. She's been a great help to me.'

'Although she's a year younger than you, the hardship of the past two years has left its mark on Margaret. She looks a little thin, and her face is pale.'

'Margaret worries that Jonas has become withdrawn since his father's disappearance.'

'I've seen a difference in them both.' I smiled. 'At first, Margaret wouldn't look me in the eye – and I believe young Jonas is like his uncle Harry. He says little, yet his questions often surprise me.'

Mary agreed. 'Although they had no choice, I know they are grateful to be welcomed into our household.'

'Have you seen how the boys follow Diego? He's asked if I'll allow him to build them a Cimarron hut in the garden, complete with a circle of stones for cooking!'

'Will you allow it?' Mary smiled. 'Diego seems able to turn his hand to anything.'

'I believe I will. I'm engaging a tutor, as it's time the boys learned to read and write. Diego can share their lessons, and teach them some practical skills.'

A log fire burned in the hearth, and tall candles flickered in silver holders, lighting up our faces as we sat at the dining table for supper. The family evening meal had become something of a ritual. We clasped our hands in prayer as I said grace.

'*God guide our ways, and give us grace our Lord to please. For what we are about to receive, may the Lord make us truly thankful.*'

Annie, our serving maid, brought a basket of freshly baked bread, and plates of steaming-hot roast lamb in gravy, with honeyed parsnips and onions fried in butter. I washed my hands in my fingerbowl as Mary, sitting at my side, did the same, drying them on a linen napkin.

Opposite us sat her younger sister Margaret, with Jonas and my young nephew John. He'd arrived on the coach late one evening, and had grown into a tall ten-year-old. Looking across at him I sensed an unexpected stab of grief, as he reminded me of my late brother, John.

I'd been right to hope my nephew would be company for Jonas, who was only a year older. They'd both been raised by women, and lacked a father figure, which might explain why they seemed a little in awe of me.

I broke some bread and dipped it in the rich gravy, tasting the red wine. 'I've been reflecting on how our lives have changed since the move to Notte Street.' I looked around the table at their faces. 'I'd like to thank you all for helping to make this house our home.'

Mary turned to me. 'I once believed this house was too large but, between us, we seem to have filled every room.'

I smiled, and cut a slice of lamb with my sharp knife. Flavoured with mint, the meat was tender and succulent. 'Once I could carry all I owned in the world in one small bag, but soon enough I needed my sea chest!'

Mary laughed. 'It's taken a wagon drawn by two cart horses to move our furniture from the old house.' She smiled across at her sister. 'I must confess I don't think I could have managed to have all the rooms made ready without Margaret's help.'

Annie served wine, and small beer for the boys, and Margaret raised her glass. 'We thank you for inviting us to share your new home. I truly don't know what we would have done—'

Mary held up a hand. 'If our situation was reversed, Margaret, you would do the same.'

I raised my own glass and proposed a toast. 'To family – and the future.'

They all raised their glasses in reply. 'To our family, and the future.'

12

APRIL 1575

William Hawkins rode at my side as we made the twenty-five mile journey to Dartington Hall. We'd set off at first light for a meeting with the Admiral of Devon, following the rutted road along the edge of Dartmoor. The reason for the admiral's invitation was a mystery to us both.

I looked across at William. 'How do you know Admiral Champernowne?'

'Through my brother.' He smiled. 'In business, such connections can be important.'

'I trust this is a business matter.'

William Hawkins nodded. 'I'm hopeful this could be a turning point in our Irish venture.'

'God knows we could use a little luck.' I frowned as I recalled Harry's return from his first voyage. 'We might have covered our costs, but we made no profit.'

'Your brother-in-law wasn't to know the Irish merchants would take advantage of his inexperience.'

'Harry Newman proved himself a good captain, capable of taking a cargo to Dublin and returning safely home, despite gales around Land's End.'

'He's brought us to the admiral's attention. I'd no idea he has interests in Ireland, but it doesn't surprise me. He's a good Protestant, and his aunt was the queen's governess, so he's well connected. When the Spanish fleet sought sanctuary in Plymouth, Sir Arthur escorted their treasure to the Tower, and they say more than half was used by Her Majesty to fund her navy.'

'The queen made him an admiral as reward?'

'And Vice Admiral of Devon, for life.'

I stared up at the high-vaulted roof of the great hall, and the oak hammer beams reminded me of the cavernous hold of a galleon. The admiral's coat of arms decorated the gable wall, and the stone fireplace was the grandest I'd seen. Dartington Hall was a display of old money and power, intended to impress.

Despite William's company, I worried about the reason for this summons. No one knew about the Spanish gold I'd hidden for my retirement. If the admiral guessed my secret, he might be offering me a chance to surrender my prize to the Crown, or face the consequences.

A servant ushered us into the admiral's study. Brightly lit by high-arched windows, shelves of leather-bound books filled one wall, while a magnificent old tapestry of a sea battle covered another. Admiral Champernowne waved a hand for us to take a seat.

Only his silver-grey hair suggested his age. He wore a blue velvet doublet with a white ruff and a gold chain of office. I glanced at his collection of books, and was reminded he'd been the Member of Parliament for Plymouth, and Sheriff of Devon.

William Hawkins gestured towards me. 'Admiral Champernowne, this is Captain Francis Drake.'

'Captain Drake. I hear you preach to your men twice a day.'

The admiral's educated voice carried an air of natural authority with a hint of good humour.

'My father was a preacher, Admiral, and when at sea I like to lead the daily prayers.'

The admiral gave me an appraising look. 'What do you know about the situation in Ireland?'

I glanced at William Hawkins, relieved he'd been right about the reason for our visit. 'I've not been to Ireland myself, but have begun to explore the opportunities for trade.'

'Permit me to enlighten you. Our western shores are vulnerable, unless we control Ireland. Two years ago, Sir Walter Devereux, Earl of Essex, led a mission to colonise part of the north of Ireland. Although he has the support of Her Majesty, the venture is at his own risk – and his own expense.'

William Hawkins nodded. 'My brother John has an investment in the earl's venture.'

'As does the queen's treasurer, Sir William Cecil, and Sir Robert Dudley – and, between us, Her Majesty invested ten thousand pounds. The stakes are high, as lands and titles will be granted by the Crown once we succeed, but our forces in Ireland have been reduced by sickness and desertion. They are resisted by Irish Catholics, who are aided by the Scots.'

William Hawkins leaned forward in his chair. 'How would we be able to assist, Admiral?'

'Her Majesty wishes this matter resolved. It seems the key is to control the Irish Sea, and prevent the Scots from interfering.' He looked across at me. 'If I were younger, I'd take this on myself, but my experience supporting the Huguenots has taught me I'm growing too old for such work. I asked John Hawkins to come out of retirement, and he recommended you, Captain Drake.'

'I only have one ship, the *Falcon*.'

The admiral nodded. 'The Earl of Essex has a fleet of ships

in Ireland, but his commanders are soldiers, without your experience of fighting at sea, particularly in shallow estuaries.' He studied me, waiting for my answer.

The opportunity to build my reputation was too good a chance to miss. 'We should take advantage of the favourable weather, Admiral. I can be ready to sail to Ireland within a week.'

My nephew John pulled off his cap and waved it to Jonas, who stood at the quayside with Margaret and Mary. I'd kept my promise to my wife, as more than a year had passed since I'd last been to sea.

We carried a full cargo of supplies for the Earl of Essex, and even Harry, retained as my deputy on the *Falcon*, believed we were on merchant business. I'd not told anyone the true purpose of our mission, as we had to take the Scots by surprise.

As John watched the last of Plymouth disappear in our wake, I had a grim recollection of the tearful face of Captain Hawkins' young nephew on the burning *Jesus of Lubeck*, unable to jump to safety. There'd been no word of what became of him. He might have been rescued by the Spanish, but I doubted it.

I swore not to put my own nephew in such danger, and aimed to leave the fighting to the earl's soldiers. I'd invested in a new swivel gun for the *Falcon*, and we carried a good supply of shot but, like the new sword I wore at my belt, I hoped I would never need to use it.

Harry Newman joined us as we headed down the Cornish coast. 'South-westerly winds. Favourable for Dublin, although I recommend we allow Land's End a wide berth.' He grinned at John, and pointed to the distant headland of the Lizard Point. 'A good many ships have foundered here. They call it the sailors' graveyard.'

I smiled at my nephew's frown of concern. 'One of your first lessons, John. It's not the sea you need to worry about – it's the land. Come with me, and I'll show you how we plot a safe course to Ireland.'

Dublin harbour bustled with activity and we were lucky to find a space at the busy quayside. Harry and Diego went in search of the harbour master and returned with a well-dressed man of about thirty. Like me, he wore a felt hat, a black doublet, and a sword which looked as if it had seen little use.

'Welcome to Ireland, Captain Drake.' He touched his hat in courtesy. 'Thomas Doughty, agent to the Earl of Essex. I have papers for you to sign, if you will.'

I invited him aboard and led him to my private cabin. Gesturing for him to take a seat, I filled two thick-bottomed glasses with my best red wine and handed him one. He took an appreciative sip and smiled, a twinkle of amusement in his questioning blue eyes.

'I've followed your adventures with interest, Captain. Are you going to allow John Oxenham to steal a march on you?'

'To be the first to explore the South Sea?' I laughed. 'I wish John Oxenham luck, crossing overland. He knows the route, and the risks. If he fails, we shall all learn from it.'

'A commendable attitude, Captain.' He took another sip of his wine, and seemed in no hurry.

'Thank you, Master Doughty. Now, where are these papers I need to sign?'

'That was a device to enable us to speak in private, Captain. I regret to tell you Dublin is full of Catholic spies, keen to learn what they can about our plans.'

'I've told no one the true reason for our voyage. Are we to unload here in Dublin, or is our cargo destined for the north of Ireland?'

'It is, Captain. I'm to ask you to remain here overnight, then sail at dawn for the harbour at Carrickfergus, where the commander of our army, Captain John Norris, is waiting.'

'With the rest of Sir Walter Devereux's fleet?'

'Captain Norris has a plan to end the Scottish interference, but it will be ten times harder if they know our intention, so the fleet is hidden in harbours along the coast. We will need to avoid drawing attention. Warn your men. There is danger in Carrickfergus.'

'Danger? From the Irish?'

'Have you been told what happened soon after the earl first arrived in Ireland?'

'I've been told next to nothing.'

'The earl was invited to a castle in Castlereagh, home of an Irish chieftain, named Brian McPhelim. The earl's soldiers took the chieftain's wife and brother prisoner, and killed more than a hundred of his men. Brian McPhelim and his family were executed in Carrickfergus Castle.'

'By Captain John Norris?'

Thomas Doughty nodded. 'Resentment simmers in Ireland, Captain Drake, like a pot of stew on a hot stove. We must take care not to stoke the fire.'

A square-turreted Norman castle guarded the cobblestoned harbour, and armed soldiers were assembling as we made our way to the headquarters building. Admiral Champernowne told me the army in Ireland had been reduced by sickness and desertion, but these men looked well disciplined, and busy preparing for action.

I'd told my men to stay aboard. Carrickfergus stank like a sewer, and I'd be glad to return to the *Falcon*. After everything I'd survived in the Indies, it would be a cruel twist of fate for me to be struck down with fever so close to home.

My instinct warned me not to trust Captain John Norris. He had a reddish pointed beard with a long moustache, and wore a black breastplate over a doublet with padded sleeves. He said little as Thomas Doughty introduced me, and before he spoke I sensed his manner would be abrupt.

He spread out a map of the northern coast of Ireland on his table, and weighted the corners with a book and a pewter tankard. 'The Scots are resourceful and the Irish must not be underestimated, Captain Drake, but I have a plan to take control of these seas.'

'I'm here to help you achieve that, Captain Norris. I doubt the Scots have more resources than the Spanish,' I smiled, 'and we made short work of them.'

He didn't return my smile, but pointed to a strange island in the shape of a boot, off the northern headland.

'Rathlin.' He glanced across at me, then stared back at his map. 'Three miles from Ireland and thirteen from Scotland. The Scots have made the island castle their base to frustrate our efforts here, so my plan is to hold them to siege until they surrender. The island has no fresh water, so they can't hold out for long, and we'll take heavy guns to blast the castle walls.' He tapped a shallow bay in the lee of the island. 'This is where we'll land, out of sight of the castle.'

I studied the map, fixing the unusually shaped shoreline in my memory. 'How many men are you taking, Captain?'

'Three hundred – as well as eighty horses.'

'Are so many horses necessary?'

'You'll see for yourself what eighty cavalrymen can do.' Captain Norris rolled up the map. 'We will be ready to sail as soon as you tell me the winds and tides are in our favour.'

We set off from Carrickfergus harbour in July sunshine, but were soon scattered by unpredictable winds. I suspected Captain Norris would be cursing my choice of departure time, although we now looked less like a fleet, which helped to conceal our true purpose.

I'd planned to hold the *Falcon* back, but the only other ships in our fleet were a flyboat, the *Fortunate*, which carried Captain Norris, and a thirty-ton sloop-rigged coastal hoy, the *Cork*. Her commander, Captain James Sydae, seemed to resent my involvement in the mission, and I suspected he saw it as a demotion.

The other boats were shallow-draft local craft, and crammed with armed soldiers. Some looked barely able to make the crossing to the island with such a load. I wondered if the rest of the earl's fleet had been held back in reserve, or if he'd run short of funds.

Harry Newman wiped the sweat from his brow and cursed under his breath. 'You were right to be concerned about taking so many horses. It's a miracle we managed to load them.'

Thomas Doughty overheard. 'Captain Norris served as a cavalry commander with the Huguenots in France, Captain Drake. It's what he knows.'

I frowned at Doughty's condescending manner. 'In my experience horses can be troublesome to unload, and the time it takes could cost us the element of surprise.'

After two days sailing we landed on Rathlin Island in the late evening, and I was relieved to see the *Fortunate* and the *Cork* close behind. The smaller boats would take longer, but the winds had been fair. We kept from the view of any lookouts in the high castle, and unloaded our horses and men as quietly as we could.

We were to patrol the waters between the island and Scotland, so we found the wind and headed for the Scottish coast. Thomas Doughty waved a hand in farewell as we left, and I said a prayer for the success of their mission.

I shielded my eyes against the setting sun, relieved there was no sign of the Scots raising the alarm, and turned to Harry. 'It seems Captain Norris's plan will work.' As I said the words, the sharp crack of shots echoed across the water.

Harry frowned. 'They haven't wasted any time, but we have the advantage of numbers, even if we've already lost the element of surprise.'

I nodded, glad to be out of it. 'I sent my nephew below as a precaution. Send Diego to tell him it's safe for him to be on deck.'

Harry frowned. 'I understood Diego was to remain on the island, with the other crewmen?'

I glanced back at the island. The landing bay was already hidden by high cliffs. 'What other crewmen?'

'Thomas Doughty told me he was to take a few of our men to help look after the horses. I thought you'd agreed—'

'I did nothing of the sort.'

Harry stared back at the island. 'How will we know when it's safe to return?'

'They'll light a beacon on the high ground as a signal. The skies are clear, so we should see it easily enough.'

Five long days passed, patrolling the waters between Rathlin Island and Scotland. Our gunners were ready if the Scots sent any ships to the island, but we only encountered a small fishing boat. At last, our lookout shouted, pointing at a column of smoke on the island's clifftop.

The landing beach bustled with men carrying sacks of grain on to the *Cork*. More arrived, driving a herd of cows which looked ready for milking. Captain Norris spotted us, and rode up on a grey horse. He wore a plumed black helmet with his black breastplate, and I found the grin on his face unsettling.

'You missed your chance to be part of a great victory, Captain. The Earl of Essex will wish to report this day to Her Majesty in person.'

I scanned the bay. 'Where are my men?' A sense of misgiving troubled me. I couldn't see Diego, or our other crewmen.

Captain Norris glanced back up at the castle. 'With Master Doughty. They'll be finished up soon enough.'

'And the Scots?' I guessed my men were being used to guard them up at the old castle.

'The Scots will not trouble us any more, Captain Drake, you have my guarantee of that.' He spurred his horse and rode off without waiting for my reply.

I left Harry to supervise the loading and followed Captain Norris up the stony track leading to the castle. A group of English soldiers came down the path, laughing and joking. I spotted Diego approaching. He looked exhausted and his clothes were dirty. He didn't smile when he saw me, and I sensed he had bad news.

'What happened?'

He stared at me with dull eyes. 'We used the horses to drag the cannons up to the castle.' Diego pointed back the way he'd come. 'It took three days to break the walls, and one of our men is badly wounded.'

'The Scots garrison surrendered?'

'Captain Norris's soldiers killed everyone, even the women and children.' He sounded numbed by what he'd witnessed.

'This wasn't what I brought you back to England for. I didn't know you'd stayed ashore.'

Diego glanced back over his shoulder. 'Captain Norris ordered his men to search the island, and kill anyone they found.' He rubbed his eyes. 'They found people hiding in caves...'

I put my hand on his shoulder. 'Return to the *Falcon*. I must find the truth of what's happened here.'

I left the path to follow the scraping sound of men digging with spades and picks. A dozen men worked in a deep pit, throwing shovels of earth high into the air. To one side lay bodies heaped on top of each other, like sides of beef in a butcher's cart.

A woman, no older than my own Mary, lay with her eyes wide and staring, as if unable to believe her fate. A young boy's throat had been cut, and flies buzzed at his jagged wound. I'd seen men killed, and the dead body of my own brothers, but nothing prepared me for the brutality of this massacre.

Staggering, as if in a dream, I made my way back to the *Falcon*. There was no need to question anyone about what had happened. The garrison's surrender had been rewarded in the cruellest way, by the hand of Captain John Norris, on the orders of Sir Walter Devereux, in the name of Queen Elizabeth of England.

The *Falcon* provided an escort to the boats ferrying supplies to and from the island, and I made a trip across the sea to Liverpool to collect the Lord Deputy of Ireland, Sir Henry Sidney.

With a fur cape and gold chain of the Order of the Garter, Sir Henry had been raised as a companion to young King Edward. Now in his late forties, he'd become an advisor to the queen.

I'd made a judgement to sacrifice my own cabin to him for the crossing, and he invited me to dine with him by way of thanks. Despite his noble background, he had the manners of a soldier, and wiped his bread around his plate, leaving it so clean it might not have been used at all.

'I heard about the attack on Rathlin Island.' He took a deep drink of the bitter ale and wiped his mouth on his sleeve. 'I took Rathlin once myself, you know? We couldn't hold it then, and I doubt we will now.'

'Is Her Majesty displeased?'

'Quite the contrary. The queen asked me to convey her gratitude to those involved. You can rest assured your part in this has done no harm to your reputation, Captain Drake.'

'Did the Earl of Essex mention me by name?'

He nodded. 'William Cecil asked me to give you this letter.' He looked curious. 'What is it you have planned, after your work in Ireland is done?'

'I'm having a new ship built for another voyage to the West Indies.'

Sir Henry Sidney raised an eyebrow. 'The Spanish will not welcome your return.'

13

MARCH 1576

London seemed busier, dirtier, and more dangerous. The once towering spire of St Paul's cathedral had not been rebuilt since being struck by a bolt of lightning. Catholics claimed the damage was a sign of God's anger at the heresy of Protestants, but for me the stump of the tower served as a different reminder.

Neither Queen Elizabeth, her government, nor the Church could afford the cost of having the spire rebuilt. The irony wasn't lost on me as I made my way down to the River Thames. The last time I met William Cecil I'd been John Hawkins' errand boy. This time, I hoped to discuss how I might boost the finances of the country.

Sir Henry Sidney's return to Ireland marked the end of my time there, as Sir Walter Devereux, Earl of Essex, had no further use for my services. I believed it was a matter of time before the Scots had their revenge for the betrayal at Rathlin Island, so I'd been glad to return to Mary and the peace of my family home in Plymouth.

I'd waited until the winter passed before travelling to visit Sir William Cecil, now Lord Burghley, Lord High Treasurer, and chief advisor to the queen. His letter was intriguingly brief, and he'd asked me to join him for dinner at his private house on the Strand in London. Whatever he had to say would not be official business.

We'd been blessed with a mild start to the spring, but the evenings could be chilly. Glad of my fur cape and leather gloves, I raised a hand to hail a wherry. The river would be the easiest way to travel, as the narrow streets were thronged with people. I'd been warned to watch for thieves and cutpurses, and to be wary of slops thrown from upper-floor windows.

The high tide of the wide River Thames lapped at the landing steps, and a flock of over a hundred swans hissed and flapped as people threw them scraps, and crusts of stale bread. There were so many boats and wherries my boatman had to use his oar to fend them off as we made our way towards the Strand.

I held my breath as a stinking dung boat passed close by, carrying its load of foul waste to dump further downriver. The Thames had become an open sewer, as the increasing number of people now living in London created new problems for the city. It was little wonder Parliament struggled to fund keeping the river clean.

I'd embarked close to London Bridge, which I'd never seen from the water before, and I stared up in fascination. With twenty huge arches, the magnificent bridge blocked out the sky, towering some sixty feet high and over twenty feet wide.

The massive stone pillars supporting the bridge were built in the shape of the bows of ships to allow the fast-flowing tides of the river to swirl through. Shops and the homes of wealthy merchants overhung the top of the bridge, some as many as six storeys high.

Like the spire of St Pauls, the ancient drawbridge tower needed rebuilding, and could no longer be raised to allow the passage of ships. I looked away from the grisly sight of severed heads on pikes, displayed as a macabre warning.

My grim-faced boatman laboured against the murky waters of an outgoing tide, but I had allowed plenty of time. We passed the Queenhithe wharf, where the air filled with the raucous shouts of men working with tall cranes, unloading the barges ferrying cargo to and from ships waiting downriver.

Only a short boat ride from Cheapside, the Strand could not have looked more different. The streets were paved and clean, and even the air seemed fresher. Connecting the Palace of Westminster to the city, the Strand had good access to the Thames and the royal mews, and the houses were the finest I'd seen.

Unlike crowded Cheapside, there were no carriages or horses in the street, and only two men on the pavement. Wearing lawyers' robes, they carried papers bound in red ribbon, and ignored me as they bustled past, deep in discussion.

I found Sir William's house halfway along the Strand, and was unsurprised to see it was one of the grandest. More of a mansion than a town house, it had red-brick chimneys, a paved forecourt with iron gates, and grounds extending to Covent Garden and open pasture beyond.

I rang the bell, and an elderly servant took my coat and showed me into a high-ceilinged room. I warmed my hands on a welcome log fire while I waited. Gilt-framed oil paintings of Sir William's ancestors decorated the walls, and the velvet upholstered furniture would not look out of place in a royal palace.

This meeting could mark a turning point for me, as Sir William had the money and influence to make my planned venture a success – or to ruin me, if he wished. My time in Ireland earned me little, but if Sir Henry Sidney was right, my reputation had been enhanced, which would make it all worthwhile.

The door creaked open and Sir William entered, followed by a stern-looking man, a little older than me. He gestured for us to be seated, although he remained standing.

'Thank you for coming to London, Captain Drake. This is Francis Walsingham, who has replaced me as the queen's principal secretary, and is the secretary of state for foreign affairs.' He glanced at Walsingham. 'I shall take my leave.' He closed the door behind him with a sharp click.

My mind raced with questions. William Cecil contrived this meeting for good reason, and could not be too busy to attend. I turned to Francis Walsingham. 'It's an honour to meet you, sir.' I tried to sound cheery, although my instinct told me this man could be dangerous to know.

Francis Walsingham looked at me with sharp eyes that revealed no clue to his thoughts, like the unblinking stare of a snake. 'Captain Drake. I understand from the Earl of Essex that you took part in the capture of Rathlin Island.'

His firm tone put me on my guard. I didn't understand the politics of court but guessed it might suit Sir Walter Devereux to misrepresent the truth. Walsingham waited for my reply, but I was determined not to have any share of the blame for the massacre of innocent women and children.

'I was commissioned to command the English fleet which carried Captain Norris and his men to the island. On my word, sir, I would not have done so if I'd known how they would deal with their prisoners.'

'I was told your men took part in the attack.' He spoke with a subtle note of accusation.

'A small number of my men were left ashore on Rathlin Island while I sailed off the coast of Scotland. I would have had no part in betraying an honourable surrender.' I struggled to retain my composure. 'I must tell you, sir, the Earl of Essex is misinformed.' My West Country accent returned in my raised voice, as it did when I felt defensive.

He studied me for a moment with an unfathomable stare before replying, 'The Earl of Essex gave me a letter recommending you for a mission which requires absolute discretion and secrecy. Walsingham's eyes narrowed. 'The security of England could be at stake.'

'I am at your service, sir.'

'Her Majesty is concerned that the King of Spain poses a threat to the peace and safety of our country. He harbours supporters of Mary Stuart, obstructs the Protestant reforms in the Netherlands, and persecutes followers of the true faith, despite our promise to tolerate Catholics.'

'I have seen how cruelly the Spanish treat good Christian men, sir. They have no honour.'

He frowned. 'If the Spanish were to launch an invasion, the treasury does not have the means to respond. We have decided to support a raid on the Spanish treasure fleet, which would reduce the power of King Philip.' He leaned back in his chair. 'Our wish is to show the Spanish that the reach of England's influence is not to be underestimated.'

My mind raced with possibilities. 'The Spanish treasure fleet is well protected, and will not be so easy to intercept. I can also confirm that the Spanish settlements have reinforced their defences, and are guarded by soldiers, but I believe I know of a vulnerability.'

For the first time, Francis Walsingham's eyes showed a flicker of interest. 'What do you propose?'

'When I crossed overland to Panama I saw the Southern Sea, where no Englishman has been, and unguarded treasure ships lie at anchor.'

'You must be aware, Captain Drake, that Richard Grenville

made a similar proposal some time ago, but our attempts to reach the Southern Sea have failed...'

'I have a map, captured from the Spanish, which shows the navigable route through the Strait of Magellan. I'm building a new ship with the aim of reaching the Southern Sea and Peru, once I have the funds. I've yet to see anything for my trouble in Ireland, so have had to delay the arrangements for my departure.'

Walsingham raised an eyebrow. 'I understood you were paid well for your services in Ireland.'

'A modest salary, and not enough to cover my costs.'

'You will appreciate why Her Majesty cannot be seen to provide King Philip with the justification to declare war. Richard Grenville's proposal was declined for that reason, but private investors might fund a voyage of exploration with a view to opening new trade routes.'

'We would need a fleet of fast ships. Well-armed and crewed by the best men we can find, we can reach the Southern Sea without drawing the attention of the Spanish.'

'Once there, you believe it will be easy enough to take them by surprise?'

I smiled at the thought. 'In Ireland, we were able to keep our true purpose secret by posing as merchant traders. The Spanish have no reason to be on their guard in the Southern Sea.'

Walsingham nodded. 'How long would you need to prepare?'

'It might take a season to complete my flagship and fit out a fleet.'

'There can be no royal commission, Captain Drake, and although one of the queen's ships could accompany you, the risks are your own. If you are captured there is nothing we can do.' Walsingham's eyes looked dark. 'If you succeed, you will be well rewarded, but anyone who betrays the involvement of Her Majesty will be charged with treason.'

William Hawkins accompanied me to inspect the progress on my new flagship, recently arrived from the shipyards at Aldeburgh, Suffolk, for her final fitting out. On the way he produced a note from the pocket of his coat and handed it to me. 'I regret to tell you that Her Majesty the queen has not consented to give her support for your voyage to the Southern Sea.'

I opened the unsealed note. It was from Sir William Cecil, signed Lord Burghley, not addressed to me, but to John Hawkins. I read it through twice before handing it back. In an instant, all I'd been working for hung by the slenderest of threads – yet I refused to lose hope.

'You have a better understanding of politics. Could this be Sir William's way of distancing himself from the venture, if we fail?'

William Hawkins raised an eyebrow. 'He says the risk of angering the Spanish is too great, which is true enough – and don't even consider sailing without permission.'

'Like John Oxenham has? By God's faith, if he claims what was mine by right—'

'You know as well as I do that John Oxenham was poorly prepared and ill equipped. We must pray he doesn't pay the price for his foolishness.' The harsh tone of his reply revealed his strength of feeling.

'I know you did your best to persuade Oxenham to wait until we could sail together.'

William Hawkins forced a smile. 'These things take time, Francis, and in the meanwhile, I have some better news to tell you. I believe I've found us a new trade route.'

'Not to Ireland, I trust?'

'Zante, in the Greek islands. My brother has a contact, a merchant named Acerbo Velutelli, from Lucca, in Tuscany. His patron is Sir Robert Dudley, Earl of Leicester, and I understand Velutelli has a licence from Her Majesty to import olive oil.'

'I've never sailed to the Mediterranean. It will be quite an experience.'

William Hawkins looked at me in surprise. 'I didn't imagine you would go.' He pointed to my unfinished ship. 'You need to be here, to oversee the finishing of your flagship.'

I had to admit he was right. Progress had been slow, but I found the sweeping lines of my new ship pleasing, and the seasoned oak timbers were the best money could buy. 'Harry Newman has proved a capable captain. Please speak to your brother, and tell him we can put the *Falcon* at his service.'

William Hawkins agreed, then turned his attention to the carpenters, who were fitting a new gun port by hammering wooden pegs to fix it in place. 'She looks more like a warship than a merchantman. Do you suppose no one will notice all those gun ports?'

I smiled, my good spirits returning after his bad news. 'I know you believe I should have refitted an older ship, but this design is based on what I learned from your own brother. Her hold can carry four pinnaces, and the gun deck has good head-room.' I ran my hand over the smooth timber of the double-planked hull. 'She only draws thirteen feet of water, so can take the shallows, and she'll have extra topgallants to help if we're becalmed.'

'Have you thought of a name for her yet?'

'I shall call her the *Pelican*, after the birds I first saw in Africa.' I smiled. 'They look innocent enough, but are able to swallow the largest fish with ease.'

William laughed. 'People will believe you chose the name

because the pelican happens to be a favourite device of Her Majesty, the symbol of Christ's sacrifice.'

I recalled Francis Walsingham's threat. 'The name is only an idea. Perhaps this ship is too sleek to be named after such an ungainly bird.'

Thomas Doughty had grown more self-assured since I'd last seen him in Ireland. He'd asked to meet me in my Plymouth harbourside offices, and I agreed out of curiosity. I knew he'd become private secretary to the influential captain of the queen's guard, Sir Christopher Hatton.

'My former master, Sir Walter Devereux, Earl of Essex, is dead.' Doughty watched for my reaction.

'I'll not pretend I'm sorry to hear that. I believe Captain John Norris followed the earl's orders when he massacred the Scots on Rathlin – after they'd surrendered.'

'The queen made Sir Walter Earl Marshal of Ireland, but he fell sick at the banquet given in his honour at Dublin Castle. It's rumoured he was poisoned.'

'Poisoned?' Although I had reason to curse Sir Walter Devereux, the thought of poison troubled me.

'Sir Walter had many enemies. The official story is that he died of natural causes, but Alice Draycott – the daughter of another guest of honour at the banquet, Judge Henry Draycott – is said to have drunk the same wine, and also died soon afterwards.'

'Do you think it could have been the Irish, taking their revenge on Sir Walter?'

'He'd given them good reason. I heard a rumour the Earl of Leicester, Robert Dudley, could be involved in Sir Walter's death.'

Although I had no time for gossip, my curiosity got the better of me. 'How would he benefit?'

Thomas Doughty smiled. 'It's a poorly kept secret at court that Robert Dudley has designs on Sir Walter's wife, Lettice Knollys, who is now a wealthy widow. He'll no doubt show his hand soon enough.' He gave me a mischievous look. 'Did you know there's talk that you were in some way involved?'

I scowled. 'You seem to hear a lot of rumours.'

'My master, Sir Christopher Hatton, is in charge of court security and has to make it his business to know what is being said – and who is saying it. He asked me if I thought there could be any truth in it.'

'What did you tell him?' The suggestion I could have been involved could be damaging. I'd made no secret of my dislike for Sir Walter's methods.

'That you are one of the most honourable men I've met.'

'That was good of you, Master Doughty – but would that have anything to do with your travelling all the way to Plymouth to tell me?'

'I mentioned to you before that I would like to accompany your voyage to the Southern Sea, together with my brother, and I have a proposal for you. I've found you a wealthy sponsor, who will meet half the costs.'

I sat back in my chair. I didn't like Thomas Doughty, but I might learn to, for such a reward. 'Who might that be?'

'My master, of course. Sir Christopher Hatton is an ambitious man, and wishes to make a name for himself.'

'Well, he might have quite a wait. The queen turned down my plan, as she did with Richard Grenville.'

Thomas Doughty smiled. 'I believe you will find Her Majesty has tired of appeasing the Spanish and, in the absence of any better plan, might be reconsidering her earlier opinion.'

I reached out and shook his hand. 'In that case, I must welcome you aboard, Master Doughty.'

The rumour spread rapidly through Plymouth, passing from one person to another like fleas on a dog. I rushed to William Hawkins' house, despite the torrential shower of rain, and found him in his study, working by the light of a candle on his accounts.

'What is it, Francis?' He raised an eyebrow. 'Your coat is dripping water on to my floor.'

'You've not heard?' I pulled off my wet hat and cloak and slumped into a chair. It took me a moment to catch my breath and compose myself. 'The *Falcon* has been lost in a storm off the Kent coast, near Deal, and there is no hope of survivors.'

William Hawkins placed his quill in his inkstand and stared at me. 'How did you hear of this?'

'A merchant ship arrived from the port of Dover this morning.' My voice sounded flat. 'They say the weather was too bad to attempt a rescue, so we must be prepared for the worst.'

'Dear God.' His eyes widened in concern. 'I am truly sorry for your loss.'

I returned home in the rain with a heavy heart. My ship, the *Falcon,* had been bound for London, with a full cargo of precious olive oil. The value would have more than compensated for my losses in Ireland, but the cargo was the least of my concerns.

I found Mary in bed, a flickering candle burning in a silver holder. She seemed to sense I'd brought bad news. 'What is it that's kept you out so late, Francis?'

I sat on the bed and pulled off my boots in silence while I chose my words, and then took her hand in mine. 'I have something to tell you, Mary. My loyal friend, your brother, has been lost at sea in a storm.'

She stared at me as if I might be making some cruel joke, then lay back on her pillow and sobbed. The disaster was no fault of mine, but I thought of my brother's wife, Alice, and I prayed that Mary wouldn't hold me responsible for Harry Newman's death.

14

MAY 1577

The royal messenger delivered the summons late in the evening, wearing a dark cape over the queen's livery of red and gold. He left as soon as he could, as if he wished no one to notice his visit to my house. Breaking the large wax seal in a mix of excitement and apprehension, I studied the formal wording.

My appointment was a week away, on the eighteenth of May, and the choice of location offered a clue. Instead of one of the royal palaces, my meeting with the queen would take place at Gorhambury Manor, home of the Lord Keeper of the Great Seal, Sir Nicholas Bacon. Whatever the queen said would remain secret from the chattering gossips of court.

I handed the folded parchment to Mary, and watched her eyes grow wide as she read. Although I'd told her I might one day meet the queen, I could tell she thought me a dreamer, and neither of us believed it would be so soon.

'The queen wants to see you?' She stared at me in amazement, then back at the summons as if she couldn't comprehend what she'd read.

I smiled at her reaction. 'This could be the making of us. If what Thomas Doughty told me is true, it might mean the queen has had a change of heart.'

'Why don't you trust Thomas Doughty?'

The note of challenge in her question surprised me. 'Doughty is well placed to know the mood in court – but my instinct is to be on my guard.'

'I'd much prefer that you sail with Her Majesty's blessing than without it.' Her eyes shone at the thought. 'This will be the talk of Plymouth.'

'You must tell no one, Mary. If Her Majesty has an interest in my new venture, it must be kept our great secret, or there will be consequences.'

'Consequences?'

'You deserve to know the truth about my plans. There should be no secrets between us, but I gave my word to Walsingham that I would keep my destination confidential.'

Mary frowned. 'You, of all people, know how sailors talk. Do you believe anyone has fallen for your story of a trading visit to Alexandria?'

'Why should they not? I'm building a merchant shipping business. It's to be expected that I will sail to foreign ports.'

'And my brother gave his life to help your story.'

The bitterness of her outburst was a reminder that it would take a long time to undo the pain I'd caused. I let the queen's summons fall to the tiled floor, took her in my arms and held her close. No words were needed for her to know how much I regretted Harry's death.

My meeting with the queen had the worst possible start. Gorhambury proved to be further from Plymouth than London, and I lost my way in failing light on country lanes. By the time I arrived, tired and exhausted, the queen had retired for the night.

The room provided for me looked like servants' quarters, low-ceilinged and simply furnished, with a rush-matting floor and a pallet bed. I'd expected better, but my host, Sir Nicholas Bacon, was entertaining the queen, as well as her travelling entourage of ladies and courtiers.

A maid brought a platter of bread and cured ham, which I ate alone, and washed down with a tankard of beer. The tiring ride from Plymouth meant I slept soundly, despite the uncomfortable straw mattress on a wooden pallet which creaked each time I moved.

Waking at dawn, I lay thinking about how my life had changed. I'd risen in the world, but wished I'd brought William Hawkins for company. He'd never had an audience with the queen, but knew the mysterious protocols of the royal court.

I used a jug of cold water to wash, and dressed in a new linen shirt, my black doublet with silver buttons and padded sleeves, black breeches and woollen stockings, finished off with a starched white ruff. I'd chosen to wear a sash of Spanish indigo silk I'd acquired on my travels. I wasn't certain if the colour was permitted, but it made me look like a man of some status.

I had no idea when I would see the queen, but I would be ready if summoned. I polished the road dust from my leather boots and paced the room, recalling William Hawkins' advice: 'Kneel and remove your cap. Don't stand until you're told to – and don't speak until you are spoken to.'

When the call came, I followed the queen's servant down the wood-panelled corridor with a growing sense of foreboding. The dull ache in my leg from my wound at Nombre de Dios returned, making me walk with a limp.

Although I'd travelled more widely than most men in England, nothing had prepared me for what I was about to do.

My heart pounded, and my palms felt moist with sweat. I took a deep breath and said a silent prayer for guidance.

The door opened and I breathed in the delicate, intoxicating scent of perfume. Queen Elizabeth sat in a gilded chair, flanked by older ladies. A high collar of lace, wired with gold thread, framed her red-gold ringlets. Her sharp eyes fixed on me with a strange intensity and, for the first time, I understood the absolute, magical power of royalty.

I removed my hat as I approached and kneeled, avoiding her eyes, but acutely conscious of their appraising gaze. A long moment passed in silence before the queen spoke. It took me a moment to understand that she'd dismissed her ladies and invited me to be seated. The door closed with a clunk behind me, and my pulse raced. I was alone with the Queen of England.

'Drake.' Her voice sounded sharp, as if annoyed. 'We would gladly be avenged on the King of Spain, for the injuries he has caused our people.'

'I am at your service, Your Majesty, and have my own score to settle with the Spanish.' My West Country accent echoed in the empty room, and her failure to respond made me wonder if I'd said too much.

Queen Elizabeth was said to be a great beauty, yet the powder dusting her pale skin failed to hide shadows under her dark-brown eyes. Her long fingers were bare of any rings and fidgeted with her necklace as she spoke. The Queen of England might be the most powerful woman in Christendom, yet her pallor reminded me she was as mortal as any of us.

'Tell me how you might injure the Spanish.'

'The Spanish believe they have the measure of us in the Indies, Your Majesty.' I looked away from her bodice, surprised at how much her low-cut dress revealed. 'They do not expect to encounter English ships in the Southern Sea.'

'Why do you believe you can succeed where other men have

failed?' She spoke more softly this time, yet with a note of challenge in her voice.

'By God's good grace, Your Majesty, my experience of the Spanish in the West Indies has prepared me well for the task.'

'Walsingham believes that Spanish spies watch over my court. How do you propose to keep our secret?'

If she had been anyone else I might have mistaken her tone for flirtation. 'I'm an honest merchant, Your Majesty, seeking new routes for trade, and Master Walsingham can let that be known to the Spanish.' I decided to take a risk. 'If we happen across a Spanish treasure ship, we shall treat them well and, of course, relieve them of their burden.'

Her red lips parted in the briefest smile, showing yellowed and uneven teeth. 'The King of Spain has put a high price on your head, Drake. It would not go well for you if you were captured.'

I smiled at her understatement. 'The Spanish had opportunities enough to capture me, Your Majesty, but each time I had the better of them. My plan is to outgun them with superior firepower, outrun them with swifter ships, and return to fill your treasury with Spanish gold.' I regretted my boast even as I said the words, but I was encouraged by the glint of amusement in her eyes.

'It would please us to use Spanish gold to build our navy.'

I judged the moment was right and reached into the pocket of my doublet to take out a small velvet purse, which I handed to her. The briefest frown showed on her face, but I'd aroused her curiosity – she pulled open the purse and dropped the large pearl into the palm of her hand.

'It's the size of a bird's egg!' The delight sounded in her voice.

'The largest pearl I've found on all my travels, Your Majesty.'

She held the pearl up to the light from the window, and

admired its translucent glow. 'I shall have the royal jeweller set this into a pendant, so I might wear it.'

'I am honoured, Your Majesty, and trust this pearl will remind you of those of us who venture into the world for the glory of England.'

'What is it like to sail to faraway lands, not knowing what dangers you might find there?'

'In truth, Your Majesty, I find it harder to remain in Plymouth.' I smiled. 'The dangers are great, yet so are the rewards. More than once I've seen more silver and gold than we could carry away, and I've seen how cruel and treacherous the Spanish can be. If it is God's will for me to avenge those they've wronged, I am ready for the task.'

I ran through our brief conversation many times on the long ride to Plymouth, fixing every detail in my memory. As I'd been about to leave, I learned that the queen and her entourage had already left for London, and was told Sir Nicholas Bacon wished to see me in his study.

'Her Majesty the queen told me to thank you, Captain Drake, and to present you with this.' He handed me a sword in a silver scabbard, engraved with the royal arms, and the queen's personal motto, *Semper Eadem*. Sir Nicholas smiled. 'It seems your meeting went as well as Her Majesty expected. You are to be made an admiral of the queen.'

I stood staring at the sword for a moment, lost for words. I unsheathed the blade, engraved and crafted from the finest polished steel. 'I confess I've been sailing in uncharted waters, Sir Nicholas, but I am truly grateful to Her Majesty.'

Captain John Wynter seemed surprised at our lack of preparation. He'd sailed the queen's eighty-ton frigate, *Elizabeth*, loaded with supplies and equipment, to Plymouth from the royal docks in London. A cousin of Admiral Sir William Wynter, Surveyor of the Navy and Master of Naval Ordinance, and son of George Wynter, an investor in my voyage, he had the rugged, tanned face of a man who'd spent his life at sea.

'Your hold is good and deep – but empty, Captain Drake.' His accusation echoed in the cavernous *Pelican* as I showed him around my new flagship.

'Admiral Drake.' I corrected his mistake. 'I prefer the title Captain General. The hold will soon be filled with four dismantled pinnaces, but work to fit her out took longer than intended.'

He studied the gun deck with an experienced eye, and lay a hand on the cold bronze barrel of one of my new guns. 'Fourteen demi-culverins.'

'All new, and four more on the upper deck.' I looked down the row. 'We'll not be outgunned, but this will be a noisy place if they are all fired at once.'

'I've also brought you a hundred new arquebuses from the royal arsenal, with a quantity of shot.' John Wynter gave me a questioning look. 'Well-armed for a merchantman, Captain General.' He added my title as an afterthought. 'We need to be on our way before the winter storms set in. Will you allow me to take charge of the arrangements?'

'I would appreciate your help, Captain Wynter, and in return will appoint you as vice admiral and my deputy for the voyage.'

He brightened at my suggestion. 'You can rely on me.'

In a flash of insight, I understood. My cousin, Captain John Hawkins, another stakeholder, had won our loyalty on my early voyages in much the same way. My old habit of leading from the front served me well in the past, but that would all change now I'd become the queen's admiral, a captain general.

More people arrived in Plymouth each day, all making demands on my time. Thomas Doughty, one of the few who knew our true destination, came to see me with a group of well-dressed gentlemen, including his half-brother, John, a botanist, and a parson, who he introduced as Francis Fletcher.

I studied their pale, eager faces. 'Have any of you ever been to sea?'

John Doughty spoke first. 'I'm a good shot with an arquebus,' he grinned, 'and will work as hard as any man aboard.'

'I recall saying much the same myself once, Master Doughty. I'm bringing my own younger brother, Thomas, on the voyage, as well as my nephew, several trumpeters and four viol players, so I suppose I should find a place for some gentleman adventurers.'

Francis Fletcher shook my hand. 'I would like to be your chaplain, Admiral Drake. I've heard how you keep up the men's spirits with your sermons, and I have a good knowledge of the Holy Bible.'

'You are right, but I know to my cost what it's like to have too many mouths to feed when supplies run low. Are you aware of the dangers we face?'

Fletcher nodded. 'I am, and I have a good eye for detail, so will help keep records of the voyage.'

I turned to Thomas Doughty. 'When we encounter a prize ship, which I've no doubt we will, you shall have your own command. In the meantime, I trust you will keep your gentlemen out of the way.' His self-satisfied smile made me hope I wouldn't have reason to regret my good intention.

Drake - Tudor Corsair

Well-wishers thronged the quayside under a darkening sky on the great day of our departure. The *Pelican*, as flagship, led our small fleet of ships, followed by the queen's ship, *Elizabeth*, and the fifty-ton supply ship, the *Swan*. Commanded by Captain John Chester, her name brought back painful memories of the ship once captained by my brother John.

At her side sailed the thirty-ton *Marigold* – owned by Sir Christopher Hatton, who'd been promoted to Vice-Chamberlain of the royal household – under Captain John Thomas. At the rear followed the fifteen-ton sloop *Benedict*, commanded by my former crewman, Thomas Moone, once my ship's carpenter, now promoted to captain.

Between us we carried some hundred and sixty-four men and boys, with supplies enough to last us eighteen months. The men included a carpenter, and a blacksmith, complete with his forge and all his tools, saws, axes and spades to build forts. We'd also loaded over a hundred boxes of ship's biscuits, barrels of beer and wine.

I'd invested in new notebooks to record the details of our voyage. I'd also brought my growing collection of books. As well as my father's book of Psalms, I had John Foxe's *Protestant Martyrs*, and next to my well-thumbed copy of *The Art of Navigation* I also had an account of the Portuguese explorer Ferdinand Magellan's voyage.

Magellan knew the Southern Sea as *Mare Pacificum*, the peaceful sea. I worried that it had proved less than peaceful for Ferdinand Magellan. Set upon by islanders, he'd been murdered with a spear. From the accounts, it seemed Magellan failed to communicate with the natives. I was pleased to have my friend Diego to help parley with islanders from the Southern Sea.

Around my neck I wore a scarf of green silk, another gift from the queen. Embroidered in golden thread were the words: *The Lord guide and preserve thee until the end*. I liked to believe the message might be Her Majesty's own handiwork and, with a sailor's superstition, I already thought it a token of good luck.

Gulls swooped and shrieked in our wake as we cleared Sutton Pool. The winds were freshening, and white foam showed on the waves ahead. Looking back, I glimpsed the distant figure of Mary, with her sister Margaret, and my little nephew Jonas, waving goodbye. I raised a hand in farewell, wondering where this adventure would end.

An unfavourable south-westerly wind scattered the fleet towards the coast of Cornwall, and developed into a gale. The untested topgallants snapped like twigs with a rending crash. Designed to help if we were becalmed, they were no match for the fierce Cornish winds, and hung precariously by the stays.

'Cut them down!'

I watched as the dangling spars tangled the mainsail, and we turned side on to the heavy swell. A white-crested breaker slapped against the hull, sluicing through the gun ports, and I heard shouts of alarm and deep curses over the sounds of the storm.

I turned to the helmsman. 'Steer a course for Falmouth!'

We would have to seek shelter or our voyage would be over before it had begun. The *Swan* and *Marigold* were close enough to follow our lead. I scanned the horizon and spotted the *Elizabeth*, but there was no sign of the fifteen-ton *Benedict*. I knew Thomas Moone well, and prayed he'd have the sense to seek shelter.

The *Pelican* strained at her anchor in Falmouth harbour as the fierce winds tested us. A wave hit us broadside, and she rolled precariously before righting. I watched as the *Marigold* broke free and drifted towards the shore.

'Man the pumps!' I cursed as I heard the rumble of our cargo shifting. I should have checked the load before we set sail.

The storm passed as quickly as it had come, yet as well as the loss of the topmast of the *Pelican,* Captain Thomas reported damage to the mainmast of the *Marigold,* which would need replacing before the long crossing. With a heavy heart, I ordered the fleet to return to Plymouth.

Once we were safely anchored back in Sutton Pool I summoned the captains to my cabin. This would be the first real test of my command, and all our lives might depend on what was agreed. They stood in grim-faced silence, until Captain John Wynter spoke for them.

'I overheard the men grumbling about the folly of setting out at the start of winter, Captain General, but I believe we no longer have a choice.'

I agreed. 'The die is cast, gentlemen.' I was pleased to see relief on their faces. Like me, they'd staked their savings on this voyage in the hope of making their fortune. 'We shall make repairs and take this opportunity to improve our stores. We'll set out in one month, on the thirteenth of December,' my hand went to my green silk scarf, 'and place our trust in God to keep us safe.'

15

JANUARY 1578

Rumours travel on a ship as quick as rainwater runs from the scuppers. Diego told me our true purpose had become common knowledge among the crew, and it took no time to trace the source to Thomas Doughty. I summoned him to my cabin to account for his indiscretion, yet he seemed unrepentant.

'We've sailed past the Strait of Gibraltar. The men know for sure we're not headed to Alexandria.' He sounded disdainful. 'How long would you keep our crew ignorant of the truth?'

'My conscience troubles me about the need to deceive the captains and their crews, Master Doughty, but I would rather the men had our sailing orders from me.'

'They would have found out soon enough.'

I chose to ignore his scorn, yet my anger rose like a spring tide. 'I would have you respect my command, Master Doughty.' I spoke sharply. 'Is that understood?'

He smiled with innocent surprise. 'Of course, Captain General.'

I dug my nails into my palms to control my frustration. There was nothing I could do, and he knew it. 'We have a long and challenging journey ahead, so let's put this matter behind us.'

After he left I wondered if I'd been too lenient. All my life I'd been talked down to by gentlemen, but now, as an admiral and captain general of the queen, I'd earned the right to respect. I'd never called Thomas Doughty a friend, yet now I worried I'd unwittingly made him my enemy.

Beating down the Barbary coast, we made good progress to the Cape Verde islands, despite heavy rain squalls and veering winds. Our lookout pointed to distant sails which proved to be Spanish ships at anchor. The time had come to show our hand, and boost the morale of the crew.

'Action stations!'

My shout triggered a flurry of activity. Everyone on board knew their role, and prepared for action. The arquebus men scrambled for their weapons and strapped on armour before clambering aboard one of our pinnaces, towed behind us.

Assembled on the island of Mogador on New Year's Eve, the work to rebuild the pinnace cost a member of our crew. He'd been taken by Berber tribesmen and, despite our best efforts, had not been seen since. I prayed he could persuade them to release him, but we'd had to leave him to take his chances.

We couldn't see anyone aboard the Spanish ships, but fired two cannons from the *Pelican*, loaded with wadding and gunpowder. The fierce boom reverberated across the water, like a crack of thunder, enough to alarm the Spanish into surrender.

Our boarding party discovered there were only two men aboard. I took the best of the ships in exchange for the *Benedict*. I renamed our prize the *Christopher*, to honour our patron, Sir

TONY RICHES

Christopher Hatton, and placed Captain Tom Moone in command.

Emboldened by our success, we pursued a hundred-ton Portuguese caravel, which surrendered after only one salvo from our guns. Laden with supplies, she carried a good quantity of sweet Madeira wine and rich sherry, which cheered the men. As well as items of gold and silver, I discovered something of even greater value to our venture – a Portuguese pilot.

At first, he refused to answer my questions, but soon agreed to offer his help when he knew the alternative was to be abandoned to take his chances in our pinnace. He brought me the caravel's sea charts, and bowed as he introduced himself.

'Nunho da Silva. *Estoy a tu servicio.*' Short, and deeply tanned, his white beard reached to his chest. He spoke no English, and I failed to understand his Portuguese-accented Spanish, so sent for Diego.

'He says he has many years working as a pilot in these waters.' Diego sounded dubious, although the usual glint of good humour showed in his eyes.

I studied Nunho da Silva with suspicion. 'Have you sailed through the Strait of Magellan?'

Diego translated my question and I saw the Portuguese pilot frown. He replied in rapid Spanish to Diego, who turned to me.

'He advises you to take care. The current is strong and there are dangerous rocks and shallows.'

'We need to find a safe anchorage to prepare our fleet for the passage. Do you know such a place?'

Unrolling one of the charts, Nunho da Silva pointed to an inlet marked with a neat cross of black ink. 'Puerto San Julián.'

I recalled the name from the account of Magellan's voyage. 'A natural harbour, where Ferdinand Magellan anchored before he found the eastern entrance to the strait which bears his name.' I'd been concerned about the worsening weather, so the

166

Portuguese pilot had already proved his worth. 'I'll take you on as a pilot, and reward you well, once we are safe in the Southern Sea.'

Nunho da Silva nodded, once Diego translated, and replied again in Spanish. Diego smiled at his reply. 'He asks that we tell the Spaniards he was held on your ship against his will – and that you set him down somewhere tolerable.'

The Portuguese caravel proved another good prize, worthy of keeping as a supply ship. We let her crew go ashore, and I renamed her from the *Santa Maria* to *Mary*, in honour of my wife. I kept my word, appointing Thomas Doughty as her captain, and the valuables were left aboard under his care.

I was cheered not to have to see Doughty's superior smile every day, or listen to his criticism of my leadership. I found he'd been training the men with arquebuses without my permission, yet his instruction proved a popular diversion. He'd laughed when I asked if he'd been in a battle at sea, and said he was only helping the men improve their aim. I'd been outmanoeuvred again.

When Doughty and the chosen crewmen transferred to the *Mary* I made sure my brother was among them. Shorter than me, but broad-shouldered, my younger brother had our mother's colouring, with freckled skin, his hair and beard a lighter red than mine.

'Keep an eye on him, Thomas.'

My brother raised an eyebrow. 'What for?'

His tone surprised me, as I'd believed everyone knew how Doughty undermined my authority. 'Report to me directly if he abuses his command.'

We settled into a routine, and our chaplain, Francis Fletcher, proved a good companion, dining in my cabin, accompanied by my viol players, and discussing my collection of books. A reasonable artist, Fletcher encouraged my young nephew John to make drawings and sketches of any islands and coastlines we saw.

Working in my cabin in the evenings, we recorded the events of the day's passage in our notebooks, drawing and making notes. Most days we had little enough to report, but on others we were kept busy with mysteries such as the shoals of flying fish which hit our sails, landing on our decks like silvery gifts from God.

The crew assembled for prayers when we reached the equator in light winds. We'd passed further south than any of us, except for Nunho da Silva, had ever sailed. I read to the men from my father's book of Psalms, and said a prayer of gratitude.

'*We give thanks for the gracious providence of God who, in his great mercy, has preserved us to see more of his excellent works.*'

Scanning the ships following in our wake on a crisp spring morning, I realised the *Mary* no longer sailed behind us. My first thought was for my younger brother. I'd sworn to do everything in my power to make sure no harm came to him, and cursed Doughty for not keeping close through the night.

I regretted agreeing that Doughty and his gentleman adventurers could join us, yet it had been my decision to place him in command of the *Mary*. Now she was missing, together with my brother and a good part of our reserves of water. I ordered the signal for the fleet to come within hailing distance and told them to keep a lookout.

A full day and night passed before our lookout sighted the *Mary* on the horizon, and slowed under light canvas for them to catch up. They remained out of hailing distance, so it wasn't until we sat at anchor in the wide, choppy estuary of the River Plate that I learned how I'd been betrayed.

When we were boys, my father used to say my brother Thomas wasn't the brightest among us. He struggled to learn to read and write, and was forever getting into trouble, yet he'd gained in confidence since being chosen for this voyage. He asked to see me in private, and closed the door to my cabin behind him.

'Thomas Doughty has taken valuables for himself, and tries to place the blame on me.'

'This is a serious matter. Are you certain?'

Thomas itched the back of his neck. He'd let his hair and beard grow long, and needed a change of clothes. We had never been close, but after the loss of our father and two brothers, I owed him the chance of a profitable future. He looked at me as if trying to decide how much to say.

'Tell me, Thomas.'

'Doughty told anyone who would listen that you called him a bad and lewd fellow. He says you blame him for conjuring up storms, and contrary winds.'

This wasn't what I expected, yet had a ring of truth. I'd blamed Doughty aloud once or twice, and perhaps called him a curse on our voyage. I guessed one of his gentlemen had been indiscreet. That would be typical of them, to band together against me. They resented my success, and scorned my humble background.

'I gave him command of our best prize ship, as I'd promised.' My raised voice betrayed me, as much as Thomas Doughty had. 'What more does he expect?' I could tell from Thomas's pained expression there was more he'd chosen to hold back. 'What is it, that you hesitate to say even to your own brother?'

He spoke softly. 'He bragged that he should put your wife with child, as you seem unable.'

I stared at him open-mouthed, my reply frozen in my throat. Frustration surged through me. 'Thomas Doughty has crossed the line! He's challenged my authority, and incited the crew to mutiny!'

My brother stared at me wide-eyed, and left without another word, banging the door behind him. I cursed the day I agreed to bring Thomas Doughty on our mission. When the time was right I would teach my crew a lesson in loyalty they would not forget.

Port St Julián, where Magellan had anchored fifty-eight years before, looked a dreary place, not helped by a chill wind, despite the bright June sunshine. Although a natural harbour, guarded by high grey cliffs, a bar of stones obstructed the shallow entrance, and we had to sail close by the northern shore to avoid grounding.

I'd dealt promptly with Doughty's disloyalty, and replaced him as captain of the *Mary*, a position I gave to my brother. I charged Doughty with treachery, theft and incitement to mutiny, and ordered him to be tied to the mast for two days as a punishment. The matter left a sour taste in my mouth, and I knew it must be addressed before the risky navigation to reach the Southern Sea.

Captain John Wynter asked to see me and confessed to being troubled by Doughty's treatment.

'I understand the need to make an example of him, Captain General, but it would be best for us all if he could be locked away out of sight, in safe custody on board the *Swan*.'

I grudgingly agreed. 'We must return home, so Master Doughty can face a proper trial.'

He looked surprised. 'Our investors will be displeased if we return with empty holds—'

'I will face ruin, and our crew's wages will not now be paid.'

'God forbid!' Captain Wynter scowled. 'We would face a mutiny. We must arrange our own trial, and deal with this matter now.'

'It would not be usual practice, but on Magellan's voyage he also suppressed a conspiracy, led by one of his captains. He hanged the ringleaders here, at Port St Julián.'

John Wynter frowned. 'Let us hope it doesn't come to that. We must choose good men as jurors. A formal court, where evidence can be heard, will allow you to offer a fair sentence – although there can only be one outcome.'

'Our first priority is to locate fresh water, then we'll hold a trial. I wish you to take command, while I lead a shore party. I read that Magellan's men fought with the natives here, and killed two of them.'

'I feel it might be best for you to remain—'

I held up a hand to silence him. 'I hope to befriend the local Indians, as I did with the Cimarrons.'

We rowed up the narrowing river in the longboat, twelve men armed with bows and arquebuses, including our master gunner, and the ship's surgeon. Steep mountains loomed ahead of us, and a soft, irritating rain began to fall as we searched for a fresh-water tributary.

My mind was on Doughty, and a memory of something Mary said before we left. *Why don't you trust Thomas Doughty?* Her words nagged at me, like a rat at a stale rind of cheese. The way she'd said his name suggested familiarity, yet as far as I knew she'd only met him briefly. My hatred of the man smouldered with the intensity of a lit fuse. I cursed the way I'd let Doughty get to me, and resolved to be even with him.

Instinct warned me we were being watched, and I scanned the shoreline for movement, but the only sounds were the leathery creak of the oars moving in the rowlocks, and the soft patter of rain on the rippling water. My hand went to my pistol when one of my crew pointed.

'Indians.'

Two men armed with bows appeared from nowhere like silent ghosts. Tall and olive-skinned, they wore cloaks of thick fur. Their faces were painted with black stripes, and bright-green feathers decorated their long dark hair. They seemed oblivious to the rain, which soaked through my doublet, and trickled down my back.

One of my gunners began readying his arquebus, but I stopped him and turned to Diego. 'Tell them we come in friend-ship, and need fresh water.'

Diego called out in his Cimarron Spanish, and the natives lowered their bows. I ordered the men to take us to a shallow beach on the riverbank, keeping a close watch on the Indians. I hadn't used my pistol for more than a year, and prayed it wouldn't let me down in the rain.

One of the Indians stepped forward as we reached the shore. He called out to Diego, and I made out the Spanish word '*esclavo*'. It seemed he asked if Diego was being held as a slave against his will, and looked reassured when Diego laughed at the suggestion and called back that we were '*Ingleses*'.

I led the men ashore and gave the Indians the loaf of bread we carried, as a gift. They were interested in our bows, which were larger than their own. One of my archers offered to show them, and fired an arrow high into the air. It flew to the opposite riverbank with ease, but alarmed the Indians, who shouted and gestured for us to leave.

As we climbed back into our boat, more Indians appeared and began shooting arrows at us. Most fell short, but an arrow hit our surgeon in the arm. He cried out in pain and fell backwards as a second arrow thudded into his chest.

Our gunner aimed his arquebus, but it failed to fire. An arrow flashed through the air and struck him with such impact the arrowhead protruded from his back, killing him instantly. I'd forgotten to ensure we wore armour, and two good men had paid for my mistake.

I raised my pistol and pulled the trigger. The powder flashed as it fired with a loud bang, echoing across the water. More by luck than skill, my shot hit one of the Indians, and his fleeing companions dragged him away. My hand shook at the realisation that after years of bravado, I'd taken a man's life, but saved us all from certain death.

The bleak stony beach where Magellan hanged his mutineers seemed a fitting place for the trial of Thomas Doughty. He denied being guilty of any crime, and showed no remorse. One by one, the men repeated what they'd seen and heard. Doughty argued with their word, called them liars, and demanded their testimony be sworn under oath.

Edward Bright scowled as he stepped forward. One of the most experienced men on the crew of the *Mary*, he surprised Doughty by calling for a Bible and swearing to tell the whole truth.

'Master Doughty said he arranged the funding for our venture and, as such, had the right to command us.' Edward Bright glanced at me, then back at the jurors. 'He said he would make me rich, if I would be ruled by him.'

One of Thomas Doughty's gentlemen companions, Leonard

Vicary, a lawyer of the Inns of Court, declared the trial illegal. He did his best to intimidate the witnesses with threats of what would happen to them once we returned to England, then he turned to me.

'It will reassure us, Captain General, if you provide proof of your commission from Her Majesty the queen.'

They all waited for my reaction to his audacious challenge to my authority. The only document I knew of was from William Cecil, forbidding me to sail without permission. Worst of all, he'd contrived for William Hawkins to witness me reading it. Her Majesty had taken care to put nothing in writing.

I pointed to the *Pelican*. 'I have the proof in my cabin, and can show it to the jury.' I gave him an innocent look, yet prayed he wouldn't dare to call my bluff.

Leonard Vicary raised his eyebrows in surprise. 'We shall hold you to that promise, Captain General, and do you also give your word to the jury that the death penalty will not apply?'

I looked across at the stern faces of the chosen jurors, and caught Captain John Wynter's eye. 'If we must, I'm prepared to abandon this venture, and return to England where Thomas Doughty will face the charge of treason against Her Majesty the queen.'

Many of the jurors frowned at the prospect. I knew they would want to find any alternative to returning home with our meagre prizes. The Southern Sea was within our reach, with only the treacherous Doughty standing between us and hopes of a fortune in gold.

Doughty looked scornful. 'There's no turning back now, Captain General. I made sure Sir William Cecil knew of your plans before we left. He cannot deny his involvement if this venture fails.'

My heart missed a beat. 'What did Sir William say?'

'That he gave a written instruction. You were not to sail without permission.'

'I assure you I have the consent of Her Majesty, but she ordered that the details should be kept from her treasurer, Sir William Cecil.' I turned to the men of the jury. 'You heard Thomas Doughty condemn himself of treason – with his own words.'

The jury needed no further evidence. Against Leonard Vicary's advice, Doughty accepted the seriousness of his actions, and confessed to the charges. Convicted of treason by a unanimous vote, it fell to me to pass sentence.

Drizzling rain began falling as I spoke. 'Thomas Doughty, I offer you the choice of returning to England, to answer for your deeds before Her Majesty's council, or to be set ashore on this coast – or to be executed.'

'If I should be set ashore among infidels, how could I be sure of a Christian burial?' He turned to the jury. 'If I should return to England, I must have a ship, and who will accompany me?' Doughty shook his head. He stared at me, with piercing blue eyes. 'All I ask is that you and I receive Holy Communion together, and that I am permitted a gentleman's death.'

Francis Fletcher's hands shook as he provided the communion in my tent, our only shelter from the cold drizzle, and I saw a look of concern pass between him and Doughty. I invited Doughty to dine with me, from my best silver. He raised his final glass of wine in a toast, yet his eyes were tearful, as if he finally felt some remorse.

'I'm sorry our friendship must end in this way, Captain General.'

For a moment I wondered if a change of heart would be seen by the men as weakness. 'This is not what I would have wished, but you leave me no choice, Master Doughty.'

He followed me back to the stony beach, where the men

waited to witness his punishment. Doughty tossed his hat away and pulled off his jerkin, despite the downpour which began to soak his white linen shirt. He stood in silence, turning his face to the soft rain as if relishing its coolness, then closed his eyes and clasped his hands in prayer. He prayed for Her Majesty the queen, and the success of our voyage, and asked forgiveness, before kneeling on the wet ground.

The man chosen by lots as executioner looked in my direction, waiting for my signal. I nodded, and his sharpened axe swished through the air and ended Doughty's life with a single stroke. Doughty surprised me with how calmly he met his end, and I knew I could not have acted as bravely. His intelligent blue eyes would haunt my dreams for the rest of my life.

16

AUGUST 1578

Relentless rain drummed on the roof of my cabin, and the anchor cable groaned as it strained against buffeting winds. I worried I'd lost the bond of trust with my crew, and left myself open to recriminations from Doughty's powerful friends when we returned to England. Men like Francis Fletcher sided with Doughty, leaving me to wonder who I could rely on for support. I prayed to the Lord for guidance, and an answer came from an unexpected source.

Thomas Doughty's property was brought to me for safekeeping, and I studied his private papers out of curiosity. Among them I found a letter of recommendation from Sir Christopher Hatton, bearing his seal and impressive coat of arms, surmounted by his badge of a golden hind.

One of the main sponsors of our voyage, Sir Christopher had much to gain from our success, and the most to lose if we failed. Whatever I thought of Doughty's betrayal, he was Sir Christopher's man, and I feared there would be consequences for me when we returned.

We needed a fresh start before entering the dangers of the Strait of Magellan, and I decided to rename the *Pelican* the

Golden Hinde, in honour of Sir Christopher's generous support, and as a good omen for the future. Our carpenter carved a new figurehead, and the crew cheered after Francis Fletcher blessed our renamed flagship.

I made the difficult decision to transfer the supplies and crew from the *Swan*, the *Christopher* and the *Mary*, which leaked beyond the capability of their pumps to keep the bilges clear. With great regret, I gave the order for them to be broken up for salvage.

A lump formed in my throat as I watched the smoke billowing from the *Mary*, and listened to the crackle as the leaping flames took hold. I'd named her after my wife, and provided Thomas Doughty with an excuse for his cruellest taunt. I had to remind myself we were reduced to three well-provisioned and fully crewed ships, ready for the most perilous leg of our journey.

The first snowflakes of the southern winter drifted in the freezing air, chilling our bones as we waited for a break in the weather. I invited my two captains to my cabin to prepare for entering Magellan's strait. I gave them a cup of hot mulled wine, but their faces looked grim at the prospect of the unknown passage ahead.

Taking the account of Ferdinand Magellan's passage from my bookshelf I turned to the bookmarked page. 'The Portuguese estimate the distance is some hundred leagues, but we've seen how the waters here can be dangerously shallow, so our progress will be slow.'

Captain John Thomas looked concerned. 'The *Marigold* isn't good at taking the ground.'

Captain Wynter nodded. 'I recommend we take soundings as often as we can.'

'I agree.' I spread out Nunho da Silva's map on the table. 'If our fleet becomes scattered it won't be easy to turn back to search for you. Keep in close company, and if we lose sight of each other, we shall meet at latitude thirty degrees, off the coast of Chile.' I refilled their cups and raised mine in a toast. 'To success, gentlemen.'

The temperature fell below freezing before the biting wind veered to northerly, and I judged it time for us to enter the Strait of Magellan. The *Golden Hinde* sailed in the lead, followed by Captain Wynter with the queen's galleon, *Elizabeth*, and Captain Thomas with our supply ship, the thirty-ton *Marigold*.

My nephew John's eyes were wide with concern. 'What happens if we run aground, Uncle?'

'We use anchors to winch ourselves into deeper water, an old sailors' trick.' I made light of it, yet the thought worried me, and no doubt most of the crew. Many good ships had tried to navigate this passage, and never been heard of again. There were great dangers, but the rewards would be worth the risk.

The spray left a bitter taste in my mouth and I shivered in the freezing wind as I stared across at the rocky shore. If we ran aground, and were forced to make landfall, the barren land would make survival a challenge. Magellan reported seeing Indians, but my experience of their welcome left me wary.

After picking our way through the narrow channel, the strait widened and grew deeper, but still dangerous with dark shadows of hidden rocks and surging, unpredictable currents. I sent for the Portuguese pilot, and Diego to help translate. Nunho da Silva studied the waters ahead, and frowned before speaking in Spanish.

Diego turned to me. 'He says there are islands ahead, Captain General, where we can anchor.'

'Tell him to stay by the helmsman.' I studied the brooding

sky. 'It would be good if we can reach these islands before nightfall.'

The scrubland-covered shore gave way to high mountains, with steep, rocky cliffs providing no chance of landing. Nunho da Silva proved his worth as the dark shapes of the islands emerged in the distance. Peering back into the gloom, I was reassured to see the *Elizabeth* and *Marigold* following close behind.

Relieved to set foot on land, we anchored in the lee of the largest of the three islands, which I named Elizabeth Island, the first foreign land to be claimed for England in the name of the queen. Diego and my brother Thomas helped our ship's carpenter fell a huge tree to take home.

They also brought back a brace of the small black-and-white seabirds we'd seen diving from the rocky foreshore as we approached. My brother grinned and held one of his lifeless trophies up for me to see.

'The men have sport pursuing them, as the little creatures can't fly, but have vicious beaks.'

I studied the bird, which had large webbed feet, oily feathers and short, stubby wings. 'They'll be a welcome change from eating limpets and seaweed. Show one to Master Fletcher, to make a drawing of it for our notes.'

Thomas nodded. 'A Welsh gunner from the *Marigold* dubbed them '*pen gwyns*', which means 'white heads' in his language. We've taken all we can catch, so I trust they will make good eating.'

The winds were against us in the morning, making the going slow, so I led the men in prayers and shared out the last of the Portuguese wine to keep up their spirits. The mountain tops were white with snow and ice, although the dull red of an erupting volcano glowed on the horizon, like a strange omen of what lay ahead.

I turned to Francis Fletcher, keen to restore our companionship. 'That must be what Magellan called Tierra del Fuego, the land of fire.'

He shook his head. 'I've read his account, and believe the land of fire refers to native campfires the Portuguese spotted on the headlands.'

'I struggle to see why anyone would choose to live in such a miserable place.'

Francis Fletcher raised an eyebrow. 'Do I sense from your tone that you might be losing spirit, Captain General?'

'Nothing of the sort.' I decided to be honest with him. 'The responsibility for the lives of so many men weighs heavily on my mind, Master Fletcher. A good few ships have vanished without trace attempting this passage.'

The helmsman roused me from my cabin to see how narrow the strait had become. 'Any narrower, and we'll be scraping the sides, Captain General.' He cursed as he tried to steer for the deepest part of the channel.

I studied the passage ahead. The steep cliffs seemed to meet some distance in front of us, although I was certain we'd followed the right channel. 'I'll take a party in the longboat and have a closer look.'

A strange canoe appeared from nowhere as we made our way into the narrow pass. I readied my pistol, mindful of what had happened at our last encounter with the local Indians. 'Have a care, men.'

Two of the crew stowed their oars to aim their arquebuses, while a third nocked an arrow in his bow. Francis Fletcher sat in the bows, and turned with a look of surprise. 'One of them is half-naked, a woman with bared breasts, and another is little more than a child.'

I smiled at the thought this would no doubt be the first time our preacher had seen such a sight. 'I wonder they don't freeze in such temperatures, Master Fletcher.'

We rowed closer to study their strange craft. Covered with animal skins, the sharply pointed bows and stern cut through the waves like a knife. Seeing the family of Indians were unarmed, I lowered my pistol and told the others to do the same. I raised a hand in greeting and they replied with a wave as they passed, with no sign of surprise at the sight of us.

Satisfied we had enough water to pass through the narrowest part of the strait, we returned to the ship, where I made a drawing of the canoe and described the occupants in my notebook. It was a mystery to me how this family survived in such a barren land, and a reminder that the native people were not all hostile or dangerous.

Once through the narrow passage, we passed a scattering of uncharted islands, which I marked on our maps with a cross and named the Elizabeth's. It had taken us two long weeks to find our way through the dangerous strait, yet that was half the time it had taken Magellan. I gathered the crew on deck and led them in a prayer of thanks to God.

We had little time to celebrate, as we were welcomed to the Southern Sea by a thunderstorm of such violence we were driven towards the rocky coast. In gale-force winds, we sailed south of the islands marked on my charts as Tierra del Fuego, but saw no sign of the legendary Terra Australis, a southern continent. The Portuguese maps of the Southern Sea, which we'd relied on and trusted with our lives, were wrong.

. . .

Tom Moone was the first to notice the price we'd paid for the storms. 'The *Marigold* is gone, Captain General.' He shaded his eyes and scanned the horizon in all directions.

I agreed. Only the *Elizabeth* followed in our wake. 'We are at least three hundred miles off course, so let's hope we find her again.' I wasn't optimistic. Captain John Thomas was an experienced man, but the *Marigold* was more suited to the calmer waters of the English coast than the storms of the Southern Sea.

That night another ferocious tempest drove us back towards the cape, and we sought shelter in a rocky bay. I closed my eyes to snatch much-needed sleep, and woke to the clanging of the ship's bell, our warning the anchor cable had broken. By God's grace we fought the highest waves I'd seen, and found our way to open water in the darkness.

The queen's ship, *Elizabeth*, had vanished, yet I held out hope that John Wynter would be waiting for us off the coast of Chile. He'd seemed dispirited last time we spoke, yet had been determined not to return to England without Spanish gold and silver in his hold.

Sailing north some thousand miles towards Chile, we kept vigilant for any signs of the *Elizabeth* or *Marigold*. Only eighty-six men remained from those who'd left Plymouth, yet now we had favourable winds, and looked forward to the prospect of reward for our hardship.

I showed my nephew John an island, marked on the chart ahead of us, named Mocha, some eighteen miles from the coast. 'With God's grace it will be a good place to rest and careen our weed-covered hull.' I saw him brighten at the prospect of land. 'We must also find fresh water and food to restore our dwindling reserves.'

He agreed. 'I'm tired of seabird stew – and picking maggots from biscuits.'

'With luck, we shall find a sweet pineapple for you, John.'

I fought back nervous memories of our last encounter with Indians, but this time we were ready for trouble. Our pinnace carried a bronze cannon, and we all wore armour and carried primed arquebuses. One of the crew, a bluff-mannered Devonian named Thomas Brewer, saw Francis Fletcher's hands clasped in prayer, and turned to me with a grin.

'Let us hope for our parson's sake we don't find more naked women!'

I smiled at his good humour, but also said a silent prayer that this time the natives would be friendly. I could not have succeeded in the past without the help of the Cimarrons, and hoped to persuade the local people that the English would treat them better than the Spanish.

One of the Indians who welcomed us wore a cape of black feathers and led a strange animal with a long neck on a leather leash. I'd never seen anything like it. The size of a cow, the beast's body was covered with lank wool and it had a face like a sheep.

I turned to Diego. 'See if you can trade that beast for one of our axes.'

I kept my primed arquebus ready for use as I watched him trying to explain to the Indian, who grinned and agreed the exchange. Too large to carry alive on our pinnace, we killed and butchered the animal on the stony beach, and found the meat looked not unlike mutton.

We tried to explain our need for fresh water, but the Indians didn't understand, so I decided we should return the next day with more oak casks and goods to trade. This could be the opportunity I'd been hoping for to form an alliance with the local people.

The following morning we set out more confident of our safety, laden with as many empty casks as we could carry. As we pulled the boat on to the shore, Thomas Brewer jumped out first, carrying an oak water cask. He turned with a warning shout as Indians appeared from the tall reeds, and began firing arrows.

Searing pain brought me to my knees as an arrow struck me on the cheek, narrowly missing my right eye, followed by another which grazed my head, causing blood to gush down my neck. The Indians were already seizing our boat to cut off our escape, and Thomas Brewer fell dead, his body bristling with arrows.

Outnumbered more than ten to one, we didn't stand a chance against the deadly onslaught. The wound on my scalp burned like a hot iron, and warm blood soaked my shirt. The injury under my eye felt numb and the metallic taste of blood in my mouth told me the wound could be serious.

I drew my dagger and lunged at the Indian holding the painter of our boat. He squirmed out of the way, long enough for our wounded crewmen to push the pinnace back into the water, and we leapt aboard. Diego had so many arrows sticking out of him I doubted he would survive, yet we managed to paddle out of range with the two remaining oars, and shouted to the ship for help.

The longboat soon appeared, full of men firing arquebuses. I looked back at the beach in time to see the Indians dismembering poor Thomas Brewer in much the same way we'd dispatched their animal. I cursed the loss of another good man, who'd died because of my carelessness.

. . .

The ship's surgeon was dead and the other physician sailed on the *Elizabeth*, so I had to be attended by Tom Moone. He tried to make up for his lack of skill with a cheery manner, yet frowned as he examined my wounds.

'You were lucky, Captain General. An inch higher and you'd have lost your eye.'

'I thank God in his mercy.' I flinched as he prodded the cut on my head. 'Do any of the men show signs of poison?'

'Not yet, but one has died from his injuries – and, of course, Thomas Brewer...' His voice tailed off.

'The men wanted to blast the Indians with our cannons, but I believe they mistook us for Spaniards.' I flinched as he began to close my wound with his needle and thread. 'I read that Magellan was killed by Indians, and now I understand how it could have happened.'

We'd sailed a good distance from the ill-fated island of Mocha before our lookout spotted a reed boat, bobbing on the water. I ordered the occupant, an Indian fisherman, brought aboard. Diego, bandaged from twenty arrow wounds, questioned him and learned of a Spanish ship, anchored in a bay close to the harbour of Valparaiso.

Nunho da Silva recognised her as we approached, and explained through Diego that she was the two-hundred-ton *Los Reyes*.

'The king's ship?' I hoped we'd stumbled on a prize which would make the voyage a success.

Nunho da Silva shook his head. 'The *Capitana* of Álvaro de Mendaña de Neira.'

I knew few Spanish words, but understood this was the flagship of one of Spain's famous adventurers. Although my wounds troubled me, the opportunity was too good to miss. I primed my pistol, feeling the old excitement of the chase return.

The *Capitana* sat at anchor in a peaceful bay. Her crew looked unconcerned at our approach, and one raised a hand in welcome. The last thing they would be expecting was an attack from an English ship in these waters. They surrendered without a fight, although at least one man managed to escape by swimming ashore.

The rest were locked up while we searched their ship. Disappointed to discover she was being used as a merchant vessel, with her hold full of wine and cedar, I found that her crew included a Greek pilot. He claimed a good knowledge of the coast of Chile and showed me his charts of the ports and harbours as far north as Lima.

My brother called to me, excitement in his voice. Our search uncovered four leather cases, which held over seventy-five pounds of gold, including a golden crucifix set with emeralds, and a good quantity of silver coins. At a stroke, we'd covered the costs of our voyage and gained a fine ship.

Concerned that the crewman who escaped would raise the alarm, I put our prisoners ashore, except for the Greek pilot. With our own crewmen aboard the *Capitana*, we sailed north to our planned rendezvous with the *Elizabeth* and *Marigold*. I stood with my brother, scanning the empty horizon.

'I confess I'm worried, Thomas. It's been two full months since we saw them last.'

Thomas seemed unconcerned. 'I think they'll have turned back, to escape the storms. It's a miracle we made it through.'

'You know how determined Captain Wynter is. He would only turn back if he thought us lost.' I frowned as a dark thought occurred to me. 'I can imagine Mary's distress if he returns alone.'

My brother looked serious. 'I wonder what account he might give of the trial of Thomas Doughty?'

'John Wynter is a fair man, and saw the danger of mutiny we faced.' I prayed I was right, but needed to focus, as our water was running short. We would soon have to abandon hope of finding the rest of our fleet.

The taciturn Greek pilot led us to a bay the Spanish called La Herradura, after its horseshoe shape, where we could take on water. Herds of black cattle roamed the hillside, a sign there must be Spanish settlers close by, so we were well-armed as we took the pinnace ashore.

I turned at a shout of alarm as we filled our casks at a stream, and saw over a hundred horsemen riding down the ridge towards us. I ran for the boat, cursing the Greek for leading us into a trap, and leapt aboard as the first shots rang out. One of our men, a Cornish sailor named Richard Minivy, fell as a bullet struck him in the back, but we had to leave him to save ourselves.

Turning to look back at the beach, I saw he'd been surrounded by the Spanish soldiers, then heard a rousing cheer from the shore. One of the riders held up a lance, and on top was the head of the man we'd had to abandon to his fate.

We'd treated our Spanish prisoners with courtesy, but I swore to avenge the loss of our crewman. A full year had passed since we departed Plymouth. We'd survived attacks from Indians, sailed through the worst storms I'd ever seen, and would show the Spanish why we'd voyaged halfway around the world.

17

JANUARY 1579

The men sang bawdy songs as they worked in the blistering heat on the careened hull of the *Golden Hinde*. Relieved to see their good spirits, I ordered a double ration of wine in reward for replacing a year's growth of weed with a thick coat of tar.

It took a day of shouting and heaving on ropes to refit her heavy cannons, removed to the *Capitana*, which I'd decided to keep as a supply ship. My brother supervised the work, and raised a hand as he saw me approach to inspect the progress.

He grinned. 'Now the last of the pinnaces is assembled, her hold is ready for a haul of Spanish gold.'

'The treasure fleet is within our grasp, Thomas, but we need fresh water.' I looked across the land of northern Chile, to the snow-topped Andes mountains. An arid desert, with thorn bushes and dry, sandy gullies, was all that remained where rivers once ran down to the sea.

'I fear we might have quite a trek inland.' Thomas shaded his eyes as he scanned the horizon, and pointed to a distant smudge of green. 'Where there are trees, Diego is bound to find water.'

'I'm worried about Diego.' He never complained, but I'd seen strong men die from lesser wounds. I called his name and he appeared, ready to come with us. 'You must stay behind and rest.'

Diego shook his head. 'I have to go with you, Captain, if you are to find water in this place.'

Anyone else would have a stern rebuke for disobeying my order, but Diego was right. Our lives might depend on his skills. I had to let him come with us, but would keep a close eye on him.

We beached the pinnace up a narrow creek, and followed a stony track leading into sparse forest. Much of the greenery we'd seen from the shore proved to be thorn bushes, and spiky cactus plants, although there were trees on the higher slopes of the hills.

I was glad of the hat I wore to guard against the fierce sun, but the aching from the wound in my leg returned, making me walk with a limp. After an hour of marching in the dry heat, the man scouting ahead returned with surprising news.

'I've found a Spaniard.' He pointed ahead, keeping his voice low. 'He has two mules, and is sleeping.'

We crept to where the Spaniard lay snoring in the shade of a tree, oblivious to our presence, and to the black flies buzzing around his head. Taking his sword, my brother searched the bags carried by the mules and held up an ingot of silver.

'He has a dozen more of these.' Thomas called to Diego. 'Can you ask him to tell us where we can find water in this godforsaken place, and if there is any more silver?'

Diego woke the startled man, and they spoke in Spanish before he turned to me. 'He says only the Indians know where to find water.' Diego smiled. 'He's waiting for his companion, who brings a train of silver.'

I couldn't believe our change of fortune. 'Ask him if there is an escort of soldiers.'

Diego questioned the man again. 'He travels alone.'

'Tell him if there are soldiers, he'll be the first to die.' I glanced back in the direction we'd come. 'It seems they're not expecting us so far inland, but keep your arquebuses ready and your wits about you.'

I studied the Spaniard's reaction to Diego's threat. Our lives depended on my judgement of whether he could be trusted. He led us up the trail, deeper into the woods. It wasn't long before approaching hooves rumbled on the stony ground, yet my instinct warned me that something felt wrong. I knew the noises of a mule train well, and this sounded different.

Signalling for the men to remain, I crept ahead with Diego, my pistol primed. As the Spaniard promised, there weren't any soldiers, only one man, in a wide-brimmed hat, leading a line of the long-necked sheep we'd seen before.

Each carried heavy woven baskets, and it seemed we were in luck. The man carried a sword at his belt, but raised his hands in surrender at our challenge, his eyes wide. My brother opened one of the baskets, and turned to me with a broad grin.

'He told the truth! These are full of silver ingots.'

I looked back down the line of strange animals. 'I believe they could be carrying over a hundred pounds of silver. Too much to risk by continuing our search for water in this barren place.' I called to Diego. 'Tell him to lead the train back to our ships – in return for his life.'

Two Spanish merchant ships anchored in the sheltered harbour of Arica, where the Greek pilot told us silver was loaded from mines on the slopes of the Andes. Boarding the first, we found only two Corsican crewmen, with a small amount of silver coins.

The second ship had one man to guard her, a former slave, but carried a welcome quantity of wine casks and precious barrels of fresh water, worth more to my thirsty crew than pearls or silver.

Anything of value was transferred to the *Golden Hinde*, and my brother put in command of the better of the two ships. I'd ordered the other ship to be disabled by cutting through the mast stays, but the men sent to do the work misunderstood and set her ablaze.

The bright flames and plume of grey smoke could be seen for miles, but I wasn't concerned. Our actions would send a message to the Spanish. We left the two Corsican crewmen on the beach, but the former slave said his name was Francisco, and agreed to join us.

Older than Diego, Francisco had earned the trust of the Spanish, and didn't seem like a slave when we captured him. He spoke no English, but spent some time in conversation with Diego. I listened and understood he spoke of a treasure ship belonging to the King of Spain.

Diego looked concerned and turned to me. 'He says a galleon laden with gold and silver sailed north two days ago, but the Spanish know we are here, and have a great many soldiers.'

We followed in pursuit, but the Spanish galleon had a two-day advantage, and by the time we found her she'd been unloaded. I cursed our luck at the sight of a train of long-necked sheep, heading for the hills. Spanish soldiers on the shore fired arquebuses at us and shouted insults. We were too late.

My brother tried to cheer my mood. 'The galleon is a good prize, and will increase our fleet to six ships.'

I disagreed. 'Now the Spanish are aware of us, we must move swiftly. Have the men salvage everything they can, then we'll set the prize ships adrift.'

'I hoped for command of the galleon.'

I put my hand on his shoulder. 'Don't worry, Thomas. You'll have your command soon enough.'

I heard him curse as he went off. He had the makings of a good captain, but six ships made us too easy a target, and I'd not forgotten how savage the Spanish could be with prisoners. I didn't expect my brother to thank me, but our best hope was to take the Spanish by surprise.

Sailing two hundred and fifty leagues north, we headed for Callao, the port of Lima, capital of Peru. Our lookout spotted a Spanish barque of about fifty tons, and I gave the order to approach within range. Our warning shot across her bows proved enough to make her surrender.

My brother led the boarding party in the pinnace, and when he returned he brought back a well-dressed man who spoke English. Introducing himself as the captain, he explained he'd spent some time in the service of the Spanish ambassador to England.

I guessed he might be one of the spies Francis Walsingham worried about, but invited him to dine with my brother and me in my cabin. While my viol players entertained us, we were served my best wine in silver goblets, then a stew in gold-rimmed silver bowls. I saw the Spanish captain nod in approval as he tasted the stew.

My brother raised his spoon with a fatty lump of meat on it. 'Made from the long-necked sheep you use to transport the silver.'

The captain raised an eyebrow. 'We call them llamas, Master Drake. They are useful pack animals, although this is the first time I've dined on one.'

I heard the note of humour in his voice. I needed to find out what he knew about the treasure fleet, and hoped it would be less difficult than I'd expected. I decided to be direct.

'I'll make a deal with you, Captain. Tell me what you know of the ships in Callao, and the treasure fleet, and you have my word that you and your ship will be allowed to continue on your way unharmed.'

He took another spoonful of the stew, and seemed to consider for a moment before replying. 'I should tell you that eighteen of your countrymen were captured trying to steal from the treasure fleet.'

'Were they led by a man named John Oxenham?'

'He is held with four others in Panama for examination by the Inquisition.'

'And the rest?' I saw the look in his eyes, and knew they'd been executed as pirates. A reckless plan formed in my mind to free my friend but, in my heart, I knew there was no hope. I recalled saying to Doughty, long ago, that if John Oxenham failed, we would all learn from it.

My brother broke the silence. 'Will you tell us about the treasure fleet, Captain?'

'A ship in Callao has been loaded with silver, and another, named the *Nuestra Señora de la Concepción* sailed a week ago with silver and gold.'

'Our Lady of the Conception?' My pulse quickened. 'The one they call the *Cacafuego*?'

'The Shitfire!' My brother grinned.

I studied the captain, who could be the making of our voyage. 'Where can we find this treasure ship?'

'She sailed for Panama, and will make a stopover at Esmeraldas.'

I made a quick calculation. 'Over six hundred leagues from our present position, but in the right direction.' I raised my goblet. 'You've earned your freedom, Captain.'

. . .

We let him go and slipped into Callao in near darkness, with only a sliver of moonlight to show our way. The shallow entrance meant we came close to running aground. Shingle scraped on our keel, as I counted seventeen ships waiting at anchor.

The only way to find the silver the Spanish captain told us about was to board each one, cutting the mast stays of the larger ships, and the anchor cables of the rest, making our search without alerting anyone ashore. It was a great risk and took all night, but our only reward was a small chest of silver coins. The likeable captain had lied.

My brother cursed. 'We should set the lot ablaze.'

I frowned as I saw the lights of another ship sailing into the harbour. Mooring close by, and armed with cannons, she could block our escape, trapping us in the harbour. Her name, *San Cristobal*, was painted in flamboyant gold lettering on her stern.

'I have a better plan. Take the pinnace.' I pointed to the *San Cristobal*. 'She's yours, if you can take her without raising the alarm.'

I watched as they paddled silently in the darkness. The sharp crackle of arquebus fire rattled from the *San Cristobal*, and one of the men in the pinnace fell with a cry of pain. I couldn't see if the victim was my brother, but ordered our gunners to fire.

Our heavy cannonball crashed through the hull of the *San Cristobal*, sending deadly splinters of wood into the air. As we were readying a second shot, her crew abandoned her in their longboat, and I was relieved to see my brother wave from the helm a short while later.

The bells of Callao town rang a warning, too late, as we sailed back out to sea. The Spanish captain made fools of us, but I believed he'd told the truth about John Oxenham, and the gold ship, *Cacafuego*. We'd lost another good man, but if we could make up the ground, a king's fortune could be won.

Plagued by lack of favourable winds, we narrowly avoided the Spanish, who pursued us in three fast ships from Callao. Despite my brother's protests, we had to abandon the wallowing *San Cristobal* with our remaining prisoners, and resort to pulling the *Golden Hinde* behind the pinnace.

Towing such a heavy ship in the rolling seas proved back-breaking work for the oarsmen, so we had to make frequent changes of crew. The sight of distant Spanish ships showed they hadn't given up the chase, but the sea conditions were against them. Even if they did come close, I was confident our gunners could see them off.

To keep the men focused, I read to them from my father's book of Psalms, and offered a prize of a gold chain, found on the *San Cristobal*, to the first man to spot the treasure ship. As we approached Esmeraldas, on the first day of March, my nephew John pointed and shouted in his shrill voice from high in the crow's nest. The galleon at anchor looked about a hundred and twenty tons, the same as the *Golden Hinde*, but an older design.

I gave the order to trail empty wine caskets as a sea anchor to slow our progress. 'We'll attack once darkness falls, but this time we must take them by surprise. Have our guns made ready to fire, but hidden from sight.'

As the sun slipped below the horizon, we steered a course to take us alongside the galleon, which we could see was unmistakeably the king's treasure ship. The men tending to her rigging seemed unconcerned as we drew within range, although one pointed in our direction and called out. It sounded like a question, although I couldn't make out what he said.

Our Spanish-speaking crewman replied with my demand for their surrender, his deep voice carrying well. The effect was unexpected, as a dozen soldiers appeared and began a ragged fusillade of gunfire. An arquebus ball splintered the handrail close to where I stood with a crack of breaking wood.

Glad I'd chosen to wear my helmet and coat of mail, I gave a single sharp blast on my silver whistle, the command our gunners had been waiting for. My ears rang with the blast as the mizzen-mast of the *Cacafuego* toppled like a fallen tree, crashing into the sea with its main spar. A trumpet sounded, and my crossbow men began shooting with deadly accuracy at close range. Their orders were not to kill, but to secure surrender.

After a short exchange of fire, the Spanish threw down their weapons. Our boarding party, already in our pinnace, all carried arquebuses and soon took control. Less than ten minutes had passed between our approaching the *Cacafuego*, and my brother Thomas giving me his thumbs-up signal.

The Spanish captain scowled as my crewmen dragged him from his cabin and brought him to mine. He'd suffered a cut to his face and held a blood-soaked cloth to it. He spoke in Spanish, and I could tell from his cultured voice he'd been well educated, although I had to wait for Diego to act as translator.

Although most of his wounds were healed, Diego suffered with pain where one of the arrows had pierced his shoulder. We'd treated him with vinegar, but I worried the festering wound would poison his blood without attention from a doctor.

'His name is San Juan de Anton.' Diego eyed the captain warily. 'He demands that you release his ship.'

'Tell him his ship and his men are in safe hands. Once we've seen to that cut, he is invited to dine with me.'

The captain looked surprised, and spoke again to Diego, with the same threatening tone.

'He says every bay and harbour as far as Panama is being searched, so it's only a matter of time before we face the questions of the Inquisition.'

'Inform the captain we are already leaving Spanish waters.

My men tell me there is much silver and gold on his ship – enough for us to take our leave.'

Once we reached a secluded stretch of coast, a full search of our haul revealed eighty pounds of gold, and some twenty-six tons of silver, as well as thirteen chests of gold coins, jewels and large pearls. The only way we could carry so much home would be to replace our ship's stone ballast with silver bars.

Francis Fletcher and my nephew John joined me in my cabin to record our recent adventures, and I spread out my newest charts on the table for them to see.

'The *Cacafuego* carried two pilots, with these charts of the coastline north of Panama. We've been lucky, and discovered a greater fortune than any of us could have hoped for, yet now we have to find a safe passage back to England, and I pray we can do so before it's too late.'

My nephew frowned. 'Too late?'

'We can't wait for the Spanish to discover us, and I have no appetite for returning through the storms and shallows of the Strait of Magellan.' I traced my finger along the chart. 'We must find a passage to the north-west, or cross the Southern Sea.'

18

MARCH 1579

Captain San Juan de Anton left with his ship and crew, together with Francisco, who would rather take his chances with the Spanish than sail with us to Plymouth. I kept one of the pilots from the *Cacafuego*, with the same promise of release I'd made to the Portuguese navigator, Nunho da Silva.

My nephew pointed a nail-bitten finger at the dark shape on the horizon. 'He's been following us at a distance for two days now.'

I recognised the stunted mizzen-mast of the *Cacafuego*, the best repair we could do at sea. 'Captain de Anton is a shrewd commander, John. He'll be assessing our destination, to report to the governor in Panama, but we'll be long gone by the time he makes his report.'

I looked back at the Spanish ship behind us. 'I wish we could have trusted Captain de Anton to take Diego to a physician, but I've seen how they treat the Cimarrons.'

'Do you think Diego will live?'

His questioning eyes studied mine for the truth. Of all the crew, Diego had become his closest friend. 'He's a fighter, John. If he'd been wounded in the arm or leg, we would know how to deal with him, but all we can do for Diego now is pray for God's mercy.'

I left him staring out to the horizon and made my way to the cramped store room which had become Diego's cabin. The smell hit me as I opened the door, even though the small porthole was propped open. Diego lay sleeping on his pallet bed, but opened his eyes and forced a smile when he saw me.

I pulled back the coverlet to inspect his injury. Of the twenty arrow wounds he'd suffered in the attack at Mocha, only this one refused to heal. Anyone else would have died weeks ago, but Diego clung to life. His shoulder looked swollen and purple, and his body glistened with sweat. I replaced the bloodstained bandage, and held his leather water bottle to his lips while he drank.

I dampened a cloth with water and placed it on his feverish forehead. 'We all pray for you, so you had better recover soon.' He gave me a nod of gratitude, and closed his eyes.

I ran my tongue over dry, cracked lips, a reminder that our first priority when we reached Cano Island, off Costa Rica, was to find fresh water. We'd only been able to last so long by catching drops of condensation from the sails at dawn each day. I couldn't recall when we'd last had rain.

The dense jungle echoed to the haunting sounds of exotic bird calls, reminding me of my first visit to the coast of Africa. We found shelter in a sandy bay, fringed with tall palms, and dropped anchor while my brother led a landing party in the pinnace.

The brilliant blue water sparkled in bright sunshine, so clear we could see a forest of corals, with shoals of bright yellow fish. The men fired at a green turtle as it grazed on the weed growing on our hull, and cheered when one of them hit a large blue shark.

I was beginning to worry about our shore party when they returned with the pinnace filled to the gunwales with their spoils. My brother looked pleased as he helped haul a six-foot-long alligator aboard.

'We found a fresh-water spring.' He grunted with the effort. 'All the casks are filled, and we shot this monster, as well as a brown monkey.'

I smiled at his enthusiasm. 'It's been some time since the men enjoyed fresh meat, although your monkey is a little small, and I wonder what our cook will make of it.'

We needed more supplies, so pursued a sleek forty-ton barque which proved to carry a welcome cargo of sweetcorn and honey. By a stroke of fortune, her pilot, a white-haired Spaniard named Sánchez Colchero, carried charts of the islands to the far west of the Southern Sea.

I sent for my Spanish-speaking crewman. 'Tell him I'll pay him a thousand pesos to show us a safe passage to Java.'

Colchero shook his head, and complained in a whining Spanish voice. I didn't need my interpreter to know the pilot refused to help us. 'Put a rope around his neck and pretend we are going to hang him. If he still doesn't agree to help, lock him in the hold until he sees sense.'

Conscious of my promise to my brother, I gave him command of the Spanish barque. 'You understand we'll have to abandon her if she slows us down?'

He studied the lines of our prize. 'The pinnace slows us when we tow her astern. We can strip out anything from the barque we don't need, and use her as a replacement.'

I agreed. 'When we can find somewhere to careen the *Golden Hinde*, your barque will be useful to store the cannons.'

'I've already been thinking of that.' Thomas leaned over the side and pointed. 'The weed isn't far below the waterline, so we can find shallows to dry out, and scrape off the worst of the fouling.'

'Then we'll put some miles between us and the Spanish.'

'Do you think they're still pursuing us?'

'I'm certain of it.' I peered at the empty horizon. 'We've been lucky, but when the Spanish come, we must be ready for them.'

The inlet we found proved ideal, and we set up three of our guns on the deck of the barque, ready to fire if any Spanish arrived. Once we'd cleaned our hull, we loaded our captives, except for our pilots, on to the old pinnace with food and water, and set them free.

A luminous full moon lit the sails of another merchant ship some way ahead. At dawn I had Sánchez Colchero hail them in Spanish, while we boarded her from our pinnace, and forced her crew to surrender. She carried silks and porcelain from China, as well as a Spanish nobleman, who said he was a cousin of the Duke of Medina Sidonia.

I crossed to the captured merchantman to see her cargo for myself, choosing silks and bowls as gifts for Mary, who had been increasingly on my mind following talk of our voyage home. We'd seen no sign of the *Elizabeth*, and I worried that if Captain Wynter returned alone, Mary would believe we'd perished in the storms.

I'd heard that among the Spanish passengers were two slaves, and was surprised to see one was a young girl, who stared at me with wary eyes, as if expecting the worst. The other slave explained in Spanish that his name was Miguel, and the girl was called Maria. I was happy for Miguel to join our crew, but the girl presented a dilemma.

My brother was forthright. 'It's bad luck to have a woman aboard. The men won't like it.'

'I can hardly leave her here, Thomas.' I tried to hide the irritation in my voice at the way he presumed to act as spokesman for the crew.

'You must put her ashore when we can, for her own good.' He gave me a meaningful look.

'I will, but in the meantime tell the men she is to be treated as our guest, or they will answer to me.'

I decided to release the Spanish merchant ship, once we'd taken everything we needed. Before we let him go, I invited the duke's cousin to dine with me. He asked me to set Sánchez Colchero free and I agreed, as he was no use to us. In return, the duke warned me our activities were the talk of Spain, but he knew nothing of the fate of John Oxenham, or the three others captured with him.

The sun set in a peach-tinted sky as the entire crew of some eighty men gathered on deck. I'd never seen them so silent. Removing their caps, their faces were grim as I read from the Book of Wisdom.

'*But the just man, though he dies early, shall be at rest. For the age that is honourable comes not with the passing of time, nor can it be measured in terms of years.*' I struggled to compose myself and continue. '*He who pleased God was loved. He who lived among sinners was transported, snatched away.*'

I looked up at the faces of the crew, and saw many were touched by these words. 'Without exception, we all counted him as a friend, and pray he finds repose with the sea on which he gave his life that we might live.'

Francis Fletcher, dressed in his black cleric's robes, clasped his hands in prayer. '*Into thy hands, Lord, we commend the soul of thy servant departed, now called unto eternal rest, and we commit his body to the deep.*'

I gave the waiting men a nod and they lowered the weighted canvas into the dark blue water. Diego fought for life but, as we feared, the fever proved too much for him. I recalled how he'd kept us cheerful during the long wait for winter storms to pass. Although he'd been happy to work as my assistant, he'd become much more to me. We would all miss him.

We reached our first port on the Mexican coast in a sombre mood. Marked on the charts as Guatulco, the port revealed one small ship sat at anchor, and people were gathered on the long sandy beach. My nephew, high in the crow's nest, called out as we came closer.

'They're whipping a slave – and look ready to hang another!'

I was relieved to note the men were dressed more like settlers and merchants than soldiers. Unlike the Spanish towns, we couldn't see cannons or fortifications. I pointed to a large, balconied building on the seafront, likely to be the governor's residence, or at least someone of importance.

'Time for some target practice. A cask of wine for the first gun crew to score a direct hit!'

The air thundered with our cannon fire, and the people of the town fled, abandoning one of the slaves bound hand and foot on the beach. Coming so soon after the death of our companion Diego, the sight of the poor man saddened me.

I sent a boat ashore to rescue him, and allowed the crew to loot the houses as they wished. They deserved reward after so many long and dangerous days at sea, but I told them not to set fires. The town looked remote and I didn't wish the inhabitants to suffer unduly.

When my men returned, I learned they'd found little of value, apart from a gold chain, a small casket of pearls, and the bronze bell, taken from the church. They'd also brought back three 'hostages', one of whom was a priest, as well as another slave, who asked to join us.

My brother came to see me. 'What's to be done about our hostages? They fear for their lives, and beg for mercy.'

'Then we shall show them God's mercy. Have the men assemble on deck for prayers. These Catholics can listen to my sermon from the *Book of Martyrs*. I'll set them free, but not until they join in our hymns.'

I enjoyed the looks on their faces when they heard our crew sing 'Old Robin of Portingale' so heartily, accompanied by my viol players.

God let never so old a man,
  Marry so young a wife,
  As did Old Robin of Portingale,
  He may rue all the days of his life.
  And he shope the cross in his right shoulder,
  Of the white flesh and the red,
  And he went him into the holy land,
  Wheras Christ was quick and dead.

When the time came to let our visitors leave, I assured them we were not pirates, but honest sailors, in the service of the Queen of England. Never would we harm our prisoners, but we expected Christian mercy in return.

The ship at anchor in the bay was deserted and of no use to us, so I gave her to the Portuguese pilot, Nunho da Silva. He complained I'd promised to leave him somewhere safe, and I hoped he was unaware that our next destination, Acapulco, was a ruse to throw the Spanish off our scent when they questioned him, as I was sure they would.

Swirling fog slowed our progress north, and made navigation impossible. We relied on the stars to guide our way, or the height of the sun over the horizon. All we could see were swirling grey mists, and even my sharp-eyed nephew was at a loss as he searched for land.

Stinging hailstones and biting, icy winds made life hard for our lookouts, so the danger of running aground was always on our minds. We were sailing further north than any other Englishmen had, and I was unsurprised when my brother came alongside in the Spanish barque, his beard glistening with crystals of ice.

He shouted across to me, so all the crew could hear. 'We've been some twenty months at sea, and I for one would rather take my chances to the west than keep up this search for a northern passage.'

I suspected he spoke for the crew, and called back. 'Even once we cross the ocean, there's no easy route home.' I saw him shake his head. 'A north-west passage would have us home in half the time—'

'At what cost to the men?'

This sounded mutinous, but I had to reply. 'One more week, then we'll have to turn back.'

My brother scowled. 'There's no going forward – and no going back, as the Spanish will be watching for us in the Strait of

Magellan. That only leaves crossing to the East Indies, and sailing around the world.' Thomas ordered his helmsman to veer away, without waiting to hear my reply, and I wondered if I could count on his loyalty for much longer.

The *Golden Hinde* had seen us through the worst storms I'd known, but green weed and barnacles thrived on her hull, as thick as if we'd never careened her. Despite our pumping, a foot of seawater swirled in her bilges, an ominous warning of the need to make repairs. With a heavy heart, I gave the order to turn back.

As if nature approved of my decision, the fog lifted to reveal a shallow bay which seemed ideal for our purposes. I set the men to work felling trees and salvaging timbers from the Spanish barque. We had to build a fort to protect our gold while the leaking hull was restored. The work was progressing well when I was alerted by a shout.

'Indians!'

Several of the men pointed to the ridge overlooking the bay. The Indians chose their vantage point well. They could see every one of us, yet it was impossible to know *their* true numbers. I called for the men to ready arquebuses and crossbows, but prayed we wouldn't have to fight.

At the end of the second day a group of Indians approached, speaking in a strange language none of us could understand. As well as older men, wearing long eagle feathers in their hair, the Indian women fell to their knees, wailing and shrieking, and tearing at their skin with their nails, as if in distress. Several carried bows and arrows, but there was no suggestion of a threat.

Francis Fletcher frowned as the Indians began a strange chant. 'It seems as if they are worshipping us. We have to find a way to communicate with them, explain why we are here.'

I agreed. 'You've told me of your desire to bring religion to heathens, Master Fletcher. If you wish, we could leave you here. I don't believe you could hope for a more attentive audience.'

He glanced at the half-naked women and shook his head. 'I shall record as much as I can of this place in my journal, Captain General, but don't wish to spend my days here.'

As we left, I turned to look back at the rich, fertile land I'd named New Albion. The Indians had set a line of bright fires along the high ridge as a sign of farewell. We'd spent four weeks in their company, and begun to learn something of each other's ways. I hoped any natives we encountered on our voyage home would be as welcoming.

Favourable winds and currents speeded our long passage west across the Southern Sea, but it was November before our lookout sighted land on the horizon. We were short of food and water, so I hoped these were the islands of the East Indies, marked on my Portuguese charts as the fabled Spice Islands.

A lone carrack sailed ahead, and I ordered the crew to pursue her, but one of the master gunners cursed and called out, 'The gun ports were fastened and sealed with pitch for the crossing, Captain General, it will take us a while to be ready.'

'Do your best.' The carrack was under full sail, heading out of range. 'There will be plenty more like her, but we must make ready.'

I was glad of our preparations later that evening when we sighted a Spanish galleon, following in our wake. I ordered the gun crews to fire when ready, and the Spanish replied with a thunderous boom of cannon fire. I flinched as a shot splashed into the water close to our bows. We were in no mood for a battle, so turned and headed for the islands to find food and water.

Drake - Tudor Corsair

Before we could make landfall, some hundred canoes paddled out to greet us. The people were naked except for a belt of woven grasses, like the Carib Indians I'd seen in the West Indies, and brought coconuts and fresh fish and fruit to trade.

In our eagerness for food, we didn't notice until too late that many of the natives had boarded us. In no time we were outnumbered as the natives scrambled from their canoes. One took a knife from a crewman and shouted as he brandished it. Others tried to carry off anything they could find.

I loaded my pistol and fired it into the air. The men in canoes began using slings to throw sharp stones, injuring several crewmen, so I ordered one of the cannons to be used to scare them off. Although my intention was to fire wadding, the gun had been loaded with grapeshot, which killed a number of the natives, but we were relieved when the canoes returned to the shore.

We found water at the next island, but nothing to eat, although we discovered two native fishermen in a small boat. The men spoke some Portuguese, and were persuaded to lead us to the island of Ternate in the Moluccas, the largest of the islands marked on our charts.

After our narrow escape with the native canoes, we had our cannons ready as two brightly painted galleys approached, rowed by men dressed in white linen. We didn't allow them to board, but managed to learn that they brought a welcome from their sultan.

I saw an opportunity, and gave them gifts of fine cloth for the sultan, explaining that we visited on behalf of the Queen of England. Luck was with us, as the next morning the air echoed to the deep, rhythmic beat of drums. Escorted by three more galleys, the sultan was rowed out by eighty men dressed in white.

He sprawled on a throne, and wore cloth of gold, with a

heavy gold chain around his neck, glittering with rubies and emeralds. I had our drummers and viol players strike up a rousing tune, which seemed to go down well.

Ropes were thrown and the galleys towed us into the harbour. A well-dressed man who spoke some Spanish came aboard and asked to see me. The crewman acting as my interpreter questioned him, and turned to me with a frown.

'He says he is the brother of the sultan, sent as surety, but warns you not to go ashore, Captain General.'

I felt a pang of disappointment, as I'd been hoping to establish a trading arrangement. 'Ask him why not.'

Again, my interpreter questioned the man, who glanced at me nervously as he replied. I sensed he feared for his life, but we'd given him no reason to be afraid. 'The sultan suffered attacks from the Spanish and Portuguese, and may take you as a hostage.'

'Tell him I shall stay aboard, and his brother the sultan will be protected from the Spanish and Portuguese by Her Majesty, the Queen of England.'

Our visitor bowed and thanked us, and I sent him back with more presents for the sultan, including a coat of Spanish mail, and a gilded helmet. We bartered for rice, sugar cane and fruit, but the real prize was six tons of precious cloves. The spices could be worth more than their weight in gold, and their rich aroma soon permeated the timbers of the entire ship.

19

JANUARY 1580

I sipped my wine, savouring the mellow taste, and studied the dour face of Francis Fletcher. He dined with me, although he'd hardly spoken since we left Crab Island. The memory of the forlorn figures on the beach haunted me, although I'd had no choice but to leave them.

'What are the men saying?' I tried to lighten my tone. 'Are they relieved to see the back of her?'

Francis Fletcher cut another thick slice of cured ham, rich with spices, one of many gifts from the Sultan of Ternate. He frowned. 'She was close to giving birth.'

'We've left her in a paradise, with two men of her own kind. Much better to have her child there. A ship is no place for an infant, Master Fletcher, and you know it.'

'We owed it to her to see her safe, Captain General.' His tone was formal, yet carried a note of contempt.

I cursed the day we'd found Maria. I understood why the men brought the slaves back to the ship, but my brother had been right. The presence of a woman unsettled the crew.

'I made sure they had a good source of fresh water, and

they'll not go hungry.' I forced a smile. 'One of those giant crabs would feed the three of them.'

'She wept when we left.'

'It's done now, and there's no going back. God willing, they will be like Adam and Eve in the Garden of Eden.'

He frowned at my reference. 'Eve has already tasted the forbidden fruit.'

I refilled our glasses with the rich Portuguese wine. Tired after a long day navigating through a maze of uncharted islands, I did my best to conceal my irritation at Fletcher's tone. The crew confided in him, and I needed his support.

'What do they say about who the father is?'

Francis Fletcher laid down his knife. 'I shall only tell you if you give me your word there will be no recriminations.'

I nodded. 'I need to know.'

Fletcher took another sip of his wine, and I suspected he enjoyed his moment of power. 'Some are saying it's you, Captain General.'

'I allowed her the privacy of my cabin out of Christian charity!' It took an effort to restrain myself from striking him. 'Is it John Doughty who casts the slur on me?'

Before he could reply, a lurching shudder shook the cabin, sending everything flying. My precious books flew from their battened shelf, and I cursed as my wine spilled, the stem of the Venetian glass cracking as it hit the floor. I grabbed the table to steady myself, but Francis Fletcher struck his head on a beam as he toppled from his chair.

It took a moment for the danger to dawn on me. Our worst fear was to run aground on a coral reef. This could be the end of us all. I dashed on deck as a wave tilted the ship further over to her side, throwing me off my feet. Scrambling to stand, I said a prayer for salvation as I sent my brother to assess the damage.

We had to right the ship before the waves capsized us on the reef. An idea occurred to me. 'Throw the port side guns overboard!'

One by one, my costly culverins, which had hardly been used, were hoisted on winches and heaved overboard, but the ship still leaned at an alarming angle. 'Throw out anything else we can spare!'

The men understood the danger we were in and began heaving our valuable sacks of cloves into the sea. Another wave slapped the side and the ship lurched, with an ominous creaking as our hull ground on the sharp coral.

My brother returned from below. He'd lost his cap, and his clothes and hair were soaked. 'We've taken on a lot of water, but the hull looks sound, for now.'

'Thank God.' I watched as another ton of priceless cloves splashed into the sea, and prayed my brother was right. 'We are in the Lord's hands now, Thomas.'

Francis Fletcher led the prayers that evening as we waited to learn our fate. Our ship settled at a rakish angle, stuck firm on the coral in less than a fathom of water. Tom Moone tried rowing out with an anchor, but the depth proved too great to pull her free. With God's grace the rising tide might lift us enough for the swell to pull us free. If not, we faced the prospect of throwing our silver bullion overboard.

I bowed my head and prayed with the men, trying to focus on Francis Fletcher's words. A purple bruise showed where he'd hit his forehead, and he looked pale. There was no singing of hymns. We all knew our futures hung in the balance. He finished his reading from the Bible, then turned to the men, and began his sermon.

'This calamity is God's judgement upon us all. We must beg his forgiveness for our sinful ways.'

His words struck home, rousing my latent anger at his attitude towards me. Since our disagreement about Maria, Fletcher never referred to me by name or looked in my direction. I saw several of my crewmen cast wary glances at me, and knew if I allowed him to continue, I could have a mutiny on my hands.

'Enough!' They all turned at my shout. 'Have faith, men. We are servants of the Queen of England, here at Her Majesty's command. You are a brave and loyal crew, who have suffered great hardship, but are well deserving of the rewards due to you.' I sensed I'd won them over, and even Francis Fletcher stopped his sermon and stared at me, open-mouthed.

'Tie the preacher to the forward hatch, where he can reflect on God's judgement – and pay no heed to his mutinous words, unless you wish your rewards to be forfeit.'

Our prayers were answered the next morning when the *Golden Hinde* lurched upright and slipped into deep water. The men gave a rousing cheer, and I fell to my knees and gave thanks to God. Our misfortune cost us most of our cloves, eight of my expensive culverins, and most of the supplies we needed for the voyage home. Our hull leaked but we kept working on the pumps, and not one bar of silver had been lost.

I ordered the parson set free, although my brother made him wear a sign which read: '*Francis Fletcher, the falsest knave that lived*'. I was unsurprised when Fletcher chose to take his meals alone. Instead, my nephew joined me in my cabin, where we made drawings of the islands we passed through and recorded the details of our progress in our notebooks.

Each day became a nail-biting challenge of picking our path through the uncharted shoals and swirling currents of more islands than we could count. Conscious of our narrow escape on the reef, we took no chances. I doubled the depth soundings and posted more men to keep a lookout.

I joined my brother for a night watch, the most dangerous time. 'Once we are free of this maze, we should find the trade winds.'

My brother cursed. 'That cannot be too soon. Everywhere I look I see dark shapes in the water.'

I strained my eyes to see into the moonless gloom ahead. 'We've not come this far to founder now, Thomas.'

We spent the night shouting to the helmsman as we tried to find the deepest channels. I couldn't believe my tired eyes as the first glimmer of dawn showed on the horizon. Ahead lay nothing but clear blue water. Our sails filled with a favourable wind, straining on the sheets, like hunting dogs with a scent of prey, as the *Golden Hinde* made her eager way towards the mysterious land of Java.

My nephew John stared at the lush green forest and turned to me. 'May I go with Thomas in the shore party?'

I studied the crowd of smiling natives, who'd been gathering on the shore since we dropped anchor. They looked welcoming enough. 'I'm sorry, John. I've sworn to keep you safe.' I saw the disappointment on his face. 'I long to feel dry land under my feet as much as you, but let's wait until my brother returns.'

I didn't tell John I'd read how Ferdinand Magellan was murdered on the neighbouring island of Mactan. Magellan led his men against the local natives. Wounded in the arm with a bamboo spear, a poisoned arrow struck his leg, causing him to fall. The account said the natives hurled themselves upon him, killing him with spears while his helpless men watched from his ship.

I'd felt an affinity with Magellan since following him to these islands. If nothing else, we would learn from his death, and I'd warned my brother to be vigilant. He was guarded by our best fighters, carrying trade goods, but also well-armed and ready.

My brother gave us a cheery wave as he returned in the boat, loaded with fish, sacks of rice, and sweet ripe fruits. I thanked God for our salvation, as we were dangerously short of rations, and too exhausted from our long and difficult passage through the islands to fight.

'The people of Java welcomed us, and were happy to trade silks.' Thomas held up a yellow fruit for me to see, and took a bite. 'We've found another paradise.'

I led the shore party to meet the local ruler. Mindful of our experience with the Sultan of Ternate, I brought my trumpeters and viol players, who played rousing music as we approached. Although supported by crewmen armed with pikes and swords, I wished to reassure the islanders of our good intentions.

My plan worked, as the people danced and cheered at the sight of us, with no sign of hostility. We were soon bartering to trade for food, including the first salted beef we'd seen since leaving Plymouth, live fowls and a pig.

My interpreter learned the area was ruled by a man named Raja Donan, so we sent presents of our finest silks, inviting him to visit our ship. An impressive figure, he wore a gold chain studded with rubies, and enjoyed the music of our viol players.

I told him we were servants of the Queen of England, and presented him with the casket of pearls we'd taken from the ship at Guatulco. Although I saw my brother's frown, this proved a wise investment, as he warned us of Spanish ships close by.

Unwilling to risk another fight, we left for the Cape of Good Hope, our ship repaired and our stores filled with supplies. I peered up at the crow's nest, the favourite spot of my nephew John. He'd grown from a boy to a man on our voyage. A skilled sailor, popular with the crew, he'd become the son I longed for.

Sierra Leone on the Guinea coast welcomed us with tropical rain, although we were glad of it after so many miles of rationed water. We'd not stopped since leaving Java, and the familiar sight of West African mangroves made home seem closer.

We'd rounded the cape in fair weather, and our temporary repairs to our leaky hull proved successful. With our crew reduced to fifty-nine, our supplies lasted well enough, supplemented by a dolphin we caught in a cargo net. Hacked into slices, it tasted like Dover sole.

The rain eased as we anchored in a sweeping bay, and I gathered the exhausted men together on deck. 'Let us thank the Lord for our salvation.' Opening my father's book, I read Psalm 95.

'*Come, let us sing for joy to the Lord. Let us shout aloud to the rock of our salvation. Let us come before him with thanksgiving and extol him with music and song.*'

My trumpeters and viol players heard their cue, and played in celebration. The men sang as they never had before. We were weakened and weary, and still some way from home, but every mile we sailed took us closer.

I'd dreamed of this moment many times over the past three years, yet as we approached the familiar waters of Plymouth Sound, I brooded about the repercussions of the death of Thomas Doughty. I also worried about the queen, in whose name we'd been pillaging the Spanish.

I was less worried about Mary, yet Doughty's cruel taunt left unanswered questions in my mind. I refused to believe my wife would be disloyal, but imagined Thomas Doughty could be a persuasive flatterer, with no conscience about using his roguish charm.

I spotted two men in a small fishing boat and hailed them with a shout. 'Does Her Majesty the queen still live?'

'She does, sir, God bless her.' The fisherman studied our ship. 'Are you thinking to come ashore?'

'I am.' I resisted the temptation to tell him my name, as his question put me on my guard. 'Why would I not?'

The fisherman pointed to the town. 'I'd bear away if I were you, sir. There's plague in Plymouth, with a good few dead of it.'

His words chilled my heart and sent a murmur through the crew. I thanked the fishermen and thought of Mary, her sister Margaret, and little Jonas, who might be grown so tall I wouldn't know him. The plague was no respecter of rank or status, age or vulnerability.

I turned to the crew, who waited for my decision. 'We'll anchor here, until the situation can be confirmed. I need a volunteer to take a message to my wife. If she is well enough, she is to come out to the ship and tell me how we stand.' I heard muttering among the men. 'There is a risk, so I will reward whoever volunteers with a chain of gold.'

Tom Moone stepped forward. 'I'll go, Captain General.' He looked towards the rooftops of Plymouth. 'I confess I long to feel dry land under my boots, plague or not.'

I waited in a restless mood, and decided to move the *Golden Hinde* to the lee of the small island, ready for a quick escape. If Tom Moone returned alone it would mean the worst. Searching in my sea chest I found my precious scarf of green silk, my gift from Queen Elizabeth, and read the words in golden thread: *The Lord guide and preserve thee until the end.*

I took out my writing materials and chose the best sheet of

parchment. I dipped my quill in the black ink but hesitated, unsure about how much information to provide in writing to the queen. After a suitable preamble, I requested an audience to provide an account of my voyage around the world, and the places I'd claimed in her name for England.

I also wrote to Sir Christopher Hatton and Francis Walsingham, requesting support in ensuring the safety of the share of the profits due to them, and others. I sent for Sir Christopher's man, the trumpeter John Brewer, and tasked him to deliver my letters to London by the fastest horse. I handed him a purse of gold coins, and promised he would have his share of our spoils.

My nephew John was on lookout when the boat was sighted, and called for me to come and see. Mary, wrapped in furs, sat with Tom Moone and two men in dark cloaks and tall hats. As they came closer I recognised William Hawkins.

Mary looked pale and anxious. As far as I knew, she'd never been so far out in a rowing boat. I said a prayer of thanks to God that she was not suffering with the plague. Tom Moone helped her aboard, and she looked up at the towering masts, then saw me and froze.

Overcome with emotion, I was at a loss for words, and took her in my arms. Her white-gloved hand went to the scar on my cheek, and she studied me as if I was a stranger.

'You've been wounded.'

'An arrow, from a South Sea Indian.' I managed a smile. 'I was one of the lucky ones.'

Something had changed. Mary didn't return my smile. Her body felt thin under her furs, and she tensed when I held her close. There would be time to talk later, but it seemed she had suffered during my time away.

Mary stepped back as William Hawkins climbed aboard and shook my hand. 'Congratulations, Francis. It's good to see you safe and well.' He turned to his companion. 'This is John Blitheman, the new Mayor of Plymouth.'

I knew John Blitheman. He'd once walked past me without any acknowledgement. Now he wore the mayoral chain of office, and looked at me with keen interest.

'I'm authorised by the council to offer you facilities for the safekeeping of your treasure, Captain General.'

'I might take up your offer, once I know Her Majesty's wishes.' I saw John Blitheman's surprise at my mention of the queen. 'Has John Wynter returned home?' I had so many questions, which had swirled in my mind all the way home.

'He has.' William Hawkins frowned. 'He said you encountered terrible storms.'

I nodded. 'The worst I've known, but this ship is sound, and kept us safe.'

The queen's reply to my letter was a shock. She wrote of her displeasure, and the need to consider restitution to the Spanish. I sensed the hand of Sir William Cecil, Lord Burghley, and worried about the ominous silence from Francis Walsingham and Sir Christopher Hatton.

Mary seemed bewildered by my presents of silks and china bowls from the other side of the world, and I sensed a strange distance between us. I'd been unable to forget Thomas Doughty's cruel taunt. Even now, his ghost lingered in my thoughts, but before I could confront her, Mary surprised me with a confession.

She waited until the servants had retired for the night. We were alone in the darkness of our bedchamber, with the embers in the hearth casting a dull red glow on the walls. Turning to me with tear-filled eyes, she begged for my forgiveness.

'I spoke with Captain John Wynter. He told me of the fearsome storms, and he believed you were lost with all your crew.' She wiped a tear from her eye. 'I had a friend, a gentleman, who offered to marry me.'

I stared at her in amazement. Although I'd worried this might happen, and sensed some tension between us, I'd allowed myself to believe I'd worried for nothing. I took her hand in mine, struggling to come to terms with her news.

'Who is he?'

'He was a good man, but died in a riding accident.' She looked at me, wide-eyed. 'I had to tell you, Francis, before some mischief-maker did.'

'Did you marry him?' I recalled the wary glances from William Hawkins and John Blitheman, the day I returned to Plymouth.

'No – but he left me a substantial sum in his will.'

I lay back in our bed, took her in my arms and pulled her close. 'I can't hold this against you, Mary. In fact, I asked William Hawkins to ensure you were well provided for if I did not return.'

She didn't reply, but fell asleep in my arms. I lay awake, relieved that the air had finally been cleared between us. I was glad Mary had the courage to tell me herself. She was right: it would have been much worse to hear from anyone else.

We'd transferred much of the gold and silver to the stone keep of Trematon Castle in Saltash, when a former Member of Parliament for Plymouth, Edmund Tremayne, now clerk to the Privy Council, brought a summons from the queen. I was to report to Her Majesty at Richmond Palace with samples of my spoils, to account for my actions.

With Tremayne, my brother Thomas, and a few armed and trusted men, we'd loaded packhorses with the finest gold, silver and jewels. As the time came for my audience, I led a small procession of men carrying three wooden caskets, which they set down in a row before being dismissed.

I bowed to the queen, knowing my life and liberty hung in the balance. I would be powerless if she ordered me arrested for piracy, yet Edmund Tremayne told me I need not be overly concerned by Her Majesty's letter, which was merely her official position.

'Sit by me, Drake.' She gestured to a chair, close to her own. 'Tell me of your adventures, and leave nothing out.'

'Your Majesty.' I looked up at her and felt my heartbeat quicken as she stared at me, her sharp eyes noting the pale scar on my tanned cheek.

Her face seemed thinner, her lips a more vibrant red. This time she wore gold and diamond rings on her long fingers. The puffed sleeves of her embroidered gown shone with gold and silver thread, and the pins fastening her red-haired wig gleamed with pearls. Long necklaces of pearls reached to her waist, and around her slender throat she wore a golden collar of large rubies.

I'd had plenty of time to plan how I might turn her curiosity to advantage, as a fisherman might play a fish caught on his hook. I carried my journal, and my largest world map, which my nephew John and I had annotated with our sketches of flying fish, pen-guins, llamas, Spanish galleons and Indians.

Rolling out the map in front of her, I opened the first of the three caskets. Filled to the brim with Spanish silver coins, I allowed them to cascade on to the tiled floor, and looked into her brown eyes, relieved to see a glint of excitement – or, at the very least, anticipation.

The next chest held my collection of glittering emeralds and rubies, sapphires and diamonds in a sea of pure white pearls. I carried it closer for her to see, and she picked up one of the largest emeralds.

'Burghley would have me return these to the King of Spain.' She turned the emerald in the light.

'My Lord Burghley didn't risk his life to bring this treasure to Your Majesty.' I held my breath as I waited for her reaction. She didn't reply, but I saw her glance at the third casket.

Unfastening the leather strap, I lifted the lid to reveal my greatest prize. An exquisitely crafted coronet sat on a heap of golden ducats, jewellery and gold bars which glowed with an ethereal light. I'd planned to remind the queen of my promise to return to fill her treasury with Spanish gold, but there was no need.

A look of understanding passed between us. Opening my journal at the first page, I began to describe our adventures, and could not have wished for a more attentive listener. Elizabeth gasped as I told her of wild storms and savage Indians, and wiped away a tear when I told her of the death of my loyal friend Diego.

Several hours passed before my work was done. I believed Elizabeth looked at me with renewed respect, and understood when she told me to ensure my crew and I had our proper shares before the treasure was registered by her officials in the Tower of London.

20

APRIL 1581

The *Golden Hinde* sat in the dry dock at Deptford Creek looking as good as new. A canopy stretched high over the main deck, and the cross of St George flew proudly from the topgallant. Anyone could be forgiven for doubting she'd been through such adventures. Her carved figurehead had been freshly gilded, and her topsides painted in royal red, Tudor green and white.

The row of bronze culverins, some of which had never fired in anger, gleamed in the spring sunshine. Even the rusting iron anchors were treated to a coat of black paint. The sweet scent of cloves permeated her hold, but the light breeze hadn't carried away the tang of a thick new layer of tar, concealing the ravages and repairs to the hull.

Curious crowds of Londoners thronged around the dock, chattering and laughing. Eager for sight of their queen, they cheered when they recognised me. The nobility made no secret of how they resented my success, calling me a pirate, and worse, behind my back. The self-important courtiers were mystified by my close association with the queen, but I'd become a national hero to the common people.

Her Majesty ordered the *Golden Hinde* to be sailed to London from Plymouth and repainted to be put on public display. My proud ship had suffered on her long voyage. Her sails were worn and fraying, and she needed a new hull, but we'd patched her up and kept working on the pumps as we limped around the south coast and up the River Thames.

I was proud to point out to anyone who would listen that the *Golden Hinde* was the first English ship to sail around the world, and return with her captain, and most of her crew, safe and well. I was forbidden to add that we'd brought back a king's ransom in silver and gold, jewels and pearls, worth more than most men could dream of.

The last three months had been a whirl of royal engagements. As well as the queen's New Year celebrations at Richmond Palace, I'd been invited to many private meetings with Her Majesty. I'd dined at her table and walked at her side in her gardens. Elizabeth could be stern and formal in public, but encouraged me to regale her with stories of crocodiles and sultans, and laughed at my jokes, in private.

I'd been guest of honour at receptions at Windsor Castle, and a grand banquet in the great hall at Hampton Court Palace. I would have liked Mary to accompany me, but she'd complained of feeling unwell. Instead, my nephew John attended the receptions and banquet, a worthy reward for his courage during our long journey.

Much to the annoyance of Ambassador Mendoza of Spain, the queen wore the gold coronet, emblazoned with emeralds from the mines of Peru, while insisting I'd returned with nothing of value. In truth, the fortune brought from Trematon Castle in Saltash, now lodged in the Tower of London, cleared her debts of the Irish wars, with plenty left over.

The queen ordered the details to be kept secret, which only increased speculation and exaggeration. She knew the gold, silver and precious gems recorded by Edmund Tremayne had been only part of the fortune. After paying off all my sponsors, and rewarding every member of my crew, my own share of the treasure made me one of the wealthiest men in England.

I wore my silver sword, a gift from the queen, and a black velvet doublet. Mary and her sister Margaret looked elegant in silk gowns and pearls, as they waited nervously to meet the queen. With them stood my brother Thomas – also dressed in black, and uncomfortable in his new ruff – with young Jonas and my nephew John.

Mary's face looked pale, yet she refused to tell me what ailed her. I took her white-gloved hand in mine. 'All you need to do is curtsey.' I smiled, recalling the advice from William Hawkins the first time I'd met with the queen. 'You don't need to speak to Her Majesty unless she asks you a question.'

Mary looked doubtful, and glanced at the excited crowds. 'I should never have come to London. I've done nothing to deserve meeting the queen, and I don't know what I would have to say to her.'

'You can tell the queen you've had the hardest job of all.' I gave her hand a gentle squeeze. 'It can't have been easy to wait for the best part of three years, not knowing if I would return.'

Her answer was drowned out by cheering and applause, which told us the royal party had finally arrived. The queen made the two-mile journey upriver from Greenwich Palace at the head of a procession of gilded royal barges. Rowed by dozens of red-liveried oarsmen, they were an impressive sight as they lined up at the quay.

First came the queen's heralds, followed by Sir Christopher Hatton, with the yeomen of the queen's guard, armed with swords and shining halberds. Her yeomen held back the crowds as Sir Christopher led the queen and her ladies-in-waiting to the widened gangplank.

Behind them followed a group of richly dressed nobles and

courtiers. Sir William Cecil wasn't among them, and I regretted offering him ten bars of Spanish gold to try to win his favour. Sir William's terse refusal made me worry I'd made an enemy of him, although I had other equally influential supporters at court. I couldn't see Francis Walsingham, but recognised the French ambassador, Monsieur de Marchaumont.

At my signal, my trumpeters played a fanfare, accompanied by a rattling drum roll. The red-and-blue royal standard, with its golden leopards, quartered with the lilies of France, unfurled from the top of the mainmast. Colourful silk banners, gifts from the Sultan of Ternate, streamed in the breeze. I removed my hat and bowed to the queen in welcome, and Mary and Margaret gave her a graceful curtsey.

On the scrubbed deck, where sailors once fought off savage Indians, battled storms and caught flying fish, trestle tables were covered with fresh white linen. They groaned under the weight of a seafood banquet of oysters and sturgeon, conger eels and lampreys, chines of salmon, with sweet sugar delicacies, and gilded goblets of wine for our guests.

Queen Elizabeth took her place in a throne with a cushion of purple velvet, commissioned for her visit, flanked by her ladies-in-waiting, and seemed to be enjoying herself as my viol players struck up a melodic tune, accompanied by my drummers. My nephew John danced a jig, applauded by the queen, courtiers and watching crowds.

Then came the moment I'd been sworn on oath not to mention to anyone. The queen ordered me to kneel, and the onlookers fell silent while Ambassador de Marchaumont drew his sword and lay it on my shoulder.

'I dub thee knight. Rise, Sir Francis Drake.' The watching crowds gave a rousing cheer.

After so many years of being looked down upon by the nobility, treated as a commoner, and being called a man of low birth, I'd become a man of importance, a knight of the realm. If anyone now dared to call me a pirate, they would be answerable to the queen.

I bowed my head. *'God bless our queen, guide our ways, and give us grace our Lord to please. For what we are about to receive, may the Lord make us truly thankful.'*

Servants dressed as sailors poured wine and ale, bringing baskets of bread and silver platters of fish of every kind. Another fanfare brought more applause as the centrepiece, a baked porpoise swimming in a sea of small silver fish, was placed on the queen's table.

After the long banquet, I presented the queen with a gift of a golden astrolabe, and precious silks brought from the East Indies. To more cheers from the crowds, the royal procession began to make their way back to the waiting barges.

Cries of alarm and panic made me turn to see the wooden gangplank break in two with a rending crash, throwing people into the mud. The queen, her ladies, and the nobles had all crossed safely, but the aldermen and guild masters who followed proved too much for the makeshift gangway.

I would have thought the accident a bad omen, but the queen laughed at the sight of the pompous dignitaries. Dressed in their finest clothes, they cursed and scrambled to escape the slippery Thames mud at the bottom of the dry dock. I thanked God it looked as if no one had been hurt, especially Her Majesty.

After the queen and her party left I contrived a moment alone in my cabin with Mary. 'I know it is small compensation for the long months we've been parted, but now you are Lady Drake, and shall have your proper place in society.'

Mary looked at me as if the thought hadn't occurred to her. 'Will we have to move to London?'

I heard the note of concern in her voice, and smiled. 'Buckland Abbey has always been a special place to me. It's only seven miles from Crowndale, where I was born. Now it will become our family home, safe from the plague in Plymouth. There's more room for Margaret and the boys, and grounds where you can go riding. I'm content with my rented rooms, but we shall find a London house, in keeping with our position.'

She shook her head in despair at my ambition, but kissed me on the cheek. 'Why were you knighted by the ambassador of France, instead of the queen?'

'It was a ploy, another of Queen Elizabeth's tricks.'

'But why?'

'Monsieur de Marchaumont is here to arrange for the queen to marry the King of France's younger brother, Francis, Duke of Anjou and Alençon.'

'Do you think she *will* marry him?'

'I doubt it. She calls him her little frog.'

'You gave the queen a present of a little gold frog!'

I grinned. 'Duke Francis is half her age, and heir to the throne of France, but his face is disfigured by the pox and he has a crooked spine.'

'You've seen him?'

'He attended a reception at Windsor Castle. Everyone at court talks of the match, but Walsingham plays his game of keeping an alliance with the French. The Spanish will be furious when they learn who has knighted me – so Queen Elizabeth has drawn the French closer, without having to marry anyone.'

Buckland Abbey had been converted into a comfortable family home at great expense by the younger Richard Grenville. The Grenville family would never have consented to sell the abbey to me, so negotiations were completed through agents.

The only change I'd made was to paint over the Grenville family crest in the great hall. In its place was my new coat of arms, with a wavy line representing the sea, silver stars for the poles and a ship on top of a globe.

We'd not been in residence at Buckland for long before I had to tell Mary my bad news.

'I have to return to London, on legal business.'

'Would you like me to come with you?'

I could tell from her tone she didn't relish the prospect of the long journey. 'I don't expect I'll be away for long. It concerns John Doughty. He's determined to have me tried for the death of his brother, and I need to put an end to it.' My hand formed a fist in frustration.

'What are you going to do?' Mary looked concerned.

I took her in my arms and held her close. 'I'm going to call in a few favours, that's all.' I kissed her. 'You have my word.'

Her thin body relaxed a little, and she returned my kiss. 'The first time we met, you gave a sermon in the church about how faith keeps a ship on a true course.' She smiled. 'I shall pray for your safe return.'

Francis Walsingham seemed unsurprised at my request, and no doubt felt obliged to help. 'A vengeful man is dangerous, if he has the law in his favour.'

I had to agree. 'Doughty has the approval of the Lord Chief Justice to proceed against me in the courts over the death of his brother.'

Walsingham nodded. 'So I understand.'

'Is there anything that can be done to stop him?'

'There is always something that can be done, Sir Francis.

Accounts of your voyages are the queen's secrets of the realm, and all participants are sworn to secrecy, on pain of death.'

I heard the sinister note in Walsingham's voice. 'I thought to challenge the jurisdiction of the courts over actions taken at sea, on the other side of the world.'

'As the matter was outside the realm, this case would have to be heard by the Earl Marshal and the Lord High Constable, a position which is currently vacant.'

'There will be a delay?'

Walsingham's eyes narrowed. 'I need a little time to complete my investigations, but there has been an allegation that the Spanish offered John Doughty twenty thousand ducats to kidnap and kill you.'

My throat felt dry at the thought. 'Is there any evidence of this?'

'We have a witness in custody. In the meantime, I'm sure Her Majesty will be in no hurry to appoint a new Lord High Constable.'

I thanked Francis Walsingham, but glanced over my shoulder as I walked back to my rooms at Elbow Street. One problem was solved, but now I'd learned of another, more serious danger. My hand went to the handle of my dagger. An assassin would have ample opportunity to take me by surprise, and I must be on my guard.

Our bedchamber, above the former nave at Buckland Abbey, was twice the size of our room at Notte Street. Mary had asked for the mullioned windows to be covered, and the light from flickering candles cast their waxy yellow pall over her pale face. Mary opened her eyes as I sat on the bed and pulled off my riding boots.

'How are you feeling?' I put my hand to her forehead. It felt cool, with no sign of a fever.

'I'm tired, all the time.' She groaned as she sat up, and I used a down-filled pillow to support her back.

A chill draft made me glance at the fireplace. The servants had let the fire burn to ash, and I would have to speak to them. The icy rooms might have suited the Cistercian monks who built the original abbey, but Mary needed to be kept warm.

'The councillors have elected me Mayor of Plymouth.' I forced a smile. 'The stipend is only twenty pounds a year, but it's a great honour – and I become captain of the fort.'

'Who would have thought it?' She spoke softly, her words little more than a whisper.

'John Blitheman has offered to take me around the city boundaries, and show me what I need to do. I think they hope I'll help to fatten the city coffers. I've also been made a Justice of the Peace, so I believe I'll be busy enough.'

Mary's brow furrowed in concern. 'Won't you be too busy to stay here with me?'

'I shall ask for a leave of absence.' I forced a smile. 'I wish to remain until you are well again.'

I crossed to the window and pulled back the heavy velvet coverings. In the courtyard John and Jonas, the sons I'd longed for, now grown into young men, practised archery with the yew bows I'd bought them.

I would soon have to tell them that my plan to take them in a flotilla to wrest Portugal from Spain had come to nothing. They would be disappointed, but not as much as I had been. The venture proved a financial disaster. A fleet of eight warships had been assembled, crews recruited and supplies purchased.

The whole business had been a poorly kept secret, so we should not have been surprised when news of our plans reached the ears of Ambassador Mendoza. King Philip sent word to

Queen Elizabeth that supporting any claim to the throne of Portugal would be taken as a declaration of war.

The queen commanded the entire enterprise to be abandoned, and we were forbidden from sailing. The money recovered from selling the stores went back to the investors, but not one penny had been returned to me. I cursed at how another opportunity to have my revenge on the King of Spain slipped through my fingers like a handful of elvers.

William Hawkins had tried to console me with a new, equally ambitious plan. He proposed a voyage to the East Indies to establish trade in spices and silks with the wealthy Sultan of Ternate. I looked down as my nephew raised his powerful bow, and wondered if he was ready to command a ship of his own.

I opened the window to let in fresh air, then turned to Mary. I thought she'd be amused to hear that I was to have my portrait painted for the first time, but in miniature, by our neighbour Nicholas Hilliard. I'd been godfather to his son, named Francis in my honour, and the portrait was his way of thanking me. Mary's eyes were closed. I kissed her on the cheek, and left, closing the door as silently as I could.

21

JANUARY 1582

Francis Walsingham's young maidservant gave me a curious glance as she brought a silver tray with a bottle and two glasses. I watched as she set it down on the polished table, and poured us each a drink. Walsingham dismissed her with a wave of his hand, and frowned as she closed the door behind her with a heavy clunk.

He had been as good as his word. The troublesome John Doughty had been locked up in Marshalsea prison in Southwark. That meant the end of his vindictive plans to hold me to account for the treachery of his brother. I expected now would be the time for me to return the favour.

Walsingham handed me my glass with a pitying frown. 'I'm sorry to hear your wife is unwell.'

I nodded in acknowledgement. 'Mary's physicians are at a loss.' I sipped my drink, surprised to feel the rich, warming heat in my throat. 'I try to stay close to her at Buckland Abbey, but confess I'm glad of an excuse to return to London, and was intrigued by your note.'

Walsingham swirled his drink in his glass. 'Armagnac, a gift from our ambassador of France.' He savoured the taste before

234

continuing. 'My stepson, Christopher Carleill, has an interest in the Muscovy Trading Company. They plan to expand trade to the East Indies, and have secured the backing of the Earl of Leicester.'

'You want me to lead another venture?' I raised an eyebrow. 'I lost a great deal of money when Her Majesty cancelled our last escapade.'

He shook his head. 'By your own account, you have enough on your hands. Martin Frobisher is to be in command, and I should tell you that one of the ships proposed is the *Elizabeth*.'

'I should have guessed. Once again, the queen's hand is firmly on the tiller.'

Walsingham frowned at my tone, but the resentment of being passed over left a bitter taste in my mouth; I was better qualified than Martin Frobisher, with more relevant experience, but I understood. Frobisher was an experienced commander, and must have seen an opportunity to redeem his tarnished reputation, after the disaster of his last venture.

'What would you have me do?'

'I would be more confident about investing if we had the benefit of your support.' Walsingham gave me a rare smile, not echoed in his eyes. 'I've no doubt Sir Christopher Hatton and, of course, my stepson would be equally appreciative.'

I took another sip of the rich Armagnac, savouring the taste as I considered the implications.

'I've been thinking of offering my nephew the chance of his own command. My new barque, the *Francis*, can be made ready by the spring. She's only forty tons, but built for speed.'

'Then you're with us?'

'I am, and I can find you men with experience of sailing through the Strait of Magellan.'

'We must learn from what happened last time. I have a man within Mendoza's network who tells me the ambassador suspects something is being planned. Take care to keep our intentions secret, or we'll find the Strait of Magellan is full of Spanish warships.'

'Why do we allow Mendoza to live here so freely, when we know he reports everything to King Philip?'

Walsingham scowled. 'Her Majesty hopes for peace with Spain, and if I deport Bernardino de Mendoza, he'll simply be replaced with someone else.'

'You could let it be known that our plan is to sail around the Cape of Good Hope, and across the Indian sea.'

Walsingham raised his glass in a toast. 'To the East Indies venture.'

John stared at me in amazement when I told him the news. I was glad of the need to busy myself with the meetings and preparations, and immediately set to work. New swivel guns were fitted to the *Francis*, and a pinnace was built, then dismantled and fitted inside her hold.

I briefed the captains on the perils of the Strait of Magellan, and showed them where fresh water could be found. I had copies made of several of my charts, marked with secret symbols showing where to watch for dangerous natives, and the best islands for trade.

I helped John with the selection of his crew, including William Markham, our sailing master from the *Golden Hinde*, and Will Hawkins, eldest son of my old friend William, who'd sailed with Captain John Wynter on the *Elizabeth*.

I also found a minister named Richard Maddox, to keep up their spirits. He had no experience of life at sea, but Maddox promised to keep notes of the voyage.

In no time I found myself in the bustling port of Southampton, ready to see the fleet depart. If Walsingham believed this venture could be kept secret he was mistaken. The crowded quayside had the air of a May fair, with street traders selling pies and ale, and many small boats circling the great sailing ships.

As well as the *Elizabeth* and the *Francis*, the Earl of Leicester purchased an impressive four-hundred-ton galleon, the *Bear*, and renamed it as his flagship *Leicester*. Mindful of the need to protect their interests, the Muscovy Trading Company paid for a forty-seven-gun warship, the *Edward Bonaventure*.

I made my way through the crowds of noisy onlookers, and found my barque *Francis* straining at her moorings at the quay. My nephew John had sailed her around the south coast from Plymouth without incident, and he looked pleased with himself as he greeted me.

'Welcome aboard, Uncle.' He grinned. 'The *Francis* might be the smallest in our fleet, but she's fast, and sails well to windward.'

'I wish you success, John. Do well, and the *Francis* shall be yours when you return.' I smiled at his wide eyes. 'I made my start in much the same way – and I trust you'll take good care of her if you have a vested interest.'

'I'll not disappoint you, Uncle, you have my word.' He gave me a questioning look. 'What do you make of the news about our captain general?'

'All I know is Martin Frobisher has fallen out of favour with the Muscovy Company about some financial matter. Your new commander, Edward Fenton, served as his second in command on his last two voyages – and is also John Hawkins' brother-in-law.'

John frowned at the implication. 'He's not liked by the men, and has a temper. I wish you were coming with us. Is it too late for you to take Frobisher's place?'

I smiled at his naivety. 'I confess I would have liked to, but

Mary is no better, and I've promised to remain at her side. I've also been persuaded to put my name forward as Member of Parliament for Bossiney, and hope to have a more active role than I could in the past.'

'Please tell Mary I shall pray for her, and give my regards to Jonas.'

'I shall.' I placed my hand on his shoulder. 'I know you think I'm wrong to keep Jonas at home, but this venture is too long and too dangerous for his first sea voyage.' I reached into a pocket of my doublet and handed him my silver whistle. 'I wish you to have this for good luck. It served me well for many years, and has seen action in the East and West Indies.'

John studied the whistle. 'I shall treasure it, Uncle.' He smiled, like the boy I remembered. 'Thank you.'

A strange foreboding troubled me as I watched the fleet sail. I shared my nephew's misgivings about Edward Fenton's reputation. He'd not made the best start, sailing without several of his crew, including Will Hawkins, who had to be taken aboard the *Francis*. If not for my promise to Mary, I could have appealed to the queen to permit me to sail as captain general, but it was too late.

John was the closest I'd ever have to a son. I'd done all I could to teach him everything I knew, yet as I rode back home I worried that I'd pushed him too far. Even Captain John Wynter failed to cope with the storms at the cape, but he'd had the experience to know when to turn back and save his crew.

A crescent moon, surrounded by bright stars, glowed in the dark sky by the time I returned to Buckland Abbey, tired after the hundred-and-thirty mile journey. The ride from Southampton had taken the best part of four days, and I was relieved to be home.

I expected to find only servants awake, so was surprised to be greeted by Mary's sister Margaret. She'd become indispensable to me since Mary's illness. After a succession of unsuitable housekeepers, Margaret offered to take responsibility for the daily running of the Buckland estate, and I trusted her decisions.

An unspoken bond had formed between us, and I thought of her as the sister I'd never had. Margaret proved to be the best nurse Mary could wish for, and knew how to keep Jonas working with his tutors, when he'd rather be out riding in the grounds.

'I'm relieved you're back.' Margaret glanced up the staircase, as if worried we might be overheard. 'I regret to tell you Mary has taken a turn for the worse. She hasn't eaten properly since you left. I've tried feeding her broth each day, but cook despairs of finding anything to restore her appetite.'

'Have you sent for her doctor?'

She nodded. 'I told him we were expecting you to return today, and he's waiting in your study.' Margaret looked as if she was going to say something else, but decided against it.

'What is it, Margaret?' I put my hand on her arm, surprised by her soft warmth after Mary's coldness. 'You can speak freely with me.'

She frowned before answering. 'Mary begged me not to summon the doctor. She says his potions make her feel worse.'

'Thank you, Margaret. It's late. You should go to bed. I'll take care of her now.'

I entered the room I'd chosen as my study. Once belonging to Sir Richard Grenville, the huge hearth of local stone kept it warm, even in the winter months. The impressive antlers of a long-dead stag still decorated one wall, while a faded tapestry of a hunting scene filled most of another.

The doctor stood as I entered, and I noticed he'd been reading my well-thumbed translation of the voyages of Ferdinand Magellan. A stern-faced man, he had a reputation as one of the best doctors in Devon, and was a member of the London College of Physicians. I'd never seen him smile.

'Tell me as it is, doctor.' I'd grown tired of the mystery surrounding Mary's ailment, and he seemed to understand.

'Your wife has an imbalance of humours, which makes her melancholic.'

'What can you do for her?'

The doctor stroked his pointed beard, as if he'd not been expecting my question. 'She needs rest, Sir Francis. I've prescribed her a potion of wormwood and balm, with some mint, which has restorative powers.'

'Thank you, doctor.'

I doubted he had any more idea than I did about what ailed her. I would care for Mary myself, with the help of Margaret. My wife had survived the plague, which took so many of our neighbours in Plymouth, and with God's grace would survive this mystery illness as well.

After the doctor left I called for a cup of warmed milk, and carried it up to our bedchamber. A platter of plums, which Margaret had left to tempt her, sat untouched on Mary's side table. I pulled up a chair and helped myself to a plum, savouring the sweet taste as I wondered how much to tell her.

'The doctor says you will soon be well, but need to rest. I've brought some milk. You should drink it while it's still warm.'

Mary took the cup with both hands and sipped the warmed milk. Her eyes met mine and I could tell even this was an effort. She'd always been slim, but her pale arms and hands looked worryingly thin.

'How was your journey?' Her voice sounded weak.

'Long as ever, but at least the weather held.' I smiled. 'John looks a proper ship's captain now. I was proud of him.'

'He seems young to be in command.'

The hint of disapproval annoyed me. 'He's a Drake. John was born to live at sea, and has our sailing master from the *Golden Hinde* as his second in command.' I handed her a plum. 'You must eat, Mary. You need to build your strength.'

She didn't put it in her mouth. Instead she held the plum in her thin fingers, in much the same way as the queen had held the large emerald I'd given to her. Mary took a bite, then dropped the plum back on to the plate. It was a start.

William Hawkins tutted like a foraging hen as he studied the yellowed parchment deeds of the properties I'd been granted by the queen. The legal notes were in such small handwriting he had to squint to see them. He traced the words with his finger and tut-tutted again, shaking his head, and looked up at me, a glint of humour in his eyes.

'Granted in reversion. The manor of Sherford has a sitting tenant. You'll have to pay the wages of a bailiff, some six or seven shillings a year.' He passed the deed back to me. 'I recommend you transfer this when you can, or put the rent to a good cause, such as alms to the poor.'

'I'm glad of your advice, William.' I folded the deed and retied the red legal ribbon, handing him another. He unfolded it and laughed when he saw the title. 'The bishopric of Durham?'

'The grant includes Durham Castle, but I understand it's in poor repair, and I fear the upkeep will be something of a liability.'

William nodded. 'I don't doubt it. Durham is at least four hundred miles from here, so you'd have to rely on your agents.'

I stared at the pile of deeds in disappointment as I guessed the remainder would be much the same. 'I'm sure Her Majesty's gifts were well-intended.'

He nodded. 'It seems her advisors have taken the opportunity to offload some liabilities.'

I looked across at William, now an important local landlord. 'The profits from merchant ventures can be high, but so are the risks, as we both know to our cost. I need to invest in local property, while I have the means to do it.'

'You are right. I can sell you the leases of good houses in Plymouth, and a half share in the mills at Plympton if you like. The manor of Yarcombe, north-east of Honiton, has come up for sale.' He grinned. 'You'd be lord of the manor. The whole village and surrounding farms are all part of the Yarcombe estate.'

I frowned. 'The owner of Yarcombe Manor is a kinsman of mine, the son of Sir Bernard Drake. I've been in dispute with Sir Bernard about my claim to the Drake family wyvern for the crest of my coat of arms.'

'They are saying he's threatened to box your ears.' William laughed at the thought.

I didn't share his amusement. 'That's typical of his attitude – but I suspect he's been more underhand, and complained to the Master of Arms to prevent me from using it, although I have the right to do so.'

'If you think he'd refuse to sell to you, I could act on your behalf, and secure Yarcombe at a fair price.'

I liked the idea. 'My Buckland Abbey estate has plenty of land. If I add the manors of Sherford and Yarcombe...'

'You would become one of the most important landowners in the West Country.'

'I would also like to buy as many freehold properties in

Plymouth as you can sell to me, but I need to take my time, to avoid drawing attention to the source of my funds.'

'I'm afraid we don't have much time, Francis, as I'm going to be away at sea for a while. In fact, I could be away for more than a year.'

I stared at him in amazement, my head full of questions. 'Where are you going? When were you going to tell me?'

William hesitated for a moment. 'I'm sworn to secrecy, so you must not tell anyone. The mission is to meet up with Edward Fenton's flotilla, and seize the Moluccas from the Portuguese.'

'Have I been excluded because of Mary's illness?'

'I'm sorry, Francis. I'm sixty-three, and this is my last chance to put to sea as captain general.'

I sat back in my chair. 'You are right, as ever, William, and have always been a true friend to me. Mary needs me here, but I hope you'll let me pay for the fitting out of two ships to escort you.'

After he left I sat alone in my study, staring at my charts of the Southern Sea. In the corners, my talented nephew had drawn a war canoe, rowed by Indians, and the *Golden Hinde* in full sail. I worried about John, and would give anything to join him, but took some comfort from William's mission to find him.

22

JANUARY 1583

Apart from a dusting of snow, the parish church in St Budeaux looked the same as the day I'd been married there. On that bright summer's day, I was young and ambitious, with my whole future ahead of me. Mary had said her vows in a clear voice, her shining, deep-brown eyes never once leaving mine.

The bells, high in the church tower, abruptly stopped their mournful clanging, leaving a haunting silence. I shivered as drifting flakes of snow settled on my beard and heavy coat. My brother Thomas brushed the snow from my shoulders, breaking through my reverie. He glanced at the half-open church door.

'It's time.'

Struggling to compose myself, I hesitated to enter the church. I wasn't ready to say goodbye, and part of me wished I could be away at sea, in some far-off land, as I had been when my father died. Then, it was my brother John, back in Medway, who had to deal with the arrangements. This time I'd relied on Thomas.

Memories swirled through my mind like misted breath in the frozen air. My mother's gold ring had fitted her slender finger perfectly. A good omen – or so I'd believed. I recalled how

Diego fought for every precious moment of life. Mary had surrendered to her illness, accepting her fate as God's judgement.

'It wasn't her fault.'

Thomas turned to me. 'I'm sorry?'

I'd muttered my thoughts aloud, but needed to talk. 'I wished for a son, to inherit, but that was not God's will. Mary blamed herself, but I could not have wished for a better son than our nephew John.'

'He has the makings of an able sailor.' He smiled. 'And that young rascal Jonas is brighter than the two of us put together.' Thomas stepped towards the church. 'We must go in, Francis. They're waiting.'

Margaret, like her sister's ghost in her black mourning gown, greeted me and led me past friends and family to the front pew. My eyes went to the oak coffin with brass handles, standing on wooden trestles. I choked back tears at the knowledge my wife lay inside, so close but forever out of reach. I would never hold her in my arms again.

I'd never asked her about Thomas Doughty, or about the mysterious man who offered to marry her when they thought I'd been lost at sea. I'd never mentioned Maria, or how we left her to take her chances with her child. I'd not kept my promise to be a better husband to Mary. So many regrets weighed heavily, like a sea anchor on my spirit.

I tried to listen to the service, but my thoughts returned to our happy wedding day, in this same church, all those years ago. Harry Newman had been determined to match me with his sister. I'd repaid his great compliment by sending him on a fool's errand, from which he never returned.

My younger brother John had refused to wear a starched white ruff, or the tall felt hat I'd bought him in place of his sailor's cap, until I insisted. Now he lay in an unmarked grave on a deserted island in the West Indies, shot in the back by the Spanish. To my regret, we'd not been on speaking terms when I saw him last.

All eyes turned to me. The time had come for me to say a few words. I took a deep breath as I tried to draw strength from my faith. I'd left my father's book of Psalms behind, yet I knew enough by heart. I took my place and stared at the waiting congregation.

'Jesus said to her, I am the resurrection and the life. The one who believes in me will live, even though they die...'

The familiar words of the Gospel of John wouldn't come to me, and I stood in silence, struggling to control my thoughts. Someone at the back of the church stifled a cough, and I managed to continue.

'Whoever lives by believing in me will never die. Amen.'

Tears formed in my eyes and I stumbled to my pew, glad I had my back to the congregation. Margaret took my hand in hers with a comforting squeeze. For a brief moment, it felt as if Mary had returned to me. I'd loved my wife, and made a lady of her, yet would regret the lost years, when I could have been at her side, for the rest of my days.

Admiral John Hawkins' grey eyes were as sharp and impassive as ever as he studied me. As always, I found it hard to read his thoughts. I guessed he might be thinking I'd put on weight. Life as a Member of Parliament included a good number of meetings like this, over dinner.

'Congratulations on your appointment to the Navy Review Board, Francis. It needs more men with experience of the challenges of life at sea.' He stabbed a slice of veal loin with his fork, and dipped it in the spiced German sauce.

I nodded in agreement. 'Our chairman is Lord Burghley. As far as I know he's never been aboard a ship – and he cares little for the pay of common sailors.'

I took another mouthful of succulent meat, a little too rare for my taste, wondering when he was going to ask the favour. I'd had to learn entirely new skills in Westminster, as well as a different set of values. Connections mattered, and I'd learned the hard way that politics was about patronage. Results weren't achieved by honest toil, but by who you knew, and whether they owed you favours.

John Hawkins was one of the many important people who'd treated me differently, although not as an equal, since my knighthood. At first I'd been pleased, but I would rather be acknowledged for my achievements than for my title.

'I hear Her Majesty refused to sign royal assent to your Sunday Bill.' His tone carried an unexpected hint of challenge.

I'd become used to envious comments about my closeness to the queen. The summons could come at any time. I might find myself presented to a foreign ambassador, taken for a walk in the ornamental gardens, or called upon to be witty and amusing for the queen and her gossiping ladies. Sometimes I wondered if I'd become the court jester, and if they mocked my Devon accent behind my back.

'All I wanted was greater respect for the Sabbath day. I supported the proposal for a ban on bear-baiting, a savage form of entertainment. Only last month eight men were killed on the Sabbath when the bear-baiting pit collapsed at Paris Gardens – a sure sign of God's displeasure!' I took a sip of the Gascony claret, savouring the earthy aftertaste. 'I was persuaded to add amendments to ban hawking and hunting on a Sunday.'

'I'm not surprised there were so many objections.' John Hawkins smiled. 'It's a brave politician who comes between a gentleman and his sport.'

'I've never claimed to be brave, only to do what I thought right.' I regretted the defensive note in my voice, a weakness I'd never overcome.

'Which is what you will do on the Navy Review Board.'

I waited while a servant refilled my glass. 'Tell me about Sir William Wynter.'

John Hawkins scowled at the name. 'My reforms of the navy were bound to be opposed by those with vested interests. William Wynter is one of the most outspoken. You know he's accused me of corruption?' His face flushed with anger at the thought.

'The review might be the best way to clear your name.'

He scowled. 'I've served for four years as Treasurer of the Navy, and deserve better.'

I was surprised to find myself feeling sorry for him. There would have been questionable contracts awarded, and opportunities missed. That was the way of things. John Hawkins did his best, and deserved a knighthood more than I did. At least my new position meant I had the power to help restore his reputation. Together we would prepare the English navy for war with the Spanish, which would surely come.

I'd met Luke Warde when I briefed the captains of Edward Fenton's fleet before they sailed. I'd been impressed by his questions, which showed his experience as a commander. He told me he'd been on all three of Martin Frobisher's previous voyages, and seemed a good choice as Fenton's vice admiral.

Troubled by news that the *Edward Bonaventure* had returned home unexpectedly, I made the long and tiring journey back to Southampton to find out why. Captain Warde welcomed me aboard his ship, but his face looked grim as he led me to his spartan, white-painted cabin.

'You must be wondering about the rest of the fleet, and your nephew, Sir Francis?'

'I am. I believe myself a good judge of character, Captain Warde, and you don't seem the sort of man to return early without good reason.'

'I'll tell you what I can – although, in truth, I've no idea what's become of your barque, the *Francis*.'

My pulse quickened with concern for John, yet my own fleets had been scattered often enough by storms, and still found each other again. 'Please, Captain, I'd like to know what happened.'

Luke Warde frowned. 'We were making good headway off the coast of Portuguese Brazil, in the second week of December. That's when we told our crews of our true plan, to sail through the Strait of Magellan instead of around the cape.'

'How did they take it?'

'You know how rumours spread on a ship. It came as little enough surprise, until we captured a Spanish carrack bound for the River Plate. She carried settlers, who told us the strait is well fortified. I didn't witness it myself, but Captain Fenton disagreed with his second in command about the best course of action.'

'You mean young Will Hawkins?'

'Will had set his sights on following your route, and was against rounding the cape.'

'I understand, but it shows his lack of experience. What did Captain Fenton do?'

'He ordered us to reverse course, and we headed north towards São Vicente. The weather worsened, and that night a storm scattered the fleet. I regret to say that was the last we saw of the *Francis*.'

'Do you think there's a chance my nephew has gone for the strait on his own?'

'It's possible – he could have run aground or been cast up on the shore. He could also have been attacked by the Spanish, as we were threatened by three Spanish galleons one night. I believe they thought us easy prey, and didn't expect us to be so heavily armed. We defeated them at São Vicente. One was sunk and the other two suffered serious damage.'

'How did you end up returning alone?' The question had been on my mind from the moment I'd heard.

'The captain general declared our mission over. Our supplies were running short, we couldn't find anywhere safe to resupply, and we didn't have the ammunition to risk another encounter with Spanish warships. We also had injured men. Our chaplain, Richard Maddox, was one of those who died of his wounds.'

'I'm sorry to hear that. Maddox seemed a good man, and I'd thought to make him my own chaplain.'

Luke Warde sat in silence for a moment, then looked up at me. 'Captain Fenton will be here soon. God willing, he might have more information about what's become of your nephew's ship.'

I returned to my London lodgings with a heavy heart. I should never have encouraged my nephew to sail with Captain Fenton. John proved himself capable of commanding the *Francis*, and I didn't believe he'd been lost in a storm. I cheered myself with the thought that he'd given Captain Fenton the slip and made his own way to the Southern Sea.

What troubled me was the news that the Spanish defended the Strait of Magellan. It should not come as a surprise, and Luke Warde seemed certain that what the Spanish settlers told him was true. I knew there were many narrow passages, islands and headlands within the strait to set up a fort. It would be easy enough to capture an unwary ship with an inexperienced captain.

My servants had a welcome fire burning in the hearth and brought me a goblet of mulled wine, together with two letters. I sat in my favourite chair by the fire and broke open the red wax seal of the first. My old friend William Hawkins was back in Plymouth, and wanted my help. He'd returned with his fleet of seven ships from raids in the West Indies. His holds were filled with Spanish gold, and he wanted to know how news of his success might be received.

By chance, the second letter contained the answer to his question. Francis Walsingham's terse note advised me that the Spanish had tried to seize English merchant ships in their ports. Queen Elizabeth had the excuse she needed for reprisals, and William Hawkins' treasure would provide the means to achieve it.

23

FEBRUARY 1585

I stared into the polished silver plate, trying to see my own reflection. The frowning man who stared back at me looked tired, his face scarred under one eye and a wart on the side of his nose. The chill of self-doubt made me reconsider the wisdom of what I planned to do.

Elizabeth Sydenham was beautiful, sophisticated – and twenty years younger than me. Young enough, as my scornful brother Thomas pointed out, to be my daughter. Most importantly, Elizabeth was the only child of the influential landowner Sir George Sydenham, Sheriff of Somerset.

Her mother, also named Elizabeth, told me her late father was the famous judge and Master of the Rolls, Sir Christopher Hales. In the service of King Henry VIII, he'd presided over the trial of Her Majesty's mother, Queen Anne Boleyn.

Once, Elizabeth Sydenham would have been out of my reach, but now her father welcomed my proposal. Like many old families, he had the name and vast estates in Somerset, yet his wealth had been invested in property. As well as my collection of manors, I had access to a greater fortune than he could imagine.

My first recollection of seeing Elizabeth was on an autumn

morning, in the queen's rose garden at Hampton Court. Her Majesty preferred to surround herself with elderly matrons, a grey backdrop to her own magnificence. I'd been surprised to see one of her maids of honour so young and attractive – and giving me a warm smile.

Even the queen joked I was one of her most eligible subjects, and if I waited any longer I'd be too elderly to remarry. In truth, I'd been too busy to give the matter much thought. As well as my work on the navy reforms, I'd been making secret preparations for the grandest fleet to ever sail from Plymouth.

I might have settled for the life of a widower, had fate not intervened at a reception given by my neighbour at Fitzford House. My host, John Fitz, mischievously sat Elizabeth Sydenham at my side. Her flawless young face framed by a fashionable ruff, her auburn hair was tucked under a velvet hat, ringed with a jewelled band of gold.

She'd placed her gloved hand on my arm and leaned close. 'Father told me your great secret, Sir Francis.'

My pulse raced, and my head filled with urgent questions. Had her father learned of my secret cache of gold? Had a crewman from the *Golden Hinde* gossiped about Maria, who haunted my conscience like a restless ghost, or was someone spreading rumours to ruin me?

'I confess I've no idea—'

'Don't look so worried.' She'd smiled, revealing perfect white teeth, like those of a child. 'I promise not to tell a living soul.'

Elizabeth's warmth surprised me. Her whispered voice had a flirtatious tone, and her attention took me completely by surprise. I looked into her brown eyes and saw a twinkle of amusement. In an instant my hard-won sense of self-importance evaporated like a morning mist in sunshine.

My arm tingled with her possessive grip, as if she had laid claim to me, and rendered me powerless to her charms. In the two years since Mary's death I'd not been so close to another woman, particularly one so young and lively. Even now, my face flushed as I recalled how tongue-tied I'd been that day, like an innocent boy.

I later discovered that the secret she'd been referring to was the flotilla assembling in Plymouth Sound. The secret became common knowledge soon afterwards, but Walsingham stressed the need to keep preparations confidential. Even William Cecil supported our plan and warned of the need for urgency, before the queen had a change of heart.

Now Elizabeth and I were to be married, something I struggled to come to terms with. I still missed Mary, and there'd not been time to think about my true feelings for Elizabeth. I didn't believe she could have fallen in love with me, although I enjoyed the envious glances of other men when we were out together.

Elizabeth's parents had been quick to have Sir George Sydenham's lawyers draw up a marriage settlement, whereby I bequeathed my manors and estates to Elizabeth and our heirs. He'd acted as if it was a formality, but I understood he wished to protect his daughter's interests, as his only heir.

The Norman church of All Saints in Monksilver, a village in north-west Somerset, was festooned with garlands of white roses. My brother Thomas had grudgingly agreed to help me with the arrangements, although I sensed he would rather not have been asked. He seemed uncomfortable in Elizabeth's company, and I suspected he was jealous.

Unlike my first marriage, when the church had been crowded to the rafters with friends and neighbours, several rows of wooden pews stood empty. We fitted comfortably into the south chapel. Elizabeth's parents sat at the front, with a group of her giggling young friends behind, and some older ladies who I presumed were her aunts.

Elizabeth looked beautiful in an elegant satin gown and

kirtle with a plunging neckline. I found it hard not to stare at the diamond pendant on a gold necklace which drew attention to the soft curves of her body. The white silk ruff at her neck matched the cuffs of her gown and, for once, her long auburn hair was worn loose, a symbol of purity.

Our voices echoed as we repeated our vows, my Devon accent contrasting with Elizabeth's cultured and confident tone. I'd thought of reading from my father's book of Psalms, and brought the precious volume with me, but the dour minister seemed in a hurry to conclude the ceremony.

I was mystified at how happy Elizabeth seemed. People pretended friendship while seeking patronage because of my fortune, or after I'd become a national hero, yet her affection seemed genuine. As if in a dream, I placed the gold ring on her finger and heard us being pronounced man and wife.

She took my hand in hers and kissed me on the cheek, as if I was some kindly uncle. I overheard someone call her Lady Drake, and felt a fleeting moment of sadness. Mary had been a little bewildered to discover she'd gained the title. Elizabeth took it as hers by right, as she had been born to do.

We rode in the carriage through narrow, winding country lanes to her father's home for the reception. I glanced across at her slender waist and realised that my dream of having children of my own may be within reach. God willing, I might have a son to inherit my fortune. The thought of children reminded me of my nephew John, risking his life in the Strait of Magellan, and Jonas, not forgotten at Buckland Abbey.

Combe Sydenham Hall, a grand manor house, was surrounded by woodland and a five-hundred-acre deer park. Minstrels played in a gallery, raised over the great hall which was set for our wedding banquet with some eighty guests, the great and good of Somerset.

An impressive centrepiece of a sailing ship made from sugar

in a sea of small fish dominated the top table. A procession of liveried servants carried plates of roasted venison, spiced suckling pigs, sturgeon cooked in parsley and vinegar, herons and capons covered with powdered ginger.

I sat down to enthusiastic applause after my rambling speech, in which I suggested marriage was a greater challenge than sailing around the world. My new wife was deep in discussion with her father, so I turned to my brother, seated at my side. He toyed with a dish of roasted quail in a rich claret sauce, and had been unusually quiet.

'This banquet is better attended than the ceremony.'

Thomas took a deep drink of his wine before replying. 'It seems Sir George wishes to impress everyone of note in the county.'

I glanced across at my father-in-law, still talking to Elizabeth. 'She's his only daughter, and from the look of Lady Sydenham, I doubt there's any prospect of more.'

Thomas frowned as he dismembered one of the tiny quails in search of meat. 'Why did you not invite Margaret?'

'Margaret?' His question touched a nerve. I'd not given Margaret a thought since meeting Elizabeth.

'Do you have any idea how she feels about you?'

'She's always treated me like her older brother, especially after her own brother was lost at sea – and I think of her like the sister we never had.'

'Why do you think Margaret works so hard to run Buckland Abbey?'

I stared at my brother, surprised at the note of challenge in his voice. Margaret always waited up to welcome me home, regardless of the hour. She'd sacrificed two years of her life caring for Mary, and I'd never thanked her. I heard my new wife laugh at some witty remark. Draining my glass, I watched as a young serving girl refilled it. I had no answer for Thomas.

Plymouth harbour thronged with the towering masts of the largest fleet to sail from England in living memory. Elizabeth decided the cold September breeze was reason enough for her to remain at Buckland, but Margaret, faithful as ever, waited at the quay to see me off.

I'd chosen the queen's six-hundred-ton warship, the *Elizabeth Bonaventure*, as my flagship. Although some eighteen years old, I'd refitted her with new guns, and repainted her in the queen's colours of black and white. As well as a hundred and fifty mariners, I'd recruited twenty-four of the best gunners I could find.

My flag captain, Tom Fenner, was an experienced naval commander from Chichester, of similar age to me. Although he came from a famous seafaring family, he'd worked his way up through the ranks. His booming voice rang out across the deck, leaving no one aboard in any doubt of his authority.

We also carried seventy-six professional soldiers, one of several divisions spread across the fleet. As lieutenant general, Christopher Carleill, Walsingham's stepson, commanded the soldiers as well as the *Tiger*. He'd reassured me they were well-armed and more than a match for the Spanish.

I scanned the rest of our flotilla of twenty-two smaller vessels and six other large ships, including another Royal Navy galleon, the *Aid*, captained by Edward Wynter. A cousin of John Wynter, Edward was the son of John Hawkins' nemesis, the garrulous old admiral Sir William Wynter.

At the urging of my brother, I'd invested in the refit of a fast merchantman and renamed her the *Thomas Drake*. Now under his command, I'd sworn to keep a close eye on him. I'd already lost two brothers and, after so long with no news, feared I might never see my nephew John again.

I would also have to keep an eye on Francis Knollys. The son of the Treasurer of the Household and a blood relative of the queen, he'd turned up uninvited with other courtiers and members of parliament, including Sir Philip Sidney. Sir Philip was married to Francis Walsingham's daughter, so it had been easy enough to ask his father-in-law to recall him to court, but I'd had to allow Knollys to command the galleon *Leicester*.

Raising a hand to Margaret on the shore, I recalled how Mary always took the trouble to see me off, whatever the weather, and despite her illness. Her small gifts at my departure were of great comfort to me on longer voyages. Elizabeth seemed indifferent about seeing me go, and I knew the reason.

Goaded by my brother Thomas, I'd drunk too much wine at our wedding banquet. I woke the next morning alone and fully dressed – except for my boots, which stood together at the side of our bed, silent witnesses to my unconsummated marriage.

I had vague memories of Thomas and others helping me to my room, and Elizabeth's attempt to rouse me. Since that night, our lovemaking had become a routine in which love played no part. She did her best to please me, but from wifely duty, and without passion.

A consummate actress, she'd played the part of a loving wife at civic receptions in Plymouth, yet we shared no interests and lived separate lives. I'd thought she might ask for Margaret to be sent away but, to my surprise, they became close friends. I believe it proved convenient to them both for Margaret to run Buckland.

I turned at the thump of boots to see Jonas waving his cap at his mother. Now a handsome and well-educated young man, he'd persuaded Margaret to allow him to sail as my steward. With a jolt, I realised it was Jonas she'd come out in the cold to see off, not me.

'All set to sail, Admiral.' Tom Fenner's words cut through my reverie like a sharp rigging axe through a mooring rope.

'Weigh anchor, Captain.' I glanced up at the sails. 'Let's make the best of this wind.'

My heart raced at the familiar rattle of chains and shouted commands. I'd been ashore too long, and had forgotten the thrill of getting under way. Even if Her Majesty changed her mind, there would be no turning back. This was my chance to take the West Indies from Spain, and claim them in the name of Queen Elizabeth.

After seizing supplies from a Spanish ship in the Bay of Biscay and raiding the coastal town of Vigo, we sailed to Las Palmas. The shore batteries opened fire. A heavy cannonball struck *Elizabeth Bonaventure* above the waterline, and others damaged the *Aid* and *Leicester*.

I decided we should make our escape, rather than waste ammunition in reply. We filled our water casks at the undefended island of La Gomera and, despite storms, reached Santiago by mid-November.

Christopher Carleill was rowed from the *Tiger* and stood at my side as we studied the defences from a safe distance. 'They've strengthened the Portuguese battery covering the anchorage, Admiral. They have some fifty guns, but look poorly manned.'

'That's why I'm glad to have you with us, Lieutenant General Carleill. What do you recommend?'

'I'll take our soldiers ashore to seize the batteries from the rear.' He pointed to a cove, a few miles to the east of the town. 'We'll land under the cover of darkness, then you can bombard the town at dawn, as a diversion.'

'Tomorrow is Her Majesty's accession day, so we'll show the Spanish how we celebrate our queen.'

Christopher Carleill nodded. 'I'll hoist the flag of St George once we have control of the town.' He smiled. 'Take care to look out for it, Admiral. I don't want my men to be on the receiving end of your cannons.'

The booming guns of the *Elizabeth Bonaventure* shattered the tranquil peace, rousing the Spanish from their beds. The gunners on the *Aid* took over while my crews reloaded, leaving the townspeople no respite. The shore batteries returned fire but, as we'd hoped, their aim was poor and the heavy cannonballs fell short.

Jonas cheered as one of our gunners scored a direct hit on the tower of the cathedral, silencing the clanging bells. I flinched as a stray cannonball splashed into the water, too close for comfort. I'd promised Margaret I'd bring Jonas back safe and well, and called out to him.

'Fetch my helmet and breastplate from my cabin, Jonas.'

People were fleeing the town, and I prayed it wouldn't be long before Carleill's men seized the shore battery. Our lookout pointed and a cheer rang out as Carleill's white flag with the red cross of St George flew from one of the largest buildings in the town. Santiago was ours.

By the time I was rowed ashore, my brother Thomas had started boarding the ships at anchor in the harbour. We'd agreed to take the best to add to our fleet, and strip the rest of anything we could use. Carleill's soldiers had the task of dismantling the batteries, keeping the best guns, cannonballs and gunpowder.

I chose an impressive building on the seafront as my headquarters, and began questioning the prisoners. It seemed the governor was in São Domingos, a few miles inland. I marched there with Carleill and six hundred of his best soldiers, but we found the people had fled, taking anything of value. Carleill's men burned the town after news of the murder of a young soldier, captured by the Spanish.

Carleill's face looked stern as he explained. 'I tasked two men to keep a rearguard. We found one of them, little more than a boy, on the path.' He cursed at the memory. 'They'd cut off his head, but not before disembowelling him – by the looks of it while he still lived.'

The inhabitants of the port of Praia, some nine miles east along the coast, must have been warned of our approach, as they'd fled to safety. We looted what we could carry away, and in reprisal for their cruelty to our young soldier, I ordered Praia to be razed to the ground.

On the last day of November, I led our fleet westward, out into the Atlantic Ocean. My chaplain, Philip Nichols, acted as my secretary and assistant, making detailed notes of the voyage. A likeable, softly spoken man, he preached to the crew twice a day. He also made the often risky journey in a small boat to read sermons to the other crews, but I doubted they realised he also acted as my eyes and ears.

He returned from a visit to the *Leicester* with news. 'More of the crew suffer with the fever, Admiral.'

I could tell from his tone there must be a good number. 'How many is that altogether?'

Nichols frowned as he consulted his notebook. 'Together with our crewmen, and the eleven men on the *Primrose*, the total is now one hundred and forty-nine, and sixty-four have died.'

I studied my charts. 'We'll stop at St Kitts, where the sick men can rest while we clean the worst affected ships.'

'I regret to tell you there is more bad news. Captain Knollys asked me if I believe the fever is God's judgement upon us.'

'I confess I've been expecting trouble from him, ever since he refused to swear our oath of loyalty. We must deal with it, before others become disaffected.'

'He says he is being excluded from decisions, Admiral. It would be easy enough to involve him more. He also accuses Lieutenant General Carleill of allowing his men to keep valuables looted in Santiago.'

'He's probably right. I know what soldiers are like.' I sat back in my chair, wondering how best to proceed. 'I either have to send Francis Knollys home – or reward his insubordination.'

Nichols looked thoughtful. 'If you send him home, he would have the opportunity to misrepresent this matter.'

'You are right. He could cause no end of trouble for me. Let me think on this and, in the meantime, let me know if you hear any more mutinous talk.'

Rows of men removed their caps and stood in sombre reflection on the volcanic island of St Kitts. I watched as they hammered the last of the wooden crosses into place. Twenty good men had reached the West Indies but would sail no further.

The fever raged through our fleet like a forest fire from which no one was safe. We all knew that but for the grace of God we could have been remaining on this island. I took my father's book of Psalms, and turned to Psalm 116.

'*Return unto thy rest, O my soul, for the Lord hath dealt bountifully with thee. For thou hast delivered my soul from death, mine eyes from tears, and my feet from falling. I will walk before the Lord in the land of the living. Amen.*'

24

JANUARY 1586

We sailed west on a crisp New Year's Day, and met Lieutenant General Carleill in the *Tiger*. He'd been on a scouting mission, assessing the defences of Santo Domingo, capital of the island of Hispaniola, and rowed across to brief me in my cabin.

Carleill studied my parchment chart of the island. 'The city is too well defended for an assault from the sea, Admiral, but they won't be expecting us to attack by land, as we did at Santiago.' He raised an eyebrow. 'They've begun to build a wall, but the work is unfinished. There's a gap wide enough to march an army through.'

I pointed to the depth soundings on my chart. 'The Haina river could be a landing place, but the approach is shallow – and would mean a hike across ten miles of rough ground.'

Carleill frowned. 'It's the only way to surprise the Spanish. I'll lead the attack on the main gate, while Sergeant Major Powell leads a storming party to the rear.'

I agreed. 'We'll attack tonight. Our pinnaces will ferry your men to the beach before the light fails, and the rest of the fleet will provide a diversion.'

. . .

The lights of Santo Domingo flickered in the darkness like a thousand votive candles, revealing the sprawling city to be better defended than Santiago. The gunners of the Spanish shore battery were waiting for us, and began firing. My captain, Tom Fenner, pointed to three ships nosing their way from the harbour.

'If I'm not wrong, Admiral, they plan to block the entrance to the port.'

'Let's offer them a hand, Captain. Have the gun crews open fire on them as soon as we are within range.'

Our heavy guns boomed. Deafened, my ears rang with the noise and the air filled with the sulphurous tang of gunpowder. A shot from the shore battery hit the *Elizabeth Bonaventure*, crashing into her bows in a shower of splintering timber, but most of the cannonballs splashed into the sea around us.

Captain Wynter on the *Aid* fired a broadside at the battery, and a lucky shot must have hit a munitions store. The sky glowed bright orange as a massive explosion shook the city. The batteries ceased firing as the Spanish gunners fled, but the sharp rattle of distant musket fire told us Carleill's men faced a battle at the gates.

The first light of dawn showed the damage our guns had inflicted. The seafront buildings were ruined. One blazed with flames and billowing smoke, like a beacon lit to celebrate our success. Once again, our flag of St George marked another victory.

Ferried ashore with Jonas and my chaplain, Philip Nichols, we picked our way through the rubble of ruined buildings, and found Lieutenant General Carleill, who'd set up his headquarters in the fort. He had a cut on his cheek and a bandaged hand, but grinned when he saw me.

'They put up a fight this time, Admiral, but were mostly mili-

Drake - Tudor Corsair

tiamen, armed with rusty pikes and swords – no match for our muskets.'

I glanced at his bloodstained bandage. 'How many casualties, Lieutenant General?'

'Twenty wounded, and seven men killed.' He had a soldier's matter-of-fact bravado, but I guessed the battle had been a test of his men.

'We saw people fleeing the city. Have we captured anyone we might be able to ransom?'

'There are over two hundred prisoners, including a Spanish lady who says she is the governor's wife.'

I raised an eyebrow. 'And what of the governor?'

'My men are searching for him, but I expect he's escaped inland with the others.'

'I'll set up my headquarters in the cathedral. Have your men do what they can to repair the city's defences, in case of a counter-attack – and try to prevent them from looting.'

The impressive, gold-tinted limestone facade of the cathedral had escaped damage, and by making it my base it would be safe from our soldiers. A notice in Spanish proclaimed it the first cathedral of the New World. I stared up at the high ceiling, awed by the stillness of the cavernous space, and said a prayer of thanks.

There were twelve private side chapels, one of which held the tomb of Christopher Columbus, as well as rooms used by the clergy. Choosing the grandest of these as my temporary study, I sent Jonas to forage for food and drink, then helped Philip Nichols record the details of our victory, while they were fresh in our minds.

A soldier arrived with a flagon of wine, and silver goblets. Jonas followed with a loaf of bread and a leg of cured ham so large he struggled to carry it. He produced an orange from one of his bulging pockets and began peeling it.

'There are ships on fire in the harbour, Admiral.'

I frowned at the news. 'I left my brother Thomas in charge of salvaging what he could.'

'I saw soldiers smashing the windows of a church and ripping down tapestries.' Jonas pulled the orange in two and handed half to me. 'It seems they didn't have your message about looting.'

The orange tasted sweet and juicy, but I cursed Carleill's failure to control his men. I turned to Philip Nichols. 'We need to record as much of the spoils taken from here as we can. So far, this venture has failed to recover its costs, and our investors will hold us to account when we return.'

I began the laborious work of interrogating prisoners, trying to find someone I could trust to act as an intermediary. The governor's Spanish wife arrived, accompanied by Sergeant Major Powell, with an escort of two burly soldiers and my interpreter. She had a look of wary defiance in her dark eyes, and her overgown was torn, revealing a glimpse of white silk.

'Tell her she'll be kept safe here at the cathedral.' The crewman acting as my interpreter explained, and I saw her relax a little. I hoped to hold her to ransom, but it wouldn't be easy to get a message to the Spanish, hiding somewhere inland.

I gestured at the rip in her gown. 'How did this happen, Sergeant Major?'

'She tried to make a run for it, Admiral. My men were under orders to stop her.'

'Leave one man to keep an eye on her, then I want you to put an end to the looting. The Spanish won't pay a ransom to save their town if your men have destroyed it.'

After seeing several merchants, there came a well-dressed man, who introduced himself as Juan Malarejo. He showed me his papers confirming he was a high sheriff and city magistrate. He made a passionate speech once he knew who I was, and I understood he begged for an end to the desecration of the churches.

I turned to my interpreter. 'Tell Señor Malarejo he is to take our demand for one million ducats to the governor. In return, I give my word to release the governor's wife, and leave their city without further damage – including his churches!'

We spent the week, while we waited for Malarejo's return, repairing our ships, and loading them with captured guns, ammunition, food and wine. Philip Nichols recorded the details as reports came in. I studied his notes, disappointed to see that only sixteen thousand gold ducats were found in the city treasury.

'This makes it even more important to secure a ransom.'

Nichols nodded. 'Carleill's men found a warehouse full of hides, and another used to store barrels of Spanish wine, but we'll only know the true value once we return home.'

Worried a Spanish fleet might be somewhere in the West Indies, I ordered the city gates to be repaired and posted lookouts to keep watch. Two ships were sent out to patrol the harbour approaches, and provide us with an early warning by firing their cannons.

My interpreter explained that Juan Malarejo had returned with bad news. 'He claims the governor offers less than a quarter of the ransom amount.'

I cursed our luck. 'Tell him if he doesn't come back with a better offer in two days, the civic buildings and churches will be burned to the ground!'

Another week passed with no news. I reluctantly ordered the soldiers to begin slighting the buildings, and to set fire to three of the churches. I sent for one of the governor's former slaves, a bright young boy who reminded me of Diego.

I turned to the crewman acting as my interpreter. 'Ask him if he knows where to find the governor.'

I watched as the boy pointed to the hills, and spoke in rapid Spanish. My interpreter smiled. 'He says he can find him soon enough, sir.'

'Tell him I've decided to reduce my demand to twenty-five thousand ducats.' I pointed up to the high-vaulted ceiling. 'We will destroy this cathedral if our demands are ignored.'

I saw the boy nod, his eyes wide at my threat, and a thought occurred to me. I turned to my interpreter. 'Tell the boy he can have a place on my flagship if he brings us good news.'

I'd grown tired of Santo Domingo, and the men were restless. Francis Knollys came to see me, concerned the Spanish were delaying while they prepared to return with a fleet of warships. I did my best to remain civil, but suspected he'd been conspiring against my ransom plan behind my back.

The following evening my brother Thomas brought a flagon of wine and filled two silver goblets. 'The men want us to cut our losses and raid Cartagena.'

'In good time, Thomas.' The dry heat made me thirsty, and I drained the blood-red wine in one gulp. He refilled my goblet with a grin.

'The Spanish think they've trapped us in this godforsaken place.' He scowled up at shadows in the vaulted roof of the cathedral. 'The last thing they'll expect is for us to slip away in the night and attack another city.'

Several goblets of wine improved my mood, and I could see

his point, but wasn't ready to give up – at least until my messenger returned. I could imagine Francis Knollys taking the credit if I changed my plan too soon.

'Have faith, Thomas. I've no doubt the Spanish governor can find twenty-five thousand ducats, then we'll be on our way.'

'I hope you're right. The men know we've no chance of catching the treasure fleet – and there's meagre pickings here.' This time the critical edge to his voice was unmistakeable.

'Have you been sent by that jackal Knollys and the other captains to persuade me?'

My brother's reply was interrupted by a heavy knock at the door. A soldier led my young message boy into the room. The former slave had taken a savage beating. His left eye was bruised and swollen shut, and the front of his shirt was red with congealing blood.

'He's been stabbed, sir.' The soldier shook his head. 'A deep wound, with a sword, by the look of it.' As he spoke the boy dropped to the ground, striking his head on the tiled floor.

'Take him to the doctor. Now!' It might have been the strong wine, frustration at the Spanish, my brother's collusion with Knollys, or the memory of Diego, but my rage flared like a match to gunpowder. I turned to Thomas. 'Find Sergeant Major Powell. Tell him to hang two of the prisoners where the Spanish will be sure to see them!'

Juan Malarejo returned in the last week of January with a rose-wood chest containing the ransom of twenty-five thousand ducats. He told me the Spanish were sorry my young messenger had been killed, and the man responsible had been sentenced to death, and hanged.

Sergeant Major Powell misunderstood my orders, or had his own reasons, as the two men hanging from the harbour-front gibbet were Dominican friars, whose only crime was not having escaped our soldiers. Their deaths would be added to the others on my conscience.

I still had the challenge of dealing with the troublesome Francis Knollys, and summoned him – together with Philip Nichols, tasked to make a note of our meeting. Knollys wore his best sword, and a flamboyant ostrich plume in his hat.

'I understand you wish to have a greater role in our venture, Captain Knollys.'

'I do.' He glanced at Nichols. 'It cannot be right that I hear of events at the same time as the ship's boy.'

'I propose to appoint you as my rear admiral.'

Knollys studied me as if the promotion might be some sort of trick. 'I shall think on it.'

I struggled to control my frustration. 'You will accept my offer, or be sent home in disgrace, Captain.'

We sailed from Santo Domingo leaving a scene of devastation. The town had been ruined, and twenty Spanish ships were burned or sunk, the best taken to replace three of ours. I renamed the best of our prizes, a six-hundred-ton armed galleon, *New Year's Gift*.

We'd replaced our crewmen lost through fever with freed slaves. I'd only chosen those who asked to sail with us, and although many were unused to life at sea, they were quick to learn. Many also spoke Spanish, so could help as interpreters.

We'd learned some important lessons at Santo Domingo, and our raid on Cartagena was over in a day. Carleill's soldiers crossed the marshy ground on the undefended side of the city on an inky-black, moonless night, taking the defenders by surprise.

The harbour was protected by a heavy chain, strung across

the entrance, but this also trapped the Spanish ships inside. I made my headquarters in the governor's mansion, and began to take stock of our situation.

Philip Nichols consulted his notes. 'Twenty-eight of Carleill's soldiers are dead, Admiral, and Captain Thomas Moone was shot in the thigh, and died of loss of blood.'

'I'll miss Tom. He was one of my most loyal friends.'

Philip Nichols looked up from his records. 'They didn't die for nothing, Admiral. The Spanish paid a hundred thousand ducats.'

'The merchants were not to know we had no time to plunder their city. How many men have we lost through fever?'

Philip Nichols frowned. 'I've not been keeping count, Admiral, but if we don't return home soon I fear—'

'We have one last mission before we can turn for home. I've promised to call at Sir Walter Raleigh's colony at Roanoke Island. I know their governor, Captain Ralph Lane. He was a Member of Parliament.'

The settlers lined the shore, staring at us in amazement. Ralph Lane stepped forward and raised a hand in welcome. He'd allowed his beard and hair to grow long and unkempt, and his hand felt calloused from hard work as he shook mine.

'Welcome to the Roanoke Colony, Sir Francis. We thank the Lord you've come.' He seemed overcome by emotion as he looked at our ships. 'We were expecting Sir Richard Grenville with supplies, two months ago.'

'He's not been here?'

Ralph Lane shook his head. 'We arrived too late for planting, and had trouble with the Indians, after we killed their chief in a fight. I've had to ration our supplies.'

'We have little enough to share, but one of our ships, the

Bark Bonner, is undermanned, so any of you who wish to return with us may do so.'

Ralph Lane smiled for the first time since we'd arrived. 'I'll put it to the vote, but know there isn't a man among us who doesn't long for the sight of England.'

Midsummer was upon us by the time we docked in Portsmouth. Jonas helped me dress in my best sword and sash as we prepared to be rowed ashore. Crowds of people appeared on the quay, drawn by the spectacle of so many ships.

'Word of our return will be speeding to our backers in Westminster, Jonas, so I'm keen to put my side of the story, before others spread half-truths and rumours.'

Jonas hesitated as we were about to leave my cabin. 'Have we made a profit on this voyage, Admiral?'

'A good question – and one many will soon be asking. We aren't loaded with gold and silver, as our investors might have wished, but we've taught the Spanish a lesson they'll not forget.'

25

MARCH 1587

William Cecil wished to see me in his private rooms in Westminster Palace. His note had been brief, and seemed more like a summons than an invitation, but I hoped I knew the reason. He'd become even more important as the queen's advisor since the execution of Mary, Queen of Scots, at Fotheringhay Castle the previous month.

As I entered his dark-panelled room I recalled the day we'd first met, some eighteen years before. I'd been an ambitious young messenger for William and John Hawkins. My circumstances could not now be more different, but I felt the same flicker of unease as he studied me, as if making a judgement.

'I understand you've been badgering Her Majesty with your plans to attack the Spanish fleet.' He made it sound like an accusation, yet had a glint in his eye.

'Am I to languish here, like some desk admiral, while King Philip prepares to invade our country?' My raised voice revealed my frustration. 'I've been prevented from returning to the West Indies, yet the queen seems unwilling to listen to my advice.'

William Cecil frowned at my irreverent tone. 'You know it's a matter of timing. Walsingham has been reliably informed that the Spanish fleet is being refitted in the harbour of Cadiz.'

'So I've heard – but can you secure me a commission to find out if this is true, my lord?'

'Your wish is granted, Sir Francis. I've advised Her Majesty that you should be sent to assess the capability of the Spanish fleet – and cause them as much damage as you can.'

'By God's faith!' This was the chance I'd been longing for, and my head filled with questions. A thought occurred to me. 'I'll need to leave as soon as possible. Will Her Majesty allow me the *Elizabeth Bonaventure*?'

William Cecil nodded. 'As well as three warships.' He ticked them off on his fingers. 'The *Golden Lion*, *Rainbow* and the *Dreadnought*. Your vice admiral will be the Comptroller of the Navy, William Burough, but it will be up to you to choose the rest of your flotilla, as well as the crews.' He sat back in his chair. 'If the Spanish fleet has sailed, you are to prevent their reaching England by whatever means you can.'

'I'll start preparing straight away, but we'll need government funds. I doubt there will be much of a return for investors, unless we're lucky enough to find a Spanish treasure ship.'

'The royal coffers will meet half the cost, but I don't need to say you are to keep the queen's involvement strictly confidential. The remainder must be found from London merchants.' He smiled. 'They do, after all, have a vested interest in a successful outcome for this venture.'

No one waited on the windswept quay in Plymouth as we set sail. We'd learned to keep our preparations secret, dispersing our ships, ordering supplies from different merchants, and leaving at first light. I wished to secure the best chance of taking the Spanish by surprise, as this might be our only opportunity.

The storms off the Galician coast were as violent as any I'd seen. Torrential rain squalls lashed the deck, and fierce winds began to scatter our fleet. Even the heavy *Elizabeth Bonaventure* broached like a whale in the heavy swell, her sails straining at the sheets.

Jonas appeared at my cabin door, rainwater dripping from his heavy cape. His eyes were wide, and his face as pale as a corpse, as if he might be suffering from seasickness. I realised this would be his first experience of a serious storm at sea.

'The *Elizabeth Bonaventure* is a tough, well-built ship.' I tried to reassure him. 'We're well clear of land, so you needn't worry.'

'One of the pinnaces has been dismasted, Admiral. Should we try to save her crew?'

I grabbed my hat and cape. 'We'll do our best, Jonas, God willing.'

Following him, I stared into the stormy seas. At first, I couldn't see anything in the downpour. A flash of lightning lit up one of our smaller pinnaces, a navy messenger boat. She rose on the crest of a great wave, and disappeared again into a deep trough as thunder rattled in the blackened sky. I called to our helmsman to steer for the stricken craft.

Jonas shouted in alarm as a heavy wave crashed over the pinnace. 'A man has fallen overboard!'

As we watched, the crewman's dark shape bobbed into view, and I glimpsed the terror on his face before he vanished beneath the turbulent water. A second man sat hunched over the tiller, battling for his life against the unforgiving sea as another wave swamped his dismasted boat.

I found a coil of rope and tied one end around a cleat. We swept past the pinnace, so close we nearly struck her, and I threw the rope to the crewman at the helm. He made a desperate grab for the end, but it slipped through his hands.

'Turn about!' I shouted at the top of my voice against the

howling wind, knowing at least one man's life depended on our help.

The *Elizabeth Bonaventure* lurched heavily in the swell as we turned broadside into the waves. Once we were back on course I scanned the grey sea ahead of us, and called for Jonas and our crew to do the same. Nothing remained of the dismasted pinnace or her crewmen – only a dark object I recognised as a sailor's cap, floating on the water.

Once the storm subsided, we sighted a Dutch merchant ship heading from Cadiz. We overhauled her and I sent a boarding party to fetch the captain. A portly man with a wide-brimmed hat and a large ruff, he spoke some English. When he realised he might be released if he was helpful, he confirmed Walsingham's report.

'I've never seen so many vessels in the Bay of Cadiz.'

'How many warships, Captain?'

He stared at me with wary eyes, no doubt wondering if I planned to seize his ship, and shrugged. 'More than fifty, but less than a hundred. When we were unloading our cargo, I heard they were sailing on to Lisbon.'

We set the Dutchmen free, and reached the sheltered Bay of Cadiz at sunset on the last day of April. Anchoring behind the headland, out of sight of Spanish lookouts, we waited for the rest of our fleet to catch up. After a wait of over an hour, our lookout spotted Captain Burough being rowed from the *Golden Lion*.

Although I'd agreed for him to be my second in command, we'd crossed in the past over my proposals to reform the navy. He'd also blocked John Hawkins' plans for faster warships, arguing there was nothing wrong with the ageing fleet. Famous for his treatise on compass errors, he seemed a poor choice for this mission.

Captain Burough scowled as he clambered aboard, and followed me to the privacy of the upper deck. 'I understand you plan to take on over sixty warships, Admiral, with only half that number?'

'This is our best chance to destroy the Spanish fleet. With luck, we have them trapped like rats in a barrel. What would you have us do?'

'I know how well Cadiz is defended. There are batteries at the fort, as well as in the harbour.' He shook his head. 'The entrance to the bay is narrow, with dangerous shoals. If you don't listen to my counsel, it's us who'll be trapped, not the Spanish.'

As if to support his concern, the still night air filled with the roar of the shore battery at the fort. I ducked instinctively as great splashes surged from the water, and they began to find the range.

'We will attack, while we can – and if it is the will of God for this to be my last battle, then I'll take as many Spanish ships with me as I can.'

William Burough stared at me as if I was mad. I sent him back to the *Golden Lion* and, sailing line astern to provide the smallest target, we headed in the fading light into the bay, towards the largest of the Spanish galleons. I held up a hand to signal to the gunnery master.

'Hold your fire until we're close enough to make every shot count.'

A lantern flickered aboard the Spanish warship, and men with muskets began taking pot-shots at us from her deck as we approached. Luck was with us; she sat at anchor, and the outgoing tide took her bows to the shore, making it difficult to use her guns against us. I thanked God for the breeze which offered us an advantage.

I spared a thought for our gunners, crouched in the cramped darkness of the gun deck below my feet, waiting for their signal. I'd hoped the gunnery commanders of Cadiz fort would fear hitting their own ships, once we were among the Spanish fleet. Unfortunately their guns continued to fire, and although their shots fell well astern, we faced the constant threat of a direct hit.

Holding my breath, I watched as we sailed so close to the galleon I could see the faces of her Spanish crewmen. Her gun ports were open, the dark gun barrels ready for action. I glanced back at the rest of our ships, following in our wake, and gave the command.

'Open fire!'

The thunderous booming of our cannons was followed by panic and chaos aboard the Spanish galleon. Our muskets and swivel guns dealt with anyone who showed on deck, while our culverins punched ragged holes through the thick planking of her hull. A fine ship, she would have made a good prize, but we hastened past and fired a devastating broadside at the next closest ship, a fat-bellied Genoese merchantman.

Her crew struggled to launch their tender as she began to take on water. In different circumstances I would have saved them, but I had my orders. I watched as the *Rainbow*, a new ship commanded by Captain Henry Bellingham, fired on a second galleon, scoring a direct hit. The towering mast came crashing down on to the deck, ripping the sails in a tangle of rigging.

Captain Tom Fenner on the *Dreadnought*, a galleon built for speed, blockaded the narrow entrance to the harbour. Several ships trying to escape sailed straight into her deadly forty-one guns, but others scraped over the shoals to the safety of the open sea.

I turned at the sound of a shout in time to see the Spanish

had set one their ships on fire, and set it adrift on a collision course. Flames roared and crackled in the tarred rigging as the fireship bore down on the *Golden Lion*. Her commander, William Burough, took swift avoiding action, heading back out into the open sea. The fireship careered into an anchored merchant ship with a crash of breaking timbers.

I ordered our fleet into the inner harbour, where we began attacking every Spanish ship in sight. The fighting continued for the next day and night, and we boarded and looted any ships we could. Several were loaded with supplies for long sea voyages, leaving no doubt about King Philip's planned invasion.

Any ships not taken as prizes were set alight, the billowing smoke and leaping flames adding to the panic and confusion. By dawn, some twenty-seven ships were destroyed, and more severely damaged. Some twenty smaller ships had managed to slip past the *Dreadnaught*'s deadly guns, but our plan had succeeded, with the loss of only one ship, and the pinnace sunk by the storm.

One of our prizes was a new galleon, a flagship of the High Admiral of Spain, of one thousand two hundred tons. Another, of a thousand tons, was filled with barrels and staves, iron spikes and horseshoes. We seized such quantities of wine and biscuit they could provision us for several months.

At dawn the next day we set off along the south-west coast of Spain, pursued by ten armed Spanish galleys, which were soon seen off by our gunners. We continued to Portugal, destroying all the shipping we could find and, after two weeks, arrived at the Algarve.

While we sat at anchor that night, I sent for Captain William Burough. He sat in my cabin and refused a cup of looted Spanish wine with a dismissive wave of his hand.

'Explain why you withdrew from the fighting.' I struggled to keep my tone civil.

'We'd been hit by the shore battery, below the waterline. One of my men had his arm torn off and died, another has been blinded. We worked hard on the pumps, but the water kept rising, so we had to sail out of range while we made repairs.'

His excuse seemed convenient, but the truth could be proved easily enough. 'I plan to land and attack the forts here in Portugal. Can I rely on you to support us?'

'Our orders were clear, Admiral. We've achieved more than we could have hoped for in Cadiz.' William Burough scowled. 'You know the risks of shore-based attacks. The Spanish will be waiting for us. I consider your plan to be unnecessary and reckless—'

'You will *not* question my authority.' I dug my nails into my palms as I struggled to control my anger. 'I am relieving you of command, and you can return to England with our sick and wounded men.'

We attacked the fort at Sagres at night, landing some eight hundred soldiers on the shingle beach. The thick walls were defended by high cliffs, but the entrance gates were made from ancient timbers. We piled wood against them and set it ablaze.

The garrison fought bravely, killing two of our soldiers, but were outnumbered. I sent a Portuguese-speaking messenger under a flag of truce, and they soon surrendered, in return for safe passage. The other forts were abandoned without a fight, and we began two days of destruction, throwing their guns over the cliffs and looting the town.

When we returned to the fleet I found the *Golden Lion* had gone. The sergeant major of her soldiers, who I'd put in temporary command, was spotted in the ship's boat. I cursed William Burough, and swore he would answer for it if he'd persuaded his crew to mutiny and return to the safety of England.

That night, a galleon appeared on the horizon twenty miles from the island of São Miguel, but she slipped away in the darkness. At dawn, Jonas shouted from the crow's nest, and pointed to a distant ship under full sail. 'She flies the Spanish flag!'

I squinted at the distant ship. 'With luck, she could be an East Indiaman – and she sits low in the water, so is likely to be fully laden.' I called to the bosun. 'Action stations!'

We struck our flags and drew as close as we could, while Tom Fenner, now my rear admiral, fired shots across her bows and, after an exchange of fire, her crew surrendered. Named the *São Filipe*, after the King of Spain, we discovered her hold filled with caskets of gold, aromatic spices and colourful silk from the West Indies.

I presented Jonas with a silver dagger. 'Your reward for being first to sight a treasure ship.'

He unsheathed the weapon and admired how it shone in the sunlight. 'Thank you, Admiral.' He grinned. 'I wouldn't have missed this for the world.'

'One day you can tell your grandchildren how you helped to singe the beard of the King of Spain.'

I brimmed with pride at how he'd conducted himself as we turned for England. We'd taken great risks, but our mission was a success, with over a hundred Spanish ships destroyed or captured. I looked forward to telling William Cecil that Spanish plans for the invasion of England would have to be postponed.

26

MAY 1588

Elizabeth had become used to my bad-tempered outbursts since I returned from the raid on the Bay of Cadiz. I'd been disappointed by the queen's unwillingness to acknowledge our success, despite our valuable prizes, and seventeen shiploads of treasure and booty delivered to London.

To increase my frustration, the inquiry into William Burough's mutiny concluded that I'd overreacted to his insubordination. It was said I'd misunderstood his concerns, although I had no shortage of witnesses. He'd called my plans rash and ill-conceived, and should thank the Lord's mercy that I only sent him home in disgrace.

Elizabeth took my arm to stop me pacing the great hall at Buckland Abbey. 'Why does the arrival of Lord Howard of Effingham trouble you so much?'

'By God's faith, Elizabeth, the man hasn't been further than Calais. He's never seen action at sea, yet they make him Commander of the Royal Navy, and give him the *Ark Royal* as his flagship!'

She frowned at my raised voice. 'You mustn't take this personally. Charles Howard is a cousin of the queen, and he's been Lord High Admiral of England for years. You should be pleased he's chosen to base his fleet in Plymouth.'

I stared into her mysterious brown eyes, wondering if I knew her at all. Margaret told me Buckland Abbey had been a busy place while I'd been at sea, with Elizabeth's friends coming and going, and social events which lasted well into the night. I'd decided not to ask her who'd been staying in our home, or why.

'He's supposed to be guarding the Channel approaches and the Isle of Wight. By turning up here, Howard robs me of my own command, and will take the credit for our victory.' I cursed my bad luck. 'When I was knighted I thought it would put an end to the nobility looking down their noses at me. I should have known better.'

'At least the queen had the good sense to make you second in command of the fleet. As vice admiral, it's you they turn to for advice.' She kissed me on the cheek without affection. 'Father says the Spanish talk of a holy crusade, and believe they defend the Catholic faith. Does that not make them more dangerous?'

'Much of King Philip's invasion fleet lies at the bottom of the Bay of Cadiz.' I took her hands in mine. 'The Spanish are no match for us, Elizabeth.'

'I hope you are right.' She sounded doubtful.

'At William Cecil's war council, we agreed we must present the threat of a Spanish invasion as a serious danger, to encourage men like your father to raise and arm their militias. I don't believe a single Spanish soldier will set foot in Plymouth, but you should know I've made my will, and named you as executor, with my brother Thomas.'

Francis Walsingham frowned as he consulted his notes. 'Our sources inform us the Spanish war fleet has sailed from Lisbon, with some hundred and thirty ships and over thirty thousand men.'

'Less than half their ships will be armed and capable of fighting.' I made a quick calculation, and glanced at William Cecil. 'At best, only two-thirds of the men will be trained soldiers.'

Walsingham fixed me with his unblinking gaze. 'That may be right, but even twenty thousand is a formidable army.' He returned to his notes. 'We understand they are heading for Flanders, where they hope to join forces with the army of the Duke of Parma, Alexander Farnese, Governor of the Spanish Netherlands, who has some thirty thousand battle-hardened Italian soldiers.'

I spread out my chart of the English Channel on his table. 'Do your informants know where they plan to land?'

Walsingham shook his head. 'We'll find out soon enough, but can make an educated guess. The port of Gravelines is the closest Spanish territory to England – but they will know Dover is well defended, so they might plan to surprise us.'

'Then we must be ready for them.' I turned to William Cecil. 'We need to set up a line of warning beacons along the coast, with lookouts day and night. The Spanish must not be allowed to take us by surprise.'

Church bells clanged their discordant alert, and the towering beacons blazed in warning on the headlands. The country had been rife with rumour and speculation for weeks. The queen had heard that King Philip had changed his mind, and she'd ordered half our fleet to be paid off.

We'd delayed for as long as we could, and now the Spanish

fleet they called the 'Armada' had been reported forty miles west of Plymouth.

Our flagship, the *Revenge*, at four hundred and sixty tons, was the best of the queen's warships. Well-armed, with forty-six of the latest guns, she'd been built for speed, able to sail closer to the wind than the heavy Spanish galleons. I'd had her careened and tarred, and the topsides painted in the queen's Tudor harlequin of green and white.

At our side was my brother's ship, the two-hundred-ton *Thomas Drake*. My former flagship, the refitted *Elizabeth Bonaventure* – commanded by the blunt-speaking northern peer Sir George Clifford, Earl of Cumberland – waited close behind. More ships were being readied under the command of John Hawkins in Kent, but if Walsingham's reports proved to be right, we were likely to be outnumbered.

'Wind and tide are against us, Admiral.' My captain, John Grey, scowled as he welcomed me aboard. A gruff man, with a broad Devon accent, frown lines were set into his weather-beaten face, like the cracks in dried earth, and he was one of the most experienced coastal navigators in the fleet. 'We'll need to be warped out with a tow to clear the Sound.'

'Good idea, Captain.' I glanced at Lord Admiral Howard's *Ark Royal*, still at anchor while he waited for the tide to turn. 'We'll use one of the larger pinnaces to give us an advantage.'

Jonas, appointed as my lieutenant, clambered down from his high vantage point on the fighting platform, a serious look on his young face. 'There's no sign yet of the Spanish fleet. Is there any chance they'll use this south-westerly breeze to attack us in port?'

His grasp of the danger we were in surprised me. 'They might, Jonas.' I scanned the empty horizon out of habit. 'The Spanish were sighted close to the Scillies, then off Falmouth. My guess is they want to reach the English Channel, and the Duke of Parma in Flanders, with their fleet intact.' I grinned. 'Our task is to make sure they don't.'

I'd had no hesitation in having Jonas at my side, as he'd proved his worth. His question reminded me of Elizabeth's concern. Half of England's Catholics could rise up in support of the Spanish if we allowed the Armada to make landfall. I'd bragged they were no match for us, yet until we joined the rest of our ships, they outnumbered us two to one.

The setting sun turned the sky lavender pink, and a chill breeze carried the threat of storms. I'd wanted all fifty-four ships at sea before nightfall, yet they'd taken too long. I cursed Lord Admiral Howard's lack of urgency, a sign of his limited experience of fighting at sea, but none of us had been tested in such conditions.

I tried to ignore the nagging doubt, but there was a great difference between surprising a lone Spanish ship, and facing over a hundred well-armed galleons. Philip of Spain was bringing the fight to Plymouth, and his Armada was the most powerful fleet ever assembled.

We suspected he had spies in Plymouth, so the *Revenge* could be a prime target for the Spanish gunners. With a jolt I realised I might be leaving Plymouth for the last time. The exciting thrill of the chase was tempered with a pang of regret. I stared back in the direction of Buckland Abbey, but doubted Elizabeth would miss me.

I ordered the crew to assemble on the main deck, and told them the Spanish Armada was no match for our new guns. We said the Lord's Prayer, before I read Psalm 20.

'*The Lord gives victory to his chosen king; he answers him from his holy heaven and by his power gives him great victories. Some trust in their war chariots and others in their horses, but we trust in the power of the Lord our God.'*

Ahead of us was a spectacle I'd only imagined in my dreams. The great Armada sailed in a crescent-shaped battle formation, some two miles across. Supply ships were flanked by great war galleons, with towering fore- and sterncastles.

I had to admit so many ships were an impressive sight, yet I'd been right – many were lumbering transports, rather than men-of-war. Few of their crews would have experience of fighting at sea, and the outdated Italian galleasses would make easy targets for our new guns.

As planned, Lord Admiral Howard led half our fleet to the landward side, while I took the seaward. Even from such a distance I could see great numbers of soldiers crowding the decks, armed with pikes and muskets. Any attempt to board them would carry high risks. Instead, we took turns to release a barrage of cannon fire into the heart of the Armada.

Captain Grey called out to me. 'The range is too great, Admiral. Our shots are falling short. Shall we close on them?'

'Hold your course, Captain. Our orders are to shadow the Spanish, with a light burning at our stern after sunset.'

Jonas pointed. 'It seems our work has not been in vain, Admiral.'

One of the grandest of the Spanish ships broke formation. Over a thousand tons, she looked like a flagship, and would no doubt be carrying a valuable cargo. I studied the wallowing galleon. Men struggled at the bows to retrieve her bowsprit and foremast, which were broken off and floating in the sea.

I ducked instinctively as she fired a single shot, then realised it must be a distress signal to her fleet. Her call for help went unheeded, as the Armada regrouped and continued sailing east in their determined formation. It looked as if the damaged galleon drifted with the current, and I guessed she was unable to steer.

'Keep behind her, Captain. We'll wait until nightfall, then see if we can take her by surprise.'

Clouds drifted over a waning moon, casting dark shadows over the sea as we approached the drifting Spanish ship after midnight. A stiff breeze whipped foam from the wave crests, and the fat-bellied galleon rolled in the swell, at the mercy of the worsening weather.

I knew there would be consequences of ignoring Howard's orders to shadow the Armada, but the chance was too good to miss. We waited for dawn, then I ordered our cannons to be fired at the stricken ship, and for men to stand ready with grappling hooks. Others lined up with primed muskets as our crewman shouted in Spanish for the galleon to surrender.

To our amazement, her crew threw up their hands without a fight. They shouted back that their commander, Admiral General Don Pedro de Valdés, would agree to surrender in return for my word his men would not be mistreated.

Grappling hooks were thrown, and in a moment we were boarding the first captured ship of the Armada. The *Nuestra Señora del Rosario* – Our Lady of the Rosary – was mine. We didn't have much time, but my men began a thorough search. Our greatest prize was a wooden strongbox containing more than fifty thousand gold ducats, freshly minted, from the Spanish king's treasury.

We also found silver goblets engraved with a Spanish crest, and a dozen jewelled swords. I drew one of the weapons from its scabbard and showed Jonas the workmanship.

Drake - Tudor Corsair

'No doubt intended as King Philip's rewards.'

Jonas looked puzzled. 'For who?'

'For English Catholic nobles, awaiting their chance to betray our country.'

As well as her commander, General Don Pedro de Valdés, we took over a hundred sailors and a hundred and forty Spanish soldiers prisoner. I ordered the two Englishmen found hiding in the hold to be thrown into the brig as spies and traitors.

I returned to the *Revenge* and wrote a note for Lord Admiral Howard. Mindful that he might accuse me of failing to follow his orders, I explained I'd pursued some ships we saw at midnight, believing them to be Spanish.

I hoped he would be appeased by the news of the *Rosario*'s armament. Although one of the newer galleons, her guns were outdated. Ours were capable of five times the rate of fire as those we'd found on the *Rosario*. We'd taken a good supply of cannon-balls and powder from our prize, but I asked for more powder and shot, as we were already running low.

One of the message boats delivered my sealed note to the *Ark Royal*, although I doubted the resupply would come soon enough. William Cecil had mentioned how the royal coffers were running low, although I'd warned him we couldn't fight without the supplies.

Our concern was that the Spanish might find sanctuary somewhere in the Solent, off the poorly defended Isle of Wight. We'd tried to keep it secret that the soldiers there had only four cannons, and were armed with bows and arrows against the most formidable army in Europe.

At first light we sighted the slow-moving Armada and the *Ark Royal* began the attack, driving into the heart of the rearmost ships. Knowing how difficult it had been to find our range at sea, we sailed within a hundred paces of the nearest Spanish galleon, close enough to do greater damage, but not within grappling distance.

Our guns blasted again and again, smashing into Spanish hulls, until the wind and tide began to take the Armada into the dangerous shoals off the eastern end of the island. The deephulled galleons had no choice other than to bear away, and head out into the deeper Channel.

I stood at the rail, watching them go. 'Twice we've engaged the Spanish fleet, and twice we've seen them off, thank the Lord.' I turned to Jonas. 'Now we have to stop them joining forces with the Prince of Parma in Flanders.'

Jonas studied the distant fleet. 'They still sail in good formation, Admiral. Do you believe we've done them enough damage?'

'Three of their warships have been sunk, and several more badly damaged. One looked as if its powder store exploded, as both the after decks were blown up.'

Jonas frowned. 'I saw men jumping into the sea, and drowning. We should pray for them.'

'Let us pray our Lord Admiral persuades Her Majesty to provide the powder and shot we need to finish the task. The Channel is no more than twenty miles wide at its narrowest point. Twenty miles, Jonas, which will decide the fate of our country.'

A burning torch flickered in the darkness, then a second and a third. The light breeze fanned the flames, until they lit up the midnight sky to reveal a row of eight blazing fireships. Among them was my own ship, the *Thomas Drake*, loaded with as much gunpowder as we could spare, her guns primed to explode when the fire reached them.

The tarred rigging caught alight, and our fireships became

ferocious, floating bonfires, drifting on the tide into the Spanish fleet, anchored off Calais. The guns exploded one after the other, sending shrapnel and sharp splinters of wood into the air. Spanish captains yelled and crewmen cursed as they hacked through their anchor cables with axes to escape the danger.

Several ships were rammed and some set on fire, causing great panic and alarm among their desperate crews as they stared in horror at the roaring flames. Some, no longer anchored, drifted into the shallows, where jagged rocks waited. A few were sunk, and five ran aground, canted over like beached whales while their crews tried to struggle ashore.

At six in the morning we were ready to launch our final attack. A freshening wind blew from the south-west, and a heavy rain shower told us storms were on the way. I'd expected the Armada to be in disarray, yet a formidable fleet of seaworthy ships formed up to face us. I didn't need to count to know we remained outnumbered.

I thought of my last will and testament, held for safekeeping by William Hawkins. Elizabeth would be well provided for, and my brother Thomas, and Jonas – if they survived this battle. If this was my time to die, I would be ready, but prayed for a swift and painless end. I wore my new armour, and my scarf of green silk, my token of good luck, a treasured gift from Queen Elizabeth. I often recalled her words, embroidered in golden thread: *The Lord guide and preserve thee until the end.*

The men gave a rousing cheer, and I turned to see a forest of masts behind us. Admiral John Hawkins had waited until the last moment to join us with his fleet of thirty-five fresh ships from Kent. I hoped they carried the much-needed supply of powder and shot.

For the first time, our fleet outnumbered the Spanish, and

the air filled with thick smoke and the sharp tang of gunpowder as we began the battle, pounding the nearest ships with full broadsides. I'd never seen anything like it as our barrage made up for accuracy with the sheer quantity of cannon shot.

I felt unexpected exhilaration at being in such danger, but flinched as another cannonball smashed through our hull. The *Revenge* could not take much more of such a beating. The scream of a man suffering amputation with a bone saw could be heard over the noise of the cannons, and I said a prayer for him.

After many hours of fighting we were rewarded by the sight of a Spanish crew abandoning their ship before it disappeared beneath the waves. The first ship of the Armada to be sunk by our cannons, only a few fragments of timber and the corpse of a sailor, floating face down, showed where the great galleon had been.

Despite our efforts, firing for the best part of the day, the capricious weather in the Channel proved our best ally. Blustery prevailing winds and the powerful ebbtide left the Armada no choice but to run for the north of Scotland, to find a route back to Spain. England and our queen were safe – for now, at least.

I called to the men. 'Are we happy?'

They replied with a roaring cheer of relief.

27

JANUARY 1589

This would not be a private meeting. The queen sat in her high-backed, gilded chair surrounded by her whispering ladies and courtiers. She clearly wished there to be witnesses to what I had to say. I'd been expecting her summons, but as I removed my cap and bowed, I wondered what mood I would find her in.

At Tilbury fort the queen had made a rousing victory speech to her soldiers, mounted on a white horse. As I'd expected, Lord Admiral Howard took the credit for vanquishing the Armada, and had been well rewarded, despite retreating to a safe distance during the final battle.

My own part in the action was barely mentioned, apart from the suggestion that my capture of the *Rosario* meant I'd disobeyed orders. Howard kept me silent with the threat that we'd had orders from the queen, warning on pain of death that no ship of his fleet was to come to close quarters with the Spanish Armada.

I might have to explain my actions, although the *Rosario*'s money and silver was long gone. I'd spent most of it on the lease of my London house by the river in Dowgate Street, but there'd been questions since we returned about the true value of what we'd found.

'Sir Francis.' Her voice sounded welcoming, although her sharp eyes fixed me with a stern gaze. 'We wish to know what became of the Armada after it left Gravelines.' She gestured to a footman, who brought a chair for me.

My mind raced as I studied her pale, powdered face for any clue to her intentions. At least she'd not called me 'Drake'. Her eyes glinted like diamonds and her thin lips were as red as blood. She would have been briefed by William Cecil or Francis Walsingham, neither of whom were now present. I'd heard Walsingham had fallen out of favour. Was this a test of my loyalty, to her or to them?

'A gale drove fifteen of the Spanish ships on to the rocks of the Irish shore. Among those wrecked was the galleon *San Martin*, flagship of the Spanish commander, the Duke of Medina Sidonia. I regret to report he wasn't on board, Your Majesty—'

She held up a thin-fingered hand. 'We understand most of the crews were drowned, and the few who landed were killed by our soldiers.' Again, her voice had a note of challenge, as if it had been my fault.

'That's true, Your Majesty, but others returned to Santander. I sent Captain Thomas Fenner to Portugal and Spain to discover the status of the returned Armada ships.' I saw the queen's brief nod. 'He reports that few of the men who sailed against us are still alive.'

'What became of the Duke of Medina Sidonia?'

'I understand the duke escaped on a smaller ship. He is disgraced, Your Majesty, and King Philip has banished him.'

'Does that mean we need no longer be concerned about the threat from Spain?' She must know the answer, yet played her game with me.

'Spanish galleys attacked Captain Fenner's ships off the coast of Lisbon. I'm pleased to report he had the better of them.' I didn't mention that he'd also taken a merchant ship loaded with a valuable cargo of Greek wine. 'We must finish the task, Your Majesty.'

'What do you propose, Sir Francis?'

I saw my chance. 'We cannot rest until King Philip's reign is ended. With your approval, Your Majesty, I will lead an *English* Armada, and end this threat to our country, once and for all.'

She stared at me in silence for a moment. I sensed her ladies and courtiers were holding their breath. I'd enjoyed my special relationship with the queen, yet my heart pounded. I'd seen good men dragged off to the Tower of London for risking Her Majesty's displeasure.

'Go, with my blessing, and may God be with you.' She spoke softly, perhaps knowing many lives could be put at risk by her decision.

I bowed once more and left before she changed her mind. I knew better than to ask how my new venture would be funded. William Cecil confided that three years of war, and raising troops for the threatened invasion, had emptied the royal coffers. I would have to beg, borrow, and find investors.

There was much to arrange. My head filled with the names of ships to refit, captains and crews to commission. This time I would be the general of my own campaign, not sailing under a vice admiral's flag as second in command. As I stepped out into the fresh spring sunshine, I hummed an old sailors' tune, cheered by my renewed sense of purpose.

My wife seemed proud of my new role. 'I shall arrange a party in the great hall here at Buckland, to celebrate your departure.'

I stared at her in disbelief. 'We'll celebrate when we return victorious, Elizabeth. We need to offer the Spanish as little warning of our plans as possible and you, of all people, know how easily gossip can spread at court.'

'I have to tell you that your great secret is already out, Francis. I've been approached by several of my friends, seeking appointments with your fleet.'

I swore under my breath. 'I'll have no more gentlemen adventurers. Against my better judgement, I've already been persuaded to allow the young Earl of Essex, Robert Devereux, to sail with us.'

She raised an eyebrow. 'Essex is a cousin of the queen, but only through his great-grandmother, Mary Boleyn. I confess I'm surprised you agreed to take him.'

'Essex is betrothed to Walsingham's daughter, Frances, and was William Cecil's ward. I didn't have any choice.' Despite myself, the ghost of Thomas Doughty still haunted me, and I prayed Robert Devereux would not give me cause to regret my decision.

I'd hoped to secure Christopher Carleill as the commander of my soldiers, but he'd been made Governor of Ulster. Instead, I found someone from my past. Since the massacre at Rathlin, John Norris had been knighted for his campaigns in the Low Countries, as well as the defence of Dover the previous year. He still had an annoying air of superiority, but brought nineteen thousand experienced soldiers to our venture.

He arrived in the late afternoon at Buckland Abbey with a mounted escort of armed yeomen and a man wearing a silver breastplate over his velvet doublet. John Norris wore a sword low on his belt, and looked weather-beaten, as if he'd just returned from battle.

Drake - Tudor Corsair

He gestured to his companion as I welcomed them. 'This is my younger brother Edward, my second in command.'

I knew Sir Edward Norris as a distinguished commander, knighted in reward for fighting in the Netherlands. 'I'm glad to have you with us, Sir Edward.'

I recalled how the other gentlemen rallied with Doughty against me, all those years before. I worried about having both of them to deal with, but had no choice. Their father, Baron Norris, a lifelong friend of the queen, had agreed to invest twenty thousand pounds in our venture.

John Norris frowned. 'I know our task is to destroy the last of the Armada ships, but I also know you, General Drake. Are we going to take the opportunity to finish this?' His steel-grey eyes fixed on me, as if daring me to agree.

'We are, Sir John. We're preparing a fleet of a hundred and fifty warships, many of which were victorious against the Spanish Armada, and with your men we'll have more than twenty-three thousand soldiers and crew. Once we've dealt with any ships we find in northern Spain, we'll take Lisbon, and capture King Philip.' I enjoyed seeing their surprise.

'I understand Her Majesty wishes him to be replaced with Dom António. Has anyone told the queen he's a bastard, with no claim to the throne?' John Norris made no effort to hide his scorn.

I began to regret having to work with him, but our success could depend on his ruthlessness. 'Dom António is our secret weapon, as the heir to the Aviz dynasty. He's here in Plymouth with his son, Dom Emmanuel. They'll sail with us, and when we land in Lisbon, will lead the Portuguese in a revolt against the Spanish.'

Edward Norris looked thoughtful. 'Will we be returning with our holds filled with Spanish treasure, General Drake?'

'Pray God we do, Sir Edward. Before we return home, we

shall find the Spanish treasure fleet – and take the Azores in the name of Queen Elizabeth!'

I cursed the blustery south-westerly winds, which yet again threatened our plans. John Norris used the time while we waited to sail by training my men. I was pleased he'd agreed to my plan, although as I watched the men landing ashore, I could see how few were the battle-hardened veterans I'd been promised.

Instead of nineteen thousand experienced soldiers, there were only thirteen thousand and, by the look of them, most were volunteers, hoping to earn easy money in the queen's service. Worse still, the siege equipment Norris needed to attack the Spanish forts had yet to arrive. I prayed I'd not been too ambitious with my plan to seize Lisbon.

It would be my crowning success to sail up the Thames to London with King Philip in chains as my prisoner. I worried that the Spanish knew we were coming, and would not be taken by surprise – but we had only one roll of the dice, and I had bet everything on winning.

I watched as a lone figure rowed across to the *Revenge*. The waves rocked his boat but he kept his course with a steady stroke of his oars. As he drew closer I recognised my brother Thomas. I raised a hand in greeting and said a silent prayer of thanks. He'd been away at sea throughout our preparations and I helped him aboard and led him to my cabin, where I poured him a cup of ale.

He took a deep drink. 'I've brought you a gift.' Reaching into the leather bag he carried, he produced a bottle of wine. 'We took a merchant trader bound for Spain. Her hold turned out to be full of supplies.'

'We'll be needing them, Thomas. The men have been living off my stores for the past two weeks.'

He nodded. 'I'm surprised to find you still in Plymouth. We hit a few squalls, but nothing to worry about.'

'You are right.' An idea occurred to me as I watched him empty his cup of ale. 'I planned to captain the *Revenge* myself, but I've grown too cautious in my old age. I'd like you to take the post, if you will.'

'I will, Francis.' He smiled. 'We'll need to watch out for the nobility. Have you been told about the Earl of Essex?'

'What's happened?' I could tell from my brother's face the news wasn't good.

'It seems the queen ordered Essex not to take part in your mission, but he's disobeyed her. I heard he galloped here on a fast horse and has already set sail.'

'On one of my ships?'

Thomas nodded. 'One of the queen's ships – the *Swiftsure*.'

I cursed the young earl's nerve, although I wasn't surprised. 'I fear I'll be held to blame.' I peered out at the grey skies. 'We'll set sail as soon as we can, and pray the weather improves. When we catch up with the Earl of Essex he'll answer to me.'

Salt spray lashed my face as I tried to count the ships following in our wake. Storms in the Bay of Biscay had scattered my flotilla to the four winds. Worse still, we'd been swept west, past the port of Santander, where Walsingham believed many Spanish ships were sheltered.

Thomas called out over the howling wind. 'Are we to steer for Coruña?'

'We have no choice!' I ducked as a wave splashed over the

rail and sluiced across the deck, soaking my clothes. 'Let us pray the others follow, and don't choose to turn back!'

The *Revenge* groaned in protest as we changed course, and she heeled hard into the wind. I tied a rope around my waist for safety as I watched to see if our new plan had been understood. Our fleet, even larger than that which took on the Armada, looked to be reduced to no more than twenty vessels. I prayed none were lost as a consequence of my decision to sail in worsening weather.

Jonas was first to spot the Tower of Hercules, an ancient Roman lighthouse marking the headland of Coruña. A few ships sheltered in the natural harbour, a wide-mouthed bay safe from the storm-force winds. One was the thousand-ton Portuguese flagship *San Juan*, a good prize – but apart from two men-of-war, the others were supply ships and galleys.

The fort high on the headland began firing as we entered the bay, but none of our fleet were hit, and we anchored out of range while I waited for the rest of our flotilla to arrive. I used the time to scan the shore defences. The high wall encircling the lower town didn't reach to the water, so we could land our men at night and attack at dawn.

A swinging lantern in the darkness told us John Norris had his men in place and ready. I could have directed the assault from the *Revenge*, but left Thomas and Jonas to keep an eye on our ships while I joined the small boats ferrying one and half thousand men ashore at first light. I stared up at the dark outline of the fort, knowing we would make easy targets for their gunners, but luck was on our side. The guns remained silent as we scrambled ashore in the shadows like harbour rats.

I fired my pistol into the air and we charged into the lower town. Men leapt from their beds and some returned fire, but most ran for the protection of the fort, leaving Coruña open for the taking. Despite my orders to secure as many supplies as we could, our soldiers began looting and burning, killing anyone who stood in their way.

I stood back watching Coruña burn, and knew John Norris had been up to his old tricks. He cared for nothing but the complete annihilation of his enemy. Turning to look back at the *Revenge*, I saw a pall of smoke rising into the early-morning sky, followed by a flash of flame. The crew of the flagship *San Juan* had robbed us of her by running the great galleon aground and setting her ablaze.

Thomas welcomed me back to the *Revenge*. 'The wind has veered against us.' He frowned. 'We might be stuck here for days – a week even.'

'I pray not, Thomas. I doubt our supplies will last.' I studied the remaining Spanish ships in the harbour. 'It seems the galleys have already escaped.'

Jonas had been listening. 'The rest appear abandoned. Shall we seize them as prizes to make up for those we've lost?'

I stared up at the high headland. 'John Norris and his brother have taken our soldiers to attack the fort, so we've time to kill. We'll search the ships for anything we can salvage, then we'll use them as target practice for our gunners.'

Two weeks passed before the winds turned westerly. The captains were against beating back along the exposed coast to Santander, so we agreed to leave for Lisbon. We'd missed our chance to catch much of the remaining Spanish fleet, but the capture of King Philip would more than make up for it.

The siege of Coruña fort had been a disaster. Twenty of our men died when a tower collapsed on top of them, and the Norris brothers were lucky to escape. Undaunted, they'd returned with a colourful Spanish standard, and claims of wiping out an army of eight thousand men, sent to reinforce the town.

Thomas came to see me, looking grim-faced. 'Another dozen of the crew are suffering with a fever.'

I cursed our luck. 'We're not turning back.'

Thomas scowled. 'The wind's against us again, so it's going to take a while to reach Lisbon. How do we take a city if half our men are dead?'

'They knew the risks when they signed up. Do your best, Thomas.' I didn't tell him I'd woken sweating with a fever in the night. If I fell ill, I'd provide him with the excuse to return home early, and all would be lost.

Jonas shouted from his vantage point at the fighting top. 'A ship, Captain!'

I stared out to sea. 'One of ours, I swear.'

We watched as the ship changed course and came towards us. Thomas turned to me with a grin. 'She's the *Swiftsure*. Someone has some explaining to do.'

Robert Devereux wore a shining silver breastplate over his doublet and raised his ostrich-plumed hat as he spotted us. 'Good day to you, Admiral Drake!' He looked as if he'd been out for a day sail in the Solent, rather than halfway down the enemy coast.

Despite myself, I had to admire his nerve. I raised a hand in acknowledgement and called back. 'We have some men with fever, so I'll not ask you to board, but we'll meet at the Tagus estuary, north of Lisbon!'

Although glad to have another ship to swell our numbers, I wanted to know where they'd been while we were waiting for the weather in Coruña. The Earl of Essex could prove a liability, but his captain was an experienced man I could rely on.

We made landfall at Cape Roca and I called my commanders together. 'This will not be an easy task, as we don't have the equipment or resources for a siege, and the city is well defended, with a castle out of range of our guns. We will first take the town of Perniche, to the north of the city.' I glanced at Dom António. 'We understand the militia is mostly Portuguese, who we hope will be persuaded to join our cause.'

'And if they don't?' John Norris sounded doubtful.

'Then your army will rout them, Sir John. The fleet will follow, and together we will end this.'

Robert Devereux turned to me. 'What would you have me do, Admiral Drake?'

I hadn't had time to confront him about his actions. 'You will lead a detachment of soldiers in the attack, and have the opportunity to redeem yourself, my lord of Essex.'

The shore at Perniche proved a dangerous landing place, and one of our longboats overturned in the surf, drowning twenty men. Robert Devereux leapt out too soon and floundered in the waves, dragged down by his armour, yet somehow made it to the shore and raised his sword in the air, shouting encouragement to the men.

Most of the townspeople ran at the sight of us, but several were paid to take Dom António's letter to the castle commander. John Norris left with his land army of six thousand men to march over the steep hills to Lisbon, while we waited to see if my plan would work.

Our Portuguese messenger returned with good news, and I gathered the men together. 'The commander of Lisbon Castle offers his surrender. We shall wait until our soldiers are in place, then finish our work here. In the meantime, find whatever provisions you can.'

Robert Devereux took the best of our soldiers, and planned to meet up with our army at the gates of Lisbon. I would have liked to have gone with them, but still felt weak from the sweating fever, and the old wound in my leg meant I found it painful to march such a distance.

Instead, I led the fleet against the shipping in the approaches, where we captured French, German and Dutch merchantmen carrying goods and supplies to Lisbon. When we returned to Perniche, we found our army had failed in their assault on the city, at a cost of some two thousand men.

Devereux's tunic was torn and he had a black eye, but remained defiant. 'We hammered on the city gates, Admiral, but were outnumbered two one.'

'Her Majesty ordered that taking Lisbon is contingent on the people accepting Dom António as their king.'

John Norris stood unusually silent with his brother, who had a bloodstained bandage across his chest. He finally spoke up. 'We've too many wounded or sick with the fever. I recommend we forget about taking the Azores.' He glanced at his wounded brother, who nodded. 'We should cut our losses, and return to England.' He looked around at our faces. 'Is it agreed?'

There would be consequences of our failure to achieve any of our ambitions, but the fever drained my last reserves of strength. Enough good men had died, and the lives of those left were in my hands. I glanced at my brother Thomas, who stood with Jonas at his side, and saw his nod.

'Agreed. We've done our best, and now it's time to take our leave of this godforsaken place.'

The congregation had filled the whitewashed chapel by the time I arrived, but William Hawkins reserved me a seat in the front pews. He'd grown to look like his father, who'd been my best friend and mentor since I'd first arrived in Plymouth.

'A good turnout.' I glanced back at the congregation, which included the mayor and aldermen of Plymouth.

William nodded. 'My father would have been pleased.'

'He was a good man. One of the best.' A lump formed in my throat at the thought I would never see him again.

'He told me he would have liked to sail with you one last time, Sir Francis, but I suppose his health wasn't up to it?'

I nodded. 'Did you know he asked for a command in the fight against the Spanish Armada?' I gave him a wry look. 'I put him in charge of the Plymouth militia, and the fortification of St Nicholas Island.'

The service began and I found myself recalling my first meeting with William Hawkins, at his London home, a lifetime ago. He'd seen something in me, and had always been ready with helpful advice. I would miss him now, when I needed such friends more than ever.

We'd limped home at the start of July having achieved little. I'd squandered our chance to destroy the weakened Spanish navy with my 'English Armada'. I consoled myself with the knowledge that we'd taken the war to the ports of Spain. Hundreds of enemy militiamen had been killed or wounded, and many Spanish ships sunk or captured. We'd lost few men in fighting, but too many had died in accidents or from fever.

William Cecil warned that the funding of my expedition had depleted England's treasury, and the Privy Council had charged both myself and Sir John Norris with neglecting our duty. We gave good accounts of our venture, and never blamed each other. I prayed the matter was closed, but waited to discover what Queen Elizabeth might say.

28

APRIL 1595

I opened the leaded-glass window of my quayside merchant shipping office to let in the fresh sea air. I missed the excitement of setting off on a voyage across the ocean, but enjoyed seeing ships come and go. My business had proved successful, yet profit seemed less important than keeping friends in the seafaring community in work.

The queen had not sought to punish me for the failure of the 'English Armada', yet no longer sought my advice. I only made the long journey to London for my duties as a Member of Parliament or Deputy Lord Lieutenant for Devon. My wife liked to accompany me on my rare visits to court – a chance to learn all the latest gossip.

We'd reached an understanding over the past five years. I indulged her many friends, and supported her extravagant spending. In turn, Elizabeth played the part of my charming and dutiful wife. No one would guess we lived separate lives.

I kept busy enough as a Plymouth magistrate, passing judgement over everything from stolen corn to evicted tenants, and even the occasional murder case. I also served as a prize commissioner, deciding ownership of goods captured from foreign shipping. People joked at the irony of my appointment, but I made many useful contacts.

After years of campaigning, I'd won the battle to build a fort in Plymouth. The work wasn't complete, yet I'd secured a guard of five hundred soldiers to protect the harbour. I'd not forgotten how close the Armada came. If the Spanish found the nerve to bring the fight to us again, we would be ready.

I'd also not forgotten the misfortune of Dom António. I let him have one of my cottages in Buckland Monachorum, and visited him when I could. He lived by selling items from the crown jewels of Portugal, his only reminder of what might have been. When they ran out I paid his passage to Paris, where he'd been offered a pension by the King of France.

Dom António became the unwitting cause of the rift between Jonas and my brother. I'd never known Thomas in such a rage, even when he disagreed with my decisions. We'd seen much less of each other since his marriage to Elizabeth Elford, an attractive widow from Plympton. I spoiled his two children with gifts of sweet comfits – particularly his son, named Francis after me.

'Jonas is defrauding you, Francis.' Thomas clutched a handful of papers which he waved in the air. 'I found these by chance, and it's clear he's cheating you!'

I gestured for him to sit. 'A serious charge, Thomas.' I glanced at the papers in his hand. 'Let me take a look.'

Thomas handed me a letter, written in the spidery hand of Dom António. Addressed to Jonas, he expressed thanks for the generous loan of one thousand five hundred pounds. Another document, from a land agent in Ireland, confirmed details of land purchases there.

Thomas calmed a little, yet still sounded bitter. 'He's betrayed your trust, Francis. What are you going to do?'

With a sinking heart, I knew Jonas could only come by such

sums from my own account. His mother ran Buckland Abbey, so it made sense for Jonas to oversee the expenses. I trusted him, and never checked all was as it should be. Thomas no doubt worried that Jonas embezzled his inheritance.

I lay the letters on my desk. 'Leave these with me. I will have to discover the truth, and soon.'

Sir John Hawkins called at my London house in Dowgate Street. He looked tired, perhaps even frail, and walked with the aid of a stick which he brandished to make his point. We were working on a plan to provide for destitute mariners, particularly those who'd fought against the Spanish Armada.

Last year we'd opened our second hospital to care for mariners, and were now devising a welfare insurance scheme. He'd brought papers to discuss, but before we began work he sat back in his chair and looked across at me. 'I hear you've bought the *Defiance*, and are having her refitted. Does this mean you're planning to put to sea?'

I smiled at the thought. 'She's over five hundred tons, and fast, with forty-six guns, but I intend her for the defence of Plymouth. Adventuring is for younger men.'

'Nonsense!' He gave me an appraising look. 'How old are you, fifty?'

'I'm fifty-five this year.'

'Well, I'm sixty-three, and I want to see the Southern Ocean before I die. Will you sail with me?'

I laughed at the idea. 'I barely managed to serve as Howard's vice admiral, and swore I never would again. You've been a good friend to me, John, but can you imagine a fleet with two such strong-headed commanders?'

He ignored my protest. 'Ever since Edward Wynter was

exchanged for General de Valdés, I've hoped for the return of my son Richard, who is imprisoned in Seville. As well as intercepting the Spanish treasure fleet, we'll bring back a Spanish governor as our hostage. We'll assemble two fleets, and sail in support of each other. Half the risk, twice the firepower. What do you say?'

'I've unfinished business in the West Indies, and a similar idea has been on my mind since I heard my nephew John had been captured by the Spanish. I fear the Strait of Magellan is too well guarded but, in truth, I've always longed to return to Nombre de Dios, and take an army overland to Panama.'

'We'd need a capable military commander.'

'Sir John Norris is thankfully back in Ireland, so I'm spared the challenge of sailing with him again. The Earl of Essex recommends Sir Thomas Baskerville. He's a professional general, and has the experience.'

'I know him.' John Hawkins frowned. 'He has a high enough opinion of his own ability, but might invest his own money in the venture.'

I looked across at John Hawkins and smiled. 'When do we sail?'

Preparations were well under way when Jonas woke me from my bed one night. 'Spanish ships have attacked and burned the Cornish harbour towns!'

It took me a moment to understand. 'Ride to the fort as fast as you can, and make sure they've lit the beacons. Plymouth could be next.'

After Jonas left I hurriedly dressed and strapped on my sword and breastplate. Elizabeth appeared from her bedchamber in her silk nightgown. She looked concerned to see me preparing to leave. 'My maid told me the news. What are you going to do?'

'The *Defiance* is armed and ready to sail.'

She put her hand on my arm. 'You have enough men in the fort to defend Plymouth. You should wait until Sir John Hawkins arrives with the queen's ships.'

'You're right, Elizabeth.' I looked at her with new respect. 'I'm not going to jeopardise my voyage to the West Indies on a fool's errand. I'll stay, and guard the approaches until reinforcements arrive.'

John Hawkins rowed across to the *Defiance* from his flagship, the magnificent six-hundred-ton *Garland*. He'd arrived in Plymouth with six of the queen's warships, as well as a dozen smaller ships sailed by adventurers, bringing our combined fleet to some twenty-seven vessels.

Queen Elizabeth commanded us to search the western coast and Irish Sea for Spanish ships. We knew the Spanish were long gone, and it would soon exhaust our supplies, but a stroke of good fortune saved our venture. Word reached England that a treasure galleon, dismasted at sea, sought refuge in the harbour of San Juan, Puerto Rico.

Sir John had a glint in his eye. 'We believe she's the flagship of the Spanish treasure fleet. I told Her Majesty there could be as much as two and a half million ducats aboard.'

I didn't need persuading. I'd sold the lease on my London house to fund this voyage. 'We must put to sea. Plymouth has more Spanish agents than weevils in a ship's biscuit. We won't take them unaware, but they cannot expect us to bring an entire Armada for one treasure ship!'

The *Defiance* needed more provisions, but my brother Thomas carried my share of our soldiers on his ship, the *Adven-*

ture, and I hoped we might capture more supplies at the Azores. Thomas had been in a surly mood since learning Jonas had been made captain of the *Defiance*, but I hoped he would understand. I'd agreed with Judge James Whitelocke to take his errant twin brother William as my steward, and I believed Jonas deserved a second chance – for his mother's sake.

I breathed the refreshing air as we headed out to the open sea, and thanked God for giving me this chance to fulfil my destiny. The sleek lines of the *Defiance* meant we soon overhauled John Hawkins' fleet, and I led the greatest English Armada ever to sail.

Plymouth slipped from sight, and I thought of my wife, Elizabeth. I'd looked back at the quayside as we sailed, and saw she'd come to see us off, with Margaret and some other ladies of our household. I raised my cap and saw her wave a white-gloved hand in farewell.

Her gesture touched me more than I expected. Thomas made no secret of his dislike of her, but Elizabeth did her best for me in her own way. We remained childless, though, and I promised myself to show her more affection once we returned.

My good mood darkened by the time we reached the islands of Guadeloupe. Short of supplies, I'd asked John Hawkins to take three hundred of our soldiers to ease our burden. His terse refusal meant a diversion to stop at Las Palmas to resupply, so I formed a plan to take the town by force.

Las Palmas proved better defended than expected, and we were beaten into a retreat. One of my pinnaces, the *Francis*, fell too far astern of the fleet, and was captured by a Spanish caravel. We had other pinnaces, but I feared her crew could reveal our plans.

Sir John sent a message that he would use Guadeloupe to

prepare our fleet for the attack on the treasure ship in San Juan. I visited the *Garland*, intending to insist we must continue, but found him in his bunk, suffering from a fever.

'A few days, that's all I ask.' His voice rasped.

'Each day we stay allows the Spanish to prepare their welcome.' His shirt looked soaked, and drops of sweat beaded on his forehead, despite the moderate heat. I had no choice. 'Two days, but then we must be ready.'

'Thank you.' He forced a smile. 'I must rest awhile.'

'I wish you a speedy recovery, John. We'll use the time to mount the guns and assemble the remaining pinnaces.'

The captain of the *Garland*, Master Michael Merryall, brought the news in person once we'd anchored off Puerto Rico, close to the town of San Juan. His face looked grim as he removed his hat and bowed his greying head.

'I regret to inform you that Sir John Hawkins is dead.'

I stared at him, lost for words. John Hawkins had been someone I'd looked up to all my life. He'd been my teacher, the inspiration for my voyages, and the yardstick by which I measured success. The world would be a different place without him.

'I'm sorry, General, we had to bury Sir John at sea. The fever, you see...' His voice tailed off. There was no need to explain.

I struggled to regain my composure. 'You must join my officers for supper, Captain, and we'll raise a glass in memory of Sir John.'

My cabin on the *Defiance* was large enough to seat three each side of the mahogany table, with me at the head in my captain's chair. On one side sat my brother, next to Captain Brutus Brown, who'd commanded the *Rainbow* against the Armada, then Jonas, as my captain. Sir Thomas Baskerville sat opposite with his second in command, Sir Nicholas Clifford, and Captain Merryall of the *Garland*. In sombre mood, we clasped our hands in prayer as I said grace.

'*God guide our ways, and give us grace our Lord to please. For what we are about to receive, may the Lord make us truly thankful.*'

My steward, William Whitelocke, filled each of our tankards with beer from a jug. Tall, with unruly blond hair, he couldn't be more different from his twin brother, Sir James Whitelocke, a respected judge – yet I valued his unquestioning loyalty.

I raised my tankard to propose a toast. 'To the everlasting memory of Sir John Hawkins, may God—'

The explosion threw me from my chair. I struck my head, and lay on the floor, my ears ringing with the noise of the blast. I couldn't think or see. The air filled with dust and smoke, stinging my eyes, and leaving a metallic taste in my mouth.

The thump of heavy guns pounded, and I guessed we'd anchored within range of the shore battery. Bright light flashed through a jagged, gaping hole in the side of my cabin, and the ship reverberated as our gunners returned fire.

A man cried out in a wail of agony, like the cry of a wounded animal. Thomas helped me up, and we stared at a scene of carnage. Nicholas Clifford called out again. His shattered bone protruded from his thigh as Thomas Baskerville tried to stem the gush of blood with his hands.

Captain Brutus Brown, who'd lost an eye to a sharp splinter of wood, lay slumped over in a pool of blood and spilled beer. Captain Merryall sat open-mouthed in shock, still holding his tankard. William Whitelocke yelled for help as a second direct hit from the battery was followed by a scream and shouted curses.

My cabin door burst open as our crewmen rushed to our aid. Jonas stripped off his linen shirt and began tearing bandages. A crewman led Brutus Brown away for treatment, while I swept the table clear of clutter and debris. We lifted Nicholas Clifford on to it to try to stop his bleeding.

Thomas pulled a splinter from his hand and turned to me. 'Are you hurt, Francis?'

'By the grace of God, I am not – but we must withdraw out of range, or it will be the end of all of us.'

The flickering lights of San Juan sparkled on the dark water as I studied the line of Spanish frigates. 'They're anchored across the bay to prevent us reaching the town. We'll have to sacrifice one of our fleet as a fireship.'

My brother frowned. 'They must be dealt with, but if we make a good quantity of incendiaries, I'll lead a squadron of pinnaces, and we'll see if we can set them alight.'

I glanced at the silent shore batteries. 'It's a moonless night tonight. You might stand a chance if we use the cover of darkness.'

'We'll have to take the risk.' I watched Thomas leave to make the arrangements, and realised he'd now become a better leader than I was.

A shout and flare of flame marked the start of the attack, but also lit up our boats, making them easy targets for the Spanish gunners. I watched with Jonas as several of the frigates were set on fire, but their crews were ready with buckets, and soon doused the flames.

Jonas pointed. 'They've succeeded!'

Fire took hold of the largest Spanish frigate, and in no time the roaring flames were as high as the mast. Bright embers and ash floated in the air, and the desperate shouts of the crew echoed across the water. We heard splashes as men dived into the sea to escape the flames. She would burn to the waterline in an hour, but the other ships sat in darkness.

The shore batteries began firing and soon found their range, scoring a direct hit and sinking one of our pinnaces. I prayed it wasn't the one with Thomas aboard, but couldn't tell in the dark. With a heavy heart I gave the order for a single shot from our cannon, the signal for our boats to return.

I thanked God as I spotted my brother returning to his ship, and watched as they manhandled wounded men aboard. I regretted my decision not to admit I'd been ready to give up the fight and return home. Too many good men were now dead. Sir Nicholas Clifford mercifully died of his wounds before our ship's surgeon could do his work. My old friend Brutus Brown lingered on for a whole day, and had time to make his will before we also committed his body to the sea.

We might have sailed home, but we needed fresh water and supplies. I studied the charts and decided to return to Rio de Hacha, which I'd attacked twenty-seven years before. Even if the Spanish had improved the defences, I knew where to find fresh water and, with luck, should be able to uncover something of value.

Jonas frowned as the long sandy beach, with its leaning palm trees, and the thatched-roofed huts of Rio de Hacha came into view. 'It looks deserted.'

'We'll find out soon enough.' We could be sailing into a trap, but there was no going back now.

I led the landing party to a beach at the eastern end of the town. The governor's white-painted house, ruined all those years ago, had been rebuilt, but the doors stood open, as if hastily abandoned. The town was deserted, so we called the rest of the crew ashore and the men began looting and burning the houses.

A Spanish woman in a red satin gown stepped from her home and demanded to know who was in charge. Through my interpreter, she offered a handful of large pearls for her house to remain untouched. Impressed by her confident courage, I relented.

'Tell her she can keep her pearls – and we will leave her house alone. We represent the Queen of England, and would not rob a woman.'

As we sailed to Nombre de Dios, I gathered the men together for prayers, and thanked God for his providence. We'd found fresh water and enough food for our journey. I could finally achieve my dream of raiding the great treasure fleet in the city of Panama, planned many years before.

29

JANUARY 1596

A shout woke me from my dream. 'Sir Thomas Baskerville is returning!'

I'd sent him to scout ahead and prepare the way to Panama, while we readied our pinnaces for the voyage up the River Chagres. He'd left with his army of eight hundred men, and wasn't due to return so soon. His weary soldiers staggered into our camp at Nombre de Dios, which we'd captured without a fight.

I hardly recognised Sir Thomas. His usually immaculate tunic was soiled with brown mud, his lank hair dripping, and his helmet replaced by a bloodstained linen bandage. He stood before me like a beaten man.

'The rain turned the road to mud, and slowed our progress. Our powder was soaked, and our rations spoiled.' He glanced back at his men. 'We ran into an ambush. They chose their ground well, as we couldn't get around them, and lost some sixty of my soldiers before I ordered the retreat.'

The men were dirty and exhausted, many with bandaged wounds. I cursed our luck. The Spanish had seen us off at Las Palmas, and again at San Juan. I knew how word of such defeats could travel in the Indies. My reputation as 'El Drako', which made towns flee at our approach, was at risk of being compromised.

I gathered my officers together. 'When I was here last, the Spanish thought they had the better of us, but we returned, and won the day with more silver than we could carry.'

Sir Thomas frowned. 'The road is ruined by the weather, General, and the Spanish will be waiting for us. It will be impossible to reach Panama from here.'

'Which is why we'll use the River Chagres to the way station at Casa de Las Cruces. We'll adapt the pinnaces to carry more men – but success depends on convincing the Spanish we've left. Tell your men to salvage what we can, then burn the town. We'll withdraw a good distance, and return under cover of darkness.'

The warm air filled with the earthy scent of burning wood, and I looked back at billowing smoke rising into the clear blue sky. Flames glowed from the windows of the governor's white-fronted house, and the roof collapsed in a shower of broken tiles. My men had been thorough, even setting fire to the servants' houses.

Nombre de Dios, a place of so many memories, would soon be nothing but charred timbers and ashes. The Spanish might celebrate another victory, but we would have the last laugh when we returned to strike at the heart of their empire.

I'd chosen the isolated island of Escudo as our sanctuary. Thirty leagues from the mainland coast, there were mangrove swamps and perilous coral reefs to the north, but the sandy bays to the south provided sheltered anchorage for our fleet.

Crystal clear water meant the brightly coloured fish were easy to catch, and those few who could swim had sport diving for lobsters and crabs. The thick forest of Escudo provided good timber for repairs to our pinnaces, as well as plentiful fruit trees and game birds.

I planned that we should stay at the island for a week to allow our injured soldiers to recover, while we stripped down the pinnaces for the journey up the River Chagres. Our ship's carpenters oversaw the work of strengthening the hulls of the shallow-draft boats, removing unnecessary weight to make them easier to row.

The sharp crack of musket fire was followed by a cheer. I ran from my cabin to see what was going on, in time to see the men hauling a large sea turtle aboard. I watched as they butchered it, the axe cracking into the thick shell while its scaly flippers paddled in the air. There would be enough meat to feed the crew for a day or so.

Jonas rowed me to the shore and we went foraging for coconuts under the towering palms. We sat on a sun-bleached fallen tree, looking out to the tranquil, turquoise blue sea. Jonas used his dagger to dig the white flesh from a coconut, which he'd smashed open with a rock.

The damp heat of sweat trickled at my neck, and I unfastened my collar. We'd not walked far along the sandy beach, but I suffered with the sun more than Jonas, and there wasn't a cloud in the blue sky. I'd planned to arrive in the West Indies summertime, so was surprised that Thomas Baskerville found the road from Nombre de Dios impassable. The rainy season wasn't supposed to begin until May.

'The West Indies has changed.' I spoke as if to myself. Jonas didn't comment, but handed me a piece of coconut. I relished the fresh taste, recalling the first time I'd tried it, many years ago. 'I remember when we would be welcomed by the Cimarrons. They were brave fighters, always ready to help us against the Spanish.'

'What became of them?'

'I'd like to think they've settled on some remote island, like this. The Spanish only gave them the same choice they would offer us – slavery or death.' I heard the bitterness in my voice as I remembered my old friend Morgan, and my nephew John, who I doubted I would ever see again.

Jonas dug out another chunk of coconut and bit into it. 'Am I forgiven?'

His question surprised me. 'You betrayed my trust, Jonas, but I believe you meant well in helping Dom António.' I managed a smile. 'You have the chance to redeem yourself.'

'Will you restore my inheritance?' There was an edge to his question, and I suspected he'd been arguing with my brother again.

'Thomas will be the executor of my will, Jonas, so you would do well to make your peace with him. I might make you joint executor, and grant you a manor.'

We returned to the beach to find a deputation waiting for us, led by Captain Merryall of the *Garland*. 'The fever has spread, General. We don't know what to do.'

'How many men are ill?'

'Eighteen at the last count, but there are more each day.' Captain Merryall glanced back at his ship. 'We must turn for home, or put the sick men ashore.'

'We are not going home, Captain. We'll put back to sea when the work on the pinnaces is done. In the meantime, any men who wish to rest ashore may do so.'

I woke in the night bathed in sweat, my head pounding. I'd had a restless night, wondering if I should send the sick and wounded men home while the rest of us returned to Nombre de Dios. Captain Merryall was right to be concerned. Fever could spread through a ship's company.

I splashed cold water from the jug over my face and called for William Whitelocke to bring me a fresh shirt. My vison blurred and I fell back on my bunk, shivering as the fever took hold. My poor appetite meant I hadn't eaten enough the previous day, and now I would pay the price.

My head throbbed and I gasped as the pain in my stomach was like being stabbed with a knife. I called out again for William Whitelocke, but there was no answer. I cursed my idle steward, and closed my eyes to rest a moment. My last thought was of my old friend John Hawkins, begging me to let him rest.

'Francis. Wake up!'

I opened my eyes, not sure where I was.

Thomas shook me, his face a frown of concern. 'The men have noticed you've not shown yourself.' He put his hand on my forehead and cursed. 'By God, I knew you had the fever!' He made it sound like an accusation, but withdrew his hand swiftly, as if I'd burned him.

'I need you to take command of this venture, Thomas. I must rest.' My dry throat was swollen, and my voice sounded weak.

'Sir Thomas Baskerville has taken command.'

'Thomas Baskerville is a soldier. He knows nothing of commanding a fleet.'

'It's only until you are well enough.'

I sensed my grip on the venture slipping through my fingers. 'Will you send the surgeon to come and see me?'

Thomas stood back and shook his head. 'The surgeon is dead of the fever. We buried him with the others, before we left Escudo.'

I stared at him. I could barely recall leaving the island, and had no recollection of any funerals. 'How many men have died?'

'I've lost count.' Thomas shrugged. 'A dozen. A few more died in the night.'

I pulled myself up and peered through the porthole window. We'd anchored in the lee of another wooded island which looked vaguely familiar. 'Where are we?'

'Buena Ventura, outside Porto Bello.'

'The beautiful port.' I smiled. 'We're within easy reach of the Chagres river. I trust we are out of range of the Spanish forts in Porto Bello?' The memory of Sir Nicholas Clifford's shattered thigh was still painfully fresh in my mind.

Thomas nodded. 'There are a few Spanish ships in Porto Bello harbour. I've posted lookouts to alert us if any try to leave.' He poured a cup of beer and handed it to me. 'You should drink.'

My hand trembled with the weight of the cup in my weakened state, but I managed to drink a few sips of the warm ale. The bitter taste made me choke, but soothed my aching throat.

'We've waited long enough, Thomas. It's time we were going ashore.'

He studied me for a moment, as if trying to decide. 'You're not well enough to make the journey to Panama. As your captain, and as your brother, I'm ordering you to rest.'

With an effort, I emptied the cup of ale and dropped back on to my bunk. Thomas was right. I was in no condition to go ashore, much less to make the long march across the country, and lead the attack on Panama.

I awoke to someone shaking me and calling my name. I'd had a disturbing dream about my nephew John being burned at the stake by the Spanish, and worried I might be losing my mind. I rubbed my eyes and recognised the familiar voice of Jonas. He stood over me, holding a document and my quill.

'You must sign this, or I'll never clear my name.'

'What is it?' He wasn't making sense, and his tone was abrupt and demanding.

'A legal acquittance.' He dipped my quill in ink and placed it in my shaking hand. 'All you need to do is sign. I will take care of everything.'

I took the goose-feather quill, yet struggled to focus on the words on the parchment, which floated before my eyes. The door to my cabin opened and Thomas stood open-mouthed as he saw me with my quill in my hand.

'Stop!' He grabbed Jonas by the collar and dragged him outside, leaving me still holding the document.

I heard him threaten Jonas, who argued back with unexpected vehemence. I would have intervened, but my legs were unsteady as I tried to pull myself up. I dropped the quill and sat on my bunk until Thomas returned, my aching head in my hands.

'He was trying to cheat you again.' Thomas scowled. 'I'll have him arrested when we return to Plymouth. A spell in jail will teach him—'

'You'll do no such thing. No harm has been done, and your arrival was timely, as I need to speak with you.'

Thomas muttered under his breath but sat in my captain's chair. 'I won't be persuaded to allow you ashore.'

'I want you to be the executor of my will, Thomas, and I've chosen your son Francis as my heir. All I ask is that you make your peace with Jonas, and allow him to assist you.'

Thomas cursed. 'What about Elizabeth? Is she not to be your executor?'

'Elizabeth shall have my mills and the furniture at Buckland. I was too hasty to agree to her father's demands, but I'm sure you can reach a settlement about the manors.' A thought occurred to me. 'I shall write a codicil to my will. I wish to leave you my houses in Plymouth, including the property in High Street.'

Thomas shook his head. 'Enough of this talk of wills. You must rest, and recover your strength – and then we will march on Panama.'

'We will, but I'll rest easy when the codicil is written and witnessed, so please attend to it.'

I awoke in near darkness and peered through my small window. The first glimmering light of a peaceful dawn reflected on a calm sea, lapping at the shores of the island of Buena Ventura. My fever had eased for the first time in days, and I thanked God I was well enough to dress, and face the world.

I pulled on a fresh shirt, but fell to my knees as the nausea returned. 'William!'

My steward appeared, rubbing his eyes and still wearing his nightshirt. His grubby feet were bare, and he frowned at the sight of me on my knees. 'Are you all right, sir?'

'Help me put on my best armour, William, and I need my ceremonial sword.'

William looked confused, but took my silver breastplate from my sea chest and unwrapped the velvet covering, staring at his reflection for a moment as he polished the surface. William never learned to read or write, yet shipboard routine had been the making of him.

'Are we going to fight, sir?'

I staggered unsteadily to my feet so he could fasten the leather straps. 'I must look like a soldier if I'm to have the respect of the men.'

William fastened my sword belt around my waist and handed me my sword. I'd carried the sword with me on every voyage, yet rarely wore it, and had never used it in anger. I studied the engraving of the royal arms, and the royal motto, *Semper Eadem* – Always the Same.

I had only seen Queen Elizabeth from a distance since that fateful day when she agreed for me to command an English Armada. I'd replayed every detail of that last meeting in my mind, and recalled her last words to me: 'Go, with my blessing, and may God be with you.'

'You wish me to go now, sir?'

I realised I'd spoken the queen's words aloud. 'Find my brother, and send him to me.'

William left without closing the lid of my sea chest. I bent to shut it, but first reached inside for my scarf of green silk, my token of good luck – another treasured gift from my queen, Elizabeth. I read her words, embroidered in thread of gold: *The Lord guide and preserve thee until the end.*

Tying the scarf around my neck, I chose my father's book of Psalms from my precious row of books, and sat in my captain's chair. Exhausted, I closed my tired eyes to rest a moment while I waited for my brother Thomas.

My father's leather-bound book slipped from my hand and fell to the floor with a thump, but I knew the Psalm by heart, and heard his familiar, soft Devon voice as he spoke the words.

'*Return unto thy rest, O my soul, for the Lord hath dealt bountifully with thee. For thou hast delivered my soul from death, mine eyes from tears, and my feet from falling. I will walk before the Lord in the land of the living. Amen.*'

The Parting Glass

Oh all the money that e'er I spent
I spent it in good company
And all the harm that e'er I've done
Alas, it was to none but me
And all I've done for want of wit
To memory now I can't recall
So fill to me the parting glass
Good night and joy be with you all

Oh all the comrades that e'er I've had
Are sorry for my going away
And all the sweethearts that e'er I've had
Would wish me one more day to stay
But since it falls unto my lot
That I should rise and you should not
I'll gently rise and I'll softly call
Good night and joy be with you all

(Traditional Folk Song)

AUTHOR'S NOTE

My aim in writing this book was to rely on primary sources where I could, so all events are as accurate as possible. In a first-hand account, from one of Drake's crewmen, Richard Hakluyt's *Principal Navigations* records:

The 28 at 4 of the clocke in the morning our Generall Sir Francis Drake departed this life, having bene extremely sicke of a fluxe, which began the night before to stop on him. He used some speeches at or a little before his death, rising and apparelling himselfe, but being brought to bed againe within one houre died.

He made his brother Thomas Drake and captaine Jonas Bodenham executors, and M. Thomas Drakes sonne [the later Sir Francis Drake, first baronet] his heire to all his lands except one manor which he gave to captain Bodenham.

The same day we ankered at Puerto Bello, being the best harbour we found along the maine both for great ships and small. After our comming hither to anker, and the solemne buriall of our Generall sir Francis in the sea: Sir Thomas Baskervill being aboord the Defiance, M. Bride made a sermon, having to his audience all the captaines in the fleete.

Author's Note

Francis Drake asked to be dressed in his armour, and buried like a soldier. His lead-lined coffin was lowered into the sea near Portobelo, to a fanfare of trumpets and salute of cannons, off the coast of present day Colón in Panama. Several diving expeditions have tried to locate Drake's coffin since 1883, without success.

His ill-fated flotilla returned to England, and Thomas Drake began the long process of resolving the issues with his brother's will. As Francis no doubt expected, his wishes were contested by his wife, as well as Jonas Bodenham. Elizabeth remarried within a year, but died after a short illness in 1598.

John Hawkins' son Richard was released through a prisoner exchange with the Spanish in 1602, and became Member of Parliament for Plymouth and Vice Admiral of Devon. John Drake was captured by Indians, who handed him over to the Spanish. He was tried and sentenced to a lifetime of captivity, and never returned.

Thomas Drake's son Francis was admitted to Exeter College, Oxford in 1604 aged fifteen. King James made him a baronet by 1622, and in 1624 he became Member of Parliament for Plympton Erle. Elected MP for Devon in 1628, he was made High Sheriff of Devon in 1633.

His son, also named Francis, succeeded to the baronetcy. This tradition continued in successive generations until the fifth baronet, Sir Francis Henry Drake, died unmarried in 1794 and the baronetcy ended.

I discovered many fascinating details during my research for this book, and recommend a visit to the replica *Golden Hinde*, displayed at St Mary Overie Dock in Southwark, London. This faithful replica sailed from Plymouth to San Francisco on her maiden voyage, arriving in 1975 to commemorate Sir Francis Drake's claiming of New Albion.

Standing on the deck of the replica ship, I had a new respect

Author's Note

for the bravery of Drake and his crew. Only a hundred and fifty-one feet overall, it's easy to imagine how vulnerable the crew must have been in the stormy seas around Cape Horn.

Readers might wonder why there is no mention of Drake playing bowls when the Spanish Armada arrives. There was a bowling green at Buckland Abbey, but the story was added thirty-seven years after his death, one of many myths which surround his life.

I would like to thank my wife, Liz, and my editor, Nikki Brice, for their support during the research and writing of this book. I would also like to take this opportunity to thank the many readers around the world who have encouraged me to explore the real stories of the Tudors.

If you enjoyed reading this book, please consider leaving a short review. It would mean a lot to me. Details of all my books can be found at my author website **www.tonyriches.com** which also has links to my podcasts about the stories of the Tudors.

Tony Riches, Pembrokeshire.

ESSEX - Tudor Rebel
Book Two of the Elizabethan Series

Robert Devereux, Earl of Essex, is one of the most intriguing men of the Elizabethan period. Tall and handsome, he soon becomes a 'favourite' at court, so close to the queen many wonder if they are lovers.

The truth is far more complex, as each has what the other yearns for. Robert Devereux longs for recognition, wealth and influence. His flamboyant naïveté amuses the ageing Queen Elizabeth, like the son she never had, and his vitality makes her feel young.

Continuing the story of the Tudors, begun in Tony Riches' best-selling Tudor trilogy, this epic tale of loyalty, love and adventure follows Robert Devereux from his youth to his fateful rebellion.

Available as paperback and eBook

OWEN

Book One of The Tudor Trilogy

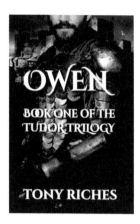

England 1422: Owen Tudor, a Welsh servant, waits in Windsor Castle to meet his new mistress, the beautiful and lonely Queen Catherine of Valois, widow of the warrior king, Henry V.

Her infant son is crowned King of England and France, and while the country simmers on the brink of civil war, Owen becomes her protector.

They fall in love, risking Owen's life and Queen Catherine's reputation, but how do they found the dynasty which changes British history – the Tudors?

Available as paperback, audiobook and eBook

MARY ~ Tudor Princess
Book One of the Brandon Trilogy

Midsummer's Day 1509: The true story of the Tudor dynasty continues with the daughter of King Henry VII. Mary Tudor watches her elder brother become King of England and wonders what the future holds for her.

Born into great privilege, Mary has beauty and intelligence beyond her years. Her brother Henry plans to use her marriage to build a powerful alliance against his enemies – but will she dare to risk his anger by marrying for love?

Meticulously researched and based on actual events, this 'sequel' follows Mary's story from book three of the Tudor Trilogy and is set during the reign of King Henry VIII.

Available in paperback, audiobook and eBook

Printed in Great Britain
by Amazon